CITY
OF GIRLS

CITY
OF GIRLS

ELIZABETH
GILBERT

BLOOMSBURY PUBLISHING
LONDON • OXFORD • NEW YORK • NEW DELHI • SYDNEY

BLOOMSBURY PUBLISHING
Bloomsbury Publishing Plc
50 Bedford Square, London, WC1B 3DP, UK

BLOOMSBURY, BLOOMSBURY PUBLISHING and the Diana logo
are trademarks of Bloomsbury Publishing Plc

First published in 2019 in the USA as *City of Girls* by Riverhead Books
First published in Great Britain 2019

A catalogue record for this book is available from the British Library

ISBNs:
HB: 978-1-4088-6704-4
Airside/India/ South Africa TPB: 978-1-4088-6705-1
ANZ TPB: 978-1-5266-1042-3
eBook: 978-1-4088-6707-5

2 4 6 8 10 9 7 5 3 1

Book design by Gretchen Achilles
Printed and bound in Great Britain by CPI Group (UK) Ltd, Croydon CR0 4YY

To find out more about our authors and books visit
www.bloomsbury.com and sign up for our newsletters

For Margaret Cordi—

my eyes, my ears, my beloved friend

You will do foolish things,
but do them with enthusiasm.

—COLETTE

I received a letter from his daughter the other day.

Angela.

I'd thought about Angela many times over the years, but this was only our third interaction.

The first was when I'd made her wedding dress, back in 1971.

The second was when she'd written to tell me that her father had died. That was in 1977.

Now she was writing to let me know that her mother had just passed away. I'm not sure how Angela expected me to receive this news. She might have guessed it would throw me for a loop. That said, I don't suspect malice on her part. Angela is not constructed that way. She's a good person. More important, an interesting one.

I was awfully surprised, though, to hear that Angela's mother had lasted this long. I'd assumed the woman had died ages ago. God knows everyone else has. (But why should anyone's longevity surprise me, when I myself have clung to existence like a barnacle to a boat bottom? I can't be the only ancient woman still tottering around New York City, absolutely refusing to abandon either her life or her real estate.)

It was the last line of Angela's letter, though, that impacted me the most.

"Vivian," Angela wrote, "given that my mother has passed away, I wonder if you might now feel comfortable telling me what you were to my father?"

Well, then.

What was I to her father?

Only he could have answered that question. And since he never chose to discuss me with his daughter, it's not my place to tell Angela what I was to him.

I can, however, tell her what he was to me.

ONE

n the summer of 1940, when I was nineteen years old and an idiot, my parents sent me to live with my Aunt Peg, who owned a theater company in New York City.

I had recently been excused from Vassar College, on account of never having attended classes and thereby failing every single one of my freshman exams. I was not quite as dumb as my grades made me look, but apparently it really doesn't help if you don't study. Looking back on it now, I cannot fully recall what I'd been doing with my time during those many hours that I ought to have spent in class, but— knowing me—I suppose I was terribly preoccupied with my appearance. (I do remember that I was trying to master a "reverse roll" that year—a hairstyling technique that, while infinitely important to me and also quite challenging, was *not very Vassar*.)

I'd never found my place at Vassar, although there were places to be found there. All different types of girls and cliques existed at the school, but none of them stirred my curiosity, nor did I see myself reflected in any of them. There were political revolutionaries at Vassar that year wearing their serious black trousers and discussing their opinions on international foment, but I wasn't interested in international foment. (I'm still not. Although I did take notice of the black trousers, which I found intriguingly chic—but only if the pockets didn't bulge.) And there were girls at Vassar who were bold academic explorers, destined to become doctors and lawyers long before many women did that sort of thing. I should have been interested in them, but I wasn't. (I couldn't tell any of them apart, for one thing. They all wore the same shapeless wool skirts that looked as though they'd been constructed out of old sweaters, and that just made my spirits low.)

It's not like Vassar was *completely* devoid of glamour. There were some sentimental, doe-eyed medievalists who were quite pretty, and some artistic girls with long and self-important hair, and some high-bred socialite types with profiles like Italian greyhounds—but I didn't befriend any of them. Maybe it's because I sensed that everybody at this school was smarter than me. (This was not entirely youthful paranoia; I uphold to this day that everybody there *was* smarter than me.)

To be honest, I didn't understand what I was doing at college, aside from fulfilling a destiny whose purpose nobody had bothered explaining to me. From earliest childhood, I'd been told that I would attend Vassar, but nobody had told me why. What was it all *for*? What was I meant to get out of it, exactly? And why was I living in this cabbagey little dormitory room with an earnest future social reformer?

I was so fed up with learning by that time, anyhow. I'd already studied for years at the Emma Willard School for Girls in Troy, New York, with its brilliant, all-female faculty of Seven Sisters graduates—and wasn't that enough? I'd been at boarding school since I was twelve years old, and maybe I felt that I had done my time. How many more books does a person need to read in order to prove that she can read a book? I already knew who Charlemagne was, so leave me alone, is how I saw it.

4

Also, not long into my doomed freshman year at Vassar, I had discovered a bar in Poughkeepsie that offered cheap beer and live jazz deep into the night. I'd figured out a way to sneak off campus to patronize this bar (my cunning escape plan involving an unlocked lavatory window and a hidden bicycle—believe me, I was the bane of the house warden), thereby making it difficult for me to absorb Latin conjugations first thing in the morning because I was usually hungover.

There were other obstacles, as well.

I had all those cigarettes to smoke, for instance.

In short: I was busy.

Therefore, out of a class of 362 bright young Vassar women, I ended up ranked at 361—a fact that caused my father to remark in horror, "Dear God, what was that *other* girl doing?" (Contracting polio as it turned out, the poor thing.) So Vassar sent me home—fair enough—and kindly requested that I not return.

My mother had no idea what to do with me. We didn't have the closest relationship even under the best of circumstances. She was a keen horsewoman, and given that I was neither a horse nor fascinated by horses, we'd never had much to talk about. Now I'd embarrassed her so severely with my failure that she could scarcely stand the sight of me. In contrast to me, my mother had performed quite well at Vassar College, thank you very much. (Class of 1915. History and French.) Her legacy—as well as her generous yearly donations—had secured my admission to that hallowed institution, and now look at me. Whenever she passed me in the hallways of our house, she would nod at me like a career diplomat. Polite, but chilly.

My father didn't know what to do with me, either, though he was busy running his hematite mine and didn't overly concern himself with the problem of his daughter. I had disappointed him, true, but he had bigger worries. He was an industrialist and an isolationist, and the escalating war in Europe was spooking him about the future of his business. So I suppose he was distracted with all that.

As for my older brother, Walter, he was off doing great things at Princeton, and giving no thought to me, other than to disapprove of my irresponsible behavior. Walter had never done an irresponsible thing in his life. He'd been so respected by his peers back in boarding school that his nickname had been—and I am not making this up—*the Ambassador*. He was now studying engineering because he wanted to build infrastructure that would help people around the world. (Add it to my catalogue of sins that I, by contrast, was not quite sure I even knew what the word "infrastructure" meant.) Although Walter and I were close in age—separated by a mere two years—we had not been playmates since we were quite little. My brother had put away his childish things when he was about nine years old, and among those childish things was me. I wasn't part of his life, and I knew it.

My own friends were moving forward with their lives, too. They were heading off to college, work, marriage, and adulthood—all subjects that I had no interest in or understanding of. So there was nobody around to care about me or entertain me. I was bored and listless. My boredom felt like hunger pains. I spent the first two weeks of June hitting a tennis ball against the side of our garage while whistling "Little Brown Jug" again and again, until finally my parents got sick of me and shipped me off to live with my aunt in the city, and honestly, who could blame them?

Sure, they might have worried that New York would turn me into a communist or a dope fiend, but anything had to be better than listening to your daughter bounce a tennis ball against a wall for the rest of eternity.

So that's how I came to the city, Angela, and that's where it all began.

———

They sent me to New York on the train—and what a terrific train it was, too. The Empire State Express, straight out of Utica. A gleaming, chrome, delinquent-daughter delivery device. I said my polite farewells to Mother and Dad, and handed my baggage over to a Red Cap, which made me feel important. I sat in the diner car for the whole ride, sipping malted milk, eating pears in syrup, smoking cigarettes, and paging through magazines. I knew I was being banished, but still . . . *in style!*

Trains were so much better back then, Angela.

I promise that I will try my best in these pages not to go on and on about how much better everything was back in my day. I always hated hearing old people yammering on like this when I was young. (*Nobody cares! Nobody cares about your Golden Age, you blathering goat!*) And I do want to assure you: I'm aware that many things were *not* better in the 1940s. Underarm deodorants and air-conditioning were woefully inadequate, for instance, so everybody stank like crazy, especially in the summer, and also we had Hitler. But trains were unquestionably better back then. When was the last time *you* got to enjoy a malted milk and a cigarette on a train?

I boarded the train wearing a chipper little blue rayon dress with a skylark print, yellow traceries around the neckline, a moderately slim skirt, and deep pockets set in at the hips. I remember this dress so vividly because, first of all, I never forget what anyone is wearing, *ever,* and also I'd sewn the thing myself. A fine job I'd done with it, too. The swing of it—hitting just at midcalf—was flirty and effective. I remember having stitched extra shoulder pads into that dress, in the desperate hope of resembling Joan Crawford—though I'm not sure the effect worked. With my modest cloche hat and my borrowed-from-Mother plain blue handbag (filled with cosmetics, cigarettes, and not much else), I looked less like a screen siren and mostly like what I actually was: a nineteen-year-old virgin, on her way to visit a relative.

Accompanying this nineteen-year-old virgin to New York City were two large suitcases—one filled with my clothes, all folded neatly in tissue, and the other packed with fabrics, trimmings, and sewing supplies, so that I could make more clothes. Also joining me was a sturdy crate containing my sewing machine—a heavy and unwieldy beast, awkward to transport. But it was my demented, beautiful soul-twin, without which I could not live.

So along with me it came.

That sewing machine—and everything that it subsequently brought to my life—was all thanks to Grandmother Morris, so let's talk about her for just a moment.

You may read the word "grandmother," Angela, and perhaps your mind summons up some image of a sweet little old lady with white hair. That wasn't my grandmother. My grandmother was a tall, passionate, aging coquette with dyed mahogany hair who moved through life in a plume of perfume and gossip, and who dressed like a circus show.

She was the most colorful woman in the world—and I mean that in all definitions of the word "colorful." Grandmother wore crushed velvet gowns in elaborate colors—colors that she did not call pink, or burgundy, or blue, like the rest of the imagination-impoverished public, but instead referred to as "ashes of rose" or "cordovan" or "della Robbia." She had pierced ears, which most respectable ladies did not have back then, and she owned several plush jewelry boxes filled with an endless tumble of cheap and expensive chains and earrings and bracelets. She had a motoring costume for her afternoon drives in the country, and her hats were so big they required their own seats at the theater. She enjoyed kittens and mail-order cosmetics; she thrilled over tabloid accounts of sensational murders; and she was known to write romantic verse. But more than anything else, my grandmother loved *drama*. She went to see every play and performance that came through town, and also adored the moving pictures. I was often her date, as she and I possessed exactly the same taste. (Grandmother Morris and I both gravitated toward stories where innocent girls in airy gowns were abducted by dangerous men with sinister hats, and then rescued by other men with proud chins.)

Obviously, I loved her.

The rest of the family, though, didn't. My grandmother embarrassed everyone but me. She especially embarrassed her daughter-in-law (my mother), who was *not* a frivolous person, and who never stopped wincing at Grandmother Morris, whom she once referred to as "that swoony perpetual adolescent."

Mother, needless to say, was not known to write romantic verse.

B ut it was Grandmother Morris who taught me how to sew.

My grandmother was a master seamstress. (She'd been taught by *her* grandmother, who had managed to rise from Welsh immigrant maidservant to affluent American lady of means in just one generation, thanks in no small part to her cleverness with a needle.) My grandmother wanted me to be a master at sewing, too. So when we weren't eating taffy together at the picture shows, or reading magazine articles aloud to each other about the white slave trade, we were sewing. And that was serious business. Grandmother Morris wasn't afraid to demand excellence from me. She would sew ten stitches on a garment, and then make me sew the next ten—and if mine weren't as perfect as hers, she would rip mine out and make me do it again. She steered me through the handling of such impossible materials as netting and lace, until I wasn't intimidated by any fabric anymore, no matter how temperamental. And structure! And padding! And tailoring! By the time I was twelve, I could sew a corset for you (whalebones and all) just as handily as you please—even though nobody but Grandmother Morris had needed a whalebone corset since about 1910.

Stern as she could be at the sewing machine, I did not chafe under her rule. Her criticisms stung but did not ache. I was fascinated enough by clothing to want to learn, and I knew that she only wished to foster my aptitude.

Her praise was rare, but it fed my fingers. I grew deft.

When I was thirteen, Grandmother Morris bought me the sewing machine that would someday accompany me to New York City by train. It was a sleek, black Singer 201 and it was murderously powerful (you could sew *leather* with it; I could have upholstered a Bugatti with that thing!). To this day, I've never been given a better gift. I took the Singer with me to boarding school, where it gave me enormous power within that community of privileged girls who all wanted to dress well, but who did not necessarily have the skills to do so. Once word got out around school that I could sew anything—and truly, I could—the other girls at Emma Willard were always knocking at my door, begging me to let out their waists for them, or to fix a seam, or to take their older sister's formal dress from last season and make it fit them right now. I spent those years bent over that Singer like a machine gunner, and it was worth it. I became popular—which is the only thing that matters, really, at boarding school. Or anywhere.

I should say that the other reason my grandmother taught me to sew was because I had an oddly shaped body. From earliest childhood, I'd always been too tall, too lanky. Adolescence came and went, and I only got taller. For years, I grew no bosom to speak of, and I had a torso that went on for days. My arms and legs were saplings. Nothing purchased at a store was ever going to fit right, so it would always be better for me to make my own clothes. And Grandmother Morris—bless her soul—taught me how to dress myself in a way that flattered my height instead of making me look like a stilt walker.

If it sounds like I'm being self-deprecating about my appearance, I'm not. I'm just relaying the facts of my figure: I was long and tall, that's all there was to it. And if it sounds like I'm about to tell you the story of an ugly duckling who goes to the city and finds out that she's pretty, after all—don't worry, this is not that story.

I was always pretty, Angela.

What's more, I always knew it.

My prettiness, to be sure, is why a handsome man in the diner car of the Empire State Express was staring at me as I sipped my malted milk and ate my pears in syrup.

Finally he came over and asked if he could light my cigarette for me. I agreed, and he sat down and commenced with flirting. I was thrilled by the attention but didn't know how to flirt back. So I responded to his advances by staring out the window and pretending to be deep in thought. I frowned slightly, hoping to look serious and dramatic, although I probably just looked nearsighted and confused.

This scene would have been even more awkward than it sounds, except that eventually I got distracted by my own reflection in the train window, and that kept me busy for a good long while. (Forgive me, Angela, but being captivated by your own appearance is part of what it means to be a young and pretty girl.) It turns out that even this handsome stranger was not nearly as interesting to me as the shape of my own eyebrows. It's not only that I was interested in how well I'd groomed them—though I was absolutely *riveted* by that subject—but it just so happens that I was trying that summer to learn how to raise one eyebrow at a time, like Vivien Leigh in *Gone with the Wind*. Practicing this effect took focus, as I'm sure you can imagine. So you can see how the time just flew by, as I lost track of myself in my reflection.

The next time I looked up, we had pulled into Grand Central Station already, and my new life was about to begin, and the handsome man was long gone.

But not to worry, Angela—there would be plenty more handsome men to come.

Oh! I should also tell you—in case you were wondering whatever became of her—that my Grandmother Morris had died about a year before that train deposited me into New York City. She'd passed away in August of 1939, just a few weeks before I was meant to start school at Vassar. Her death had not been a surprise—she'd been in decline for years—but still, the loss of her (my best friend, my mentor, my confidante) devastated me to the core.

Do you know what, Angela? That devastation might've had something to do with why I performed so poorly at college my freshman year. Perhaps I had not been such a terrible student, after all. Perhaps I had merely been *sad*.

I am only realizing this possibility at this moment, as I write to you. Oh, dear.

Sometimes it takes a very long while to figure things out.

TWO

Anyway, I arrived in New York City safely—a girl so freshly hatched that there was practically yolk in my hair.

Aunt Peg was supposed to meet me at Grand Central. My parents had informed me of this fact as I'd gotten on the train in Utica that morning, but nobody had mentioned any particular plan. I'd not been told exactly *where* I was supposed to wait for her. Also, I'd been given no phone number to call in case of an emergency, and no address to go to should I find myself alone. I was just supposed to "meet Aunt Peg at Grand Central," and that was that.

Well, Grand Central Station was grand, just as advertised, but it was also a great place for not finding someone, so it's no surprise that I couldn't locate Aunt Peg when I arrived. I stood there on the platform for the longest time with my piles of luggage, watching the station teeming with souls, but nobody resembled Peg.

It's not that I didn't know what Peg looked like. I'd met my aunt a few times before then, even though she and my father weren't close. (This may be an understatement. My father didn't approve of his sister Peg any more than he'd approved of their mother. Whenever Peg's name came up at the dinner table, my father would snort through his nose and say, "Must be nice—gallivanting about the world, living in the land of make-believe, and spending it by the hundreds!" And I would think: *That does sound nice. . . .*)

Peg had come to a few family Christmases when I was young—but not many, because she was always on the road with her theatrical touring company. My strongest memory of Peg was from when I'd come to New York City for a day trip at age eleven, accompanying my father on a business venture. Peg had taken me to skate in Central Park. She'd brought me to visit Santa Claus. (Although we both agreed I was *far* too old for Santa Claus, I would not have missed it for the world, and was secretly thrilled to meet him.) She and I had also eaten a smorgasbord lunch together. It was one of the more delightful days of my life. My father and I hadn't stayed overnight in the city because Dad hated and distrusted New York, but it had been one glorious day, I can assure you. I thought my aunt was terrific. She had paid attention to me as a *person*, not a child, and that means everything to an eleven-year-old child who does not want to be seen as a child.

More recently, Aunt Peg had come back home to my hometown of Clinton in order to attend the funeral of Grandmother Morris, her mother. She'd sat next to me during the service and held my hand in her big, capable paw. This gesture had both comforted and surprised me (my family were not predisposed toward hand-holding, you may be shocked to learn). After the funeral, Peg had embraced me with the strength of a lumberman, and I'd dissolved into her arms, spewing out a Niagara of tears. She'd smelled of lavender soap, cigarettes, and gin. I'd clung to her like a tragic little koala. But I hadn't been able to spend much time with her after the funeral. She needed to leave town right away, because she had a show to produce back in the city. I felt that I'd embarrassed myself by falling to bits in her arms, comforting though she had been.

I barely knew her, after all.

———

n fact, what follows is the sum total of everything I knew about my Aunt Peg, upon my arrival in New York City at the age of nineteen:

I knew that Peg owned a theater called the Lily Playhouse, located somewhere in midtown Manhattan.

I knew that she had not set out for a career in the theater, but had come by her work in a rather random way.

I knew that Peg had trained as a Red Cross nurse, curiously enough, and had been stationed in France during World War I.

I knew that, somewhere along the way, Peg had discovered that she was more talented at organizing entertainments for the injured soldiers than she was at tending to their wounds. She had a knack, she found, for turning out shows in field hospitals and barracks that were cheap, quick, gaudy, and comic. War is a dreadful business, but it teaches everyone *something;* this particular war taught my Aunt Peg how to put on a show.

I knew that Peg had stayed in London for a good long while after the war, working in the theater there. She was producing a revue in the West End when she met her future husband, Billy Buell—a handsome and dashing American military officer who had also decided to stay in London after the war to pursue a career in the theater. Like Peg, Billy came from "people." Grandmother Morris used to describe the Buell family as "sickeningly wealthy." (For years, I wondered what that term meant, exactly. My grandmother revered wealth; how much more of it would qualify as "sickening"? One day I finally asked her this question, and she answered, as if it explained everything: "They're *Newport,* darling.") But Billy Buell, Newport though he may have been, was similar to Peg in that he shunned the cultured class into which he had been born. He preferred the grit and glitter of the theater world to the polish and repression of café society. Also, he was a playboy. He liked to "make fun," Grandmother Morris said, which was her polite code for "drinking, spending money, and chasing women."

Upon their marriage, Billy and Peg Buell returned to America. Together, they created a theatrical touring company. They spent the better part of the 1920s on the road with a small cadre of troupers, barnstorming towns all across the country. Billy wrote and starred in the revues; Peg produced and directed them. The couple never had any highfalutin ambitions. They were just having a good time and avoiding more typical adult responsibilities. But despite all the effort they made not to be successful, success accidentally hunted them down and captured them anyhow.

In 1930—with the Depression deepening and the nation tremulous and afraid—my aunt and her husband accidentally created a hit. Billy wrote a play called *Her Jolly Affair*, which was so joyful and fun that people just ate it up. *Her Jolly Affair* was a musical farce about an aristocratic British heiress who falls in love with an American playboy (portrayed by Billy Buell, naturally). It was a light bit of fluff, like everything else they'd ever plunked down on the boards, but it was a riotous success. All across America, pleasure-starved mine workers and farmers shook out the last bits of loose change from their pockets in order to see *Her Jolly Affair*, making this simple, brainless play into a profitable triumph. The play picked up so much steam, in fact, and garnered such bountiful praise in the local papers, that in 1931, Billy and Peg brought it to New York City, where it ran for a year in a prominent Broadway theater.

In 1932, MGM made a movie version of *Her Jolly Affair*—which Billy wrote but did not star in. (William Powell did the acting job instead. Billy had decided by this point that a writer's life was easier than an actor's life. Writers get to set their own hours, they aren't at the mercy of an audience, and there's no director telling them what to do.) The success of *Her Jolly Affair* spawned a series of lucrative motion picture sequels (*Her Jolly Divorce, Her Jolly Baby, Her Jolly Safari*), which Hollywood churned out for a few years like sausages from a hopper. The whole *Jolly* enterprise made quite a pile of money for Billy and Peg, but it also signaled the end of their marriage. Having fallen in love with Hollywood, Billy never came back. As for Peg, she decided to close the touring company and use her half of the *Jolly* royalties to buy herself a big, old, run-down New York City theater of her very own: the Lily Playhouse.

All this happened around 1935.

Billy and Peg never officially divorced. And while there didn't seem to be any bad blood between them, after 1935 you couldn't exactly call them "married," either. They didn't share a home or a work life, and at Peg's insistence, they no longer shared a financial life—which meant that all that shimmering Newport money was now out of reach for my aunt. (Grandmother Morris didn't know why Peg was willing to walk away from Billy's fortune, other than to say about her daughter, with open disappointment, "Peg never cared about money, I'm afraid.") My grandmother speculated that Peg and Billy never legally divorced because they were "too bohemian" to concern themselves with such matters. Or maybe they still loved each other. Except theirs was the sort of love that best thrives when a husband and wife are separated by the distance of an entire continent. ("Don't laugh," my grandmother said. "A lot of marriages would work better that way.")

All I know is that Uncle Billy was out of the picture for the entirety of my young life—at first because he was touring, and later because he had settled in California. He was so much out of the picture, in fact, that I'd never even met him. To me, Billy Buell was a myth, composed of stories and photos. And what glamorous stories and photos they were! Grandmother Morris and I frequently saw Billy's picture in the Hollywood tabloid magazines, or read about him in Walter Winchell's and Louella Parsons's gossip columns. We were *ecstatic*, for instance, when we found out he'd been a guest at Jeanette MacDonald and Gene Raymond's wedding! There was a picture of him at the wedding reception right there in *Variety*, standing just behind luminous Jeanette MacDonald in her blush-pink wedding gown. In the photo, Billy was talking to Ginger Rogers and her then husband, Lew Ayres. My grandmother had pointed out Billy to me and said, "There he is, conquesting his way across the country, as usual. And look at the way Ginger is grinning at him! If I were Lew Ayres, I'd keep an eye on that wife of mine."

I'd peered closely at the photo, using my grandmother's jeweled magnifying lens. I'd seen a handsome blond man in a tuxedo jacket, whose hand was resting on Ginger Rogers's forearm, while she, indeed, sparkled up at him with delight. He looked more like a movie star than the actual movie stars who were flanking him.

It was amazing to me that this person was married to my Aunt Peg. Peg was wonderful, to be sure, but she was so *homely*.

What on earth had he ever seen in her?

I couldn't find Peg anywhere.

Enough time had passed that I now officially gave up the hope of being met on the train platform. I stashed away my baggage with a Red Cap and wandered through the rushing crush of humanity that was Grand Central, trying to find my aunt amid the confluence. You might think I would've been more disquieted at finding myself all alone in New York City with no plan and no chaperone, but for some reason I wasn't. I was sure it would all end up all right. (Maybe this is a hallmark of privilege: certain well-bred young ladies simply cannot *conceive* of the possibility that somebody will not be along shortly to rescue them.)

Finally I gave up my wandering and sat down on a prominently placed bench near the main lobby of the station, to await my salvation.

And, lo, eventually I was found.

My rescuer turned out to be a short, silver-haired woman in a modest gray suit, who approached me the way a Saint Bernard approaches a stranded skier—with dedicated focus and serious intent to save a life.

"Modest" is actually not a strong enough word to describe the suit that this woman was wearing. It was a double-breasted and square little cinderblock of an item—the kind of garment that is intentionally made to fool the world into thinking that women do not possess breasts, waists, or hips. It looked to me like a British import. It was a fright. The woman also wore chunky, low-heeled black oxfords and an old-fashioned boiled-wool green hat, of the type favored by women who run orphanages. I knew her sort from boarding school: she looked like a spinster who drank Ovaltine for dinner and gargled with salt water for vitality.

She was plain from end to end, and furthermore she was plain *on purpose.*

This brick of a matron approached me with much clarity of mission, frowning, holding in her hands a disconcertingly large picture in an ornate silver frame. She peered at the picture in her hands, and then at me.

"Are you Vivian Morris?" she asked. Her crisp accent betrayed the truth that the double-breasted suit was not the only severe British import in town.

I allowed that I was.

"You've grown," she said.

I was puzzled: Did I know this woman? Had I met her when I was younger?

Seeing my confusion, the stranger showed me the framed picture in her hands. Bafflingly, this item turned out to be a portrait of my own family, from about four years prior. It was a photo we'd taken in a proper studio, when my mother had decided that we needed to be, in her words, "officially documented, for once." There were my parents, enduring the indignity of being photographed by a tradesman. There was my thoughtful-looking brother, Walter, with his hand on my mother's shoulder. There was a ganglier and younger version of myself, wearing a sailor dress that was far too girlish for my age.

"I'm Olive Thompson," announced the woman, in a voice that indicated she was accustomed to making announcements. "I'm your aunt's secretary. She was unable to come. There was an emergency today at the theater. A small fire. She sent me to find you. My apologies for making you wait. I was here several hours ago, but as my only means of identifying you was this photo, it took me some time to locate you. As you can see."

I wanted to laugh then and I want to laugh now, just remembering it. The idea of this flinty middle-aged woman wandering around Grand Central Station with a giant photograph in a silver frame—a frame that looked as though it had been ripped in haste off a rich person's wall (which it had been)—and staring at every face, trying to match the person before her to a portrait of a girl taken four years earlier, was wickedly funny to me. How had I missed her?

Olive Thompson did not seem to think this was funny, though.

I would soon discover that this was typical.

"Your bags," she said. "Collect them. Then we'll taxi over to the Lily. The late show has already begun. Hurry up now. Make no flimflam about it."

I walked behind her obediently—a baby duck following a mama duck.

I made no flimflam about it.

I thought to myself, *"A small fire?"*—but I did not have the courage to ask.

THREE

A person only gets to move to New York City for the first time in her life *once*, Angela, and it's a pretty big deal.

Perhaps this idea doesn't hold any romance for you, since you are a born New Yorker. Maybe you take this splendid city of ours for granted. Or maybe you love it more than I do, in your own unimaginably intimate way. Without a doubt, you were lucky to be raised here. But you never got to *move* here—and for that, I am sorry for you. You missed one of life's great experiences.

New York City in 1940!

There will never be another New York like that one. I'm not defaming all the New Yorks that came before 1940, or all the New Yorks that came after 1940. They all have their importance. But this is a city that gets born anew in the fresh eyes of every young person who arrives here for the first time. So *that* city, *that* place—newly created for my eyes only—will never exist again. It is preserved forever in my memory like an orchid trapped in a paperweight. That city will always be my perfect New York.

You can have your perfect New York, and other people can have theirs—but that one will always be mine.

It wasn't a long ride from Grand Central to the Lily Playhouse—we just cut straight across town—but our taxi took us through the heart of Manhattan, and that's always the best way for a newcomer to feel the muscle of New York. I was all atingle to be in the city and I wanted to look at everything at once. But then I remembered my manners and tried for a spell to make conversation with Olive. Olive, however, wasn't the sort of person who seemed to feel that the air needed to be constantly filled up with words, and her peculiar answers only brought me more questions—questions that I sensed she would be unwilling to further discuss.

"How long have you worked for my aunt?" I asked her.

"Since Moses was in nappies."

I pondered that for a bit. "And what are your duties at the theater?"

"To catch things that are falling through midair, right before they hit the ground and shatter."

We drove on for a while in silence, and I let *that* sink in.

I tried one more time: "What sort of show is playing at the theater tonight?"

"It's a musical. It's called *Life with Mother.*"

"Oh! I've heard of it."

"No, you haven't. You're thinking of *Life with Father.* That was a play on Broadway last year. Ours is called *Life with Mother.* And ours is a musical."

I wondered: *Is that legal?* Can you just take a title of a major Broadway hit like that, change a single word, and make it your own? (The answer to that question—at least in 1940, at the Lily Playhouse—was: sure.)

I asked, "But what if people buy tickets to your show by mistake, thinking that they're going to see *Life with Father?*"

Olive, flatly: "Yes. Wouldn't that be unfortunate."

I was starting to feel young and stupid and annoying, so I stopped talking. For the rest of the taxi ride, I got to just look out the window. It was plenty entertaining to watch the city go by. There were glories to see in all directions. It was late in the evening in midtown Manhattan on a fine summer night, so nothing can be better than that. It had just rained. The sky was purple and dramatic. I saw glimpses of mirrored skyscrapers, neon signs, and shining wet streets. People sprinted, bolted, strolled, and stumbled down the sidewalks. As we passed through Times Square, mountains of artificial lights spewed out their lava of white-hot news and instant advertising. Arcades and taxi-dance halls and movie palaces and cafeterias and theaters flashed by, bewitching my eyes.

We turned onto Forty-first Street, between Eighth and Ninth Avenues. This was not a beautiful street back then, and it still isn't beautiful today. At that time, it was mostly a tangle of fire escapes for the more important buildings that faced Fortieth and Forty-second Streets. But there in the middle of that unlovely block was the Lily Playhouse, my Aunt Peg's theater—all lit up with a billboard that read *Life with Mother.*

I can still see it in my mind today. The Lily was a great big lump of a thing, crafted in a style that I know now is Art Nouveau, but which I recognized then only as *heavy duty*. And boy howdy, did that lobby go out of its way to prove to you that you'd arrived somewhere important. It was all gravity and darkness—rich woodwork, carved ceiling panels, bloodred ceramic tiles, and serious old Tiffany light fixtures. All over the walls were tobacco-stained paintings of bare-breasted nymphs cavorting with gangs of satyrs—and it sure looked like one of those nymphs was about to get herself in trouble in the family way, if she wasn't careful. Other murals showed muscular men with heroic calves wrestling with sea monsters in a manner that looked more erotic than violent. (You got the sense that the muscular men didn't *want* to win the battle, if you see my point.) Still other murals showed dryads struggling their way out of trees, tits first, while naiads splashed about in a river nearby, throwing water on each other's naked torsos in a spirit that was very much *whoopee!* Thickly carved vines of grapes and wisteria (and lilies, of course!) climbed up every column. The effect was quite bordello. I loved it.

"I'll take you straight to the show," Olive said, checking her watch, "which is nearly over, thank God."

She pushed open the big doors that led into the playhouse itself. I'm sorry to report that Olive Thompson entered her place of work with the demeanor of one who might rather not *touch* anything within it, but I myself was dazzled. The interior of the theater was really something quite stunning—a huge, golden-lit, fading old jewel box of a place. I took it all in—the sagging stage, the bad sight lines, the hefty crimson curtains, the cramped orchestra pit, the overgilded ceiling, the menacingly glittery chandelier that you could not look at without thinking, "Now, what if that thing should fall down . . . ?"

It was all grandiose, it was all crumbling. The Lily reminded me of Grandmother Morris—not only because my grandmother had loved gawdy old playhouses like this, but also because my grandmother had *looked* like this: old, overdone, and proud, and decked to the nines in out-of-date velvet.

We stood against the back wall, although there were plenty of seats to be had. In fact, there were not many more people in the audience than onstage, it appeared. I was not the only one who noticed this fact. Olive took a quick head count, wrote the number in a small notebook which she had pulled out of her pocket, and sighed.

As for what was going on up there on the stage, it was dizzying.

This, indeed, had to be the end of the show, because there was a *lot* happening at once. At the back of the stage there was a kick line of about a dozen dancers—girls and boys—grinning madly as they flung their limbs up toward the dusty heavens. At center stage, a good-looking young man and a spirited young woman were tap-dancing as though to save their lives, while singing at full bellow about how everything was going to be just fine from now on, my baby, because you and me are in *love*! On the left side of the stage was to be found a phalanx of showgirls, whose costumes and movements kept them just on the correct side of moral permissibility, but whose contribution to the story—whatever that story may have been—was unclear. Their task seemed to be to stand with their arms outstretched, slowly turning, so that you could take in the full Amazonian qualities of their figures from every angle, at your leisure. On the other side of the stage, a man dressed as a hobo was juggling bowling pins.

Even for a finale, it went on for an awfully long time. The orchestra banged forth, the kick line pounded away, the happy and breathless couple couldn't believe how *terrific* their lives were about to get, the showgirls slowly displayed their figures, the juggler sweated and hurled—until suddenly, with a crash of every instrument at once, and a swirl of spotlights, and wild flinging up of everyone's arms in the air at the same time, it ended!

Applause.

Not thunderous applause. More like a light drizzle of applause.

Olive didn't clap. I clapped politely, though my clapping sounded lonely there at the back of the hall. The applause didn't last long. The performers had to exit the stage in semisilence, which is never good. The audience filed past us dutifully, like workers heading home for the day—which is exactly what they were.

"Do you think they liked it?" I asked Olive.

"Who?"

"The audience."

"The *audience?*" Olive blinked, as though it had never occurred to her to wonder what an audience thought of a show. After a bit of consideration, she said, "You must understand, Vivian, that our audiences are neither full of excitement when they arrive at the Lily, nor overwhelmed with elation when they leave."

From the way she said this, it sounded as though she approved of the arrangement, or at least had accepted it.

"Come," she said. "Your aunt will be backstage."

So backstage we went—straight into the busy, wanton clamor that always erupts in the wings at the end of a show. Everyone moving, everyone yelling, everyone smoking, everyone undressing. The dancers were lighting cigarettes for each other, and the showgirls were removing their headdresses. A few men in overalls were shuffling props around, but not in any way that would cause them to break a sweat. There was a lot of loud, overripe laughter, but that's not because anything was particularly funny; it's just because these were show-business people, and that's how they always are.

And there was my Aunt Peg, so tall and sturdy, clipboard in hand. Her chestnut-and-gray hair was cut in an ill-considered short style that made her look somewhat like Eleanor Roosevelt, but with a better chin. Peg was wearing a long, salmon-colored twill skirt and what could have been a man's oxford shirt. She also wore tall blue knee socks and beige moccasins. If that sounds like an unfashionable combination, it was. It was unfashionable then, it would be unfashionable today, and it will remain unfashionable until the sun explodes. Nobody has ever looked good in a salmon-colored twill skirt, a blue oxford shirt, knee socks, and moccasins.

Her frumpy look was only thrown into starker relief by the fact that she was talking to two of the ravishingly beautiful showgirls from the play. Their stage makeup gave them a look of otherworldly glamour, and their hair was piled in glossy coils on the tops of their heads. They were wearing pink silk dressing gowns over their costumes, and they were the most overtly sexual visions of womanhood I had ever seen. One of the showgirls was a blonde—a *platinum*, actually—with a figure that would've made Jean Harlow gnash her teeth in jealous despair. The other was a sultry brunette whose exceptional beauty I'd noticed earlier, from the back of the theater. (Though I should not get any special credit for noticing how stunning this particular woman was; a Martian could have noticed it . . . *from Mars*.)

"Vivvie!" Peg shouted, and her grin lit up my world. "You made it, kiddo!"

Kiddo!

Nobody had ever called me kiddo, and for some reason it made me want to run into her arms and cry. It was also so encouraging to be told that I had *made it*—as though I'd accomplished something! In truth, I'd accomplished nothing more impressive than first getting kicked out of school, and then getting kicked out of my parents' house, and finally getting lost in Grand Central Station. But her delight in seeing me was a balm. I felt so welcome. Not only welcome, but *wanted*.

"You've already met Olive, our resident zookeeper," Peg said. "And this is Gladys, our dance captain—"

The platinum-haired girl grinned, snapped her gum at me, and said, "Howyadoin?"

"—and this is Celia Ray, one of our showgirls."

Celia extended her sylphlike arm and said in a low voice, "A pleasure. Charmed to meet you."

Celia's voice was incredible. It wasn't just the thick New York accent; it was the deep gravelly tone. She was a showgirl with the voice of Lucky Luciano.

"Have you eaten?" Peg asked me. "Are you starved?"

"No," I said. "Not *starved*, I wouldn't say. But I haven't had proper dinner."

"We'll go out, then. Let's go have a few gallons of drinks and catch up."

Olive interjected, "Vivian's luggage hasn't been brought upstairs yet, Peg. Her suitcases are still in the lobby. She's had a long day, and she'll want to freshen up. What's more, we should give notes to the cast."

"The boys can bring her things upstairs," Peg said. "She looks fresh enough to me. And the cast doesn't need notes."

"The cast always needs notes."

"Tomorrow we can fix it" was Peg's vague answer, which seemed to satisfy Olive not at all. "I don't want to talk about business just now. I could *murder* a meal, and what's worse I have a powerful thirst. Let's just go out, can't we?"

By now, it sounded like Peg was begging for Olive's permission.

"Not tonight, Peg," said Olive firmly. "It's been too long a day. The girl needs to rest and settle in. Bernadette left a meat loaf upstairs. I can make sandwiches."

Peg looked a little deflated, but cheered up again within the next minute.

"Upstairs, then!" she said. "Come, Vivvie! Let's go!"

Here's something I learned over time about my aunt: whenever she said "Let's go!" she meant that whoever was in earshot was also invited. Peg always moved in a crowd, and she wasn't picky about who was in the crowd, either.

So that's why our gathering that night—held upstairs, in the living quarters of the Lily Playhouse—included not only me and Aunt Peg and her secretary, Olive, but also Gladys and Celia, the showgirls. A last-minute addition was a fey young man whom Peg collared as he was heading toward the stage door. I recognized him as a dancer in the show. Once I got up close to him, I could see that he looked about fourteen years old, and he also looked as if he could use a meal.

"Roland, join us upstairs for dinner," Peg said.

He hesitated. "Aw, that's all right, Peg."

"Don't worry, hon, we've got plenty of food. Bernadette made a big pile of meat loaf. There's enough for everyone."

When Olive looked as though she were going to protest something, Peg shushed her: "Oh, Olive, don't play the governess. I can share my dinner with Roland here. He needs to put on some weight, and I need to lose some, so it works out. Anyway, we're semisolvent right now. We can afford to feed a few more mouths."

We headed to the back of the theater, where a wide staircase led to the upstairs of the Lily. As we climbed the stairs, I could not stop staring at those two showgirls. Celia and Gladys. I'd never seen such beauties. I'd been around theater girls back at boarding school, but this was different. The theater girls at Emma Willard tended to be the sort of females who never washed their hair, and always wore thick black leotards, and every single one of them thought she was Medea, at all times. I simply couldn't bear them. But Gladys and Celia—this was a different category. This was a different *species*. I was mesmerized by their glamour, their accents, their makeup, the swing of their silk-wrapped rear ends. And as for Roland, he moved his body just the same way. He, too, was a fluid, swinging creature. How fast they all talked! And how alluringly they threw out abbreviated hints of gossip, like bits of bright confetti.

"She just gets by on her looks!" Gladys was saying, about some girl or another.

"Not even on her looks!" Roland added. "Just on her *legs*!"

"Well, that ain't enough!" said Gladys.

"For one more season it is," said Celia. "*Maybe.*"

"That boyfriend of hers don't help matters."

"*That* lamebrain!"

"He keeps lapping up that champagne, though."

"She should up and tell him!"

"He's not exactly panting for it!"

"How long can a girl make a living as a movie usher?"

"Walking around with that nice-looking diamond, though."

"She should try to think more reasonable."

"She should get herself a butter-and-egg man."

Who were these *people* that were being talked about? What was this *life* that was being suggested? And who was this poor girl being discussed in the stairwell? How was she ever going to advance past being a mere movie usher, if she didn't start thinking more *reasonable*? Who'd given her the diamond? Who was paying for all the champagne that was being lapped up? I *cared* about all these things! These things mattered! And what in the world was a butter-and-egg man?

I'd never been more desperate to know how a story ended, and this story didn't even have a plot—it just had unnamed characters, hints of wild action, and a sense of looming crisis. My heart was racing with excitement—and yours would have been, too, if you were a frivolous nineteen-year-old girl like me, who'd never had a serious thought in her life.

We reached a dimly lit landing, and Peg unlocked a door and let us all in.

"Welcome home, kiddo," Peg said.

"Home" in my Aunt Peg's world consisted of the third and fourth floors of the Lily Playhouse. These were the living quarters. The second floor of the building—as I would find out later—was office space.

The ground floor, of course, was the theater itself, which I've already described for you. But the third and fourth floors were *home,* and now we had arrived.

Peg did not have a talent for interior design, I could instantly see. Her taste (if you could call it that) ran toward heavy, outdated antiques, and mismatched chairs, and a lot of apparent confusion about what belonged where. I could see that Peg had the same sort of dark, unhappy paintings on her walls as my parents had (inherited from the same relatives, no doubt). It was all faded prints of horses and portraits of crusty old Quakers. There was a fair amount of familiar-looking old silver and china spread around the place as well—candlesticks and tea sets, and such—and some of it looked valuable, but who knew? None of it look used or loved. (There were ashtrays on every surface, though, and those certainly looked used and loved.)

I don't want to say that the place was a hovel. It wasn't dirty; it just wasn't *arranged.* I caught a glance of a formal dining room—or, rather, what might have been a formal dining room in anyone else's home, except that a Ping-Pong table had been placed right in the middle of the room. Even more curiously, the Ping-Pong table was directly situated beneath a low-hanging chandelier, which must have made it difficult to play a game.

We landed in a generously sized living room—a big enough space that it could be overstuffed with furniture while also containing a grand piano, which was jammed unceremoniously against the wall.

"Who needs something from the bottle and jug department?" asked Peg, heading to a bar in the corner. "Martinis? Anyone? Everyone?"

The resounding answer seemed to be: *Yes! Everyone!*

Well, almost everyone. Olive declined a drink and frowned as Peg poured the martinis. It looked as though Olive were calculating the price of each cocktail down to the halfpenny—which she probably was doing.

My aunt handed me my martini as casually as if she and I had been drinking together for ages. This was a delight. I felt quite adult. My parents drank (of course they drank; they were WASPs) but they never drank with me. I'd always had to execute my drinking on the sly. Not anymore, it seemed.

Cheers!

"Let me show you to your rooms," Olive said.

Peg's secretary led me down a rabbit warren and opened one of the doors. She told me, "This is your Uncle Billy's apartment. Peg would like you to stay here for now."

I was surprised. "Uncle Billy has an apartment here?"

Olive sighed. "It is a sign of your aunt's enduring affection for her husband that she keeps these rooms for him, should he need a place to stay while passing through."

I don't think it was my imagination that Olive said the words "enduring affection" much the same way someone else might say "stubborn rash."

Well, thank you, Aunt Peg, because Billy's apartment was wonderful. It didn't have the clutter of the other rooms I'd seen—not at all. No, this place had *style*. There was a small sitting room with a fireplace and a fine, black-lacquered desk, upon which sat a typewriter. Then there was the bedroom, with its windows facing Forty-first Street, and its handsome double bed made of chrome and dark wood. On the floor was an immaculate white rug. I had never before stood on a white rug. Just off the bedroom was a good-sized dressing room with a large chrome mirror on the wall, and a glossy wardrobe containing not one item of clothing whatsoever. In the corner of the dressing room was a small sink. The place was spotless.

"You don't have your own bath, unfortunately," said Olive, as the men in overalls were depositing my trunks and sewing machine in the dressing room. "There is a common bath across the hall. You'll be sharing that with Celia, as she is staying at the Lily, just for now. Mr. Herbert and Benjamin live in the other wing. They share their own bath."

I didn't know who Mr. Herbert and Benjamin were, but I figured I'd soon enough be finding out.

"Billy won't be needing his apartment, Olive?"

"I sincerely doubt it."

"Are you very sure? If he should ever need these rooms, of course, I can go somewhere else. What I'm saying is that I don't need anything so nice as all this. . . ."

I was lying. I needed and wanted this little apartment with all my heart, and had already laid claim to it in my imagination. This is where I would become a person of significance, I decided.

"Your uncle hasn't been to New York City in over four years, Vivian," Olive said, eyeballing me in that way she had—that unsettling way of making you feel as though she were watching your thoughts like a newsreel. "I trust that you can bunk down here with a certain sense of security."

Oh, bliss!

I unpacked a few essentials, splashed some water on my face, powdered my nose, and combed my hair. Then it was back to the clutter and chatter of the big, overstuffed living room. Back to Peg's world, with all its novelty and noise.

Olive went to the kitchen and brought out a small meat loaf, served on a plate of dismal lettuce. Just as she had intuited earlier, this was not going to be enough of a meal for everyone in the room. Shortly, however, she reappeared with some cold cuts and bread. She also scared up half a chicken carcass, a plate of pickles, and some containers of cold Chinese food. I noticed that somebody had opened a window and turned on a small fan, which helped to eliminate the stuffy summer heat not in the least.

"You kids eat," Peg said. "Take all you need."

Gladys and Roland lit into the meat loaf like a couple of farm-hands. I helped myself to some of the chop suey. Celia didn't eat any-thing, but sat quietly on one of the couches, handling her martini glass and cigarette with more panache than anything I'd ever seen.

"How was the beginning of the show tonight?" Olive asked. "I only caught the end."

"Well, it fell short of *King Lear*," said Peg. "But only just."

Olive's frown deepened. "Why? What happened?"

"Nothing happened per se," said Peg. "It's just a lackluster show, but it's nothing to lose sleep over. It's always been lackluster. Nobody in the audience seemed unduly harmed by it. They all left the theater with the use of their legs. Anyway, we're changing the show next week, so it doesn't matter."

"And the box office receipts? For the early show?"

"The less we speak of such matters the better," said Peg.

"But what was the take, Peg?"

"Don't ask questions that you don't want to know the answers to, Olive."

"Well, I will *need* to know. We can't keep having crowds like tonight."

"Oh, how I love that you call it a crowd! By actual count, there were forty-seven people at the early show this evening."

"Peg! That's not *enough*!"

"Don't grieve, Olive. Things always get slower in the summer, re-member. Anyway, we get the audiences we get. If we wanted to draw larger crowds, we would put on baseball games instead of plays. Or we would invest in air-conditioning. Let's just turn our attention now toward getting the South Seas act ready for next week. We can get the dancers rehearsing tomorrow morning, and they can be up and running by Tuesday."

"Not tomorrow morning," said Olive. "I've rented the stage out to a children's dance class."

"Good for you. Resourceful as ever, old girl. Tomorrow afternoon, then."

"Not tomorrow afternoon. I've rented the stage out for a swimming class."

This caught Peg up short. "A *swimming* class? Come again?"

"It's a program that the city is offering. They'll be teaching children from the neighborhood how to swim."

"To *swim*? Will they be flooding our stage, Olive?"

"Of course not. It's called dry swimming. They teach the classes without water."

"Do you mean to tell me that they will teach swimming as a *theoretical concept*?"

"More or less so. Just the basics. They use chairs. The city is paying for it."

"How about this, Olive. How about you tell Gladys when you *haven't* rented our stage out to a children's dance class, or to a dry swimming school, and then she can call a rehearsal to begin working on the dances for the South Seas act?"

"Monday afternoon," said Olive.

"Monday afternoon, Gladys!" Peg called over to the showgirl. "Did you hear that? Can you gather everyone together for Monday afternoon?"

"I don't like rehearsing in the mornings, anyhow," said Gladys, although I wasn't sure this constituted a firm reply.

"It shouldn't be hard, Gladdie," said Peg. "It's just a scratch revue. Throw something together, the way you do."

"I want to be in the South Seas show!" said Roland.

"Everyone wants to be in the South Seas show," said Peg. "The kids love performing in these exotic international dramas, Vivvie. They love the costumes. This year alone, we've had an Indian show, a Chinese maiden story, and a Spanish dancer story. We tried an Eskimo romance last year, but it was no good. The costumes weren't very becoming, to say the least. Fur, you know. Heavy. And the songs were not our best. We ended up rhyming 'nice' with 'ice' so many times, it made your head ache."

"You can play one of the hula girls in the South Seas show, Roland!" Gladys said, and laughed.

"I sure am pretty enough for it!" he said, and struck a pose.

"You sure are," agreed Gladys. "And you're so tiny, one of these days you're just gonna float away. I always gotta be careful not to put you right next to me on the stage. Standing next to you, I look like a great big cow."

"That could be because you've gained weight lately, Gladys," observed Olive. "You need to monitor what you eat, or soon you won't fit into your costumes at all."

"What a person eats doesn't have *anything* to do with her figure!" Gladys protested, as she reached for another piece of meat loaf. "I read it in a magazine. What matters is how much *coffee* you drink."

"You drink too much *booze*," Roland cried out. "You can't hold your liquor!"

"I surely cannot hold my liquor!" Gladys agreed. "Everybody knows *that* about me. But I'll tell you another thing—I wouldn't have as big a sex life as I have, if I could hold my liquor!"

"Boot me your lipstick, Celia," said Gladys to the other showgirl, who silently pulled out a tube from the pocket of her silk robe and handed it over. Gladys painted her lips with the most violent shade of red I'd ever seen, and then kissed Roland hard on both his cheeks, leaving big, bright imprints.

"There, Roland. Now you *are* the prettiest girl in the room!"

Roland didn't appear to mind the teasing. He had a face just like a porcelain doll, and to my expert eye, it looked as though he tweezed his brows. I was shocked that he didn't even *try* to act male. When he spoke, he waved his hands around like a debutante. He didn't even wipe off the lipstick from his cheeks! It's almost as though he *wanted* to look like a female! (Forgive my naïveté, Angela, but I hadn't been around a lot of homosexuals at that point in my life. Not male ones, anyhow. Now lesbians, on the other hand—*those* I'd seen. I did spend a year at Vassar, after all. Even I wasn't *that* oblivious.)

Peg turned her attention to me. "Now! Vivian Louise Morris! What do you want to do with yourself while you're here in New York City?"

What did I want to do with myself? I wanted to do *this*! I wanted to drink martinis with showgirls, and listen to Broadway business talk, and eavesdrop on the gossip of boys who looked like girls! I wanted to hear about people's big sex lives!

But I couldn't say any of that. So what I said, brilliantly, was: "I'd like to look around a bit! Take things in!"

Everyone was looking at me now. Waiting for something more, maybe? Waiting for *what*?

"I don't know my way around New York City, is my primary obstacle," I said, sounding like an ass.

Aunt Peg responded to this inanity by grabbing a paper napkin off the table, and sketching upon it a quick map of Manhattan. I do wish I had managed to preserve that map, Angela. It was the most charming map of the city I would ever see: a big crooked carrot of an island, with a dark rectangle in the middle representing Central Park; vague wavy lines representing the Hudson and East Rivers; a dollar sign down at the bottom of the island, representing Wall Street; a musical note up at the top of the island, representing Harlem, and a bright star right in the middle, representing right where we were: Times Square. Center of the world! Bingo!

"There," she said. "Now you know your way around. You can't get lost here, kiddo. Just follow the street signs. It's all numbered, couldn't be easier. Just remember: Manhattan is an island. People forget that. Walk far enough in any direction, and you'll run into water. If you hit a river, turn around and go in the other direction. You'll learn your way around. Dumber people than you have figured out this city."

"Even Gladys figured it out," said Roland.

"Watch it, sunshine," said Gladys. "I was *born* here."

"Thank you!" I said, pocketing the napkin. "And if you need anything done around the theater, I would be happy to help out."

"You'd like to help?" Peg seemed surprised to hear it. Clearly, she had not expected much of me. Christ, what had my parents told her? "You can help Olive in the office, if you go for that sort of thing. Office work, and such."

Olive blanched at this suggestion, and I'm afraid I might have done the same. I didn't want to work for Olive any more than she wanted me working for her.

"Or you can work in the box office," Peg went on. "You can sell tickets. You're not musical, are you? I'd be surprised if you were. Nobody in our family is musical."

"I can sew," I said.

I must've said it quietly, because nobody seemed to register that I'd spoken.

Olive said, "Peg, why don't you have Vivian enroll at the Katharine Gibbs School, where she can learn how to type?"

Peg, Gladys, and Celia all groaned as one.

"Olive is always trying to get us girls to enroll at Katharine Gibbs so we can learn how to type," Gladys explained. She shuddered in dramatic horror, as though learning how to type were something akin to busting up rocks in a prisoner-of-war camp.

"Katharine Gibbs turns out employable young women," Olive said. "A young woman ought to be employable."

"I can't type, and I'm employable!" Gladys said. "Heck, I'm already *employed*! I'm employed by *you*!"

Olive said, "A showgirl is never quite *employed*, Gladys. A showgirl is a person who may—at *times*—be in possession of a job. It's not the same thing. Yours is not a reliable field of work. A secretary, by contrast, can always find employment."

"I'm not just a showgirl," said Gladys, with miffed pride. "I'm a *dance captain*. A dance captain can always find employment. Anyhow, if I run out of money, I'll just get married."

"Never learn to type, kiddo," Peg said to me. "And if you *do* learn to type, never tell anybody that you can type, or they'll make you do it forever. Never learn shorthand, either. It'll be the death of you. Once they put a steno pad in a woman's hand, it never comes out."

Suddenly the gorgeous creature on the other side of the room spoke, for the first time since we'd come upstairs. "You said you can sew?" Celia asked.

Once again, that low, throaty voice took me by surprise. Also, she had her eyes on me now, which I found a bit intimidating. I don't want to overuse the word "smoldering" when I talk about Celia, but there's no way around it: she was the kind of woman who smoldered even when she wasn't intentionally trying to smolder. Holding that smoldering gaze was uncomfortable for me, so I just nodded, and said in the safer direction of Peg, "Yes. I can sew. Grandmother Morris taught me how."

"What sort of stuff do you make?" Celia asked.

"Well, I made this dress."

Gladys screamed, "*You made that dress?*"

Both Gladys and Roland rushed at me the way girls always rushed at me when they found out that I'd made my own dress. In a flash, the two of them were picking at my outfit, like two gorgeous little monkeys.

"You did *this*?" Gladys said.

"Even the *trim*?" Roland asked.

I wanted to say, "This is nothing!"—because truly, compared to what I could do, this little frock, cunning though it appeared, *was* nothing. But I didn't want to sound cocky. So instead I said, "I make everything I wear."

Celia spoke again, from across the room: "Can you make costumes?"

"I suppose so. It would depend on the costume, but I'm sure I could."

The showgirl stood up and asked, "Could you make something like this?" She let her robe drop to the floor, revealing the costume beneath it.

(I know that sounds dramatic, to say that she "let her robe drop," but Celia was the kind of girl who didn't just take her clothes off like any other mortal woman; she always *let them drop*.)

Her figure was astonishing, but as for the costume, it was basic—a little two-piece metallic number, something like a bathing suit. It was the sort of thing that was designed to look better from fifty feet away than up close. It had tight, high-waisted shorts decorated in splashy sequins, and a bra that was decked out in a gaudy arrangement of beads and feathers. It looked good on her, but that's only because a hospital gown would have looked good on her. I thought it could have fit her better, to be honest. The shoulder straps were all wrong.

"I could make that," I said. "The beading would take me awhile, but that's just busywork. The rest of it is straightforward." Then I had a flash of inspiration, like a flare shot up in a night sky: "Say, if you have a costume director, maybe I could work with her? I could be her assistant!"

Laughter burst out across the room.

"A *costume director*!" Gladys said. "What do you think this is, Paramount Pictures? You think we got Edith Head hiding down there in the basement?"

"The girls are responsible for their own costumes," Peg explained. "If we don't have anything that will work for them in our costume closet—and we never do—they have to provide their own outfits. It costs them, but that's just how things have always been done. Where'd you get yours, Celia?"

"I bought it off a girl. You remember Evelyn, at El Morocco? She got married, moved to Texas. She gave me a whole trunk of costumes. Lucky for me."

"Sure, lucky for you," sniffed Roland. "Lucky you didn't get the clap."

"Aw, give it a rest, Roland," said Gladys. "Evelyn was a good kid. You're just jealous because she married a *cowboy*."

"If you'd like to help the kids out with their costumes, Vivian, I'm sure everyone would appreciate it," said Peg.

"Could you make me a South Seas outfit?" Gladys asked me. "Like a Hawaiian hula girl?"

That was like asking a master chef if he could make porridge.

"Sure," I said. "I could make you one tomorrow."

"Could you make *me* a hula outfit?" asked Roland.

"I don't have a budget for new costumes," Olive warned. "We haven't discussed this."

"Oh, Olive," Peg sighed. "You are every inch the vicar's wife. Let the kids have their fun."

I couldn't help but observe that Celia had kept her gaze on me since we started talking about sewing. Being in her line of vision felt both terrifying and thrilling.

"You know something?" she said, after studying me more closely. "You're pretty."

Now, to be fair, people usually noticed this fact about me sooner.

But who could blame Celia for having paid me so little attention up until this point, when she was in possession of *that* face and *that* body?

"Tell you the truth," she said, smiling for the first time that night, "you kinda look like me."

Let me be clear, Angela: I didn't.

Celia Ray was a goddess; I was an adolescent. But in the sketchiest of terms, I suppose I could see that she had a point: we were both tall brunettes with ivory skin and wide-set brown eyes. We could have passed for cousins, if not sisters—and decidedly not twins. Certainly our figures had nothing in common. She was a peach; I was a stick. Still, I was flattered. To this day, though, I believe that the only reason Celia Ray ever took notice of me at all was because we looked a *tiny* bit alike, and that drew her attention. For Celia, vain as she was, looking at me must have been like looking in a (very foggy, very distant) mirror—and Celia never met a mirror she didn't love.

"You and me should dress up alike sometime and go out on the town," Celia said, in that low Bronx growl that was also a purr. "We could get ourselves into some real good trouble."

Well, I didn't even know what to say to *that*. I just sat there, gaping like the Emma Willard schoolgirl I so recently had been.

As for my Aunt Peg—my *legal guardian*, at this point, please remember—she heard this illicit-sounding invite and said, "Say, girls, that sounds fun."

Peg was over at the bar again mixing up another batch of martinis, but at that point, Olive put a stop to things. The fearsome secretary of the Lily Playhouse stood up, clapped her hands, and announced, "Enough! If Peg stays up any later, she will not be the better for it in the morning."

"Darn it, Olive, I'll give you a poke in the eye!" Peg said.

"To bed, Peg," said the imperturbable Olive, tugging down her girdle for emphasis. "*Now.*"

The room scattered. We all said our good nights.

I made my way to my apartment (*my apartment!*) and unpacked a bit more. I couldn't really focus on the task, though. I was in a buzz of nervous joy.

Peg came by to check on me as I was hanging up my dresses in the wardrobe.

"You're comfortable here?" she asked, looking around at Billy's immaculate apartment.

"I like it so much here. It's lovely."

"Yes. Billy would accept nothing less."

"May I ask you something, Peg?"

"Certainly."

"What about the fire?"

"Which fire, kiddo?"

"Olive said there was a small fire at the theater today. I wondered if everything is all right."

"Oh, that! It was just some old sets that accidentally got ignited behind the building. I have friends in the fire department, so we were fine. Boy, was that *today*? By golly, I'd forgotten about it already." Peg rubbed her eyes. "Oh, well, kiddo. You will soon enough find out that life at the Lily Playhouse is nothing but a series of small fires. Now off to sleep or Olive will have you detained by the authorities."

So off to sleep I went—the first time I would ever sleep in New York City, and the first (but decidedly not the last) time I would ever sleep in a man's bed.

I do not recall who cleaned up the dinner mess.

It was probably Olive.

FOUR

Within two weeks of moving to New York City, my life had changed completely. These changes included, but were not limited to, the loss of my virginity—which is an awfully amusing story that I shall tell you shortly, Angela, if you'll just be patient with me for a moment longer.

Because for now, I just want to say that the Lily Playhouse was unlike any world I'd ever inhabited. It was a living animation of glamour and grit and mayhem and fun—a world full of adults behaving like children, in other words. Gone was all the order and regimentation that my family and my schools had tried to drill into me thus far. Nobody at the Lily (with the exception of the long-suffering Olive) even attempted to keep the normal rhythms of respectable life. Drinking and reveling were the norm. Meals were held at sporadic hours. People slept until noon. Nobody started work at a particular time of day—nor did they ever exactly stop working, for that matter. Plans changed by the moment, guests came and went with neither formal introductions nor organized farewells, and the designation of duties was always unclear.

I swiftly learned, to my head-spinning astonishment, that no figure of authority was going to be monitoring my comings and goings anymore. I had nobody to report to and nothing was expected of me. If I wanted to help out with costumes, I could, but I was given no formal job. There was no curfew, no head count in the beds at night. There was no house warden; there was no mother.

I was *free.*

Allegedly, of course, Aunt Peg was responsible for me. She was my actual family member, and had been entrusted with my care in loco parentis. But she wasn't overprotective, to say the least. In fact, Aunt Peg was the first freethinker I'd ever met. She was of the mind that people should make their own decisions about their own lives, if you can imagine such a preposterous thing!

Peg's world ran on chaos, and yet somehow it worked. Despite all the disorder, she managed to put on two shows a day at the Lily—an early show (which started at five, and attracted women and children) and a late show (which started at eight, and was a bit racier, for an older and more male audience). There were matinees on Sunday and Wednesday, too. On Saturdays at noon, there was always a magic show for free, for the local children. Olive was usually able to rent out the space for neighborhood usage during the daytime, though I don't think there was danger of anybody getting rich off dry swimming lessons.

Our audience was drawn from the neighborhood itself, and back then, it really *was* a neighborhood—mostly Irish and Italians, with a scattering of Catholic Eastern Europeans, and a good number of Jewish families. The four-story tenements surrounding the Lily were crammed full of recent immigrants—and by "crammed," I mean dozens of souls living in a single flat. That being the case, Peg tried to keep the language in our shows simple, to accommodate these new English speakers. Simpler language also made the memorizing of lines easier for our performers, who were not exactly classically trained thespians.

Our shows did not attract tourists, or critics, or what you might call "theatergoers." We provided working-class entertainment for working-class people, and that was it. Peg was adamant that we not kid ourselves that we did anything more. ("I'd rather put on a good leg show than bad Shakespeare," she said.) Indeed, the Lily did not have any of the hallmarks that you would associate with a proper Broadway institution. We did not have out-of-town tryouts, or glamorous parties on opening nights. We didn't close down in August, like so many of the Broadway houses did. (Our patrons didn't go on vacations, so neither did we.) We were not even dark on Mondays. We were more like what used to be called "a continuous house"—where entertainment just kept being served up, day after day, all the year round. As long as we kept our ticket prices comparable to those at the local movie houses (which were, along with arcades and illegal gambling, our biggest competition for the neighborhood dollars) we could fill our seats fairly well.

The Lily was not a burlesque theater, but many of our showgirls and dancers had come from the world of burlesque (and they had the immodesty to prove it, bless them). We were not quite vaudeville, either—only because vaudeville was nearly dead by that point in history. But we were almost vaudeville, considering our slapdash, comic plays. In fact, it would be a stretch to claim that our plays were *plays* at all. It would be more accurate to say that they were revues—cobbled-together bits of stories that were not much more than excuses for lovers to reunite and for dancers to show off their legs. (There were limits to the scope of the stories that we could tell, anyhow, given that the Lily Playhouse only had three backdrops. This meant that all the action in our shows had to take place on either a nineteenth-century city street corner, in an elegant upper-class parlor, or on an ocean liner.)

Peg changed the revues every few weeks, but they were all more or less the same, and they were all forgettable. (What's that you say? You never heard of a play called *Hopping Mad*, about two street urchins who fall in love? Why, of course you didn't! It ran at the Lily for only two weeks, and it was swiftly replaced by a nearly identical play called *Catch That Boat!*—which, of course, took place on an ocean liner.)

"If I could improve on the formula, I would," she once told me. "But the formula works."

The formula, to be specific, was this:

Delight (or at least distract) your audience for a short while (never more than forty-five minutes!) with an approximation of a love story. Your love story should star a likable young couple who can tap-dance and sing, but who are kept apart from each other's arms by a villain—often a banker, sometimes a gangster (same idea, different costume)—who gnashes his teeth and tries to destroy our good couple. There should be a floozy with a notable bustline making eyes at our hero—but the hero must only have eyes for his one true girl. There should be a handsome swain who tries to woo the girl away from her fellow. There should be a drunken hobo character for comic relief—his stubble indicated by application of burnt cork. The show always had at least one dreamy ballad, usually rhyming the word "moon" with the word "swoon." And there was always a kick line at the end.

Applause, curtain, do it all over again for the late show.

Theater critics did an excellent job of not noticing our existence at all, which was probably best for everyone.

If it sounds like I'm denigrating the Lily's productions, I'm not: I loved them. I would give anything to sit in the back of that rotting old playhouse and see one of those shows again. To my mind, there was never anything better than those simple, enthusiastic revues. They made me happy. They were designed to make people happy without making the audience work too hard to understand what was going on. As Peg had learned back in the Great War—when she used to produce cheerful song-and-dance skits for soldiers who'd just lost limbs, or had their throats burned out with mustard gas—"Sometimes people just need to think about something else."

Our job was to give them the something else.

As for the cast, our shows always needed eight dancers—four boys and four girls—and also always needed four showgirls, because that's just what was expected. People came to the Lily for the showgirls. If you're wondering what the difference was between "dancer" and "showgirl," it was height. Showgirls had to be at least five foot ten. That was *without* the heels and the feather headdresses. And showgirls were expected to be far more stunning than your average dancer.

Just to further confuse you, sometimes the showgirls danced (such as Gladys, who was also our dance captain), but the dancers never showgirled, because they weren't tall enough or beautiful enough, and never would be. No amount of makeup or creative padding could turn a moderately attractive and medium-sized dancer with a fairly decent figure into the spectacle of Amazonian gorgeousness that was a mid-century New York City showgirl.

The Lily Playhouse caught a lot of performers on their way up the ladder of success. Some of the girls who started out their careers at the Lily later moved on to Radio City or to the Diamond Horseshoe. Some of them even became headliners. But more often, we caught dancers on their way down the ladder. (There is nothing more brave or touching than an aging Rockette auditioning to be in the chorus line of a cheap and lousy show called *Catch That Boat!*)

But we had a small group of regulars, too, who performed for the Lily's humble audiences in show after show. Gladys was a staple of the company. She had invented a dance called the "boggle-boggle," which our audiences loved, and so we put it in every performance. And why wouldn't they love it? It was nothing but a free-for-all of girls *boggling* about the stage with the most jiggling of body parts imaginable.

"Boggle-boggle!" the audience would shout during the encores, and the girls would accommodate them. Sometimes we would see neighborhood children on the sidewalks doing the boggle-boggle on their way to school.

Let's just say it was our cultural legacy.

would love to tell you exactly how Peg's little theater company remained solvent, but the truth is that I do not know. (It could be a case of that old joke about how to make a small fortune in show business: by starting with a large fortune.) Our shows never sold out, and our ticket prices were chicken feed. Moreover, although the Lily Playhouse was marvelous, she was a white elephant of the highest degree, and she was *expensive*. She leaked and creaked. Her electrical wiring was as old as Edison himself, her plumbing was occult, her paint was everywhere peeling, and her roof was designed to withstand a sunny day with no rain, and not much more than that. My Aunt Peg poured money into that collapsing old theater the way an indulgent heiress might pour money into the drug habit of an opium-addicted lover—which is to say bottomlessly, desperately, and uselessly.

As for Olive, her job was to try to stem the flow of money. An equally bottomless, desperate, and hopeless task. (I can still hear Olive crying out, "This is not a French hotel!" whenever she'd catch people running the hot water too long.)

Olive always looked tired, and for good reason: she had been the only responsible adult in this company since 1917, when she and Peg first met. I soon learned that Olive wasn't joking when she said she'd been working for Peg "since Moses was in nappies." Just like Peg, Olive had been a Red Cross nurse in the Great War—although she'd been trained in Britain, of course. The two women had met on the battle-fields of France. When the war ended, Olive decided to abandon nurs-ing and follow her new friend into the field of theater instead—playing the role of my aunt's trusted and long-suffering secretary.

Olive could always be seen marching about the Lily Playhouse, rap-idly issuing commands, edicts, and corrections. She wore the strained and martyred expression of a good herding dog charged with bringing order to an undisciplined flock of sheep. She was full of rules. There was to be no eating in the theater ("We don't want more rats than audi-ence members!"). There was to be *promptitude* at all rehearsals. No "guests of guests" were allowed to sleep overnight. There were to be no refunds without receipts. And the taxman must always be paid first.

Peg respected the rules of her secretary, but only in the most ab-stract way. She respected those rules in the manner of someone who has lapsed from their faith but who still has a fundamental regard for church law. In other words: she respected Olive's rules without actually obeying them.

The rest of us followed Peg's lead, which meant that nobody obeyed Olive's rules, although we sometimes pretended to.

Thus Olive was constantly exhausted, and we were allowed to re-main like children.

Peg and Olive lived on the fourth floor of the Lily, in apartments separated by a common living area. There were several other apart-ments up there on the fourth floor, too, that were not in active use when I first moved in. (They'd been built by the original owner for his mis-tresses, but were now being saved, Peg explained to me, "for last-minute drifters and other sundry itinerants.")

But the third floor, where I got to live, is where all the interesting activity happened. That's where the piano was—usually covered by half-empty cocktail glasses and half-full ashtrays. (Sometimes Peg would pass by the piano, pick up someone's leftover drink, and knock it back. She called it "taking a dividend.") It was on the third floor where everyone ate, smoked, drank, fought, worked, and lived. This was the *real* office of the Lily Playhouse.

There was a man named Mr. Herbert who also lived on the third floor. Mr. Herbert was introduced to me as "our playwright." He created the basic story lines for our shows, and also came up with the jokes and gags. He was also the stage manager. He also served, I was told, as the Lily Playhouse's press agent.

"What does a press agent do, exactly?" I once asked him.

"I wish I knew," he responded.

More interestingly, he was a disbarred attorney, and one of Peg's oldest friends. He'd been disbarred after embezzling a considerable amount of money from a client. Peg didn't hold the crime against him because he'd been off the wagon at the time. "You can't blame a man for what he does when he's drinking" was her philosophy. ("We all have our frailties" was another of her adages—she, who always gave second and third and fourth chances to the frail and the failing.) Sometimes in a pinch, when we didn't have a better performer on hand, Mr. Herbert would play the role of the drunken hobo character in our shows—bringing to that position a natural pathos that would just break your heart.

But Mr. Herbert was *funny*. He was funny in a way that was dry and dark, but he was undeniably funny. In the mornings when I got up for breakfast, I would always find Mr. Herbert sitting at the kitchen table in his saggy suit trousers and an undershirt. He'd be drinking from his mug of Sanka and picking at his one sad pancake. He would sigh and frown over his notepad, trying to think of new jokes and lines for the next show. Every morning, I would bait him with a sunny greeting, just to hear his depressed response, which always changed by the day.

"Good morning, Mr. Herbert!" I would say.

"The point is debatable," he might respond.

Or, on another day: "Good morning, Mr. Herbert!"

"I will half allow it."

Or: "Good morning, Mr. Herbert!"

"I fail to see your argument."

Or: "Good morning, Mr. Herbert!"

"I find myself unequal to the occasion."

Or, my favorite ever: "Good morning, Mr. Herbert!"

"Oh, you're a satirist now, are you?"

Another inhabitant of the third floor was a handsome young black man named Benjamin Wilson, who was the Lily's songwriter, composer, and piano player. Benjamin was quiet and refined, and he always dressed in the most beautiful suits. He was usually to be found sitting at the grand piano, either riffing on some jaunty tune for an upcoming show, or playing jazz for his own entertainment. Sometimes he would play hymns, but only when he thought nobody was listening.

Benjamin's father was a respected minister up in Harlem, and his mother was the principal of a girls' academy on 132nd Street. He was Harlem royalty, in other words. He had been groomed for the church, but was lured away from that vocation by the world of show business. His family didn't want him around anymore, as he was now tainted with sin. This was a standard theme, I would learn, for many of the people who worked at the Lily Playhouse. Peg took in a lot of refugees, in that respect.

Not unlike Roland the dancer, Benjamin was far too talented to be working for a cheap outlet like the Lily. But Peg gave him free room and board, and his duties were light, so he stuck around.

There was one more person living at the Lily when I moved in, and I've saved her for last, because she was the most important to me.

That person was Celia—the showgirl, my goddess.

I had been told by Olive that Celia was lodging with us only temporarily—just until she got things "sorted out." The reason Celia needed a place to stay was because she'd recently been evicted from the Rehearsal Club—a respectable and inexpensive hotel for women on West Fifty-third Street, where a good many Broadway dancers and actresses stayed back in the day. But Celia had lost her place at the Rehearsal Club because she'd been caught with a man in her room. So Peg had offered Celia a room at the Lily as a stopgap measure.

I got the sense that Olive disapproved of this offering—but then again, Olive mostly disapproved of everything that Peg offered to people for free. This wasn't a palatial offering in any case. Celia's little room down the hall was far more humble than my fancy setup over in Uncle Billy's never-used pied-à-terre. Celia's bolt-hole wasn't much more than a utility closet with a cot and a tiny bit of floor upon which to strew her clothing. The room had a window, but it faced a hot, stinking alley. Celia's room didn't have a carpet, she didn't have a sink, she didn't have a mirror, she didn't have a closet, and she certainly didn't have a large, handsome bed, like I had.

All of this probably explains why Celia moved in with me my second night at the Lily. She did so without asking. There was no discussion about it whatsoever; it just happened—and at the most unexpected time, too. Somewhere in the dark hours between midnight and dawn on Day Two of my sojourn in New York City, Celia stumbled into my bedroom, woke me up with a hard bump to the shoulder, and uttered one boozy word:

"Scoot."

So I scooted. I moved over to the other side of the bed as she tumbled onto my mattress, commandeered my pillow, wrapped the entirety of my sheet around her beautiful form, and fell unconscious in a matter of moments.

Well, *this* was exciting!

This was so exciting, in fact, that I couldn't fall back to sleep. I didn't dare to move. For one thing, I'd lost my pillow, and I was now pressed against the wall, so I was no longer comfortable. But the more serious issue here was this: what is protocol when a drunk and fully dressed showgirl has just collapsed onto your bed? Unclear. So I lay there in stillness and silence, listening to her thick breathing, smelling the cigarette smoke and perfume on her hair, and wondering how we would manage the inevitable awkwardness when morning came.

Celia finally roused herself around seven o'clock, when the sunlight that was glaring into the bedroom became impossible to ignore. She gave a decadent yawn and stretched fully, taking up even *more* of the bed. She was still wearing all her makeup and was dressed in her reckless evening gown from the night before. She was stunning. She looked like an angel who had fallen to earth, straight through a hole in the floor of some celestial nightclub.

"Hey, Vivvie," she said, blinking away the sun. "Thanks for sharing your bed. That cot they gave me is torture. I couldn't take it anymore."

I hadn't been fully confident at this point that Celia even knew my name, so to hear her use the affectionate diminutive "Vivvie" flooded me with joy.

"That's all right," I said. "You can sleep here anytime."

"Really?" she said. "That's terrific. I'll move my things in here today."

Well, then. I guess I had a roommate now. (That was fine with me, though. I was just honored that she'd chosen me.) I wanted this strange, exotic moment to last as long as possible, so I dared to make conversation. "Say," I asked, "where'd you go out to last night?"

She seemed surprised that I cared.

"El Morocco," she said. "I saw John Rockefeller there."

"*Did* you?"

"He's the pits. He wanted to dance, but I was out with some other fellows."

"Who'd you go out with?"

"Nobody special. Just a couple of guys who aren't about to take me home to meet their mothers."

"What kind of guys?"

Celia settled back into the bed, lit a smoke, and told me all about her night. She explained that she had gone out with some Jewish boys who were pretending to be gangsters, but then they ran into some *real* Jewish gangsters, so the pretenders had to scram, and she ended up with a fellow who took her to Brooklyn and then paid for a limousine to take her home. I was entranced by every detail. We stayed in bed for another hour as she narrated for me—in that unforgettably gruff voice of hers—every detail of an evening in the life of one Celia Ray, New York City showgirl.

I drank it all down like spring water.

By the next day, all of Celia's belongings had migrated into my apartment. Her tubes of greasepaint and pots of cold cream now cluttered up every surface. Her vials of Elizabeth Arden competed for space on Uncle Billy's elegant desk against her compacts of Helena Rubinstein. Her long hairs laced my sink. My floor was an instant tangle of brassieres and fishnets, garters and girdles. (She had such prodigious quantities of undergarments! I swear, Celia Ray had a way of making negligees *reproduce*.) Her used, perspiration-soaked dress shields were hiding under my bed like little mice. Her tweezers bit into my feet when I stepped on them.

She was outrageously entitled. She wiped her lipstick on my towels. She borrowed my sweaters without asking. My pillowcases became stained with black smudges from Celia's mascara, and my sheets were dyed orange from her pancake makeup. And there wasn't anything this girl wouldn't use as an ashtray—including once, while I was in it, the bathtub.

Incredibly, I didn't mind any of this. On the contrary, I never wanted her to leave. If I'd had a roommate this interesting back at Vassar, I might've stayed in college. To my mind, Celia Ray was perfection. She was New York City's very distillation—a glittering composite of sophistication and mystery. I would endure any filth or befouling, just to have access to her.

Anyhow, our living arrangement seemed to suit us both perfectly: I got to be near her glamour, and she got to be near my sink.

I never asked my Aunt Peg if this was all right with her—that Celia had moved into Uncle Billy's rooms with me, or that the showgirl seemed intent on staying at the Lily indefinitely. This seems awfully ill-mannered, when I think back on it now. It would have been the most basic act of politeness to at least clear this arrangement with my host. But I was far too self-absorbed to be polite—and so was Celia, of course. So we just went ahead and did whatever we wanted to do, without giving it another thought.

What's more, I never *really* worried about the mess that Celia left behind in that apartment, because I knew that Aunt Peg's maid, Bernadette, would eventually take care of it. Bernadette was a quiet and efficient soul who came to the Lily six days a week to clean up after everyone. She tidied up our kitchen and our bathrooms, waxed our floors, cooked dinner for us (which we sometimes ate, sometimes ignored, and sometimes invited ten unannounced guests to). She also ordered the groceries, called in the plumber nearly every day, and probably did about ten thousand other thankless tasks, as well. In addition to all that, she now had to clean up after me and Celia Ray, which hardly seems fair.

I once overheard Olive remark to a guest: "Bernadette is Irish, of course. But she is not *violently* Irish, so we keep her on."

This is the kind of thing that people used to say back then, Angela. Unfortunately, that's all I can remember about Bernadette.

The reason I don't remember any particular details about Bernadette is because I didn't pay much attention to maids back then. I was so very accustomed to them, you see. They were nearly invisible to me. I just expected to be served. And why was that? Why was I so presumptuous and callow?

Because I was rich.

I haven't said those words yet in these pages, so let's just get it out of the way right now: I was rich, Angela. I was rich, and I was spoiled. I'd been raised during the Great Depression, true, but the crisis never affected my family in any pressing manner. When the dollar failed, we went from having three maids, two cooks, a nanny, a gardener, and a full-time chauffeur to having just two maids, one cook, and a part-time chauffeur. So that didn't *quite* qualify us for the breadline, to put it mildly.

And because my expensive boarding school had ensured that I never met anybody who wasn't like me, I thought everyone had grown up with a big Zenith radio in the living room. I thought everyone had a pony. I thought every man was a Republican, and that there were only two kinds of women in the world—those who had gone to Vassar, and those who had gone to Smith. (My mother went to Vassar. Aunt Peg went to Smith for one year, before dropping out to join the Red Cross. I didn't know what the difference was between Vassar and Smith, but from the way my mother talked, I understood it to be crucial.)

I certainly thought everyone had maids. For my entire life, somebody like Bernadette had always taken care of me. When I left my dirty dishes sitting on the table, somebody always cleaned them up. My bed was beautifully made for me, every day. Dry towels magically replaced damp ones. Shoes that I tossed carelessly upon the floor were straightened out when I wasn't looking. Behind it all was some great cosmic force—constant and invisible as gravity, and just as boring to me as gravity—putting my life in order and making sure that my knickers were always clean.

It may not surprise you, then, to learn that I didn't lift a finger to help out with the housekeeping, once I moved into the Lily Playhouse— not even in the apartment that Peg had so generously bestowed upon me. It never occurred to me that I should help. Nor did it occur to me that I couldn't keep a showgirl in my bedroom as a pet, just because I felt like it.

I cannot comprehend why nobody ever throttled me.

You will sometimes encounter people my age, Angela, who grew up experiencing real hardship during the Depression. (Your father was one such person, of course.) But because everybody around them was also struggling, these people will often report that they were not aware as children that their deprivations were unusual.

You will often hear such people say: "I didn't even know I was poor!"

I was the opposite, Angela: I didn't know I was rich.

FIVE

Within a week, Celia and I had established our own little routine. Every night after the show was finished, she would throw on an evening gown (usually something that, in other circles, would've qualified as lingerie) and head out on the town for a night of debauchery and excitement. Meanwhile, I would eat a late dinner with Aunt Peg, listen to the radio, do some sewing, go to a movie, or go to sleep—all the while wishing I were doing something more exciting.

Then at some ungodly hour in the middle of the night I'd feel the bump on my shoulder, and the familiar command to "scoot." I'd scoot, and Celia would collapse onto the bed, devouring all my space, pillows, and sheets. Sometimes she would conk right out, but other nights she'd stay up chatting boozily until she dropped off in midsentence. Sometimes I would wake up and find that she was holding my hand in her sleep.

In the mornings, we would linger in bed, and she would tell me about the men she'd been with. There were the men who took her up to Harlem for dancing. The men who took her out to the midnight movies. The men who had gotten her to the front of the line to see Gene Krupa at the Paramount. The men who had introduced her to Maurice Chevalier. The men who paid for her meals of lobster thermidor and baked Alaska. (There was nothing Celia would not do—nothing she had not done—for the sake of lobster thermidor and baked Alaska.) She spoke about these men as if they were meaningless to her, but only because they *were* meaningless to her. Once they paid the bill, she often had a tough time remembering their names. She used them much the same way she used my hand lotions and my stockings—freely and carelessly.

"A girl must create her own opportunities," she used to say.

As for her background, I soon learned her story:

Born in the Bronx, Celia had been christened Maria Theresa Beneventi. While you'd never guess it from the name, she was Italian. Or at least her father was Italian. From him, she'd inherited the glossy black hair and those sublime dark eyes. From her Polish mother, she'd inherited the pale skin and the height.

She had exactly one year of high school education. She left school at age fourteen, after having a scandalous affair with a friend's father. ("Affair" may not be the accurate word to describe what transpires sexually between a forty-year-old man and a fourteen-year-old girl, but that's the word Celia used.) Her "affair" had gotten her thrown out of her home, and had also gotten her pregnant. This situation, her gentleman suitor had graciously "took care of" by paying for an abortion. After her abortion, her paramour had no wish to further engage with her, so he returned his devotions to his wife and family, leaving Maria Theresa Beneventi all on her own, to make do in the world as best she could.

She worked in an industrial bakery for a while, where the owner gave her a job and offered her a place to stay in exchange for frequent

"J.O.'s"—a term that I'd never heard before, but which Celia helpfully explained to me were "jerk offs." (This is the image that I think of, Angela, whenever I hear people talk about how the past was a more innocent time. I think of fourteen-year-old Maria Theresa Beneventi, fresh off her first abortion, with no roof over her head, masturbating the owner of an industrial bakery so that she could keep her job and have somewhere safe to sleep. *Yes, folks—those were the days.*)

Soon young Maria Theresa discovered she could earn more money as a dime-a-dance girl than by baking dinner rolls for a pervert. She changed her name to Celia Ray, moved in with a few other dancers, and began her career—which consisted of putting forth her gorgeousness into the world, for the sake of personal advancement. She started working as a taxi dancer at the Honeymoon Lane Danceland on Seventh Avenue, where she let men grope her, perspire on her, and cry with loneliness in her arms for fifty dollars a week, plus "presents" on the side.

She tried for the Miss New York beauty pageant when she was sixteen, but lost to a girl who played the vibraphone onstage in a bathing suit. She also worked as a photographer's model—selling everything from dog food to antifungal creams. And she'd been an artist's model—selling her naked body for hours at a time to art schools and painters. While still a teenager, she wedded a saxophone player whom she'd met while briefly working as a hatcheck girl at the Russian Tea Room. Marriages to saxophone players never do work out, though, and Celia's was no exception; she was divorced before you knew it.

Right after her divorce, she and a girlfriend moved to California with the intention of becoming movie stars. She managed to get herself some screen tests, but never landed a speaking part. ("I got twenty-five dollars a day once to play a dead girl in a murder picture," she said proudly—naming a movie I had never heard of.) Celia left Los Angeles a few years later, having realized that "there were four girls on every corner out there with better figures than me, and no Bronx accent."

When she came back home from Hollywood, Celia got a job at the Stork Club as a showgirl. There, she met Gladys, Peg's dance captain, who recruited her for the Lily Playhouse. By 1940, when I arrived, Celia had been working for my Aunt Peg for almost two years—the longest period of stability in her life. The Lily was not a glamorous venue. It was certainly no Stork Club. But the way Celia saw it, the job was easy, her pay was regular, and the owner was a woman, which meant she didn't have to spend her workdays dodging "some greasy boss with Roman hands and Russian fingers." Plus, her job duties were over by ten o'clock. This meant that once she was done dancing on the Lily stage, she could go out on the town and dance until dawn—often *at* the Stork Club, but now it was for fun.

How all that life experience adds up to someone who was claiming to be only nineteen years old, you tell me.

To my joy and surprise, Celia and I became friends.

To a certain extent, of course, Celia liked me because I was her handmaiden. Even at the time, I knew that she regarded me as her handmaiden, but that was all right with me. (If you know anything about the friendships of young girls, you will know that there is always one person playing the part of the handmaiden, anyhow.) Celia demanded a certain level of devoted service—expecting me to rub her calves for her when they were sore, or to give her hair a rousing brushing. Or she'd say, "Oh, Vivvie, I'm all out of ciggies again!"—knowing full well that I would run out and buy her another pack. ("That's so *bliss* of you, Vivvie," she'd say, as she pocketed the cigarettes, and didn't pay me back.)

And yes, she was vain—so vain that it made my own vanities look amateurish by comparison. Truly, I've never seen anyone who could get more deeply lost in a mirror than Celia Ray. She could stand for ages in the glory of her own reflection, nearly deranged by her own beauty. I know it sounds like I'm exaggerating, but I'm not. I swear to you that she once spent *two hours* looking at herself in the mirror while debating whether she should be massaging her neck cream *upward* or *downward* in order to prevent the appearance of a double chin.

But she had a childlike sweetness about her, too. In the mornings, Celia was especially dear. When she would wake up in my bed, hungover and tired, she was just a simple kid who wanted to snuggle and gossip. She would tell me of her dreams in life—her big, unfocused dreams. Her aspirations never made sense to me because they didn't have any plans behind them. Her mind skipped straight to fame and riches, with no apparent map for how to get there—other than to keep looking like *this,* and to assume that the world would eventually reward her for it.

It wasn't much of a plan—although, to be fair, it was more of a plan than I had for my own life.

I was happy.

I guess you could say that I had become the costume director of the Lily Playhouse—but only because nobody stopped me from calling myself that, and also because nobody else wanted the job.

Truth to tell, there was plenty of work for me. The showgirls and dancers were always in need of new costumes, and it wasn't as if they could just pluck outfits out of the Lily Playhouse costume closet (a distressingly damp and spider-infested place, filled with ensembles older and more crusty than the building itself). The girls were always broke, too, so I learned clever ways to improvise. I learned how to shop for cheap materials in the garment center, or (even cheaper) way down on Orchard Street. Better yet, I figured out how to hunt for remnants at the used clothing shops on Ninth Avenue and make costumes out of those. It turned out I was exceptionally good at taking tatty old garments and turning them into something fabulous.

My favorite used clothing shop was a place called Lowtsky's Used Emporium and Notions, on the corner of Ninth Avenue and Forty-third Street. The Lowtsky family were Eastern European Jews, who'd paused in France for a few years to work in the lace industry before emigrating to America. Upon arrival in the United States, they'd settled on the Lower East Side, where they sold rags out of a pushcart. But then they moved up to Hell's Kitchen to become costumers and purveyors of used clothing. Now they owned this entire three-story building in midtown, and the place was filled with treasures. Not only did they deal in used costumes from the theater, dance, and opera worlds, but they also sold old wedding gowns and occasionally a really spectacular couture dress, picked up from some Upper East Side estate sale.

I couldn't stay away from the place.

I once bought the most *vividly* violet-colored Edwardian dress for Celia at Lowtsky's. It was the homeliest looking rag you ever saw, and Celia recoiled when I first showed it to her. But when I pulled off the sleeves, cut a deep V in the back, lowered the neckline, and belted it with a thick, black satin sash, I transformed this ancient beast of a dress into an evening gown that made my friend look like a millionaire's mistress. Every woman in the room would gasp with envy when Celia walked in wearing that gown—and all that for only two dollars!

When the other girls saw what I could make for Celia, they all wanted me to create special dresses for them, as well. And so, just as at boarding school, I was soon given a portal to popularity through the auspices of my trusty old Singer 201. The girls at the Lily were always handing me bits of things that needed to be mended—dresses without zippers, or zippers without dresses—and asking me if I could do something to fix it. (I remember Gladys once saying to me, "I need a whole new rig, Vivvie! I look like somebody's uncle!")

Maybe it sounds as if I was playing the role of the tragic stepsister in a fairy tale here—constantly working and spinning, while the more beautiful girls were all heading to the ball—but you must understand that I was so grateful just to be around these showgirls. If anything, this exchange was more beneficial for me than it was for them. Listening to their gossip was an education—the only education I had ever really longed for. And because somebody always needed my sewing talents for *something,* inevitably the showgirls started to coalesce around me and my powerful Singer. Soon, my apartment had turned into the company gathering place—for females, anyhow. (It helped that my rooms were nicer than the moldy old dressing rooms down in the basement, and also nearer to the kitchen.)

And so it came to pass that one day—less than two weeks into my stay at the Lily—a few of the girls were in my room, smoking cigarettes and watching me sew. I was making a simple capelet for a showgirl named Jennie—a vivacious, adorable, gap-toothed girl from Brooklyn whom everyone liked. She was going on a date that night, and had complained that she didn't have anything to throw over her dress in case the temperature dropped. I'd told her I would make her something nice, so that's what I was doing. It was the kind of task that was nearly effortless, but would forever endear Jennie to me.

It was on this day—a day like any other, as the saying goes—that it came to the attention of the showgirls that I was still a virgin.

The subject came up that afternoon because the girls were talking about sex—which was the only thing they *ever* talked about, when they weren't talking about clothing, money, where to eat, how to become a movie star, how to marry a movie star, or whether they should have their wisdom teeth removed (as they claimed Marlene Dietrich had done, in order to create more dramatic cheekbones).

Gladys the dance captain—who was sitting next to Celia on the floor in a pile of Celia's dirty laundry—asked me if I had a boyfriend.

Her exact words were, "You got anything permanent going with anybody?"

Now, it is worth noting that this was the first question of substance that any of the girls had ever asked about my life. (The fascination, needless to say, did not run in both directions.) I was only sorry that I didn't have something more exciting to report.

"I don't have a boyfriend, no," I said.

Gladys seemed alarmed.

"But you're *pretty*," she said. "You must have a guy back home. Guys must be giving you the pitch all the time!"

I explained that I'd been in girls' schools my whole life, so I hadn't had much opportunity to meet boys.

"But you've *done it*, right?" asked Jennie, cutting to the chase. "You've gone the limit before?"

"Never," I said.

"Not even *once*, you haven't gone the limit?" Gladys asked me, wide-eyed in disbelief. "Not even by *accident*?"

"Not even by accident," I said, wondering how it was that a person could ever have sex by accident.

(Don't worry, Angela—I know now. Accidental sex is the easiest thing to do, once you get in the habit of it. I've had plenty of accidental sex in my life since then, believe me, but at that moment I was not yet so cosmopolitan.)

"Do you go to *church*?" Jennie asked, as if that could be the only possible explanation for my still being a virgin at age nineteen. "Are you *saving* it?"

"No! I'm not saving it. I just haven't had the chance."

They all seemed concerned now. They were all looking at me as if I'd just said that I'd never learned how to cross a street by myself.

"But you've *fooled around*," Celia said.

"You've *necked*, right?" asked Jennie. "You've got to have necked!"

"A little," I said.

This was an honest answer; my sexual experience up until that point was *very* little. At a school dance back at Emma Willard—where they'd bused in for the occasion the sorts of boys whom we were expected to someday marry—I'd let a boy from the Hotchkiss School feel my breasts while we were dancing. (As best as he could *find* my breasts, anyway, which took some problem solving on his part.) Or maybe it's too generous to say that I let him feel my breasts. It would be more accurate to say that he just went ahead and *handled them*, and I didn't stop him. I didn't want to be rude, for one thing. For another thing, I found the experience to be interesting. I would have liked for it to continue, but the dance ended and then the boy was on a bus back to Hotchkiss before we could take it any further.

I'd also been kissed by a man in a bar in Poughkeepsie, on one of those nights when I'd escaped the Vassar hall wardens and ridden my bike into town. He and I had been talking about jazz (which is to say that *he* had been talking about jazz, and I had been listening to him talk about jazz, because that is how you talk to a man about jazz) and suddenly the next moment—*wow!* He had pressed me up against a wall and was rubbing his erection against my hip. He kissed me until my thighs shook with desire. But when he'd reached his hand between my legs I had balked, and slipped from his grasp. I'd ridden my bicycle back to campus that night with a sense of wobbly unease—both fearing and hoping that he was following me.

I had wanted more, and I had not wanted more.

A familiar old tale, from the lives of girls.

What else did I have on my sexual résumé? My childhood best friend, Betty, and I had practiced with each other some inexpert renditions of what we called "romantic kisses"—but then again we had also practiced "having babies" by stuffing pillows under our shirts so that we looked pregnant, and the latter experiment was just about as biologically convincing as the former.

I'd once had my vagina examined by my mother's gynecologist, when my mother grew concerned that I had not yet begun menstruating by the age of fourteen. The man had poked around down there for a bit—while my mother watched—and then he told me I needed to be eating more liver. It had not been an erotic experience for anyone involved.

Also, between the ages of ten and eighteen, I'd fallen in love about twenty dozen times with some of my brother Walter's friends. The choice benefit of having a popular and handsome brother was that he was always surrounded by his popular and handsome friends. But Walter's friends were always too hypnotized by *him*—their ringleader, the captain of every team, the most admired boy in town—to pay much attention to anyone else in the room.

I was not totally ignorant. I touched myself now and again, which made me feel both electrified and guilty, but I knew that wasn't the same thing as sex. (Let's just say this: my attempts at self-pleasure were something akin to dry swimming lessons.) And I understood the basics of human sexual function, having taken a required seminar at Vassar called "Hygiene"—a class that taught us about everything without telling us about anything. (In addition to presenting diagrams of ovaries and testicles, the teacher gave us a rather concerning admonition that douching with Lysol was neither a modern nor a safe means of contraception—thus planting in my head a vision that disturbed me then and still disturbs me now.)

"Well, when will you go the limit, then?" Jennie asked. "You're not getting any younger!"

"What you don't want to have happen," said Gladys, "is that you meet a fellow now, and you really like him, and then you've got to break the bad news to him that you're a virgin."

"Yeah, a lot of guys don't care for that," Celia said.

"That's right, they don't want the responsibility," said Gladys. "And you don't want your first time to be with somebody you *like*."

"Yeah, what if it goes all wrong?" said Jennie.

"What could go wrong?" I asked.

"Everything!" said Gladys. "You won't know what you're doing, and you could look like a dummy! And if it hurts, you don't want to find yourself blubbering in the arms of some guy you *like*!"

Now, this was the direct opposite of everything I'd been taught about sex thus far in life. My school friends and I had always been given to understand that a man would prefer it if we were virgins. We had also been instructed to save the flower of our girlhood for somebody whom we not only liked, but *loved*. The ideal scenario—the aspiration which we'd all been raised to embrace—was that you were supposed to have sex with only one person in your entire life, and that person should be your husband, whom you met at an Emma Willard school prom.

But I had been misinformed! These girls thought otherwise, and they *knew* things. Moreover, I now felt a sudden sting of anxiety about how old I was! For heaven's sake, I was nineteen already; what had I been doing with my time? And I'd been in New York already for two entire weeks. What was I waiting for?

"Is that hard to do?" I asked. "I mean, for the first time?"

"Oh, God no, Vivvie, don't be dense," said Gladys. "It's the easiest thing there ever was. In fact, you don't have to do anything. The man will do it for you. But you must get started, at least."

"Yes, she must get started," said Jennie definitively.

But Celia was looking at me with an expression of concern.

"Do you *want* to stay a virgin, Vivvie?" she asked, fixing me with

69

that unsettlingly beautiful gaze of hers. And while she might as well have been asking, "Do you *want* to stay an ignorant child, seen as pitiable by this gathering of mature and worldly women?" the intention behind the question was sweet. I think she was looking out for me—making sure I wasn't being pushed.

But the truth was, quite suddenly I did not want to be a virgin anymore. Not even for another day.

"No," I said. "I want to get started."

"We'd be only too glad to help, dear," said Jennie.

"Are you on your monthlies right now? Gladys asked.

"No," I said.

"Then we can get started right away. Who do we *know* . . . ?" Gladys pondered.

"It needs to be someone nice," said Jennie. "Someone *considerate*."

"A real gentleman," said Gladys.

"Not some lunkhead," said Jennie.

"Someone who'll take precautions," Gladys said.

"Not someone who'll get rough with her," said Jennie.

Celia said, "I know who."

And that's how their plan took shape.

Dr. Harold Kellogg lived in an elegant town house just off Gramercy Park. His wife was out of town, because it was a Saturday. (Mrs. Kellogg took the train to Danbury every Saturday, to visit her mother in the country.) And so the appointment for my deflowering was set at the exceedingly unromantic hour of ten o'clock on a Saturday morning.

Dr. and Mrs. Kellogg were respected members of the community. They were the sorts of people my parents knew. This is part of the reason Celia thought he might be good for me—because we came from the same social class. The Kelloggs had two sons at Columbia University who were both studying medicine. Dr. Kellogg was a member of the Metropolitan Club. In his free time, he enjoyed bird-watching, collecting stamps, and having sex with showgirls.

But Dr. Kellogg was discreet about his liaisons. A man of his reputation could not afford to be seen about town with a young woman whose physical composition made her look like the figurehead of a sailing ship (it would be *noticed*), so the showgirls visited him at his town house—and always on Saturday mornings, when his wife was gone. He would let them in through the service entrance, offer them champagne, and entertain them in the privacy of his guest room. Dr. Kellogg gave the girls money for their time and trouble, and then sent them on their way. It all had to be over by lunchtime, because he saw patients in the afternoon.

All the showgirls at the Lily knew Dr. Kellogg. They rotated visits to him, depending on who was least hungover on a Saturday morning, or who was "down to buttons" and needed a bit of pocket money for the week.

When the girls told me the financial details of this arrangement, I said in shock, "Do you mean to tell me that Dr. Kellogg *pays* you for *sex?*"

Gladys looked at me with disbelief: "Well, what'd you think, Vivie? That we pay *him?*"

Now, Angela, listen: I understand that there is a word for women who offer sexual favors to gentlemen in exchange for money. In fact, there are *many* words for this. But none of the showgirls with whom I associated in New York City in 1940 described themselves in that manner—not even as they were actively taking money from gentlemen in exchange for sexual favors. They couldn't possibly be prostitutes; they were *showgirls*. They had quite a lot of pride in that designation, having worked hard to achieve it, and it's the only title they would answer to. But the situation was simply this: showgirls did not earn a great deal of money, you see, and everyone has to get by in this world somehow (shoes are expensive!), and so these girls had developed a system of *alternative arrangements* for earning a bit of extra cash on the side. The Dr. Kelloggs of the world were part of that system.

Now that I think about it, I'm not even sure that Dr. Kellogg himself regarded these young women as prostitutes. He more likely called them his "girlfriends"—an aspirational, if somewhat delusional, designation which surely would have made him feel better about himself, too.

In other words, despite all evidence that sex was being exchanged for money (and sex was being exchanged for money, make no mistake about it) nobody here was engaging in *prostitution*. This was merely an *alternative arrangement* that suited everyone involved. You know: from each according to their abilities; to each according to their needs.

I'm so glad we were able to clear that up, Angela.

I certainly wouldn't want there to be any misunderstandings.

N ow, Vivvie, what you have to understand is that he's boring," said Jennie. "If you get bored, don't go thinking this is always how it feels to fool around."

"But he's a doctor," said Celia. "He'll do right for our Vivvie. That's what matters this time."

(*Our Vivvie!* Were there ever more heartwarming words? I was *their Vivvie!*)

It was now Saturday morning, and the four of us were sitting at a cheap diner on Third Avenue and Eighteenth Street, beneath the shadow of the el, waiting for it to be ten o'clock. The girls had already showed me Dr. Kellogg's town house and the back entrance I was to use, which was just around the corner. Now we were drinking coffee and eating pancakes while the girls gave me excited last-minute instructions. It was awfully early in the day—on a weekend, no less—for three showgirls to be wide awake and lively, but none of them had wanted to miss *this*.

"He's going to use a safety, Vivvie," Gladys said. "He always does, so you don't need to worry."

"It doesn't feel as good with a safety," Jennie said, "but you'll need it."

I'd never heard the term "safety" before, but I guessed from context that it was probably a sheath, or a rubber—a device I'd learned about in my Hygiene seminar at Vassar. (I'd even handled one, which had been passed from girl to girl like a limp, dissected toad.) If it meant something else, I supposed I would find out soon enough, but I wasn't about to ask.

"We'll get you a pessary later," said Gladys. "All us girls have pessaries."

(I didn't know what that was, either, till I figured out later it's what my Hygiene professor called a "diaphragm.")

"I don't have a pessary anymore!" said Jennie. "My grandmother found mine! When she asked me what it was, I told her it was for cleaning fine jewelry. She took it."

"For cleaning *fine jewelry*?" Gladys shrieked.

"Well, I had to say *something*, Gladys!"

"But I don't understand how you could even *use* a pessary for cleaning fine jewelry," Gladys pushed.

"I dunno! Ask my grandma, that's what she's using it for now!"

"Well, then what are you using now?" said Gladys. "For precaution?"

"Well, gee, nothing right now . . . because my grandmother has my pessary in her jewelry box."

"Jennie!" cried Celia and Gladys at the same time.

"I know, I know. But I'm careful."

"No, you're not!" said Gladys. "You're never careful! Vivian, don't be a dumb kid like Jennie. You've got to think about these things!"

Celia reached into her purse and handed me something wrapped in brown paper. I opened it up and found a small, white terry-cloth hand towel, folded neatly, never used. It still had a store price tag on it.

"I got you this," said Celia. "It's a towel. It's for in case you bleed."

"Thank you, Celia."

She shrugged, looked away, and—to my shock—blushed. "Sometimes people bleed. You'll want to be able to clean yourself up."

"Yeah, and you don't want to use Mrs. Kellogg's good towels," said Gladys.

"Yeah, don't touch *anything* that belongs to Mrs. Kellogg!" said Jennie.

"Except her husband!" shrieked Gladys, and all the girls laughed again.

"Ooh! It's after ten, Vivvie," said Celia. "You should get moving."

I made an effort to stand up, but suddenly felt dizzy. I sat back down in the dinette booth again, hard. My legs had almost gone out from under me. I hadn't *thought* I was nervous, but my body seemed to have a different opinion.

"You okay, Vivvie?" Celia asked. "You sure you want to do this?"

"I want to do it," I said. "I'm sure I want to do it."

"My suggestion," said Gladys, "is that you don't think about it too much. I never do."

This seemed wise. So I took a few deep breaths—as my mother had taught me to do before you jump a horse—stood up, and headed for the exit.

"See you girls later!" I said, with a bright and slightly surreal sense of cheer.

"We'll be waiting for you right here!" said Gladys.

"Shouldn't take too long!" said Jennie.

SIX

Dr. Kellogg was waiting for me just inside the servants' entrance to his town house. I'd barely knocked before the door flew open and he hustled me in.

"Welcome, welcome," he said, glancing about him, to make sure no neighbors were spying. "Let's get that door shut behind you, my dear."

He was a medium-sized man with an average-looking face whose hair was one of the regular colors of hair, and who was dressed in the sort of suit that one might expect a respectable middle-aged gentleman of his class to be wearing. (If it sounds like I have completely forgotten what he looked like, it's because I *have* completely forgotten what he looked like. He was the kind of man whose face you forget even when you are standing right in front of him, looking directly at his face.)

"Vivian," he said, and extended a handshake. "Thank you for coming in today. Let's head upstairs and get ourselves situated."

He sounded every bit like the doctor he was. He sounded just like my pediatrician back home in Clinton. I might as well have been there to have an ear infection looked at. There was something both reassuring and immensely silly about this to me. I felt a giggle rising in my chest, but kept it suppressed.

We walked through his home, which was proper and elegant, but unmemorable. There were probably a hundred homes within a few blocks of us decorated exactly the same way. All I can remember were some silk-upholstered couches with doilies. I have always hated doilies. He led me straight to the guest room, where he had two glasses of champagne waiting on a small table. The curtains were drawn—so that we could pretend it wasn't ten o'clock in the morning, I suppose— and he closed the door behind him.

"Make yourself comfortable on the bed, Vivian," he said, handing me one of the champagne flutes.

I sat primly on the edge of the bed. I was half expecting him to wash his hands and come at me with a stethoscope, but instead he pulled over a wooden chair from a corner of the room, and sat directly across from me. He put his elbows on his knees and leaned forward, in the manner of one whose job it is to diagnose.

"So, Vivian. Our friend Gladys tells me that you're a virgin."

"That's correct, Doctor," I said.

"There's no need to call me Doctor. We are friends. You may call me Harold."

"Why, thank you, Harold," I said.

And from that moment on, Angela, the situation became hilarious to me. Whatever nervousness I'd felt up until that point was gone now, replaced by a sense of pure comedy. It was something about the sound of my voice saying, "Why, thank you, Harold," in that small guest room with its stupid mint-green acetate quilted bedspread (I can't remember Dr. Kellogg's face, but I cannot forget that hideous goddamn bedspread) that struck me as the pinnacle of absurdity. There he was in his suit, and there I was in my buttercup-yellow rayon day dress—and if Dr. Kellogg didn't believe that I was a virgin before we met, the little yellow frock alone should have convinced him.

The whole scene was absurd. He was accustomed to showgirls, and he was getting *me*.

"Now, Gladys informs me that you wish to have your virginity"— he was searching for a delicate word—"removed?"

"That's correct, Harold," I said. "I wish to have it expunged."

(To this day, I believe that this line was the first intentionally funny thing I'd ever said in my life—and the fact that I said it with a straight face gave me no end of satisfaction. *Expunged!* Brilliant.)

He nodded; a good clinician with a bad sense of humor.

"Why don't you get undressed," he said, "and I will also get undressed, and we'll start."

I wasn't sure if I should take off *everything*. Usually at the doctor's office, I kept on my "step-ins"—as my mother always called my underwear. (*But why was I thinking about my mother right now?*) Then again, usually at the doctor's office I wasn't about to have sex with the doctor. I made a hasty decision to strip down completely. I didn't want to look like a modest little dolt. I lay down on my back on that nauseating acetate bedspread, naked as can be. Arms straight down at my side and legs stiff. You know: like a proper temptress.

Dr. Kellogg stripped to his shorts and undershirt. This hardly seemed fair. Why was he allowed to remain partially dressed, when I had to be naked?

"Now if you'll just kindly move over an inch or so, and make a bit of room for me . . ." he said. "There we go. . . . That's it. . . . Let's have a look at you."

He lay beside me, head propped by his elbow, and had a look at me. I didn't hate this moment as much as you might think. I was a vain young woman, and something within me thought it quite right that I should be looked at. Appearancewise, my chief concern was my bosom—or, rather, my near absence of a bosom. It didn't seem to be an issue with Dr. Kellogg, though, despite the fact that he was used to a different class of figure altogether. In fact he seemed delighted with all that was offered up before him.

"Virgin breasts!" he marveled. "Never before touched by man!"

(*Well*, I thought, *I wouldn't say that.* Never before touched by an *adult* man, maybe.)

"Forgive me if my hands are cold, Vivian," he said, "but I'm going to begin touching you now."

Dutifully, he began to touch me. First the left breast, then the right, then the left again, then the right again. His hands indeed *were* cold, but they warmed up soon enough. At first I was mildly panicked, and I kept my eyes closed, but after a bit of time, it was more like: *Well, this is interesting! Off we go!*

At some point, it began to actually feel good. That's when I decided to open my eyes, because I didn't want to miss anything. I suppose I wanted to watch my own body being ravaged. (Ah, the narcissism of youth!) I gazed down at myself, admiring my slim waist and the curve of my hip. I had borrowed Celia's razor to shave my legs, and my thighs were looking beautifully smooth in the low light. My breasts looked quite pretty under his hands, too.

A man's hands! On my naked breasts! *Would you look at that?*

I stole a glance at his face and was pleased with what I saw there—the reddened cheeks and the slight frown of concentration. He was breathing heavily through his nose, and I took that as a good sign that I was successfully arousing him. And it did feel very nice to be stroked. I liked the effect his touch had on my breasts—the way the skin got all rosy and toasty.

"I'm going to put your breast in my mouth now," he said. "This is standard."

I wished he hadn't said that. He made it sound like a *procedure.* I'd been thinking a lot about sex over the years, and in none of my fantasies did my lover sound like he was making a house call.

He leaned over to take my breast in his mouth, as promised, which I also found that I liked—once he stopped talking about it, I mean. In fact, I had never felt anything quite so delicious. I closed my eyes again. I wanted to keep still and quiet, with hopes that he would just continue offering this delightful experience. But then the delightful experience ended suddenly, because now he had started talking again.

"We're going to take this in careful stages, Vivian," he said.

God help me, but it sounded like he was about to insert a rectal thermometer inside me—an experience I'd once had as a child, and which I didn't want to be thinking about just now.

"Or do you want this over with swiftly, Vivian?" he asked.

"Excuse me?" I said.

"Well, I would imagine that it's alarming to you, to lie with a man for the first time. Perhaps you wish for the deed to be done swiftly, so that your discomfort will be fast over? Or would you like me to linger and teach you some things? Some of the things that Mrs. Kellogg enjoys, for instance?"

Oh, dear God, the last thing I wanted was to be taught the things that Mrs. Kellogg enjoyed! But I truly did not know what to say. So I just stared at him dumbly.

"I need to begin seeing patients at noon," he said, not at all seductively. He seemed irritated with my silence. "But we do have enough time for a bit of creative dallying, if that interests you? We will need to make a decision soon, though."

How is one supposed to answer that? How was I supposed to know what I wanted him to do? Creative dallying could mean *anything.* I just blinked at him.

"The tiny duckling is frightened," he said, his manner softening.

I only slightly wanted to kill him for the patronizing tone.

"I'm not frightened," I replied, which was true. I wasn't frightened—just baffled. My expectation had been that I was going be ravaged here today—but this was all so *labored*. Were we meant to negotiate and discuss every point?

"It's all right, my tiny duckling," he said. "I've done this before. You're awfully bashful, aren't you? Why don't you let me chart the course?"

He slid his hand down over my pubic hair. He palmed my vulva. He kept his hand flat, the way you keep your palm flat when you're feeding a sugar cube to a horse, because you don't want the horse to bite you. He began to rub his palm over my little mound. It didn't feel that bad. It didn't feel that bad at all, actually. I shut my eyes once more and marveled at this slight but magical uprush of lovely sensation.

"Mrs. Kellogg likes it when I do this," he said—and again, I had to stop experiencing pleasure in order to think about Mrs. Kellogg and her *doilies*. "She likes when I go round and round in this direction . . . and then round and round in *this* direction . . ."

The problem, I could clearly see now, was going to be the talking.

I debated how to get Dr. Kellogg to stop speaking. I couldn't very well ask him to be quiet in his own home—and especially not when he was doing me this tremendous favor of puncturing my hymen for me. I was a well-bred young lady who was accustomed to treating men of authority with a certain deference: it would have been highly out of character for me to have said, "Could you kindly shut up?"

It occurred to me that perhaps if I asked him to kiss me, that might silence him. It *could* work. It would keep his mouth busy, without a doubt. But then I would be required to kiss him, and I wasn't sure that I wanted to kiss him. It was difficult to know which scenario would be worse in this case—silence and kissing? Or no kissing, and this bothersome voice?

"Does your little kitty cat like to be petted?" he asked, as he increased his hand's pressure on my mound. "Is your little kitty cat *purring?*"

"Harold," I said, "I wonder if I might ask you to kiss me."

Perhaps I'm not being fair to Dr. Kellogg.

He was a nice enough man, and he was only trying to help me out, without alarming me too much. I do believe he did not want to hurt me. Maybe he was applying the Hippocratic oath to this situation: *First, do no harm* and all that.

Or maybe he wasn't such a nice man. I really have no way of knowing, as I never saw him again. Let's not paint him as the hero here! Maybe he wasn't trying to help me out at all, but was only enjoying the thrill of deflowering an uncomfortable and nubile young virgin in his guest room while his wife was off visiting her mother.

He certainly had no trouble becoming aroused by this situation, as I found out soon enough when he pulled away from me to apply a "safety" to his erection. Now, this would be the first erect penis I had ever seen—and therefore a banner moment—although I didn't get to see much of it. Partially, this is because the penis in question was covered by a condom and blocked by the man's hand. But mostly it's because he was on top of me in no time.

"Vivian," he said, "I've decided that the more quickly I enter, the better it will be for you. In this case, I believe it is better *not* to move by degrees. Hold tight, for now I shall penetrate you."

Thus he said it, and thus he did it.

Well, then. There we were.

It hurt far less than I'd feared. That was the good news. The bad news was that it also felt far less pleasant than I'd hoped. I'd hoped that intercourse would be a magnification of the sensations I'd experienced when he'd kissed my breasts or rubbed my mound, but it wasn't. In fact, whatever pleasure I'd been experiencing thus far, faint as it had been, vanished quite suddenly upon his entering—replaced by something very forceful and very interrupting. Having him inside me was just an unmistakable *presence* that I could not identify as being either bad or good. It reminded me a bit of menstrual cramps. It was just tremendously *odd*.

He moaned and he thrust, and through his clenched teeth he said, "Mrs. Kellogg, I find, prefers it when I—"

But I never did find out how Mrs. Kellogg preferred her copulation, because I started kissing Dr. Kellogg again, as soon as he began talking. The kissing did help to keep him quiet, I had found. Moreover, it gave me something to do, as I was being taken. As we've established, I hadn't done much kissing in my life, but I guessed pretty well at how it was done. It's the kind of skill that you have to learn on the job, really, but I did the best that I could with it. It was a bit of a challenge to keep our mouths linked as he was pounding away at me, but my incentive was great: I *really* didn't want to hear his voice again.

At the last moment, however, he got one more word in.

He pulled his face away from mine, shouted "Exquisite!" Then he arched his back, gave one more powerful shudder, and that was the end of it.

Afterward, he got up and went to another room, presumably to wash up. Then he came back and lay next to me for a spell. He held me tight, saying, "Little duckling, little duckling, what a good little duckling. Don't cry, little duckling."

I wasn't crying—I wasn't anywhere *near* crying—but he didn't notice.

Soon enough, he got up again and asked if he could please check the coverlet for blood, as he had forgotten to put down a sheet.

"We wouldn't want Mrs. Kellogg seeing a stain," he said. "I forgot myself, I'm afraid. I'm generally more careful. That suggests a certain lack of foresight on my part, which is not typically my way."

"Oh," I said, reaching for my handbag, grateful to have something to do. "I've brought a towel!"

But there was no stain. There was no blood at all. (All those horseback rides in childhood, I suppose, had already done the puncturing job for me. Thanks, Mother!) To my great relief, I didn't even feel much pain.

"Now, Vivian," he instructed, "you will want to avoid taking a bath for the next two days, as it could create infection. It's quite all right for you to clean yourself, but just splash about—do not soak. If you find that you have any discharge or discomfort, Gladys or Celia can recommend a vinegar douche for you. But you're a big strong healthy girl, and I don't expect you to run into any difficulties. You did well here today. I'm proud of you."

I half expected him to give me a lollipop.

As we dressed, Dr. Kellogg chatted away about the fine weather. Had I taken notice last month of the peonies in bloom in Gramercy Park? No, I told him, I hadn't even been living in New York City as of last month. Well, he instructed, I *must* take notice of the peonies next year, for they are in bloom such a short while, you know, and then they are gone. (Maybe this seems like too obvious a commentary on my own "short-lasting bloom"—but let's not give Dr. Kellogg that much credit for poetry or pathos. I think he just really liked peonies.)

"Let me show you out, my little duckling," he said, walking me back down the stairs, and through the doily-strewn living room, toward the servants' entrance. As we passed by the kitchen, he took an envelope off the table and handed it to me.

"A token of my appreciation," he said.

I knew it was money, and I couldn't bear it.

"Oh, no, I couldn't, Harold," I said.

"Oh, but you must."

"No, I couldn't," I said. "I couldn't *possibly*."

"Oh, but I *insist*."

"Oh, but I *mustn't*."

My objection, I have to tell you, was not that I didn't want to be regarded as a prostitute. (Don't think so highly of me as all that!) It was more a matter of deeply ingrained social politeness. My parents provided an allowance for me every week, you see, which Aunt Peg gave to me on Wednesdays, so I truly did not need Dr. Kellogg's money. Also, some puritanical voice within me told me that I had not quite earned this money. I didn't know much about sex, but I couldn't imagine that I'd shown this man much of a good time. A girl who lies down on her back with her arms straight at her sides, not moving whatsoever other than to attack you with her mouth every time you speak—she can't be much fun in the sack, right? If I were going to be paid for sex, I'd want to have done something worth paying for.

"Vivian, I demand that you take this," he said.

"Harold, I refuse."

"Vivian, I really must insist that you do not make a scene," he said, frowning slightly, and pushing the envelope toward me with force— this moment constituting the closest I'd come to danger or excitement at the hands of Dr. Harold Kellogg.

"Very well," I said, and I took the money.

(And how do you like *that,* my fancy ancestors? Cash for sex, and on the first run out of the gate, no less!)

"You are a lovely young girl," he said. "And please don't be concerned: there is still plenty of time for your breasts to fill out."

"Thank you, Harold," I said.

"If you drink eight ounces of buttermilk a day, it should help them to grow."

"Thank you, I will do that," I said, with no intention whatsoever of drinking eight ounces of buttermilk a day.

I was about to step out the door, but then I suddenly had to know.

"Harold," I said, "may I ask what kind of doctor you are?"

It was my supposition that he was either a gynecologist or a pediatrician. I was leaning toward pediatrician. I just wanted to settle the bet in my own head.

"I'm a veterinarian, my dear girl," he said. "Now, please send my warmest regards to Gladys and Celia, and do not forget to observe the peonies next spring!"

flew down the street, absolutely howling with laughter.

I ran back into the diner where the girls were all waiting for me, and before they could even speak, I shrieked, "A *veterinarian*? You sent me to a *veterinarian*?"

"How was it?" asked Gladys. "Did it hurt?"

"He's a *veterinarian*? You said he was a *doctor*!"

"Dr. Kellogg *is* a doctor!" said Jennie. "It says so right in his name."

"I feel as though you sent me to get *spayed*!"

I dove into the booth next to Celia, crashing against her warm body with relief. My own body was in a storm of hilarity. I was all trembling now, from head to toe. I felt wild and unhinged. I felt that my life had just exploded. I was overcome with excitement and arousal and revulsion and embarrassment and pride, and it was all so disorienting, but also fantastic. The aftereffect was so much more striking than the act itself had been. I could not *believe* what I had just done. My boldness that morning—sex with a strange man!—seemed to have sprung from someone else, but I also felt more authentic to myself than ever.

Moreover, looking around the table at the showgirls, I felt a sense of gratitude so rich that tears almost overtook me. It was so *marvelous* to have the girls there. My friends! My oldest friends in the world! My oldest friends in the world whom I'd met only two weeks ago—except for Jennie, whom I'd just met two days before! I loved them all so much! They had waited for me! They cared!

"But how *was* it?" said Gladys.

"It was fine. It was *fine*."

There was a stack of cold and half-eaten pancakes in front of me from earlier that morning, and now I tore into those pancakes with a hunger that was close to violence. My hands were shaking. Dear God, I had never been so famished. My hunger had no bottom to it. I drenched the pancakes in even more syrup and shoveled more of them into my mouth.

"He never stops croaking on about his wife, though!" I said, between forkfuls.

"And how!" said Jennie. "He's the worst for that!"

"He's a drip," said Gladys. "But he's not a mean man, and that's what matters."

"But did it *hurt*?" asked Celia.

"You know something, it didn't," I said. "And I didn't even need the towel!"

"You're lucky," said Celia. "You're *so* lucky."

"I can't say it was fun," I said. "But I can't say it wasn't fun, either. I'm just glad it's over. I suppose there are worse ways to lose your virginity."

"All the other ways are worse," Jennie said. "Believe me. I've tried them all."

"I'm so proud of you, Vivvie," said Gladys. "Today you're a woman."

She raised her coffee cup to me in a toast, and I clinked it with my water glass. Never did an initiation ceremony feel so complete and satisfying as that moment when I was toasted by Gladys the dance captain.

"How much did he give you?" asked Jennie.

"Oh!" I said. "I'd almost forgotten!"

I reached into my purse and pulled out the envelope.

"You open it," I said, handing it with shaky hands to Celia, who tore it right open, thumbed through the cash expertly, and announced: "Fifty dollars!"

"*Fifty dollars!*" shrieked Jennie. "He's usually twenty!"

"What should we spend it on?" Gladys asked.

"We've got to do something special with it," said Jennie—and I felt a rush of relief that the girls considered the money *ours*, not mine. It spread around the taint of misdoing, if that makes sense. It also added to the feeling of camaraderie.

"I want to go to Coney Island," said Celia.

"We don't have time," said Gladys. "We need to be back at the Lily by four."

"We've got time," Celia said. "We'll be quick. We'll get hot dogs and look at the beach and come straight home. We'll hire a taxi. We have money now, don't we?"

So we drove out to Coney Island with the windows down, smoking and laughing and gossiping. It was the warmest day of summer so far. The sky was thrillingly bright. I was wedged in the backseat between Celia and Gladys, while Jennie chatted away with the driver up front—a driver who could not believe his luck at the assemblage of beauty that had just tumbled into his cab.

"What a bunch of figures on you gals!" he said, and Jennie said, "Now, don't you get fresh, mister," but I could tell that she liked it.

"Do you ever feel bad about Mrs. Kellogg?" I asked Gladys, feeling a small pang of concern about my deed that day. "I mean, for sleeping with her husband? *Should* I feel bad about it?"

"Well, you can't have *too* much conscience about things!" said Gladys. "Or else you'll never stop worrying!"

And that, I'm afraid, was the extent of our moral agonies. Subject closed.

"Next time I want it to be with someone else," I said. "Do you think I could find somebody else?"

"Piece of cake," said Celia.

Coney Island was all shiny and gaudy and fun. The boardwalk was overrun with loud families, and young couples, and sticky children who acted just as delirious as I felt. We looked at the signs for the freak shows. We ran down to the shore and put our feet in the water. We ate candied apples and lemon ices. We got our picture taken with a strong-man. We bought stuffed animals and picture postcards and souvenir cosmetic mirrors. I bought Celia a cute little rattan handbag with sea-shells sewn on it, and I got sunglasses for the other girls, *and* I paid for a taxi ride all the way back to midtown—and there was still nine dollars left of Dr. Kellogg's money.

"You got enough left over to buy yourself a steak dinner!" said Jennie.

We got back to the Lily Playhouse with barely enough time to make the early show. Olive was frantic with concern that the show-girls would miss the curtain, and she clucked about in circles, scolding everyone for their lack of *promptitude*. But the girls dove into their dressing rooms and came out only moments later, it seemed, simply *secreting* sequins and ostrich plumes and glamour.

My Aunt Peg was there, too, of course, and she asked me, some-what distractedly, if I'd had a fun day.

"I sure did!" I said.

"Good," she said. "You should have fun, you're young."

Celia gave my hand a squeeze just as she was about to go onstage. I grabbed her by the arm and leaned in closer toward her beauty.

"Celia!" I whispered, "I still can't believe I lost my virginity today!"

"You'll never miss it," she said.

And do you know something?

She was absolutely right.

SEVEN

And so it began.

Now that I'd been initiated, I wanted to be around sex constantly—and everything about New York felt like sex to me. I had a lot of time to make up for, was how I saw it. I'd wasted *all those years* being bored and boring, and now I refused to be bored or boring ever again, not even for an hour!

And I had so much to learn! I wanted Celia to teach me everything she knew—about men, about sex, about New York, about *life*—and she happily obliged. From that point forward, I was no longer the handmaiden of Celia (or at least not merely her handmaiden); I was her accomplice. It was no longer Celia coming home drunk in the middle of the night after a wild spree on the town; it was both of us coming home drunk in the middle of the night after a wild spree on the town.

The two of us went digging for trouble with a shovel and a pickax that summer, and we never had the slightest trouble finding it. If you are a pretty young woman looking for trouble in a big city, it's not difficult to find. But if you are *two* pretty young women looking for trouble, then trouble will tackle you on every corner—which is just how we wanted it. Celia and I cultivated an almost hysterical commitment to having a good time. Our appetites were gluttonous—not only for boys and men, but also for food, and cocktails, and anarchic dancing, and the kind of live music that makes you want to smoke too many cigarettes and laugh with your head thrown back.

Sometimes the other dancers or showgirls started off the night with us, but they could rarely keep up with me and Celia. If one of us lagged, the other would pick up the pace. Sometimes I got the feeling we were watching each other to see what we would do next, because we usually had no *idea* what we were going to do next, except that we always wanted another thrill. More than anything, I believe, we were motivated by our mutual fear of boredom. Every day had a hundred hours in it, and we needed to fill them all, or we would perish of tedium.

Essentially, our chosen line of work that summer was *romping and rampaging*—and we did it with a tirelessness that staggers my imagination even to this day.

When I think about the summer of 1940, Angela, I picture Celia Ray and I as two inky, dark points of lust sailing through the neon and shadows of New York City, in a nonstop search for action. And when I try to recall it in detail now, it all seems to run into one long, hot, sweaty night.

The moment the show was over, Celia and I would change into the thinnest little stalks of evening gowns, and we would absolutely fling ourselves at the city—running full tilt into the impatient streets, already certain that we were missing something vital and lively: *How could they start without us?*

We'd always begin our evening at Toots Shor's, or El Morocco, or the Stork Club—but there was no telling where we would end up by the wee hours. If midtown got too dull and familiar, Celia and I might head up to Harlem on the A train to hear Count Basie play, or to drink at the Red Rooster. Or we could just as easily find ourselves clowning around with a bunch of Yale boys at the Ritz, or dancing with some socialists downtown at Webster Hall. The rule seemed to be: dance until you collapse, and then keep dancing for a little bit longer after that.

We moved with such speed! Sometimes it felt like I was being dragged behind the city itself—sucked into this wild urban river of music and lights and revelry. Other times, it felt like we were the ones dragging the city behind *us*—because everywhere we went, we were followed. In the course of these heady evenings, we would either meet up with some men whom Celia already knew, or we would pick up some new men along the way. Or both. I would either kiss three handsome men in a row, or the same handsome man three times—sometimes it was hard to keep track.

Never was it difficult to find men.

It helped that Celia Ray could walk into a joint like nobody I've ever seen. She would throw her resplendence into a room ahead of her, the way a soldier might toss a grenade into a machine gunner's nest, and then she'd follow her beauty right on in and assess the carnage. All she had to do was show up, and every bit of sexual energy in the place would magnetize around her. Then she'd stroll around looking bored as can be—sopping up everyone's boyfriends and husbands in the process—without exerting the slightest bit of effort in her conquests.

Men looked at Celia Ray like she was a box of Cracker Jack and they couldn't wait to start digging for the toy.

In return, she looked at them like they were the wooden paneling on the wall.

Which only made them crazier for her.

"Show me you can smile, baby," a brave man once called out to her across the dance floor.

"Show me you got a yacht," Celia said under her breath, and turned away to be bored in another direction.

Since I was by her side, and since I looked enough like her now (in low light, anyhow—since I was not only the same height and coloring as Celia, but now wore tight dresses like hers, and styled my hair like hers, and modeled my walk after hers, and padded my bosom to slightly resemble hers), it only doubled the effect.

I don't like to boast, Angela, but we were a pretty unstoppable duo.

Actually, I do like to boast, so let an old woman have her glory: we were *stunning*. We could give whole tables of men a pretty decent case of whiplash, just by walking past.

"Fetch us a refresher," Celia would say at the bar, to nobody in particular, and in the next moment, five men would be handing us cocktails—three for her, and two for me. And in the next ten minutes, those drinks would be gone.

Where did we get all that *energy* from?

Oh, yes, I remember: we got it from youth itself. We were turbines of energy. Mornings were always difficult, of course. The hangovers could be quite unsparingly cruel. But if I needed a nap later in the day, I could always do it in the back of the theater, during a rehearsal or a show, collapsed on a pile of old curtains. A ten-minute doze, and I'd be restored, ready to take on the city once more, as soon as the applause died down.

You can live this way when you're nineteen (or pretending to be nineteen, in Celia's case).

"Those girls are on the road to trouble," I heard an older woman say about us one night, as we were staggering down the street drunk—and that woman was absolutely right. What she didn't understand, though, is that trouble is what we *wanted*.

Oh, our youthful needs!

Oh, the deliciously blinding yearnings of the young—which

inevitably take us right to the edges of cliffs, or trap us in cul-de-sacs of our design.

can't say that I got good at sex during the summer of 1940, although I will say that I grew awfully familiar with it.

But, no, I didn't get good at it.

To get "good" at sex—which, for a woman, means learning how to enjoy and even orchestrate the act, to the point of her own climax—one needs time, patience, and an attentive lover. It would be awhile before I had access to anything as sophisticated as all that. For now, it was just a game of wild numbers, executed with a considerable amount of speed. (Celia and I didn't like to hover too long in one location, or with one man, in case we were missing something better that might be happening on the other side of town.)

My longing for excitement and my curiosity about sex made me not only insatiable that summer, but also *susceptible*. That's how I see myself, when I look back on it now. I was susceptible to everything that had even the vaguest suggestion of the erotic or the illicit. I was susceptible to neon lights in the darkness of a midtown side street. I was susceptible to drinking cocktails out of coconut shells in the Hawaiian Room of the Hotel Lexington. I was susceptible to being offered ringside tickets, or backstage entrances to nightclubs that did not have names. I was susceptible to anybody who could play a musical instrument, or dance with a fair amount of panache. I was susceptible to getting into cars with just about anyone who owned a car. I was susceptible to men who would approach me at the bar with two highballs, saying, "I seem to have found myself with an extra drink. Perhaps you could help me out with this, miss?"

Why, yes, I would be delighted to help you out with that, sir.

I was so good at being helpful in that regard!

———————

In our defense, Celia and I didn't have sex with *all* the men we met that summer.

But we did have sex with most of them.

The question with me and Celia was never so much "Who should we have sex with?"—it didn't really seem to matter—but only "*Where* shall we have sex?"

The answer was: Wherever we could find a spot.

We had sex in fancy hotel suites, paid for by out-of-town businessmen. But also in the kitchen (closed for the evening) of a small East Side nightclub. Or on a ferry boat where we'd somehow ended up late at night—the lights on the water all runny and blurry around us. In the backs of taxicabs. (I know it sounds uncomfortable, and believe me it was uncomfortable, but it could be accomplished.) In a movie theater. In a dressing room in the basement of the Lily Playhouse. In a dressing room in the basement of the Diamond Horseshoe. In a dressing room in the basement of Madison Square Garden. In Bryant Park, with the threat of rats at our feet. In dark and sweltering alleyways just off the taxi-haunted corners of midtown. On the rooftop of the Puck Building. In an office suite on Wall Street, where only the nighttime janitors might hear us.

Drunk, pinwheel-eyed, briny-blooded, brainless, weightless—Celia and I spun through New York City that summer on currents of pure electricity. Instead of walking, we rocketed. There was no focus; there was just a constant search for the *vivid*. We missed nothing, but we also missed everything. We watched Joe Louis train with his sparring partner, for instance, and we heard Billie Holiday sing—but I can't remember the details of either occasion. We were too distracted by our own story to pay much attention to all the wonders that were laid before us. (For instance: the night that I saw Billie Holiday sing, I had my period and I was in a sulky mood because a boy I liked had just left with another girl. There's my review of Billie Holiday's performance.)

Celia and I would have too much to drink, and then we would run into crowds of young men who'd also had too much to drink—and the whole lot of us would crash together and behave exactly the way you might expect us to behave. We would go into bars with boys whom we'd met in *other* bars, but then flirt with the boys we discovered in the *new* bar. We caused fights to break out, and somebody would take a wicked shellacking, but then Celia would choose among the survivors for who would take us to the *next* bar, where the uproar would begin all over again. We would bounce from one stag party to the next—from one man's arms to another man's arms. We even traded dates once, right in the middle of dinner.

"You take him," Celia said to me that night, right in front of the man who was already boring her. "I'm going to the ladies' room. You keep this guy warm."

"But he's *your* guy!" I said, as the man reached for me, most obligingly. "And you're my friend!"

"Oh, Vivvie," she said to me, in a fond and pitying tone. "You can't lose a friend like me just by taking her guy!"

I had precious little contact with my family back home that summer. The last thing I wanted was for them to know anything about what I was doing.

My mother sent me a note every week, along with my allowance, filling me in on the most basic news. My father had hurt his shoulder playing golf. My brother was threatening to quit Princeton next semester and join the Navy, because he wanted to serve his country. My mother had defeated this-or-that woman in this-or-that tennis tournament. In return, I sent my parents a card every week telling them the same stale and uninformative sort of news—that I was well, that I was working hard at the theater, that New York City was very nice, and thank you for the allowance. Every once in a while I'd toss in a bit of innocuous detail, such as, "Just the other day I had a charming lunch at the Knickerbocker with Aunt Peg."

Naturally, I did not mention to my parents that I'd recently gone to a doctor with my friend Celia the showgirl, in order to get myself illegally fitted for a pessary. (Illegal, because it was not permitted back then for a doctor to outfit an unmarried woman with a birth control device—but this is why it's so good to have friends who know people! Celia's doctor was a laconic Russian woman who didn't ask questions. She suited me right up without batting an eye.)

Nor did I mention to my parents that I'd had a gonorrhea scare (which had turned out to be nothing more than a mild pelvic infection, thank goodness—though it had been a painful and frightening week until it all cleared up). Nor did I mention that I'd had a pregnancy scare (which had also cleared up on its own accord, thank God). Nor did I mention that I was now fairly regularly sleeping with a man named Kevin "Ribsy" O'Sullivan, who ran numbers around the corner in Hell's Kitchen. (I was dallying about with some other men, too, of course—all equally unsavory, but none with such a good name as "Ribsy.")

Nor did I mention that I now *always* carried prophylactics in my pocketbook—on account of the fact that I didn't want any further gonorrhea scares, and a girl can't be too careful. I also didn't tell my parents that my boyfriends regularly secured these prophylactics for me as a kind favor. (Because you see, Mother, only men are allowed to purchase prophylactics in New York City!)

No, I didn't tell her any of this.

I did, however, pass along the news that the lemon sole at the Knickerbocker was *excellent*.

Which is true. It really was.

Meanwhile, Celia and I just went right on spinning—night after night—getting ourselves into all manner of trouble, big and small.

Our drinks made us crazy and lazy. We forgot how to keep track of the hours or the cocktails or the names of our dates. We drank gin fizzes till we forgot how to walk. We forgot how to look after our security once we were good and tight, and other people—often strangers—would have to look after us. ("It ain't for you to tell a girl how to live!" I remember Celia yelling one night at a nice gentleman who was politely trying to do nothing more than escort us back home safely to the Lily.)

There was always an element of peril in the way that Celia and I thrust ourselves into the world. We made ourselves available for anything that might happen, so anything *could* happen. Often, anything *did* happen.

You see, it was like this: Celia's effect on men was to make them so obedient and subservient to her—until the instant they were no longer obedient and subservient. She would have them all lined up before us, ready to take our orders and serve our every wish. They were such good boys, and sometimes they stayed good boys—but sometimes, quite suddenly, those boys were not so good anymore. Some line of male desire or anger would be crossed, and then there was no coming back from it. After that line had been crossed, Celia's effect on men was to make them into savages. There would be a moment when everyone was having fun and flirting and playing taunting games and laughing, but then suddenly the energy of the room would shift, and now there was a threat of not only sex, but violence.

Once that shift came, there was no stopping it.

After that, it was all smash and grab.

The first time this happened, Celia saw it coming moments before it occurred, and she sent me out of the room. We were in the

Presidential Suite of the Biltmore Hotel, being entertained by three men whom we'd met earlier in the ballroom of the Waldorf. These men had a great deal of loose cash, and they were clearly in a dubious line of work. (If I had to guess, I would wager that their line of employment was: racketeers.) At first they were all in service to Celia—so deferential, so grateful for her attentions, sweating with nervousness about making the beautiful girl and her friend happy. *Would the ladies like another bottle of champagne? Would the ladies like some crab legs ordered up to the room? Would the ladies like to see the Presidential Suite at the Biltmore? Would the ladies like the radio on or off?*

I was still new at this game, and I found it amusing that these thugs were so servile to us. Cowed by our powers, and all that. It made me want to laugh at them, in all their weakness: *Men are so easy to control!*

But then—not long into our visit to the Presidential Suite—the shift came, and Celia was suddenly crammed between two of those men on the couch, and they were no longer looking servile or weak. It wasn't anything they were doing per se; it was just a change of tone, and it frightened me. Something had shifted in their faces, and I didn't like it. The third man was now eyeing me, and he didn't appear as though he were interested in joking around anymore, either. The only way I can describe the change in the room was: You're having a delightful picnic, and then suddenly there's a tornado. The barometric pressure drops. The sky goes black. The birds go silent. This thing is coming straight for you.

"Vivvie," said Celia in that exact moment, "run downstairs and buy me cigarettes."

"Right now?" I asked.

"*Go,*" she said. "And don't come back."

I made for the door, just before the third man reached me—and to my shame, I closed the door on my friend and left her in there. I left her because she'd told me to, but still—it felt rotten. Whatever those men were about to do in there, Celia was on her own. She'd sent me from the room either because she didn't want me seeing what was about to be done to her, or she didn't want it done to me, too. Either way, I felt like a child, being banished like that. I also felt afraid of those men, and afraid for Celia, *and* I felt left out. I hated it. I paced the lobby of the hotel for an hour, wondering if I should alert the hotel manager. But alert him to what?

Celia eventually came down by herself—unescorted by any of the men who had so solicitously led us to the elevator earlier that evening.

She spotted me in the lobby, walked over, and said, "Well, I call *that* a lousy way to end a night."

"Are you all right?" I asked.

"Yeah, I'm terrific," she said. She tugged at her dress. "Do I look all right?"

She looked just as beautiful as ever—except for the shiner over her left eye.

"Like love's young dream itself," I said.

She saw me looking at her swollen eye, and said, "Don't squawk about this, Vivvie. Gladys'll fix it. She's the best at covering up black eyes. Is there a cab? If a cab would be kind enough to appear, I'll take it."

I found her a cab, and we made our way home without another word.

D id the events of that evening leave Celia traumatized?
    You would think so, wouldn't you?

But I'm ashamed to say, Angela: I don't know. I never talked to her about it. I certainly never saw any sign of trauma in my friend. But then again, I probably wasn't looking for signs of trauma. Nor would I have known what to look for. Maybe I was hoping that this ugly incident would just disappear (like the black eye itself) if we never mentioned it. Or maybe I thought Celia was accustomed to being assaulted, given her rough origins. (God help us, maybe she was.)

There were so many questions I could have asked Celia that evening in the taxi (starting with "Are you *really* all right?"), but I didn't. Nor did I thank her for having saved me from certain attack. I was embarrassed that I'd needed saving—embarrassed that she saw me as being more innocent and fragile than herself. Until that night, I'd been able to kid myself that Celia Ray and I were exactly the same—just two equally worldly and gutsy women, conquering the city and having fun. But clearly that wasn't true. I had been recreationally dabbling in danger, but Celia *knew* danger. She knew things—dark things—that I didn't know. She knew things that she didn't want me to know.

When I think back on it all now, Angela, it's appalling to realize that this kind of violence seemed so commonplace back then—and not just to Celia, but also to me. (For instance: why did it never occur to me at the time to wonder how Gladys had come to be so good at covering up black eyes?) I suppose our attitude was: *Oh, well—men will be men!* You must understand, though, that this was long before there was any sort of public conversation about such dark subjects—and thus we had no private conversations about them, either. So I said nothing more to Celia that evening about her experience, and Celia said nothing more about it, either. We just put it all behind us.

And the next night, unbelievably, we were out there in the city again, looking for action *again*—except with one change: From this point forward, I was committed to never leaving the scene, no matter what. I would not allow myself to be sent from a room again. Whatever Celia was doing, I would be doing it, too. Whatever happened to Celia, it would happen to me, too.

Because I am not a child, I told myself—the way children always do.

EIGHT

There was a war coming, by the way.

There was a war happening already, in fact—and quite seriously so. It was all the way over there in Europe, of course, but there was a great raging debate within the United States as to whether or not we should join it.

I was not part of this debate, needless to say. But it was happening all around me.

Perhaps you think I should have noticed earlier that there was a war coming, but truly the subject had not yet landed in my consciousness. Here, you must give me credit for being *exceedingly* unobservant. It was not easy in the summer of 1940 to ignore the fact that the world was on the brink of full-out war, but I'd managed to do exactly that. (In my defense, my colleagues and associates were also ignoring it. I don't recall Celia or Gladys or Jennie ever discussing America's military preparedness, or the growing need for a "Two-Ocean Navy.") I was not a politically minded person, to say the least. I didn't know the name of a single individual in Roosevelt's cabinet, for instance. I did, however, know the full name of Clark Gable's second wife, a much-divorced Texas socialite named Ria Franklin Prentiss Lucas Langham Gable—a jawbreaker of a moniker that I will apparently remember till my dying day.

The Germans had invaded Holland and Belgium in May of 1940—but that was right around the time I was failing all my exams at Vassar, so I was terribly preoccupied. (I do remember my father saying that all the fuss would be over by the end of summer because the French army would soon push the Germans right back home. I'd figured he was probably correct about that because he seemed to read a lot of newspapers.)

Right around the time that I moved to New York—this would be the middle of June 1940—the Germans had marched into Paris. (So much for Dad's theory.) But there was too much excitement going on in my life for me to follow the story closely. I was far more curious about what was happening in Harlem and the Village than what had happened to the Maginot Line. And by August, when the Luftwaffe started bombing British targets, I was going through my pregnancy and gonorrhea scares, so I didn't quite register that information, either.

History has a pulse, they say—but mostly I have never been able to hear it, not even when it is drumming right in my goddamn ears.

f I'd been more wise and attentive, I might have realized that America was eventually going to get pulled into this conflagration. I might have taken more notice of the news that my brother was thinking about joining the Navy. I might have worried about what that decision would mean for Walter's future—and for all of us. And I might have realized that some of the fun young men with whom I was cavorting every night in New York City were just the right age to be put on the front lines when America inevitably did enter this war. If I'd known then what I know now—namely: that so many of those beautiful young boys would soon be lost to the battlefields of Europe or to the infernos of the South Pacific—I would have had sex with even more of them.

If it sounds like I'm being facetious, I'm not.

I wish I'd done more of *everything* with those boys. (I'm not sure when I would have found the time, of course, but I would've made every effort to squeeze into my busy schedule every last one of those kids—so many of whom were soon to be shattered, burned, wounded, doomed.)

I only wish I had known what was coming, Angela.

I truly do.

Other people were paying attention, though. Olive followed the news coming out of her home country of England with particular concern. She was anxious about it, but then again, she was anxious about everything, so her worries didn't make much of an impression. Olive sat there every morning over her breakfast of kidney and eggs, reading every bit of coverage she could get. She read *The New York Times*, and *Barron's*, and the *Herald Tribune* (even though it leaned Republican), and she read the British papers when she could find them. Even my Aunt Peg (who usually read only the *Post*, for the baseball coverage) had started following the news with more concern. She'd already seen one world war, and she didn't want to see another. Peg's loyalties to Europe would forever run deep.

Over the course of that summer, both Peg and Olive became increasingly passionate in their belief that the Americans must join the war effort. Somebody had to help out the British and rescue the French! Peg and Olive were in full support of the president as he tried to garner backing from Congress to take action.

Peg—a traitor to her class—had always loved Roosevelt. This had been shocking to me when I'd first heard about it; my father *hated* Roosevelt and was a vehement isolationist. A real pro-Lindbergh sort of fellow, was old Dad. I assumed that all my relatives hated Roosevelt, too. But this was New York City, I guess, where people thought differently about things.

"I've reached my *limit* with the Nazis!" I remember Peg shouting one morning over breakfast and the newspapers. She slammed her fist on the table in a burst of rage. "That's enough of them! They must be stopped! What are we waiting for?"

I'd never heard Peg get so upset about anything, which is why it stuck in my memory. Her reaction pierced my self-absorption for a moment and made me take notice: *Gee whiz, if Peg was this angry, things really must be getting bad!*

That said, I wasn't sure what she wanted me to do about the Nazis, personally.

The truth was, I didn't have any inkling that this war—this distant, irritating war—might have any real consequences until September of 1940.

That's when Edna and Arthur Watson moved into the Lily Playhouse.

NINE

'm going to assume, Angela, that you've never heard of Edna Parker Watson.

You're probably a bit too young to know of her great theatrical career. She was always better known in London than New York, in any case.

As it happens, I had heard of Edna before I met her—but that's only because she was married to a handsome English screen actor named Arthur Watson, who had recently played the heartthrob in a cheesy British war movie called *Gates of Noon*. I'd seen their photos in the magazines, so Edna was familiar to me. Now, this was a bit of a crime—to have known Edna only through her husband. She was by far the superior performer of the two, and the superior human being, besides. But that's just how it goes. His was the prettier face, and in this shallow world a pretty face means everything.

It might have helped if Edna made movies. Maybe then she would've achieved greater fame in her day, and maybe she'd even be remembered now—like Bette Davis or Vivien Leigh, who were every bit her peers. But she refused to act for the camera. It wasn't for lack of opportunity; Hollywood came knocking on her door many times, but somehow she never lost the stamina to keep turning down those big-shot film producers. Edna wouldn't even do radio plays, believing that the human voice loses something vital and sacred when it is recorded.

No, Edna Parker Watson was purely a stage actress, and the problem with stage actresses is that once they are gone, they are forgotten. If you never saw her perform onstage, then you would not be able to understand her power and appeal.

She was George Bernard Shaw's favorite actress, though—does that help? He famously said that her portrayal of Saint Joan was the definitive one. He wrote of her: "That luminous face, peeking out from its armor—who would not follow her into battle, if only to stare at her?"

No, even that doesn't really get her across.

With apologies to Mr. Shaw, I'll do my best to describe Edna in my own words.

met Edna and Arthur Watson during the third week of September 1940.

Their visit to the Lily Playhouse, as with so many of the guests who came and went from that institution, was not exactly planned. There was a real element of chaos and emergency to it. Even beyond the scale of our normal chaos.

Edna was an old acquaintance of Peg's. They'd met in France during the Great War and had become fast friends, though they hadn't seen each other in years. Then, in the late summer of 1940, the Watsons came to New York City so that Edna could rehearse a new play with Alfred Lunt. However, the financing for this production vanished before anyone could memorize a single line, and so the play never came into being. But before the Watsons could sail back home to England, the Germans began the bombing of Britain. Within just a few weeks of the German attacks, the Watsons' town house in London had been obliterated by a Luftwaffe bomb. Destroyed. Everything gone.

"Splintered to matchsticks, apparently" is how Peg described it.

So now Edna and Arthur Watson were trapped in New York City. They were stuck at the Sherry-Netherland hotel, which is not such a bad place to be a refugee, but they couldn't afford to go on living there, as neither of them was employed. They were artists trapped in America without jobs, without a home to return to, and without safe transit back to their besieged country.

Peg heard about their plight through the theater grapevine, and—of course—she told the Watsons to come live at the Lily Playhouse. She promised that they could remain there just as long as they needed. She told them she'd even put them into some of her shows, if they needed income and didn't mind slumming it.

How could the Watsons have refused? Where else were they going to go?

So they moved in—and that's how the war made its first direct appearance in my life.

The Watsons arrived on one of the first crisp afternoons of autumn. It happened that I was standing outside the theater talking to Peg when their car pulled up. I'd just returned from shopping at Lowtsky's, and I was carrying a bag of crinolines which I needed to fix some of the "ballet costumes" of our dancers. (We were putting on a show called *Dance Away, Jackie!*—about a street urchin who is rescued from a life of crime by the love of a beautiful young ballerina. I had been tasked with the job of trying to make the Lily's muscular hoofers look like a company of premier ballet dancers. I'd done my best with the costumes, but the dancers kept ripping their skirts. Too much boggle-boggle, I suppose. Now it was time for repairs.)

When the Watsons arrived, there was a small flurry of commotion, as they had a great deal of luggage. Two other cars followed their taxi, with the remaining trunks and parcels. I was standing right there on the sidewalk, and I saw Edna Parker Watson exit the taxi as though she were stepping out of a limousine. Petite, trim, narrow-hipped and small-breasted, she was dressed in the single most stylish outfit I'd ever seen on a woman. She was wearing a peacock-blue serge jacket—double-breasted, with two lines of gold buttons marching up the front—with a high collar trimmed in gold braid. She had on tailored dark gray trousers with a bit of flare at the bottom, and glossy black wingtip shoes, which almost looked like men's shoes—except for the small, elegant, and very feminine heel. She was wearing tortoiseshell sunglasses, and her short, dark hair was set with glossy waves. She had on red lipstick—the perfect shade of red—but no other makeup. A simple black beret sat angled on her head with jaunty ease. She looked like a teeny-tiny military officer in the chicest little army in the world—and from that day forward, my sense of style would never be the same.

Until the moment I first glimpsed Edna, I'd thought that New York City showgirls and their spangled radiance were the pinnacles of glamour. But suddenly everything (and everyone) I'd been admiring all summer looked gaudy and glitzy compared to this petite woman in her sharp little jacket, and her perfectly tailored slacks, and her men's-shoes-that-were-not-quite-men's-shoes.

I had just encountered *true* glamour for the first time. And I can say without hyperbole that every day of my life since that moment, I have tried to model my style after Edna Parker Watson's.

———

Peg rushed at Edna and pulled her into a tight embrace.

"Edna!" she cried, giving her old friend a spin. "The Dewdrop of Drury Lane makes an appearance on our humble shores!"

"Dear Peg!" cried Edna. "You look exactly the same!" Edna released herself from Peg's arms, stepped back, and took a look up at the Lily. "But is *all* this yours, Peg? The *entire* building?"

"All of it, yes, unfortunately," said Peg. "Would you like to buy it?"

"I haven't a farthing to my name, darling, or I absolutely would. It's *charming*. But look at you—you've become an *impresario*! You're a theater *magnate*! The façade reminds me of the old Hackney. It's lovely. I *do* see why you had to buy it."

"Yes, of course I had to buy it," said Peg, "because otherwise I might have ended up wealthy and comfortable in my old age, and that would've been no good for anybody. But enough about my dumb playhouse, Edna. I'm just *sick* about what's happened to your home—and what's happening to poor England!"

"Darling Peg," said Edna, and she placed her palm gently on my aunt's cheek. "It's wretched. But Arthur and I are alive. And now, thanks to you, we have a roof to sleep under, and that's a good deal more than some other people can say."

"Where *is* Arthur?" asked Peg. "Can't *wait* to meet him."

But I myself had already spotted him.

Arthur Watson was the handsome, dark-haired, movie-star-looking fellow with the lantern jaw who was, at that instant, grinning at the cab driver and pumping the man's hand with altogether too much enthusiasm. He was a well-built man with a good pair of shoulders, and he was much taller than he looked on the movie screen—which is highly abnormal for actors. He had a cigar clamped in his mouth, which somehow looked like a prop. He was the best-looking man I'd ever seen at close quarters, but there was something artificial about his good looks. He had a rakish curl that fell over one eye, for instance, which would have been a lot more attractive if it hadn't looked so deliberately cultivated. (The thing about rakishness, Angela, is that it should never seem intentional.) He looked like an *actor*, is the best way I can describe it. He looked as if he were an actor hired to play the part of a handsome, well-built man, shaking the hand of a cabdriver.

Arthur marched over to us in great, athletic strides and shook Peg's hand just as forcibly as he'd done to the poor cabbie.

"Mrs. Buell," he said. "Awfully good of you to give us a place to stay!"

"A delight, Arthur," said Peg. "I simply adore your wife."

"I adore her, too!" boomed Arthur, and he caught Edna in a tight squeeze that looked like it might hurt, but which only made her beam with pleasure.

"And this is my niece, Vivian," said Peg. "She's been staying with me all summer, learning how to run a theater company into the ground."

"The *niece*!" Edna said, as though she'd been hearing fabulous things about me for years. She gave me a kiss on each cheek, wafting a scent of gardenia. "But look at you, Vivian—you're simply stunning! Please tell me that you're not an aspiring actress and that you won't ruin your life in the theater—although you're certainly pretty enough for it."

Hers was a smile far too warm and genuine for show business. She was paying me the compliment of her undivided attention, and thus I was instantly smitten.

"No," I said. "I'm not an actress. But I do love living at the Lily with my aunt."

"But of course you do, darling. She's marvelous."

Arthur interrupted, to reach in and crush my hand in his. "Awfully nice to meet you, Vivian!" he said. "And how long did you say you've been an actress?"

I was less smitten with him.

"Oh, I'm not an actress—" I started to say, but Edna put her hand on my arm and whispered in my ear, as if we were dearest friends, "It's quite all right, Vivian. Arthur sometimes doesn't pay the *closest* attention, but he'll get it all sorted out eventually."

"Let's go have drinks on my verandah!" said Peg. "Except that I forgot to buy a home with a verandah, so let's go have drinks in the filthy living room above my theater, and we can pretend that we're having drinks on my verandah!"

"Brilliant Peg," said Edna. "How *violently* I've missed you!"

A few trays of martinis later, it was as if I'd known Edna Parker Watson forever.

She was the most charming presence I'd ever watched light up a room. She was a sort of elfin queen, what with her bright little face, and her dancing gray eyes. Nothing about her was quite what it seemed. She was pale, but she didn't seem weak or delicate. And she was awfully dainty—with the tiniest shoulders and a slender frame—but she didn't look fragile. She had a hearty laugh and a robust bounce to her step that belied her size and her pallid coloring.

I suppose you could call her a non-frail waif.

The exact source of her beauty was difficult to place, for her features were not perfect—not like the girls I'd been romping about with all summer. Her face was quite round, and she didn't have the dramatic cheekbones that were so much in vogue back then. And she wasn't young. She had to be at least fifty, and she wasn't trying to hide it. You couldn't tell her age from a distance (she had been able to play Juliet well into her forties, I would later learn—and had easily gotten away with it, too), but once you looked closely, you could see that the skin around her eyes was crumbling with fine lines, and her jawline was getting soft. There were strands of silver in that chic, short hair of hers, as well. But her spirit was youthful. She was utterly unconvincing as a fifty-year-old woman—let's just put it that way. Or maybe her age didn't matter to her, so she didn't project any concern about it. The trouble with so many aging actresses is that they don't want to let nature do as it wishes—but nature seemed to have no particular vengeance against Edna, nor did she have a gripe against it.

Her greatest natural gift, though, was warmth. She delighted in all that she beheld, and it made you want to stay near her, in order to bask in her delight. Even Olive's normally stern face relaxed into a rare expression of joy at the sight of Edna. They embraced as old friends—for that is exactly what they were. As I discovered that night, Edna and Peg and Olive had all met on the battlefields of France, when Edna was part of a British touring company, putting on shows for wounded soldiers—shows that my Aunt Peg and Olive helped to produce.

"Somewhere on this planet," said Edna, "there's a photograph of the three of us in a field ambulance together, and I would give anything to see it again. We were so young! And we were wearing those terribly practical frocks, with no waistlines."

"I remember that picture," said Olive. "We were *muddy.*"

"We were always muddy, Olive," said Edna. "It was a battlefield. I will never forget the cold and damp. Do you remember how I had to make my own stage makeup out of brick dust and lard? I was so nervous about acting in front of the soldiers. They were all so horribly wounded. Do you remember what you told me, Peg? When I asked, 'How can I sing and dance for these poor broken boys?'"

"Mercifully, my dear Edna," said Peg, "I do not remember anything I have ever said in my entire life."

"Well, then, I shall remind you. You said, 'Sing louder, Edna. Dance harder. Look 'em straight in the eyes.' You told me: 'Don't you dare degrade these brave boys with your pity.' So that's what I did. I sang loud and danced hard, and looked 'em straight in the eyes. I did not degrade those brave boys with my pity. My God, but it was painful."

"You worked very hard," said Olive, approvingly.

"It was you nurses who worked hard, Olive," said Edna. "I remember the whole lot of you having dysentery and chilblains—but then you'd say, 'At least we don't have infected bayonet wounds, girls! Chins up!' What heroes you were. Especially you, Olive. Equal to any emergency, you were. I've never forgotten it."

Receiving this compliment, Olive's face was suddenly lit up by the most unusual expression. By my stars, I do believe it was *happiness*.

"Edna was performing bits of Shakespeare for the men," Peg said to me. "I remember thinking it was a terrible idea. I thought Shakespeare would bore them to tears, but they loved it."

"They loved it because they hadn't seen a pretty little English lass in months," said Edna. "I remember one man shouting, 'Better than a trip to the whorehouse!' after I gave them my piece of Ophelia, and I still think it's the best review I've ever received. You were in that show, Peg. You played my Hamlet. Those tights really suited you."

"I didn't *play* Hamlet; I just read from the script," said Peg. "I never could act, Edna. And I detest *Hamlet*. Have you ever seen a production of *Hamlet* that didn't make you want to go home and put your head in the oven? I haven't."

"Oh, I thought our *Hamlet* was quite nice," said Edna.

"Because it was *abridged*," said Peg. "Which is the only thing Shakespeare should ever be."

"Although you did make an awfully *cheery* Hamlet, as I recall," said Edna. "Perhaps the most cheerful Hamlet in history."

"But *Hamlet* isn't meant to be cheerful!" chimed in Arthur Watson, looking puzzled.

The room paused. It was quite awkward. I would soon discover that this was often the effect that Arthur Watson had when he spoke. He could bring the most sparkling of conversations to the most grinding halt, just by opening his mouth.

We all looked to see how Edna would react to her husband's stupid comment. But she was beaming at him fondly. "That's right, Arthur. *Hamlet* is not generally known for being a cheerful play, but Peg brought her natural buoyancy to the role and quite brightened up the whole story."

"Oh!" he said. "Well, jolly good for her, then! Though I don't know what Mr. Shakespeare would've thought of *that*."

Peg saved the day by changing the subject: "Mr. Shakespeare would've rolled in his grave, Edna, if he knew that I'd been allowed to share a stage with the likes of *you*," she said. Then she turned to me again: "What you have to understand, kiddo, is that Edna is one of the greatest actresses of her age."

Edna grinned. "Oh, Peg, stop talking about my *age*!"

"I believe what she meant, Edna," corrected Arthur, "is that you are one of the greatest actresses of your *generation*. She's not talking about your *age*."

"Thank you for the clarification, darling," replied Edna to her husband, with no trace of irony or annoyance. "And thank *you* for the kindness, Peg."

Peg went on: "Edna is the best Shakespearean actress you'll ever meet, Vivian. She's always had a knack for it. Started as a baby in the cradle. Could recite the sonnets backwards, they say, before she learned them forwards."

Arthur muttered, "You'd think it would've been easier to learn them forwards first."

"Many thanks, Peg," said Edna, ignoring Arthur, thank God. "You've always been so good to me."

"We shall have to find something for you to do while you're here," announced Peg, slapping her leg for emphasis. "I'd be happy to put you in one of our terrible shows, but it's all so beneath you."

"Nothing is beneath me, dear Peg. I've played Ophelia in knee-deep mud."

"Oh, but Edna, you haven't seen our shows! It'll make you miss the mud. And I don't have much to pay you—certainly not what you're worth."

"Anything's better than what we could earn in England—if we could even get to England."

"I just wish you could get a role in one of the more reputable theaters around town," said Peg. "There are many of them in New York, rumor has it. I've never stepped foot in one myself, of course, but I understand that they exist."

"I know, but it's too late in the season," said Edna. "Middle of September—all the productions have been cast. And remember—I'm not as well known here, darling. As long as Lynn Fontanne and Ethel Barrymore are alive, I'll never get the best roles in New York. But I'd still love to work while I'm here—and I know Arthur would, too. I'm versatile, Peg—you know that. I can still play a youngish woman, if you put me at the back of the stage, in the correct lighting. I can play a Jewess, or a gypsy, or a Frenchwoman. At a pinch, I can play a little boy. Hell, Arthur and I will sell peanuts in the lobby, if need be. We'll clean out ashtrays. We only wish to earn our keep."

"Now see here, Edna," declared Arthur Watson sternly. "I don't think I'd much like to clean out *ashtrays*."

That evening, Edna watched both the early and the late performances of *Dance Away, Jackie!* She could not have been more delighted with our awful little show if she'd been a twelve-year-old peasant child seeing theater for the first time.

"Oh, but it's *fun!*" she exclaimed to me, when the performers had left the stage after their final bows. "You know, Vivian, this sort of theater is where I got my start. My parents were players and I grew up around productions just like this. Born in the wings, five minutes before my first performance."

Edna insisted on going backstage and meeting all the actors and dancers, to congratulate them. Some had heard of her, but most hadn't. To most of them, she was just a nice woman giving them praise—and that was good enough for them. The players bubbled up around her, soaking in her generous ministrations.

I cornered Celia and said, "That's Edna Parker Watson."

"Yeah?" said Celia, unimpressed.

"She's a famous British actress. She's married to Arthur Watson."

"Arthur Watson, from *Gates of Noon?*"

"Yes! They're staying here now. Their house in London got bombed."

"But Arthur Watson is *young*," Celia said, staring at Edna. "How can he be married to her?"

"I don't know," I said. "She's quite something, though."

"Yeah." Celia didn't seem so sure. "Where we going out tonight?"

For the first time since meeting Celia, I wasn't so sure I *wanted* to go out. I thought I might prefer to spend more time around Edna. Just for one night.

"I want you to meet her," I said. "She's famous and I'm mad about the way she dresses."

So I brought Celia over and proudly introduced her to Edna.

You can never anticipate how a woman is going to react to meeting a showgirl. A showgirl in full costume is intentionally designed to make all other females look and feel insignificant by comparison. You need to have a considerable amount of self-confidence, as a woman, to stand in the lavish radiance of a showgirl without flinching, resenting, or melting away.

But Edna—tiny as she was—had just that kind of self-confidence.

"You're *magnificent!*" she cried to Celia, when I introduced them. "Look at the height on you! And that face. You, my dear, could headline at the *Folies Bergère.*"

"That's in Paris," I said to Celia, who thankfully did not take note of my patronizing tone, distracted as she was by the compliments.

"And where are you from, Celia?" Edna asked—tilting her head with curiosity and shining the spotlight of her fullest attention upon my friend.

"I'm from right here. From New York City," said Celia.

(As though that accent could've been born anywhere else.)

"I noticed tonight that you dance exceptionally well for a girl of your height. Did you study ballet? Your carriage would suggest you'd been properly trained."

"No," replied Celia, whose face was now aglow with pleasure.

"And do you act? The camera must adore you. You look just like a film star."

"I act a bit." Then she added (quite archly for someone who had only ever played a corpse in a B movie): "I am not yet widely known."

"Well, you shall be known soon enough, if there's any justice. Stay at it, my dear. You're in the right field. You have a face that was made for your times."

It's not difficult to compliment people in order to try to win their affections. What is difficult is to do it in the *right way.* Everyone told Celia she was beautiful, but nobody had ever told her she had the carriage of a trained ballerina. Nobody had ever told her she had a face made for her times.

"You know, I've just realized something," said Edna. "In all the excitement, I have not yet unpacked. I wonder if you girls might be free to help me?"

"Sure!" said Celia eagerly, looking like she was about thirteen years old.

And to my wonderment, in that instant the goddess became a handmaiden.

When we arrived upstairs in the fourth-floor apartment that Edna would be sharing with her husband, we found a pile of trunks and parcels and hatboxes on the sitting-room floor—an avalanche of luggage.

"Oh, dear," said Edna. "It gives quite the impression of density, doesn't it? I do hate to trouble you girls, but shall we begin?"

As for me, I couldn't wait. I was dying to get my hands on her clothes. I had a feeling they'd be splendid—and indeed they were. Unpacking Edna's trunks was a lesson in sartorial genius. I soon noticed that there was nothing haphazard about her clothing; it was all in keeping with a particular style that I might call "Little Lord Fauntleroy meets French salon hostess."

She certainly had a lot of jackets—that seemed to be the elementary unit of her aesthetic. The jackets were all variations on a theme—fitted, jaunty, slightly martial in tone. Some were trimmed in Persian lamb, others had satin details. Some looked like formal riding jackets, but some were more playful. All of them had gold buttons of different design, and all were lined with jewel-toned silks.

"I have them specially made," she told me, when she caught me searching the labels for information. "There's an Indian tailor in London who has come to know my taste over the years. He never gets bored of creating them for me, and I never get bored of buying them."

And then there were the trousers—so many pairs of trousers. Some were long and loose, but others were narrow and looked like they would hit above the ankle. ("I got used to wearing these when I studied dance," she said of the cropped variety. "All the dancers in Paris wore trousers like that, and heavens, did they make it look chic. I used to call those girls 'the slim ankle brigade.'")

The trousers were a real revelation for me. I'd never been a firm believer in trousers on women until I saw how good they looked on Edna. Not even Garbo and Hepburn had yet convinced me that a woman could be both feminine and glamorous in pants, but looking at Edna's clothes suddenly made me think that it was the *only* way a woman could be both feminine and glamorous.

"I prefer trousers for daily wear," she explained. "I'm small, but I have a long stride. I need to be able to move about freely. Years ago, a newspaperman wrote that I had a 'titillating boyishness' to me, and that's my favorite thing a man's ever said about me. What could be better than having a bit of the titillating boy about you?"

Celia gave a puzzled look, but I understood Edna's point exactly and loved this idea.

Then we came to the trunk filled with Edna's blouses. So many of them had quaint jabots, or ornamental ruffles. This attention to detail, I grasped, is how a woman could wear a suit and still look like a woman. There was one high-necked crepe de chine chemise in the softest pink you could imagine, and it made my heart ache with longing when I touched it. Then I pulled out an elegant little ivory number of finest silk, with tiny pearl buttons at the neck, and the most infinitesimal sleeves.

"What an *impeccable* blouse!" I said.

"Thank you for noticing, Vivian. You've got a good eye. That little blouse came from Coco Chanel herself. She gave it to me—if you can imagine Coco ever *giving* somebody something for free! It must have been a weak moment for her. Perhaps she had food poisoning that day."

Celia and I both gasped, and I cried out, "You know Coco Chanel?"

"Nobody *knows* Coco, my dear. She would never allow for that. But I can say that we are acquainted. I met her years ago when I was acting in Paris and living on the Quai Voltaire. That was back when I was learning French—which is a good language to learn as an actress, because it teaches you how to use your mouth."

Well, *that* was the most sophisticated combination of words I'd ever heard.

"But what's she like?"

"What's Coco like?" Edna paused, closed her eyes, and seemed to be searching for the right words. She opened her eyes and smiled. "Coco Chanel is a gifted, ambitious, cunning, unloved, and hardworking *eel* of a woman. I'm more afraid of her taking dominion over the world than I am of Mussolini or Hitler. No, I'm teasing—she's a fine enough specimen of a person. One is only ever in danger from Coco when she starts calling you her friend. But she's far more interesting than I'm making her sound. Girls, what do you think of this hat?"

She had pulled from a box a homburg—like something a man would wear, but not at all. Soft and plum colored, and dressed with a single red feather. She modeled it for us with a bright smile.

"It's wonderful on you," I said. "But it doesn't look like anything I'm seeing people wearing right now."

"Thank you," said Edna. "I can't bear the hats that are in style just now. I can't endure a hat that substitutes a pile of miscellany on the top of your head for the pleasing simplicity of a *line*. A homburg will always give you a perfect line, if it's specially made for you. The wrong hat makes me feel cross and oppressed. And there are so many wrong hats. But alas—milliners need to eat, too, I suppose."

"I love *this*," said Celia, pulling out a long, yellow silk scarf, and wrapping it around her head.

"Well done, Celia!" said Edna. "You are the infrequent sort of girl who looks *good* with a scarf wrapped around her head. How fortunate for you! If I wore that scarf in that manner, I would look like a dead saint. Do you like it? You may keep it."

"Gee, thanks!" said Celia, parading around Edna's room, searching for a mirror.

"I can't think why I ever bought that scarf in the first place, girls. I suppose I bought it during a year when yellow scarves were in fashion. And let that be a lesson to you! The thing about fashion, my dears, is that you don't *need* to follow it, no matter what they say. No fashion trend is compulsory, remember—and if you dress too much in the style of the moment, it makes you look like a nervous person. Paris is all well and good, but we can't just follow Paris for the sake of Paris, now can we?"

We can't just follow Paris for the sake of Paris!

As long as I live, I shall never forget those words. That speech was certainly more stirring to me than anything Churchill had ever said.

Celia and I were now busy unpacking a trunk filled with the most delicious items of bath and beauty—articles of *toilette* that made us swoon with joy. There were carnation-scented bath oils, lavender alcohol rubs, pomander balls to spice up the drawers and closets, and so many alluring glass vials of lotions with French instructions. It was positively *intoxicating*. I would have been embarrassed by our overenthusiasm, but Edna seemed to be genuinely enjoying our squeaks and squeals of delight. In fact, she seemed to be having just as much fun as we were. I had the craziest sensation that Edna might actually like us. This was interesting to me then, and it is still interesting now. Older women don't always relish the company of beautiful young girls, for obvious reasons. But not Edna.

"Girls," she said, "I could watch the two of you effervesce for hours!"

And boy, did we effervesce. I'd never seen such a wardrobe. Edna even had a valise filled with nothing but gloves—each pair wrapped lovingly in its own silk.

"Never buy inexpensive or poorly made gloves," Edna instructed us. "That's not the place to save your money. Whenever you are faced with the prospect of purchasing gloves, you must ask yourself if you would be *bereft* to lose one of them in the back of a taxicab. If not, then don't buy them. You should only buy gloves so beautiful that to lose one of them would break your heart."

At some point, Edna's husband walked in, but he was inconsequential (handsome as he was) compared to this exotic wardrobe. She kissed his cheek and sent him on his way, saying, "There's no room in here yet for a man, Arthur. Go have a drink somewhere and entertain yourself until these dear girls are done, and then I *promise* I'll find space for you and your one sorry little duffel bag."

He sulked a bit, but did her bidding.

After he left, Celia said, "Say, but he's a looker, ain't he!"

I thought Edna might be offended, but she only laughed. "He is indeed, as you say, a *looker*. I've never before seen his like, to be candid with you. We've been married nearly a decade, and I haven't grown tired of looking at him yet."

"But he's *young*."

I could've kicked Celia for her rudeness, but Edna, again, didn't seem to mind. "Yes, dear Celia. He is young—far younger than me, in fact. One of my greatest achievements, I daresay."

"You don't get worried?" Celia pressed on. "There's gotta be a lot of young dishes out there who want to put the moves on him."

"I don't worry about dishes, my dear. Dishes break."

"Ooh!" said Celia, and her face lit up with something like awe.

"When you have found your own success as a woman," explained Edna, "you may do such a fun thing as marry a handsome man who is very much your junior. Consider it a reward for all your hard work. When first I met Arthur, he was just a boy—a set carpenter for an Ibsen play I was doing. *An Enemy of the People.* I was Mrs. Stockmann, and oh, it's a dull role. But meeting Arthur livened things up for me during the run of that play—and he has kept things lively for me since. I'm awfully fond of him, girls. He's my third husband, of course. Nobody's first husband looks like Arthur. My first husband was a civil servant, and I don't mind saying that he made love like a civil servant, too. My second husband was a theater director. I won't make *that* mistake again. And now there is dear Arthur, so handsome and yet so cozy. My gift, till the end of my days. I'm so fond of him that I even took his name—though my theater friends warned me not to, since my own name was already well known. I'd never taken the names of any of my other husbands before, you see. But Edna Parker Watson has a nice ring to it, don't you agree? And what about you, Celia? Have you ever had any husbands?"

I wanted to say: *She's had many husbands, Edna—but only one of them was her own.*

"Yeah," said Celia. "I had a husband once. He played the saxophone."

"Oh, dear. So we may assume that didn't last?"

"Yeah, you guessed it, lady." Celia drew a line across her own throat, to indicate, I guess, the death of love.

"And what about you, Vivian? Married? Engaged?"

"No," I said.

"Anybody special?"

"Nobody *special*," I said, and something about the way I uttered the word "special" made Edna burst out laughing.

"Ah, but you have a *somebody*, I can see."

"She has a few somebodies," Celia said, and I couldn't help but smile.

"Good work, Vivian!" Edna gave me an appraising second look. "You're growing more interesting to me by the moment!"

Later on in the evening—it must have been well after midnight by then—Peg came in to check on us. She settled into a deep chair with a nightcap in her hand and watched with pleasure as Celia and I finished unpacking Edna's trunks.

"Gadzooks, Edna," Peg said. "You have a *lot* of clothes."

"This is a mere fraction of the collection, Peg. You should see my wardrobe back home." She paused. "Oh, dear. I've just now remembered again that I've *lost* everything back home. My contribution to the war effort, I suppose. Evidently Mr. Goering needed to destroy my more-than-three-decades-in-the-making costume collection as part of his plan for making the world safe for the Aryan race. I don't quite see how it *served* him, but the sad deed is done."

I marveled at how lightly she seemed to take the destruction of her home. So, apparently, did Peg, who said, "I must admit, Edna, I was expecting to find you a bit more shaken up by all this."

"Oh, Peg, you know me better than that! Or have you forgotten how good I am at adjusting to circumstances? You can't lead the sort of patched-together life that I've lived and get too sentimental about things."

Peg grinned. "Show people," she said to me, shaking her head with an insider's appreciation.

Celia had just now pulled out an elegant floor-length, high-necked, black crepe gown with long sleeves, and a small pearl brooch set deliberately off center.

"Now *that's* something," said Celia.

"You would think so, wouldn't you?" said Edna, holding the dress up to herself. "But I've had a difficult relationship with this dress. Black can be the smartest of colors, or it can be the dowdiest, depending on the line. I wore this gown only once, and I felt like a Greek widow in it. But I've kept it because I like the pearl detail."

I approached the dress, respectfully. "May I?" I asked.

Edna handed me the dress and I laid it out on the couch, touching it here and there, and getting a better sense of it.

"The problem isn't the color," I diagnosed. "The problem is the sleeves. The material of the sleeves is heavier than the material of the bodice—can you see that? This dress should have chiffon sleeves—or none at all, which would be better for you, petite as you are."

Edna studied the gown and then looked at me with surprise.

"I believe you're on to something there, Vivian."

"I could fix it for you, if you'll trust me with it."

"Our Vivvie can sew like the devil!" Celia said, proudly.

"It's true," put in Peg. "Vivian is our resident dress professor."

"She makes all the costumes for the shows," said Celia. "She made the ballet tutus everyone was wearing tonight."

"Did you?" said Edna, more impressed than she should've been. (Your cat could sew a tutu, Angela.) "So you're not only beautiful, but gifted as well? Imagine that! And they say the Lord never gives with both hands!"

I shrugged. "All I know is that I can fix this. I would shorten it, as well. It would be better for you if it landed at mid-ankle."

"Well, it appears as if you know a good deal more about clothes than I do," said Edna, "because I was ready to relegate this poor old gown to the ash heap. And here I've been, filling your ears all night with my noise and opinions about fashion and style. I should be the one listening to *you*. So tell me, my dear—where did you learn how to understand a dress so well?"

can't imagine that it was fascinating for a woman of Edna Parker Watson's stature to listen to a nineteen-year-old girl blather on about her grandmother for the next several hours, but that's exactly what happened, and she bore it nobly. More than nobly—she hung on every word.

Somewhere during the course of my monologue, Celia wandered out of the room. I wouldn't see her again until just before dawn, when she would come tumbling into our bed at the usual hour, in her usual state of drunken disarray. Peg ended up excusing herself, as well— once she got a sharp knock on the door and a reminder from Olive that it was past her bedtime.

So it ended up being just me and Edna—curled up on the couch of her new apartment at the Lily—talking into the wee hours. The well-raised girl within me did not want to monopolize her time, but I could not resist her attentions. Edna wanted to know everything about my grandmother and delighted in the details of her frivolities and eccentricities. ("What a character! She should be put in a play!") Every time I tried to turn the subject of the conversation away from myself, Edna would turn it back to me. She expressed sincere curiosity about my love of sewing and was astonished when I told her that I could make a whalebone corset if I had to.

"Then you're born to be a costume designer!" she said. "The difference between making a dress and making a costume, of course, is that dresses are sewn, but costumes are *built*. Many people these days can sew, but not many know how to *build*. A costume is a prop for the stage, Vivvie, as much as any piece of furniture, and it needs to be strong. You never know what's going to happen in a performance, and so the costume must be ready for anything."

I told Edna about how my grandmother used to find the tiniest hidden flaws in my outfits and demand that I fix the offending article on the spot. I used to protest that "Nobody will notice!" but Grandmother Morris would say, "That is not true, Vivian. People *will* notice, but they won't know what they're noticing. They will just notice that something is wrong. Don't give them that opportunity."

"She was correct!" said Edna. "This is why I take such care with my costumes. I hate it when an impatient director says, 'Nobody will notice!' Oh, the arguments I've had about that! As I always tell the director: 'If you put me in a spotlight with three hundred audience members staring at me for two hours, they will *notice a flaw*. They will notice flaws in my hair, flaws in my complexion, flaws in my voice, and they will absolutely notice flaws in my dress.' It's not that the audience members are masters of style, Vivian: it's merely that they have nothing else to do with their time, once they are held captive in their seats, *except* to notice your flaws."

I thought I'd been having adult conversations all summer, because I'd been spending my time around such a worldly group of showgirls, but this was *truly* an adult conversation. This was a conversation about craftsmanship, and about expertise, and about aesthetics. Nobody I'd ever met (except Grandmother Morris, of course) had ever known more about dressmaking than me. Nobody had ever cared this much. Nobody understood or respected the *art* of it.

I could have stayed there talking to Edna about clothing and costumes for another century or two, but Arthur Watson finally burst in and demanded that he be allowed to go to *ruddy bed* with his *ruddy wife,* and that put an end to it.

The next day marked the first morning in two months that I did not wake up with a hangover.

TEN

By the next week, my Aunt Peg had already begun creating a show for Edna to star in. She was determined to give her friend a job, and it had to be a better job than what the Lily Playhouse currently had to offer—because you can't very well put one of the greatest actresses of her age in *Dance Away, Jackie!*

As for Olive, she was not convinced this was a good idea in the least. As much as she loved Edna, it didn't make sense to her from a business standpoint to attempt to put on a decent (or even halfway decent) show at the Lily: it would break formula.

"We have a small audience, Peg," she said. "And they are humble. But they are the only audience we have, and they are loyal to us. We must be loyal to them in return. We can't leave them behind for one play—certainly not for one *player*—or they may never come back. Our task is to serve the neighborhood. And the neighborhood doesn't want Ibsen."

"I don't want Ibsen, either," said Peg. "But I hate seeing Edna sitting about idle, and I hate even more the idea of putting her in any of our draggy little shows."

"However *draggy* our shows may be, they keep the electricity on, Peg. And just barely, at that. Don't chance it, by changing anything."

"We could make a comedy," Peg said. "Something that our audiences would like. But it would have to be smart enough to be worthy of Edna."

She turned to Mr. Herbert, who had been sitting there at the breakfast table in his usual attire of baggy trousers and shirtsleeves, staring sorrowfully at nothing.

"Mr. Herbert," Peg asked, "do you think you could write a play that is both funny and smart?"

"No," he said, without even looking up.

"Well, what are you working on now? What's the next show on deck?"

"It's called *City of Girls*," he said. "I told you about it last month."

"The speakeasy one," said Peg. "I remember. Flappers and gangsters, and that sort of fluff. What's it about, again, exactly?"

Mr. Herbert looked both wounded and confused. "What's it *about?*" he asked. It seemed that this was the first time he'd considered that one of the Lily Playhouse shows should be *about* something.

"Never mind," said Peg. "Does it have a role that Edna could play?"

Again, he looked wounded and confused.

"I don't see how it could," he said. "We have an ingénue, and a hero. We have a villain. We don't have an older woman."

"Could the ingénue have a mother?"

"Peg, she's an *orphan*," said Mr. Herbert. "You can't change that."

I saw his point: the ingénue always had to be an orphan. The story wouldn't make sense if the ingénue wasn't an orphan. The audience would revolt. The audience would start throwing shoes and bricks at the players if the ingénue wasn't an orphan.

"Who's the owner of the speakeasy, in your show?"

"The speakeasy doesn't have an owner."

"Well, could it? And could it be a woman?"

Mr. Herbert rubbed his forehead and looked overwhelmed. He looked as though Peg had just asked him to repaint the ceiling of the Sistine Chapel.

"This causes problems in all aspects," he said.

Olive chimed in: "Nobody will believe Edna Parker Watson as the owner of a speakeasy, Peg. Why would the owner of a New York speakeasy be from England?"

Peg's face fell. "Blast it, you're right, Olive. You have such a bad habit of being right all the time. I wish you wouldn't do that." Peg sat in silence for a long moment, thinking hard. Then suddenly she said, "Goddamn it, but I wish I had Billy here. He could write something smashing for Edna."

Well, *that* caught my attention.

This was the first time I'd ever heard my aunt curse, for one thing. But this was also the first time I'd ever heard her mention her estranged husband's name. And I wasn't the only one who snapped to fullest attention at the mere mention of Billy Buell's name, either. Both Olive and Mr. Herbert looked as though they'd just had buckets of ice poured down their backs.

"Oh, Peg, no," said Olive. "Don't call Billy. Please, be sensible."

"I can add whoever you want me to add to the cast," said Mr. Herbert, suddenly cooperative. "Just tell me what you need me to do, and I'll do it. The speakeasy can have an owner, sure. She can be from England, too."

"Billy was so fond of Edna." Peg seemed to be talking to herself now. "And he's seen her perform. He'll understand how best to use her."

"You don't want Billy involved in anything we do, Peg," warned Olive.

"I'll call him. Just to get some ideas from him. The man is made of ideas."

"It's five A.M. on the West Coast," said Mr. Herbert. "You can't call him!"

This was fascinating to watch. The level of anxiety in the room had risen to an undeniably hot pitch, merely with the introduction of Billy's name.

"I'll call him this afternoon, then," said Peg. "Though we can't be sure he'll be awake by then, either."

"Oh, Peg, *no,*" said Olive again, sinking into what looked like leaden despair.

"Just to get some ideas from him, Olive," said Peg. "There's no harm done with a phone call. I need him, Olive. Like I say: the man is made of ideas."

That night after the show, Peg took a whole lot of us to dinner at Dinty Moore's on Forty-sixth Street. She was triumphant. She had spoken to Billy that afternoon and wanted to tell everyone about his ideas for the play.

I was there at that dinner, the Watsons were there, Mr. Herbert was there, Benjamin the piano player was there (first time I'd ever seen him out of the house), and Celia was there, too, because Celia and I were always together.

Peg said, "Now, listen, everyone. Billy's got it all figured out. We're going to put on *City of Girls* after all, and we're setting it during Prohibition. It will be a comedy, of course. Edna—you will play the owner of the speakeasy. But in order for the story to make sense and be funny, Billy says we're going to have to make you into an aristocrat, so that your natural refinement will make sense onstage. Your character will be a woman of means who ended up in the bootlegging business somewhat accidentally. Billy suggests that your husband died, and then you lost all your money in the stock market crash. Then you start distilling gin and running a casino in your fancy home, as a way of getting by. That way, Edna, you can keep the gentility for which you are known and loved, while at the same time being part of a comic revue with showgirls and dancers—which is the kind of thing our audience likes. I think it's brilliant. Billy thinks it would be funny if the nightclub was a bordello, too."

Olive frowned. "I don't like the idea of our play being set in a bordello."

"I do!" said Edna, shining with glee. "I love all of it! I'll be the madam of a bordello *and* the owner of a speakeasy. How pleasing! You can't imagine what a *balm* it will be for me to do a comedy, after so long. The last four plays I've been in, I was either a fallen woman who murdered her lover, or a long-suffering wife whose husband was murdered by a fallen woman. It wears on one, the *drama*."

Peg was beaming. "Say what you want about Billy, but the man is a genius."

Olive looked as though there was a *lot* she wanted to say about Billy, but she kept it to herself.

Peg turned her attention to our piano player. "Benjamin, I need you to make the music *exceptionally* good for this show. Edna's got a fine alto, and I would like to hear that voice filling up the Lily properly. Give her songs that are snappier than those mushy ballads I normally make you write. Or steal something from Cole Porter, the way you do sometimes. But make it *good*. I want this show to swing."

"I don't steal from Cole Porter," said Benjamin. "I don't steal from anyone."

"Don't you? I always thought you did, because your music *sounds* so much like Cole Porter's music."

"Well, I'm not quite sure how to take that," said Benjamin.

Peg shrugged. "Maybe Cole Porter's been stealing from *you*, Benjamin—who knows? Just write some terrific tunes, is what I'm saying. And be sure to give Edna a showstopper."

Then she turned to Celia and said, "Celia, I'd like you to play the ingénue."

Mr. Herbert looked like he was about to interrupt, but Peg impatiently waved him into silence.

"No, everyone, listen to me. This is a different sort of ingénue. I don't want our heroine this time to be some little saucer-eyed orphan girl in a white dress. I'm imagining our girl as being extremely provocative in the way she walks and talks—that would be you, Celia—but still untarnished by the world, in a way. Sexy, but with an air of innocence about her."

"A whore with a heart of gold," said Celia, who was smarter than she looked.

"Exactly," said Peg.

Edna touched Celia's arm gently. "Let's just call your character a *soiled dove*."

"Sure, I can play that." Celia reached for another pork chop. "Mr. Herbert, how many lines do I get?"

"I don't know!" said Mr. Herbert, looking more and more unhappy. "I don't know how to write a . . . soiled dove."

"I can make up some stuff for you," offered Celia—a true dramatist, that one.

Peg turned to Edna. "Do you know what Billy said when I told him that you were here, Edna? He said, 'Oh, how I envy New York City right now.'"

"*Did* he?"

"He did, that flirt. He also said: 'Watch out, because you never know what you'll get with Edna onstage: some nights she's excellent, other nights she's perfect.'"

Edna beamed. "That's so sweet of him. Nobody could ever make a woman feel more attractive than Billy could—sometimes for upwards of ten consecutive minutes. But, Peg, I must ask: Do you have a role for Arthur?"

"Of course I do," said Peg—and I knew in that moment that she did *not* have a role for Arthur. In fact, it was pretty clear to me that she'd forgotten about Arthur's existence entirely. But there was Arthur, sitting there in all his simpleminded handsomeness, waiting for his role like a Labrador retriever waits for a ball.

"Of course I have a role for Arthur," Peg said. "I want him to play"—she hesitated, but only for the *briefest* moment (you might not have even noticed the hesitation, if you didn't know Peg)—"the policeman. Yes, Arthur, I plan for you to play the policeman who's always trying to shut down the speakeasy, and who's in love with Edna's character. Do you think you could manage an American accent?"

"I can manage *any* accent," said Arthur, miffed—and I instantly knew that he absolutely could not manage an American accent.

"A policeman!" Edna clapped her hands. "And you'll be in love with *me*, dear! What larks."

"I didn't hear anything before about a policeman character," said Mr. Herbert.

"Oh, no, Mr. Herbert," said Peg. "The policeman has always been in the script."

"What script?"

"The script you'll commence writing tomorrow morning, at break of day."

Mr. Herbert looked like he was about to be afflicted with a nervous disorder.

"Do I get a song of my own to sing?" asked Arthur.

"Oh," said Peg. There was that pause again. "*Yes.* Benjamin, do be sure to write that song for Arthur, which we discussed. The policeman's song, please."

Benjamin held Peg's gaze and repeated with only the *slightest* sarcasm: "The policeman's song."

"That's correct, Benjamin. As we've already discussed."

"Shall I just steal a policeman's song from Gershwin, perhaps?"

But Peg was already turning her attention to me.

"Costumes!" she said brightly, and scarcely had the word left her mouth before Olive declared, "There will be virtually no budget for costumes."

Peg's face dropped. "Drat. I'd forgotten about that."

"That's all right," I said. "I'll buy everything at Lowtsky's. Flapper dresses are simple."

"Brilliant, Vivian," said Peg. "I know you'll take care of it."

"On a strict budget," Olive added.

"On a strict budget," I agreed. "I'll even throw in my own allowance if I have to."

As the conversation continued, with everyone except Mr. Herbert getting more excited and making suggestions for the show, I excused myself to the powder room. When I came out, I almost ran into a good-looking young man with a wide tie and a rather wolfish expression, who'd been waiting for me in the corridor.

"Say, there, your friend's a knockout," he said, nodding in the direction of Celia. "And so are you."

"That's what we've been told," I replied, holding his gaze.

"You girls wanna come home with me?" he asked, dispensing with the preliminaries. "I gotta friend with a car."

I studied him more closely. He looked like a piece of very bad business. A wolf with an agenda. This was not somebody a nice girl should tangle with.

"We might," I said, which was true. "But first we have a meeting to conclude, with our associates."

"Your *associates?*" he scoffed, taking in our table with its odd and animated assortment of humanity: a coronary-inducingly gorgeous showgirl, a slovenly white-haired man in his shirtsleeves, a tall and dowdy middle-aged woman, a short and stodgy middle-aged woman, a stylishly dressed lady of means, a strikingly handsome man with a dramatic profile, and an elegant young black man in a perfectly tailored pinstripe suit. "What line of business yous in, doll?"

"We're theater people," I said.

As if we could have been anything else.

The following morning I woke up early as usual, suffering from my typical summer-of-1940 hangover. My hair stank of sweat and cigarettes, and my limbs were all tangled up in Celia's limbs. (We had gone out with the wolf and his friend, after all—as I'm sure you'll be flabbergasted beyond all reason to hear—and it had been a strenuous night. I felt like I'd just been fished out of the Gowanus Canal.)

I made my way to the kitchen where I found Mr. Herbert sitting with his forehead on the table and his hands folded politely in his lap. This was a new posture for him—a new low in dejectedness, I would say.

"Good morning, Mr. Herbert," I said.

"I stand ready to review any evidence of it," he replied, without lifting his forehead from the table.

"How are you feeling today?" I asked.

"Blithesome. Glorious. Exalted. I'm a sultan in his palace."

He still hadn't lifted his head.

"How's the script coming along?"

"Be a humanitarian, Vivian, and stop asking questions."

The next morning, I found Mr. Hebert in the same position—and several of the following mornings, too. I didn't know how somebody could sit for so long with their forehead on a table without suffering an aneurysm. His mood never lifted, and neither—at least not that I saw—did his skull. Meanwhile, his notebook sat untouched beside him.

"Is he going to be all right?" I asked Peg.

"It's not easy to write a play, Vivian," she said. "The problem is, I'm asking him to write something *good*, and I've never asked that of him before. It's got his head all screwy. But I think of it this way. During the war, the British army engineers always used to say: 'We can do it, whether it can be done or not.' That's how the theater works, too, Vivian. Just like a war! I often ask people to do more than they are capable of—or I used to do, anyway, before I got old and soft. So, yes, I have full confidence in Mr. Herbert."

I didn't.

Celia and I came in late one night, drunk as usual, and we tripped over a body that was lying on the living room floor. Celia shrieked. I switched on a light and identified Mr. Herbert, lying there in the middle of the carpet on his back, staring up at the ceiling, with his hands folded over his chest. For an awful moment, I thought he was dead. Then he blinked.

"Mr. Herbert!" I exclaimed. "What are you *doing*?"

"Prophesizing," he said, without moving.

"Prophesizing *what*?" I slurred.

"Doom," he said.

"Well, then. Have a good night." I turned off the light.

"Splendid," he said quietly, as Celia and I stumbled to our room. "I will be certain to do just that."

Meanwhile, as Mr. Herbert suffered, the rest of us went about the business of creating a play that did not yet have a script.

Peg and Benjamin had already gotten to work on the songs, sitting at the grand piano all afternoon, running through melodies and ideas for lyrics.

"I want Edna's character to be called Mrs. Alabaster," said Peg. "It sounds ostentatious, and a lot of words can rhyme with it."

"Plaster, caster, master, bastard, Alabaster," said Benjamin. "I can work with that."

"Olive won't let you say bastard. But go bigger. In the first number, when Mrs. Alabaster has lost all her money, make the song feel overly wordy, to show how fancy she is. Use longer words, to rhyme. Taskmaster. Toastmaster. Oleaster."

"Or we can have the chorus run through a series of questions about her," Benjamin suggested. "Like: *Who asked her? Who passed her? Who grasped her?*"

"Disaster! It attacked her!"

"The Depression, it smacked her—that poor Alabaster."

"It gassed her. It smashed her. She's poor as a pastor."

"Hey there, Peg," Benjamin suddenly stopping what he was playing. "My father's a pastor and *he's* not poor."

"I don't pay you to lift your hands off those piano keys, Benjamin. Keep noodling about. We were just getting somewhere."

"You don't pay me at all," he said, folding his hands in his lap. "You haven't paid me in three weeks! You haven't paid anyone, I heard."

"Is that true?" Peg asked. "What are you living on?"

"Prayers. And your leftover dinner."

"Sorry, kiddo! I'll talk to Olive about it. But not right now. Go back and start over, but add that thing you were doing that time when I walked in on you playing the piano, and I liked what I heard. You remember? That Sunday, when the Giants game was playing on the radio?"

"I can't begin to know what you're talking about, Peg."

"Play, Benjamin. Just keep playing. That's how we'll find it. After this, I want you to write a song for Celia called 'I'll Be a Good Girl Later.' Do you think you could write a song like that?"

"I can write anything, if you feed me and pay me."

As for me, I was designing costumes for the cast—but mostly for Edna.

Edna was concerned about being "swallowed" by the waistless 1920s dresses that she saw me sketching.

"That style didn't look good on me back then when I was young and pretty," she said, "and I can't see it looking good on me now that I'm old and stale. You have to give me a waistline of some sort. I know it wasn't the fashion back then, but you'll have to fake it. Also, my waist is more stoutish right now than I would like it to be. Work around it, please."

"I don't think you're stoutish at all," I said, and I meant it.

"Oh, but I am. Don't worry, though—in the week before the show, I'll live on a diet of rice water, toast, mineral oil, and laxatives, like always. I'll slim down. But for now, use gussets, so you can tighten my waistline later. If there's to be a lot of dancing, I'll need you to create *purposeful* seams—you understand, don't you, darling? Nothing can fly loose when I'm in the spotlight. My legs are still good, thank heavens, so don't be afraid to show them. What else? Oh, yes—my shoulders are narrower than they seem. And my neck is awfully short, so proceed with caution, especially if you're going to put me in some sort of a large hat. If you make me look like a stubby little French bulldog, Vivian, I'll never forgive you."

I had *such* respect for how well this woman knew the vagaries of her own figure. Most women have no idea what works for them and what doesn't. But Edna was precision incarnate. Sewing for her, I could see, was going to be its own apprenticeship in costuming.

"You are designing for the stage, Vivian," she instructed. "Rely upon shape more than detail. Remember that the nearest viewer to me will be ten strides away. You have to think on a large scale. Big colors, clean lines. A costume is a *landscape,* not a *portrait.* And I want brilliant dresses, my dear, but I don't want the dress to be the star of the show. Don't outshine me, darling. You understand?"

I did. And oh, how I loved the shape of this conversation. I loved being with Edna. I was becoming quite infatuated with her, if I'm being honest. She had nearly replaced Celia as the central object of my devoted awe. Celia was still exciting, of course, and we still went out on the town, but I didn't need her so much anymore. Edna had depths of glamour and sophistication that excited me far more than anything Celia could offer.

I would say that Edna was somebody who "spoke my own language" but that's not quite it, because I was not yet as fluent in fashion as she was. It would be closer to the truth to say that Edna Parker Watson was the first native speaker I'd ever encountered of the language that I *wanted* to master—the language of outstanding apparel.

A few days later, I took Edna to Lowtsky's Used Emporium and Notions to look for fabrics and ideas. I was a bit nervous about bringing someone of such refined taste to this overwhelming bazaar of noise, material, and color (to be honest, the smell alone would turn off most high-end shoppers), but Edna was instantly thrilled by Lowtsky's—as only somebody who genuinely understood clothing and materials could be. She was also delighted by young Marjorie Lowtsky, who greeted us at the door with her standard demand: "Whaddaya need?"

Marjorie was the daughter of the owners, and I had come to know her well over my past few months of shopping excursions. She was a bright, energetic, pie-faced fourteen-year-old, who always dressed in the most outlandish costumes. On this day, for instance, she was wearing the craziest getup I'd ever seen—big buckled shoes (like a Pilgrim in a child's Thanksgiving drawing), a gold brocade cape with a ten-foot train, and a French chef's hat with a giant fake ruby brooch pinned to it. Underneath all that, her school uniform. She looked patently ridiculous, as always, but Marjorie Lowtsky was not one to be taken lightly. Mr. and Mrs. Lowtsky didn't speak the *best* English, so Marjorie had been doing the talking for them since toddlerhood. At her young age, she already knew the rag trade as well as anyone, and could take orders and deliver threats in four languages—Russian, French, Yiddish, and English. She was an odd kid, but I had come to find Marjorie's help essential.

"We need dresses from the 1920s, Marjorie," I said. "Really good ones. Rich lady dresses."

"You wanna start by looking upstairs? In the Collection?"

The archly named "Collection" was a small area on the third floor where the Lowtskys sold their rarest and most precious finds.

"We don't have the budget just now to even be glancing at the Collection."

"So you want rich lady dresses but at poor lady prices?"

Edna laughed: "You've identified our needs perfectly, my dear."

"That's right, Marjorie," I said. "We're here to dig, not to spend."

"Start over there," Marjorie said, pointing to the back of the building. "The stuff by the loading dock just came in over the last few days.

Mama hasn't even had a chance to look through it yet. You could get lucky."

The bins at Lowtsky's were not for the faint of heart. These were large industrial laundry bins, crammed with textiles that the Lowtskys bought and sold by the pound—everything from workers' battered old overalls to tragically stained undergarments, to upholstery remnants, to parachute material, to faded blouses of pongee silk, to French lace serviettes, to heavy old drapes, to your great-grandfather's precious satin christening gown. Digging through the bins was hard and sweaty work, an act of faith. You had to believe that there was treasure to be found in all this garbage, and you had to hunt for it with conviction.

Edna, much to my admiration, dove right in. I got the sense she'd done this sort of thing before. Side by side, bin by bin, the two of us dug in silence, searching for what we did not know.

About an hour in, I suddenly heard Edna shout "a-*ha!*" and looked over to see her waving something triumphantly above her head. And triumphant she should have been, for her find turned out to be a 1920s crimson silk-chiffon and velvet-trimmed *robe de style* evening dress, embellished with glass beading and gold thread.

"Oh, *my!*" I exclaimed. "It's perfect for Mrs. Alabaster!"

"Indeed," said Edna. "And feast your eyes upon *this*." She turned over the back collar of the garment to reveal the original label: *Lanvin, Paris*. "Somebody *très riche* bought this dress in France twenty years ago, I'll wager, and barely wore it, by the looks of it. Delicious. How it will *glint* on stage!"

In a flash, Marjorie Lowtsky was at our side.

"Say, what'd you kids find in there?" asked the only actual kid in the room.

"Don't you start with me, Marjorie," I warned. I was only half teasing—suddenly afraid she was going to snatch the dress away from us to sell in the Collection upstairs. "Play by the rules. Edna found this dress in the bins, fair and square."

Marjorie shrugged. "All's fair in love and war," she said. "But it's a good one. Just make sure you bury it under a heap of trash when mama rings it up. She'd murder me if she knew I let that one get away from us. Lemme get you a sack and some rags, to hide it."

"Aw, Marjorie, thanks," I said. "You're my top-notch girl."

"You and me, we're always in cahoots," she said, rewarding me with a crooked grin. "Just keep your mouth shut. You wouldn't want me getting fired."

As Marjorie wandered off, Edna stared at her in wonder. "Did that *child* just say, 'All's fair in love and war'?"

"I told you that you'd like Lowtsky's," I said.

"Well, I *do* like Lowtsky's! And I adore this dress. And what have *you* found, my dear?"

I handed her a flimsy negligee, in a vivid, eye-injuring shade of fuchsia. She took it, held it up against her body, and winced.

"Oh, *no*, darling. You *cannot* put me in that. The audience will suffer from it even more than I will."

"No, Edna, it's not for you. It's for Celia," I said. "For the seduction scene."

"Dear me. Oh, yes. That makes more sense." Edna took a more careful look at the negligee and shook her head. "Goodness, Vivian, if you parade that girl around stage in this tiny getup, we *are* going to have a hit. Men will be lined up for miles. I'd best get started on my rice-water diet soon, or else nobody will be paying attention to my poor little figure at all!"

ELEVEN

I turned twenty years old on October 7, 1940.

I celebrated my first birthday in New York City exactly how you might imagine I would: I went out with the showgirls; we gave the jump to some playboys; we drank rank after rank of cocktails on other people's dime; we had tumults of fun; and the next thing you know we were trying to get home before the sun came up, feeling as if we were swimming upstream through bilgewater.

I slept for about eight minutes, it seemed, and then woke to the oddest sensation in my room. Something felt off. I was hungover, of course—quite possibly still even officially drunk—but still, something was strange. I reached for Celia, to see if she was there with me. My hand brushed against her familiar flesh. So all was normal on that front.

Except that I smelled smoke.

Pipe smoke.

I sat up, and my head instantly regretted the decision. I lay back down on the pillow, took a few brave breaths, apologized to my skull for the assault, and tried again, more slowly and respectfully this time.

As my eyes focused in the dim morning light, I could see a figure sitting in a chair across the room. A male figure. Smoking a pipe, and looking at us.

Had Celia brought someone home with her? Had *I*?

I felt a heave of panic. Celia and I were libertines, as I've well established, but I'd always had just enough respect for Peg (or fear of Olive, more like it) not to allow men to visit our bedroom upstairs at the Lily. How had this happened?

"Imagine my delight," said the stranger, lighting his pipe again, "to come home and find two girls in my bed! And both of you so stunning. It's as though I went to my icebox to get milk and discovered a bottle of champagne, instead. *Two* bottles of champagne, to be exact."

My mind still couldn't register.

Until then, suddenly, it could.

"Uncle Billy?" I asked.

"Oh, are you my *niece*?" the man said, and he started laughing. "Damn it. That limits our possibilities considerably. What's your name, love?"

"I'm Vivian Morris."

"Ohhhh . . ." he said. "Now this makes sense. You *are* my niece. How disheartening. I suppose the family wouldn't approve if I ravaged you. I might not even approve of myself if I ravaged you—I've become so moral in my old age. Alas, alas. Is the other one my niece, too? I hope not. She doesn't look like she could be anyone's niece."

"This one is Celia," I said, gesturing to Celia's beautiful, unconscious form. "She's my friend."

"Your very *particular* friend," Billy said, in an amused tone, "if one is to judge from the sleeping arrangements. How modern of you, Vivian!

I approve heartily. Don't worry, I won't tell your parents. Though I'm sure they'd find a way to blame me for it, if they ever found out."

I stammered, "I'm sorry about . . ."

I wasn't sure how to finish the sentence. *I'm sorry about taking over your apartment? I'm sorry about commandeering your bed? I'm sorry about the still-wet stockings that we've hung from your fireplace mantel to dry? I'm sorry for the orange makeup stains that we've smeared into your white carpet?*

"Oh, it's quite all right. I don't live here. The Lily is Peg's baby, not mine. I always stay at the Racquet and Tennis Club. I've never let my dues lapse, though God knows it's expensive. It's quieter there, and I don't have to report to Olive."

"But these are your rooms."

"In name only, thanks to the kindness of your Aunt Peg. I just came by this morning to get my typewriter, which, now that I mention it, appears to be missing."

"I put it in the linen closet, in the outside hallway."

"Did you? Well, make yourself at home, girlie."

"I'm sorry—" I started to say, but he cut me off again.

"I'm joking. You can keep the place. I don't come to New York much, anyhow. I don't like the climate. It gives me a raw throat. And this city is a hell of a place for ruining your best pair of white shoes."

I had so many questions, but I couldn't formulate any of them with my dry and foul-tasting mouth, through the buzzing haze of my gin-soaked brain. *What was Uncle Billy doing here? Who had let him in? Why was he wearing a tuxedo at this hour? And what was I wearing? Apparently nothing but a slip—and not even my own slip, but Celia's. So what was she wearing? And where was my dress?*

"Well, I've had my fun here," said Billy. "Enjoyed my little fantasy of angels in my bed. But now that I realize you're my *ward*, I'll leave you be and see if I can find some coffee in this place. You look like you could use some coffee, yourself, girlie. May I say—I *do* hope you're getting this drunk every night and tumbling into bed with beautiful women. There could be no better use of your time. You make me awfully proud to be your uncle. We'll get along famously."

As he headed to the door, he asked, "What time does Peg get up, by the way?"

"Usually around seven," I said.

"Capital," he said, looking at his watch. "Can't wait to see her."

"But how did you get here?" I asked, dumbly.

What I meant was, how did you get into this *building* (which was a silly question, because of course Peg would've made sure that her husband—or ex-husband, or whatever he was—had a set of keys). But he took the question more broadly.

"I took the Twentieth Century Limited. That's the only way to get from Los Angeles to New York in comfort, if you've got the peanuts for it. Train stopped in Chicago, to pick up some slaughterhouse high-society types. Doris Day was in the same carriage with me, the whole ride. We played gin rummy, all the way across the Great Plains. Doris is good company, you know. A great girl. Much more fun than you'd think, given her saintly reputation. Arrived last night, went right to my club, got a manicure and a haircut, went out to see some old robbers and derelicts and ne'er-do-wells that I used to know, then came here to pick up my typewriter and say hello to the family. Get yourself a robe, girlie, and come help me scare up some breakfast in this joint. You won't want to miss what happens next."

Once I was able to rouse myself and get vertical, I headed to the kitchen, where I encountered the most unusual pairing of men I'd ever seen.

There was Mr. Herbert sitting at one end of the table, wearing his usual sad trousers and undershirt, his white hair tousled and hopeless looking, his customary Sanka in a mug before him. At the other end of the table was my Uncle Billy—tall, slim, sporting a sharp-looking tuxedo and a golden California tan. Billy was not so much sitting in the kitchen as *lounging* in it, taking up space with an air of luxurious pleasure while enjoying his highball of scotch. There was something of Errol Flynn about him—if Errol Flynn couldn't be bothered to swashbuckle.

In short: one of these men looked like he was about to go to work on a coal wagon; the other looked like he was about to go on a date with Rosalind Russell.

"Good morning, Mr. Herbert," I said, as per our habit.

"I would be shocked to discover that was true," he replied.

"I couldn't find the coffee and I couldn't stomach the idea of Sanka," Billy explained, "so I settled on scotch. Any port in a storm. You might want a nip yourself, Vivian. You look as though you've got a heck of a sore dome."

"I'll be all right once I make myself some coffee," I said, not really convinced of this fact myself.

"So Peg tells me you've been working on a script," Billy said to Mr. Herbert. "I'd love to have a look at it."

"There's not much to see," said Mr. Hebert, glancing sorrowfully toward the notebook that sat before him.

"May I?" Billy asked, reaching for the notebook.

"I'd rather you . . . oh, never mind," said Mr. Herbert—a man who always managed to be defeated before the battle had even begun.

Billy slowly paged through Mr. Herbert's notebook. The silence was excruciating. Mr. Herbert stared at the floor.

"It looks as though these are just lists of jokes," Billy said. "Not even jokes, all of them, but punch lines. And a lot of drawings of birds."

Mr. Herbert shrugged in surrender. "If any better ideas should develop themselves, I'm hoping to be alerted."

"The birds aren't bad, anyway." Billy set down the notebook.

I was feeling protective of poor Mr. Herbert, whose response to Billy's teasing was to look even more tortured than usual, so I said, "Mr. Herbert, have you met Billy Buell? This is Peg's husband."

Billy laughed. "Oh, don't you worry, girlie. Donald and I have known each other for years. He's my attorney, actually—or used to be, when they still let him practice law—and I'm Donald Jr.'s godfather. Or used to be. Donald's just feeling nervous because he knows I've arrived unannounced. He's not sure how that's going to go over with the upper-echelon management around here."

Donald! It had never occurred to me that Mr. Herbert had a first name.

Speaking of upper-echelon management, at that very moment in walked Olive.

She took two steps into the kitchen, saw Billy Buell sitting there, opened her mouth, closed her mouth, and walked out.

We all sat in silence for a moment after she left. That had been quite an entrance—and quite an exit.

"You'll have to excuse Olive," said Billy at last. "She's not accustomed to being this excited to see someone."

Mr. Herbert put his forehead back down on the kitchen table and *literally* said, "Oh, moan, moan, moan."

"Don't worry about me and Olive, Donald. We'll be fine. She and I respect each other, which makes up for the fact that we dislike each other. Or, rather, I respect *her*. So that's something we share, at least. We have an excellent relationship based on a deep history of profound one-way respect, and plenty of it."

Billy took out his pipe, scratched a match into flame with his thumbnail, and turned to me.

"How are your parents, Vivian?" Billy asked. "Your mother and the mustache? I always liked them. Well, I liked your mother. What an impressive woman, that one. She's careful never to say anything nice about anyone, but I think she was fond of me, too. Don't ever ask her if she likes me, of course. She'll be forced by propriety to deny it. I never warmed to your father. Such a stiff man. I used to call him the Deacon—but only behind his back, of course, out of politeness. Anyway. How are they?"

"They're doing well."

"Still married?"

I nodded, but the question took me aback. It had never occurred to me that my parents could be anything *but* married.

"They never have affairs, do they—your parents?"

"My *parents*? Affairs? No!"

"That can't hold much novelty for them, can it?"

"Umm . . ."

"Have you been to California, Vivian?" he asked, thankfully changing the subject.

"No."

"You should come. You'd love it. They have the best orange juice. Also, the weather is outstanding. East Coast people like us do well out there. The Californians think we're so refined. They give us the sun and the moon, just for classing up the joint. You tell them you went to boarding school and you've got *Mayflower* ancestors in New England, and you might as well be a Plantagenet, as far as they're concerned. Come at them with a blue-blood accent like yours, and they'll give you the keys to the city. If you can play a decent game of tennis or golf, that's almost enough to get a man a career—unless he drinks too much."

I was finding this to be a very quick-paced conversation for seven o'clock on the morning after my birthday festivities. I'm afraid I might have been just staring at him, blinking, but honestly, I was doing my best to keep up.

Also: *did* I have a blue-blood accent?

"How are you entertaining yourself around the Lily, Vivian?" he asked. "Have you found a way to be useful?"

"I sew," I said. "I make costumes."

"That's smart. You'll always find work in the theater if you can do that, and you'll never age out of it. What you don't want to be is an actress. What about your beautiful friend in there? Is she an actress?"

"Celia? She's a showgirl."

"That's a tough gig. There's something about a showgirl that always breaks my heart. Youth and beauty—they're *such* a short lease, girlie. Even if you're the most beautiful girl in the room right now, there are ten new beauties coming up behind you all the time—younger ones, fresher ones. While the older ones are rotting on the vine, still waiting to be discovered. But your friend, she'll leave her mark while she can. She'll destroy man after man in some great romantic death march, and maybe someone will write songs about her, or kill himself for her, but soon enough it will end. If she's lucky, she might marry a rich old fossil—not that this fate is anything to envy. If she's *very* lucky, her old fossil will die on the golf course one fine afternoon and leave her everything while she's still young enough to enjoy it. The pretty girls always know it will end soon, too. They can feel how *provisional* it all is. So I hope she's having a good time being young and beautiful. Is she having a good time?"

"Yes," I said. "I think so."

I didn't know *anybody* who had a better time than Celia.

"Good. I hope you're having a good time, too. People will tell you not to waste your youth having too much fun, but they're wrong. Youth is an irreplaceable treasure, and the only respectable thing to do with irreplaceable treasure is to waste it. So do the right thing with your youth, Vivian—squander it."

———————

That's when Aunt Peg walked in, bundled up in her plaid flannel bathrobe, her hair pointing in every direction.

"Pegsy!" cried Billy, leaping up from the table. His face was instantly bright with joy. All the nonchalance was gone in a heartbeat.

"Forgive me, sir, but your name escapes me," said Peg.

But she was smiling, too, and in the next moment they were embracing. It wasn't a romantic embrace, I would say, but it was *robust*. This was an embrace of love—or at least very strong feeling. They pulled back from the embrace and just looked at each other for a while, holding each other lightly by the forearms. When they stood like that together, I could see something profoundly unexpected, for the first time: I could see that Peg was kind of *beautiful*. I'd never noticed it before. She had such a shine on her face, looking at Billy, that it changed her whole countenance. (It wasn't merely the reflected light off his good looks, either.) Standing in his radius, she looked like a different woman. I could see in her face a hint of the brave young girl who went off to France to be a nurse during the war. I could see the adventurer who'd spent a decade on the road with a cheap theatrical touring company. It wasn't only that she suddenly looked ten years younger; she also looked like the most fun gal in town.

"I thought I'd pay you a visit, honey," Billy said.

"So Olive informed me. You might have let me know."

"I didn't want to bother you. And I didn't want you to tell me not to come. I figured it'd be best if I made my own arrangements. I have a secretary now, who takes care of everything for me. She made all the travel plans. Jean-Marie is her name. She's bright, efficient, devoted. You'd love her, Peg. She's like a female version of Olive."

Peg pulled away from him. "Jesus, Billy, you never quit."

"Hey, don't be sore at me! I'm just teasing. You know I can't help it.

I'm just *nervous*, Pegsy. I'm afraid you'll throw me out, honey, and I just got here."

Mr. Herbert stood up from the kitchen table, said, "I'm going somewhere else now," and left.

Peg took Mr. Herbert's seat and helped herself to a sip of his cold Sanka. She frowned at the cup, so I got up to make her a fresh cup of coffee. I wasn't sure if I should even be in the kitchen at this sensitive moment, but then Peg said, "Good morning, Vivian. Did you enjoy your birthday celebration?"

"A bit too much," I said.

"And you've met your Uncle Billy?"

"Yes, we've been talking."

"Oh, dear. Be careful not to absorb anything he tells you."

"Peg," said Billy, "you look gorgeous."

She ran a hand through her cropped hair and smiled—a big smile that settled deeply into her lined face. "That's quite a compliment, for a woman like me."

"There *is* no woman like you. I've checked into it. Doesn't exist."

"Billy," she said, "give it a rest."

"Never."

"So what are you doing here, Billy? Do you have a job in the city?"

"No job. I'm on civilian furlough. I couldn't resist making the trip when you told me Edna was here, and that you're trying to make a good show for her. I haven't seen Edna since 1919. Christ, I'd love to see her. I adore that woman. And when you told me you'd enlisted *Donald Herbert* to write the script, of all people, I knew I had to come back east and rescue you."

"Thank you. That's terribly kind of you. But if I needed rescue, Billy, I'd let you know. I promise. You'd be the fourteenth or fifteenth person I'd call."

He grinned. "But still on the list!"

Peg lit a cigarette and handed it to me, then lit another one for herself. "What are you working on out there in Hollywood?"

"A bunch of nothing. Everything I write is proudly stamped NSA—No Significance Attempted. I'm bored. But they pay me well. Enough to keep me comfortable. Me and my simple needs."

Peg burst out laughing. "Your simple needs. Your *famously* simple needs. Yes, Billy, you're quite the renunciate. Practically a monk."

"I'm a man of humble tastes, as you know," said Billy.

"Himself, who comes to the breakfast table dressed like he's about to be knighted. Himself, with his house in Malibu. How many swimming pools do you have now?"

"None. I just borrow Joan Fontaine's."

"And what does Joan get out of that arrangement?"

"The pleasure of my company."

"Jesus, Billy, she's married. She's Brian's wife. He's your friend."

"I love married women, Peg. You know that. Ideally, happily married ones. A happily married woman is the most solid friend a man could ever have. Don't worry, Pegsy—Joan is just a pal. Brian Aherne is in no danger from the likes of me."

I could not stop looking from Peg to Billy and back again, trying to imagine these two as a romantic couple. They didn't look like they belonged together physically—but their conversation flickered so bright and sharp. The teasing, the jabs of *knowing,* the fullness of the attention they gave each other. The intimacy was more than obvious, but what *were* they, within that intimacy? Lovers? Friends? Siblings? Rivals? Who knew? I gave up trying to figure it out and just watched the lightning flash between them.

"I'd like to spend some time with you while I'm here, Pegsy," he said. "It's been too long."

"Who is she?" Peg asked.

"Who is who?"

"The woman who just left you, which has caused you to feel so suddenly nostalgic and lonely for me. Come on, spill it: who was the latest Miss Billy to leave your side?"

"I'm insulted. You think you know me so well."

Peg just gazed at him, waiting.

"If you must know," said Billy, "her name was Camilla."

"A dancer, I boldly predict," said Peg.

"Ha! There's where you're wrong! A *swimmer*! She works in a mermaid show. We had a pretty serious thing going for a few weeks, but then she decided to take another path in life, and she no longer comes around."

Peg started laughing. "A pretty serious thing, for a few weeks. Listen to you."

"Let's go out together while I'm here, Pegsy. Just you and me. Let's go out and allow some jazz musicians to waste their talents on us. Let's go to some of those bars we used to like, that close at eight o'clock in the morning. It's no fun going out without you. I went to El Morocco last night and I found it so disappointing—filled with all the same people as ever, making all the same conversation as ever."

Peg smiled. "Lucky for you that you live in Hollywood, where the conversation is so much more varied and engaging! But no, no, no. We shan't be going out, Billy. I don't have that kind of durability anymore. That kind of drinking isn't good for me, anyhow. You know that."

"Really? You're telling me you and Olive don't get drunk together?"

"You're joking, but since you asked—no. Here's how it works around here now: I try to get drunk and Olive tries to stop it from happening. It's a good arrangement for me. Not sure what Olive gets out of it, but I'm awfully glad she's there to be my guard dog."

"Listen, Peg—at least let me help you with the show. You know that this pile of pages is a long way from being a script." Billy tapped a manicured finger on Mr. Herbert's dismal notebook. "And you know

Donald can't get it any closer to being a script, no matter how hard he tries. You can't squeeze this out of him. So let me go at it with my typewriter and my big blue pencil. You know I can do this. Let's make a great play. Let's give Edna something worthy of her talents."

"Shush." Peg had put her hands over her face.

"Come on, Peg. Take a risk."

"*Hush*," she said. "I'm thinking at the top of my lungs."

Billy hushed and waited her out.

"I can't pay you," she said, finally looking up at him again.

"I'm independently wealthy, Peg. That's always been a talent of mine."

"You can't own the rights to anything that we make here. Olive won't stand for it."

"You can have all of it, Peg. And you might even make a nice lump of brass off this venture, too. If you'll only let me write this show for you—and if it's as good as I think it could be—why, you'll make so much money, your ancestors will never have to work again."

"You'll have to put that in writing—that you're not expecting to earn anything out of this. Olive will insist on it. And we'll have to produce it on my budget, not yours. I don't want to get tangled up with your money again. It never ends well for me. Those have to be the rules, Billy. It's the only way Olive will let you stick around."

"Isn't it *your* theater, Peg?"

"Technically, yes. But I can't do anything without Olive, Billy. You know that. She's essential."

"Essential but bothersome."

"Yes, but you are only one of those things. I need Olive. I don't need you. That's always been the difference between you."

"By God—that Olive! Such staying power! I never could understand what you saw in her—other than that she comes dashing to serve you whenever you have the smallest need. That must be the appeal. I never could offer you such loyalty, I suppose. Solid as furniture, that Olive. But she doesn't trust me."

"Yes. Precisely true on all counts."

"Honestly, Peg—I don't know why that woman doesn't trust me. I'm very, very, very trustworthy."

"The more 'very's' you use, Billy, the less trustworthy you sound. You do know that, right?"

Billy laughed. "I do know that. But, Peg—*you* know that I can write this script with my left hand while playing tennis with my right hand and bouncing a ball off my nose like a trained seal."

"Without spilling a drop of your booze in the process."

"Without spilling a drop of *your* booze," corrected Billy, lifting his glass. "I took this from your bar."

"Better you than me at this hour."

"I want to see Edna. Is she awake?"

"She doesn't get up till later. Let her sleep. Her country is at war and she just lost her house and everything. She deserves some rest."

"I'll come back, then. I'll head back to the club, take a shower, have a rest, come back later, and we'll get started. Hey, thanks for giving my apartment away, I forgot to mention! Your niece and her girlfriend have stolen my bed and thrown their underwear all over my precious place that I never once used. It smells like a bomb went off in a perfume factory in there."

"I'm sorry," I began, but both of them waved at me dismissively, cutting me off. It obviously didn't matter in the least. I'm not sure *I* mattered in the least, when Peg and Billy were so focused on each other. I was lucky I got to be sitting there at all. It occurred to me that I should just keep my mouth shut so I would *get* to stay.

"What's her husband like, by the way?" Billy asked Peg.

"Edna's husband? Apart from being stupid and talentless, he has no faults. I will say he's alarmingly good-looking."

"That, I knew. I've seen him act, if you can call it acting. I saw him in *Gates of Noon*. He's got the vacant eyes of a milk cow, but he looked like a million bucks in his aviator scarf. What's he like as a person? Is he faithful to her?"

"I've never heard otherwise."

"Well, that's a thing, isn't it?" said Billy.

Peg smiled. "Yes, it's a real marvel, isn't it, Billy? Imagine! Fidelity! But yes, that's a thing. So she could do worse, I suppose."

"And probably will someday," added Billy.

"She thinks he's a great actor, is the problem."

"He has offered the world no evidence of this fact. Bottom line— do we have to put him in the show?"

Peg smiled, ruefully this time. "It's slightly disconcerting to hear you use the word 'we.'"

"Why is that? I'm simply crazy about that word." He grinned.

"Until the moment you stop being crazy about it, and you disappear," she said. "Are you really part of this venture now, Billy? Or will you be on the next train back to Los Angeles as soon as you grow bored?"

"If you'll have me, I'll be part of it. I'll be good. I'll behave as if I'm on parole."

"You *should* be on parole. And yes, we do have to put Arthur Watson in the play. You'll figure out a way to use him. He's a handsome man who isn't very bright, so have him play the role of a handsome man who isn't very bright. You're the one who taught me that rule, Billy— that we must work with what we have. What did you always tell me, when we were on the road? You'd say, 'If all we've got is a fat lady and a stepladder, I'll write a play called *The Fat Lady and the Stepladder*.'"

"I can't believe you still remember that!" said Billy. "And *The Fat Lady and the Stepladder* is not such a bad title for a play, if I do say so myself."

"You do say so yourself. You always do."

Billy reached over and laid his hand on top of hers. She let him do it.

"Pegsy," he said, and that one word—the way he said it—seemed to contain decades of love.

"William," she said, and that one word—the way *she* said it—also seemed to contain decades of love. But also decades of exasperation.

"Olive's not too upset that I'm here?" he asked.

She took back her hand.

"Do us a favor, Billy? Don't pretend to care. I love you, but I hate it when you pretend to care."

"I'll tell you what," he said. "I care a lot more than people think I care."

TWELVE

Within a week of his arrival, Billy Buell had written a script for *City of Girls*.

A week is an awfully short time in which to write a script, or so I've been told, but Billy worked nonstop on it, sitting at our kitchen table in a cloud of pipe smoke, clattering away steadily at his typewriter till the thing was done. Say what you want about Billy Buell, but the man knew how to bang out words. Moreover, he didn't seem to suffer at all during his creative burst—no crises of confidence, no tearing at the hair. He hardly paused to think, or so it appeared. He just sat there in his fine doeskin trousers, and his bright white cashmere sweater, and his spotless ecru Maxwell's of London custom-made shoes, calmly typing away as though taking dictation from some invisible and divine source.

"He's monstrously talented, you know," Peg said to me, as we sat in the living room one afternoon, making sketches for costumes and listening to Billy's typing in the kitchen. "He's the kind of man who makes everything look easy. Hell, he even makes it look easy to make things easy. He produces ideas in torrents. The problem is, you can usually only get Billy to work when his Rolls-Royce needs a new engine, or when he gets back from vacationing in Italy and notices that his bank account is down a few bucks. Monstrously talented, but also monstrously inclined toward laziness. That's what you get for coming from the lolling-about class, I suppose."

"So why is he working so hard now?" I asked.

"I'm not able to say," said Peg. "Could be because he loves Edna. Could be because he loves me. Could be because he needs something from me and we just don't know what it is yet. Could be because he's gotten bored out there in California, or even lonely. I'm not going to examine his motives too fiercely. I'm glad he's doing the job, in any case. But the important thing is not to count on him for anything in the future. By future, I mean 'tomorrow' or 'in the next hour'—because you never know when he's going to lose interest and vanish. Billy doesn't like it when you count on him. If I ever want privacy from Billy, I'll just tell him that I desperately need him for something, and then he'll run straight out the door and I won't see him for another four years."

The script was intact on the day Billy typed the last word. I don't recall him editing any of it. And his script didn't just have dialogue and stage directions; it also included lyrics of the songs that Billy wanted Benjamin to write.

And it was a *good* script—or at least I thought so, based on my limited experience. But even I could understand that Billy's writing was bright and funny, fast-paced and upbeat. I could see why 20th Century Fox kept him on payroll, and why Louella Parsons had once written in her column: "Everything Billy Buell touches is box office! Even in Europe!"

Billy's version of *City of Girls* was still the tale of one Mrs. Elenora Alabaster—a wealthy widow who loses all her money in the crash of 1929 and transforms her mansion into a casino and bordello in order to keep herself afloat.

But Billy added some interesting new characters, as well. Now the play also included Mrs. Alabaster's fantastically snobbish daughter, Victoria (who would sing a comic song at the beginning of the show called "Mummy Is a Rumrunner"). There was also a gold-digging, penniless aristocrat of a cousin from England, played by Arthur Watson, who is trying to win Victoria's hand in marriage, in order to lay claim to the family mansion. ("You can't have Arthur Watson playing an American police officer," Billy explained to Peg. "Nobody would believe it. He has to be a British dolt. He'll like this role better, anyway—he gets to wear finer suits and he can pretend to be important.")

The romantic male lead would be a scrappy young kid from the wrong side of the tracks named Lucky Bobby, who used to fix Mrs. Alabaster's cars but who now helps her set up an illegal casino in her home—the result being that they both get stinking rich. The romantic female lead was a dazzling showgirl named Daisy. Daisy has a body that won't quit, but her simple dream is to get married and have a dozen children. ("Let Me Knit Your Booties, Baby," would be her signature song—performed in the manner of a striptease.) That role, of course, would be played by Celia Ray.

At the end of the play, Daisy the showgirl ends up with Lucky Bobby, and the two of them head off to Yonkers to have a dozen babies together. The snobbish daughter falls in love with the toughest gangster in town, learns how to shoot a machine gun, and goes on a bank-robbing spree in order to finance her expensive tastes. (Her big number is "I'm Down to My Last Pint of Diamonds.") The shady cousin from England is banished back to his shores without inheriting the mansion. And Mrs. Alabaster falls in love with the mayor of the city—a real law-and-order type, who has been trying and failing to shut down her speakeasy throughout the entire production. The two of them get married, and the mayor resigns his political post in order to become her bartender. (Their final duet, which would turn into the big closing number for the whole cast, was called "Let's Make Ours a Double.")

There were some new smaller roles in the play, too. There would be a purely comical drunkard character who pretends to be blind so he doesn't have to work, but who is still a mighty fine poker player and pickpocket. (Billy talked Mr. Herbert into taking the role: "If you can't write the script, Donald, at least be in the damn play!") There would be the showgirl's mother—an old floozy who still wants to be in the spotlight. ("Call Me Mrs. Casanova" was her signature tune.) There would be a banker, trying to repossess the mansion. And there would be a large company of dancers and singers—far more than our usual four boys and four girls, if Billy had anything to say about it—in order to make the play into a bigger and more energized production.

Peg loved the script.

"I can't write for free seeds," she said, "but I know what a smashing story is, and this is a smashing story."

Edna loved it, too. Billy had transformed Mrs. Alabaster from a mere caricature of a society dame into a woman of real wit and intelligence and irony. Edna had all the funniest lines in the play, and she was in every single scene.

"Billy!" exclaimed Edna, after reading the script for the first time. "This is delightful, but you're spoiling me! Doesn't anyone else in the show get to speak?"

"Why would I take you offstage for a moment?" Billy said to her. "If I have the chance to work with Edna Parker Watson, I want the world to *know* I'm working with Edna Parker Watson."

"You're a dear," said Edna. "But I haven't performed comedy in so long, Billy. I'm afraid I'll be quite stale."

"The trick of comedy," said Billy, "is not to perform it in a comic manner. Don't try to be funny, and you'll be funny. Just do that effortless thing you Brits do, of throwing away half the lines as though you can scarcely be bothered to care, and it'll be brilliant. Comedy is always best when it's thrown away."

It was interesting to watch Edna and Billy interact. They had a real friendship, it appeared—based not only on teasing and playfulness, but on mutual respect. They admired each other's talents, and genuinely had a good time together. The first night they saw each other, Billy had said to Edna, "Very much of little consequence has transpired since last we met, my dear. Let's sit down for a drink and talk about none of it."

To which she had replied, "There is nothing I would rather not talk about, Billy, and nobody whom I would rather not talk about it *with*!"

Billy once told me, in front of Edna, "So many men had the pleasure of having their hearts broken by our dear Edna, back when I knew her in London so long ago. I didn't happen to be one of them, but that's only because I was already in love with Peg. But back in her prime, Edna cut down man after man. It was something to see. Plutocrats, artists, generals, politicians—she mowed them all to bits."

"No, I didn't," Edna protested—while smiling in a manner that suggested: *Yes, I did.*

"I used to love to watch you break a man apart, Edna," Billy said. "You did it so beautifully. You broke them with such force that they would be enfeebled forever, and then some other woman could come and scoop them up and control them. It was a service to humanity, really. I know she looks like a little doll, Vivian, but never underestimate this woman. She is to be respected. Be aware that there's an iron spine hidden under all those stylish clothes of hers."

"You give me far too much credit, Billy," said Edna—but again, she smiled in a manner that suggested: *You, sir, are absolutely correct.*

A few weeks later, I was fitting Edna in my apartment. The dress I'd designed was for her final scene. Edna wanted it to be sensational, and so did I. "Make me a dress I have to live up to" had been her direct instruction—and forgive my boasting, but I had done it.

It was an evening gown composed of two layers of robin's-egg-blue silk soufflé, draped with sheer rhinestone netting. (I'd found a bolt of the silk at Lowtsky's and had spent nearly all my personal savings on it.) The dress sparkled with every movement—not in a garish way, but like light reflected on water. The silk clung to Edna's figure without clinging *too* hard (she was in her fifties, after all) and there was a slit up the right side so she could dance. The effect was to make Edna look like a fairy queen, out for a night on the town.

Edna loved it, and was spinning in the mirror, to capture every twinkle and gleam.

"I swear, Vivian, you've somehow made me look *tall*, though I can't credit how you've done it. And that blue is so refreshingly youthful. I was petrified you would put me in black, and I would look as though I should be embalmed. Oh, I cannot *wait* to show this dress to Billy. He has the best comprehension of women's fashion of any man I've ever met. He'll be just as excited as I am. I'll tell you something about your uncle, Vivian. Billy Buell is that rare man who claims to love women and actually *does*."

"Celia says he's a playboy," I said.

"But of course he's a playboy, darling. What handsome man worth his salt is not? Though Billy is a special sort. There are a million play-boys out there, you must understand, but they don't typically enjoy a woman's company past the obvious gratifications. A man who gets to conquer all the women he wants, but who does not prize any of them? Now, *that* is a man to be avoided. But Billy genuinely likes women, whether he's vanquishing them or not. We've always had a wonderful time together, he and I. He'd be just as happy talking with me about fashion as trying to seduce me. And he writes the most delicious dialogue for women, which most men cannot. Most male playwrights can't create a woman for the stage who does anything more than seduce or weep or be loyal to their husbands, and that's awfully dull."

"Olive thinks he's not trustworthy."

"She's wrong about that. You *can* trust Billy. You can absolutely trust him to be himself. Olive just doesn't like what he is."

"And what is he?"

Edna paused and thought about it. "He's *free*," she decided. "You won't meet many people in life who are, Vivian. He's a person who does quite as he pleases, and I find that refreshing. Olive is a more regimented soul by nature—and thank goodness for it, or nothing around here would function—and thus she's suspicious of anyone who is free. But I myself enjoy being around the free. They excite me. The other magical thing about Billy, I dare say, is that he's so handsome. I do love a handsome man, Vivian—as surely you have already gathered. It's always been a pleasure just to be in the room with Billy's handsomeness. But with that charm of his, beware! If he ever puts the full game on you, you're a dead pigeon."

I had to wonder if Billy had ever "put the full game" on Edna, but I was too polite to pursue it. I did, however, have the courage to ask: "About Peg and Billy . . . ?"

I wasn't even sure how to finish the question, but Edna instantly understood my gist.

"You're wondering about the nature of their alliance?" She smiled. "All I can tell you is that they do love each other. Always have. They are so similar in intellect and humor, you see. They used to positively spark off each other when they were younger. If you were a non-initiate into their brand of wit, it could be intimidating—one never quite knew how to jump into the mix. But Billy adores Peg and always did. Now, to be *loyal* to just one woman would be awfully narrowing to a man like Billy Buell, of course, but his heart has always belonged to her. And they delight in working together—as soon you shall see. The only problem is that Billy has a deft hand with chaos, and I'm not certain that Peg is seeking chaos anymore. These days, she wants loyalty more than fun."

"But are they still *married*?" I asked.

By which I meant, of course: *Do they still sleep together?*

"Married by whose standard?" Edna asked, folding her arms and looking at me with her head tilted. When I didn't answer the question, she smiled again and said, "There are subtleties, my dear. You will discover as you get older that there's practically nothing *but* subtleties. And I hate to disappoint you, but it's best you learn now: most marriages are neither heavenly nor hellish, but vaguely purgatorial. Still and all, love must be respected, and Billy and Peg possess true love. Now if you could fix this belt for me, darling, and find a way to stop it bunching about my ribs whenever I lift my arms, I will absolutely die with gratitude."

Because Edna's prestige was going to elevate the tone of the play, Billy was convinced that the rest of the production had to be of equal quality to its star. ("The Lily Playhouse just got her pedigree papers" was how he described the situation. "This is a whole new dog show, kids.") Everything we created for *City of Girls,* he instructed, would have to be far better than what we were accustomed to creating.

This would not be easily achieved, of course, given what we were accustomed to creating.

CITY OF GIRLS

Billy had sat through a few nights of *Dance Away, Jackie!* and he made no secret of his disdain for our current troupe of players.

"They're garbage, honey," he said to Peg.

"Don't butter me up," she said. "I'll think you're trying to get me into bed."

"They are twenty-four-carat garbage, and you know it."

"Just give it to me straight, Billy. Stop flattering me."

"The showgirls are fine as they are, because they don't need to do anything other than look good," he said. "So they can stay. The actors are vile, though. We'll need to get some new talent in here. The dancers are cute enough, and they all look like they come from bad families, which I *like* . . . but they're so heavy on their feet. It's assaulting. I love their tarty little faces, but let's keep them in the background and bring in some real dancers to put up front—at least six. Right now, the only dancer I can stand to watch footing around the front of the stage is that fairy, Roland. He's terrific. But I need everyone else to be of his caliber."

In fact, Billy was so impressed with Roland's charisma that he'd initially wanted to give the boy a song of his own to sing, called "Maybe in the Navy"—a tune that would *seem* to be about a boy wanting to join the Navy in order to pursue a life of adventure, but would actually be a clever and veiled reference to Roland's very obvious homosexuality. ("I'm picturing something like 'You're the Top'" is how Billy had explained it to us. "You know, a suggestive little double entendre of a song.") But Olive had instantly shut down the idea.

"Come now, Olive," Peg had begged. "Let us do it. It's funny. The women and children in the audience won't catch the reference, anyhow. This is supposed to be a racy story. Let's allow things to be more *spirited* for once."

"Too spirited for public consumption" was Olive's verdict, and that was the end of it: Roland didn't get his song.

169

Olive, I should say, was not happy about any of this.

She was the only person at the Lily who didn't get caught up in Billy's excitement. On the day he arrived, she commenced sulking, and the sulk never lifted. The truth is, I was beginning to find Olive's dourness awfully irritating. The constant niggling over every dime, the policing of sexually suggestive material, the slavish devotion to her rigid chain of habits, the way she gave Billy the brush on every clever idea he proposed, the constant fussbudgeting, and the general quashing of all fun and enthusiasm—it was just so tiresome.

For instance, let's consider Billy's plan to hire six more dancers for the show than we normally had onstage. Peg was all for it, but Olive called the idea "a lot of fuss and feathers for nothing."

When Billy argued that six more dancers would make the show feel more like a spectacle, Olive said, "Six more dancers adds up to money we don't have, with no discernible difference to the play. Rehearsal salaries alone are forty dollars a week. And you want six more of them? Where do you propose I get the funds for this?"

"You can't make money without spending money, Olive," Billy reminded her. "Anyway, I'll spot you."

"I like that idea even less," Olive said. "And I don't trust you to deliver. Remember what happened in Kansas City in 1933."

"No, I don't remember what happened in Kansas City in 1933," said Billy.

"Of course you don't," Peg put in. "What happened is that you left me and Olive holding the bag. We'd rented out that massive concert hall for the big song-and-dance spectacle you wanted me to produce, and you hired dozens of local performers, and you put everything in my name, and then you vanished to St. Tropez for a backgammon tournament. I had to empty the company's bank account to pay it all back, while you and your money were nowhere to be found for three solid months."

"Geez, Pegsy—you make it sound like I did something *wrong*."

"No hard feelings, of course." Peg gave a sardonic grin. "I know how you've always loved your backgammon. But Olive's got a point. The Lily Playhouse is barely in the black as it is. We can't go out on a limb for this production."

"Naturally, I'll be disagreeing with you now," said Billy. "Because if you ladies will go out on a limb for once, I can help you to create a show that people will actually want to *see*. When people want to *see* a show, it makes money. After all these years, I can't believe I need to remind you of how the theater business works. Come on, Pegsy—don't turn on me now. When a rescuer comes to save you, don't shoot arrows at him."

"The Lily Playhouse doesn't need rescuing," said Olive.

"Oh, yes, it does, Olive!" said Billy. "Look at this theater! Everything needs to be repaired and updated. You're still using gaslights, practically. Your seats are three-quarters empty every night. You need a *hit*. Let me make one for you. With Edna here, we have the chance. But we can't go slack on any of it. If we get some critics in here—and I *will* get critics in here—we can't have the rest of the production looking ramshackle, compared to Edna. Come on, Pegsy—don't be a coward. And remember—you won't have to work as hard as usual with this play, because I'll help you direct it, like we used to do. Come on, honey, take a chance. You can keep on producing your catchpenny little shows and creeping along toward bankruptcy, or we can do something great here. Let's do something great. You were always a reckless dame with a buck—let's give it a go, one more time."

Peg wavered. "Maybe we could hire just *four* additional dancers, Olive?"

"Don't you let him Ritz you, Peg," said Olive. "We can't afford it. We can't even afford two. I have the ledgers to prove it."

"You worry too much about money, Olive," said Billy. "You always have. Money's not the most important thing in the world."

"Thus speaketh William Ackerman Buell III of Newport, Rhode Island," said Peg.

"Give it a rest, Pegsy. You know I never cared about money."

"That's right, you never cared about money, Billy," Olive said. "Certainly not to the extent that those of us who forgot to be born into wealthy families care about it. The devil of it is—you make Peg not care about money, either. That's how we've always run into trouble in the past, and I won't let it happen again."

"There's always been plenty of money for all of us," said Billy. "Stop being such a *capitalist*, Olive."

Peg started laughing and stage-whispered to me: "Your Uncle Billy fancies himself a socialist, kiddo. But apart from the aspect of free love, I'm not sure he understands its principles."

"What do *you* think, Vivian?" asked Billy, noticing for the first time that I was in the room.

I felt deeply uncomfortable being pulled into this conversation. The experience was something akin to listening to my parents argue—except that there were *three* of them now, which was extra disconcerting. Certainly over the last few months I'd heard Peg and Olive arguing about money plenty of times—but with the addition of Billy into the story, things had gotten more heated. Navigating a dispute between Peg and Olive I could handle, but Billy was the wild card. Every child learns to negotiate delicately between two bickering adults, after all, but among *three*? This was beyond my powers.

"I think you each make a strong argument," I said.

This must have been the wrong answer, because now they were all irritated with *me*.

In the end, they settled on hiring four additional dancers, with Billy picking up the tab. It was a decision that left nobody happy—which is what my father might have called a successful business negotiation. ("Everyone should leave the table feeling as if they've gotten a bad deal," my father once taught me joylessly. "This way, you may rest assured that nobody was taken for a ride, and that nobody can get too far ahead.")

THIRTEEN

ere was another thing I noticed about the effect that Billy Buell had upon our little world: with his arrival at the Lily Playhouse, everyone started drinking more.

A whole hell of a lot more.

Having read this far, Angela, you may be wondering how it was physically possible for us to drink more than we already did, but here is the thing about drinking: one can always drink more, if one is truly committed. It's just a matter of discipline, really.

The big difference now was that Aunt Peg was drinking with us. Where once she'd stopped after a few martinis and had gone to bed at a reasonable time—as per Olive's strict schedule—now she and Billy would head out together after the show and get three sheets to the wind. Every single night. Oftentimes Celia and I would join them for a few drinks, before heading off to make revelry and trouble elsewhere.

If at first it seemed awkward for me to be gadding about town with my plainly dressed middle-aged aunt, the awkwardness soon faded when I learned what a gas Peg could be in a nightclub—especially once she had a few drinks in her. Largely this was because Peg knew absolutely everybody in the entertainment business, and they all knew her. And if they didn't know Peg, then they knew Billy, and wanted to catch up with him after all these years. Which meant that drinks arrived at our table in snappy time—usually accompanied by the owner of the establishment, who often sat with us to gossip about Hollywood and Broadway.

Billy and Peg still looked so mismatched to me—he, so handsome in his white dinner jacket and slicked-back hair, and she in her matronly B. Altman dress and no makeup whatsoever—but they were charming, and wherever we went they quickly ended up the center of any gathering.

And they lived large. Billy ordering up filet mignon and champagne (he often carelessly wandered away before it was time to eat the steak, but he never neglected to drink the champagne) and inviting everyone in the room to join us. He talked nonstop about the show that he and Peg were producing, and what a smash hit it was going to be. (As he explained to me, this was a deliberate marketing tactic; he wanted to get word out that *City of Girls* was coming and that it would be good: "I have yet to meet the press agent who can spread gossip faster than I can do at a nightclub.")

It was all fun, except for one thing: Peg was always trying to be responsible and head home early, while Billy was always trying to get her to stay out late. I remember one night at the Algonquin when Billy said, "Would you like another drink, my wife?" and I saw a look of real pain cross Peg's face.

"I shouldn't," she said. "It's not good for me, Billy. Let me collect my thoughts for a moment and try to be sensible."

"I didn't ask if you *should* have a drink, Pegsy; I asked if you wanted one."

"Well, of course I *want* one. I always want one. But make it a mild one, please."

"Shall I cut to the chase and order you three mild ones at the same time?"

"Just one mild one after another, William. That's how I like to live my life these days."

"To your very good health," he said, lifting his glass to toast her and then waving to get the waiter's attention. "As long as the man keeps 'em coming, I might be able to survive an evening of mild cocktails."

That night, Celia and I peeled off from Billy and Peg, to go have our own adventures. When we stumbled home at our standard gauzy-gray presunrise hour, we were startled to find all the lights on in the living room, and an unexpected tableaux within. There was Peg sprawled out on the couch—fully dressed, unconscious, and snoring. She had an arm flung over her face, and one of her shoes was kicked off. Billy, still wearing his white dinner jacket, was dozing in a chair next to her. On the table between them was a pile of empty bottles and full ashtrays.

Billy woke up when we walked in and said, "Oh, hello girls." His voice was slurred, and his eyes were Bing cherries.

"I'm sorry," I said, in my own slurred voice. "Didn't mean to disturb you."

"You can't disturb *her.*" Billy waved an arm vaguely in the direction of the couch. "She's pickled. I couldn't get her up the last flight of steps. Say, maybe you girls can help me . . . ?"

So the three of us drunks tried to help an even drunker person get upstairs to bed. Peg was not a small woman, and we were not at our strongest or most graceful, so this was no easy operation. We more or less dragged her up the stairs the way you would transport a rolled-up carpet—thumping our way along until we reached the door to the fourth-floor apartments. I'm afraid we laughed like sailors on leave the whole time. I'm also afraid that was an uncomfortable trip for Peg—or that it would have been uncomfortable, had she been conscious.

And then we opened the door and there was Olive—the last face you want to see when you are at your drunkest and most guilty.

In one glance, Olive took in the situation. Not that it was difficult to read.

I expected her to strike out in anger, but instead she dropped to her knees and cradled Peg's head. Olive looked up at Billy, and her face was overcome with sorrow.

"Olive," he said. "Hey. Look. You know how it is."

"Please get me a wet towel, someone," she asked in a low voice. "A cold one."

"I wouldn't know how to do *that*," said Celia, sliding down the wall.

I ran into the bathroom and flopped about until I could solve the problem of how to turn on a light, how to procure a towel, how to turn on a tap, how to discern hot water from cold, how to soak the towel without also soaking myself (I utterly failed at that step), and how to find my way out of the bathroom again.

By the time I got back, Edna Parker Watson had joined the scene (wearing an adorable red silk pajama set and a lush gold dressing gown, I couldn't help but notice) and was now helping Olive drag Peg into her apartment. The women, I'm sorry to say, looked as though they had done this before.

Edna took the damp towel from me and pressed it against Peg's forehead. "Come now, Peg, let's wake up now."

Billy was standing back a bit, wavering on his feet, looking green around the gills. He looked his age, for once.

"She just wanted to have some fun," he said weakly.

Olive stood up and said—again, in that low voice—"You always do this to her. You always give her the spur when you know she needs the reins."

Billy looked for a moment as if he were going to apologize, but then made the classic drunkard's mistake, instead, of digging in. "Ah, don't blow your lid about it. She'll be all right. She just wanted to have a few more when we got home."

"She's not *like* you," Olive said, and unless I was mistaken, her eyes were sprinkled with tears. "She can't stop after ten drinks. She never could."

Edna said gently, "I think it's time for you to go, William. You, as well, girls."

The next day, Peg stayed in bed until late afternoon. But aside from that, business went on as usual, and nobody mentioned what had transpired the evening before.

And by the *next* night, Peg and Billy were out at the Algonquin all over again, buying rounds for the whole house.

FOURTEEN

Billy had committed the outrageous act of calling auditions for the play—*real* auditions, advertised in the trade papers and everything—in order to get a higher class of performer than the Lily was accustomed to.

This was a wildly new development. We'd never had auditions before. Our shows always got cast through word of mouth. Peg and Olive and Gladys knew enough of the actors and dancers around the neighborhood to be able to pull together a cast without anyone having to try out. But Billy wanted a better class of performers than what we could find within the perimeter of Hell's Kitchen, so official auditions it was.

For an entire day, then, we had a stream of hopefuls pouring into the Lily—dancers, singers, actors. I got to sit with Billy and Peg and Olive and Edna as they reviewed the aspirants. I found it to be such an anxiety-producing experience. Watching all those people on the stage who all wanted something so *badly*—so glaringly and openly—made me nervous.

And then, very quickly, it made me bored.

(Anything can get tedious after enough time, Angela—even watching heartbreaking acts of naked vulnerability. Especially when everyone is singing the same song, doing the same dance steps, or repeating the same lines, hour after hour.)

We saw the dancers first. It was just one pretty girl after another, trying to stampede her way into our new chorus line. The sheer volume and variation of them made my head spin. Auburn curls on this one. Fine blond hair on that one. This one tall. That one short. A big-hipped, huffing, snorting, dancing dragon of a girl. A woman who was far too old to be dancing for a living anymore, but who had not yet boxed up her hopes and dreams. A girl with sharp bangs who was so awfully severe in her efforts, it looked like she was marching, not dancing. All of them breathlessly hoofing with all their hearts. Puffing away in a hot panic of tap dancing and optimism. Kicking up great clouds of dust motes in the footlights. They were sweaty and they were loud. When it came to dancers, their ambitions were not merely visible, but *audible.*

Billy made a slight effort to engage Olive in the audition process, but the effort was futile. She was punishing us, it seemed, by barely watching the proceedings. In fact, she was reading the editorial page of the *Herald Tribune.*

"Say, Olive, did you think that little birdie was attractive?" he asked her, after one very pretty girl had sung a very pretty song for us.

"No." Olive didn't even look up from her newspaper.

"Well, that's all right, Olive," said Billy. "How dull it would be if you and I always had the same taste in women."

"I like that one," Edna said, pointing to a petite, raven-haired beauty throwing her leg over her head onstage as easily as another woman might shake out a bath towel. "She doesn't look quite as desperate to please as the others do."

"Good choice, Edna," said Billy. "I like that one, too. But you *do* realize that she looks exactly like you looked, twenty-odd years ago?"

"Oh, dear me, she does a bit, doesn't she? That *would* be the one I was drawn to, wouldn't it? Heavens, I'm such a vain old bore."

"Well, I liked a girl who looked like that back then, and I *still* like a girl who looks like that," said Billy. "Hire her. In fact, let's be sure to keep the height down on all the chorus girls. Make them all match the girl we just picked. I want a bunch of cute little brunette ponies. I don't want any of them dwarfing Edna."

"Thank you, love," said Edna. "One does awfully dislike being dwarfed."

When it came time to audition the male lead—Lucky Bobby, the street-smart kid who teaches Mrs. Alabaster how to gamble and who ends up marrying the showgirl—my attention was miraculously and quite suddenly restored. Because now we had a parade of good-looking young men gracing the stage, taking their turn singing the song that Billy and Benjamin had already written for the part. ("In summertime when days are nice / a fella likes to roll his dice / and if his baby doll's a bore / he likes to roll a little more.")

I thought all the guys were terrific, but—as we have established—I wasn't that discerning in my taste for men. Billy, though, dismissed them one after another. This one was too short ("He's got to kiss Celia, for the love of God, and Olive probably won't let us invest in a stepladder"); this one was too all-American-looking ("No one's going to buy that corn-fed midwesterner as a kid from a tough New York neighborhood"); this one was too effeminate ("We already have one boy in the show who looks like a girl"); this one was too earnest ("This ain't Sunday school, folks").

And then, toward the end of the day, out of the wings came a tall, lanky, dark-haired young man in a shiny suit that was a bit too short on him in both the ankles and the wrists. His hands were stuffed in his pockets, and he had a fedora pushed way back on his head. He was chewing gum, which he didn't bother to conceal as he took the spotlight. He was grinning like a guy who knows where the money is hidden.

Benjamin started to play, but the young man put up a hand to stop him.

"Say," he said, staring out at us. "Who's the boss around here, anyhow?"

Billy sat up a bit straighter at the sound of the young man's voice, which was purest *New Yawk*—sharp and cocky and lightly amused with itself.

"She is," said Billy, pointing to Peg.

"No, *she* is," said Peg, pointing to Olive.

Olive kept reading her newspaper.

"I just like to know who I gotta impress, you know?" The young man peered closer at Olive. "But if it's *that* broad, maybe I should just quit right now and head home, if you see my point?"

Billy laughed. "Son, I like you. If you can sing, you've got the job."

"Oh, I can sing, mister. Don't you worry about that. I can dance, too. I just don't wanna waste my time singing and dancing when I don't gotta sing and dance. You hear what I'm saying?"

"In that case, I amend my offer," said Billy. "You've got the job, period."

Well, *that* got Olive's attention. She looked up from her paper in alarm.

"We haven't even heard him read," Peg said. "We don't know if he can act."

"Trust me," Billy said. "He's perfect. I feel it in my gut."

"Congratulations, mister," said the kid. "You made the right call. Ladies, you won't be disappointed."

And that, Angela, was Anthony.

fell in love with Anthony Roccella, and I'm not going to dillydally around, pretending that I didn't. And he fell in love with me, too—in his own way, and for a little while at least. Best of all, I managed to fall in love with him within the space of just a few hours, which is a model of efficiency. (The young can do that kind of thing, as you must know, without difficulty. In fact, passionate love, executed in short bursts, is the natural condition of the young. The only surprising thing was that it hadn't happened to me sooner.)

The secret to falling in love so fast, of course, is not to know the person at all. You just need to identify one exciting feature about them, and then you hurl your heart at that one feature, with full force, trusting that this will be enough of a foundation for lasting devotion. And for me, the exciting thing about Anthony was his arrogance. I wasn't the only one who noticed it, of course—that cockiness was how he got cast in our play, after all—but I was the one who fell in love with it.

Now, I'd been around plenty of arrogant young men since arriving in town a few months earlier (it was New York City, Angela; we breed them here), but Anthony's arrogance had a special twist to it: he *genuinely* didn't seem to care. All the cocky boys I'd met thus far liked to play at nonchalance, but they still had an air about them of wanting something, even if it was only sex. But Anthony had no apparent hunger or longing about him. He was fine with whatever transpired. He could win, he could lose, it didn't shake him up. If he didn't get what he wanted out of a situation, he would just stroll away with his hands in his pockets, unfazed, and try again somewhere else. Whatever life offered, he could take it or leave it.

He could even take it or leave it when it came to me—so, as you can imagine, I had no choice but to become completely smitten with him.

A nthony lived in a fourth-floor walk-up on West Forty-ninth Street, between Eighth and Ninth Avenues. He lived with his older brother, Lorenzo, who was the head chef at the Latin Quarter restaurant, where Anthony worked waiting tables when he didn't have an acting job. His mom and pop used to live in that apartment, too, he told me, but they were both dead now—a fact that Anthony relayed to me with no evident sense of loss or sorrow. (Parents: another thing he could take or leave.)

Anthony was Hell's Kitchen born and raised. He was pure Forty-ninth Street, right to the core. Grew up playing stickball on that very street, and learned how to sing just a few blocks away at the Church of the Holy Cross. I came to know that street awfully well in the next few months. I certainly came to know that apartment awfully well, and I remember it with warm fondness because it was in his brother Lorenzo's bed that I experienced my first climax. (Anthony didn't have a bed of his own—he slept on the couch in the living room—but we helped ourselves to his brother's room when Lorenzo was at work. Thankfully, Lorenzo worked long hours, giving me ample time to receive pleasure from young Anthony.)

I've mentioned before that a woman needs time and patience and an attentive lover in order to get good at sex. Falling for Anthony Roccella finally gave me access to all three of those necessary features.

Anthony and I found our way to Lorenzo's bed on the first night of our acquaintance. After the auditions were over, he'd come upstairs to sign a contract and to get a copy of the script from Billy. The adults all conducted their business, and then Anthony left. But only a few minutes after he'd walked out, Peg instructed me to run after him and speak to the young man about costumes. I snapped right to duty, yes ma'am. I'd never flown down the Lily's stairwell faster.

I caught up with Anthony on the sidewalk, grabbed him by the arm, and breathlessly introduced myself.

In truth, there wasn't much I needed to discuss with him. The suit he had worn to his audition would be perfect for his costume. Yes, it was a bit modern for our play, but with the right suspenders and a wide, garish tie it would do the trick. It looked just cheap enough, and just cute enough, to suit Lucky Bobby. And while it might not have been the most *politic* thing for me to say, I told Anthony that his existing suit would be perfect for the role, precisely because it was so cheap and so cute.

"You callin' me cheap and cute?" he asked, his eyes crinkling in amusement.

He had highly pleasant eyes—dark brown and lively. He looked like he spent most of his life amused. Examining him this closely, I could see he was older than he'd looked onstage—less of a rangy kid, and more of a lean young man. He was more like twenty-nine than nineteen. It's just that his skinniness and his carefree step made him seem a lot younger.

"I might be," I said. "But there's nothing wrong with cheap and cute."

"You, on the other hand—you look expensive," he said, and gave me a slow appraisal.

"But cute?" I asked.

"Very."

We stared at each other for a while. There was a good deal of information conveyed across the silence—a whole conversation, you might say. This is what flirtation is in its purest form—a conversation held without words. Flirtation is a series of silent questions that one person asks another person with their eyes. And the answer to those questions is always the same word:

Maybe.

So Anthony and I just looked at each other for a good long while, asking the unspoken questions, and silently replying to each other: *Maybe, maybe, maybe.* The silence went on so long that it became uncomfortable. In my stubbornness, though, I wouldn't speak, but nor would I break eye contact. Finally, he started laughing, and I laughed, too.

"What's your name, baby doll?" he asked.

"Vivian Morris."

"You free tonight to spend some time with me, Vivian Morris?"

"Maybe," I said.

"Yes?" he asked.

I shrugged.

He tilted his head and looked at me closer, still smiling. "Yes?" he asked again.

"Yes," I decided, and that was the end of the *maybe.*

But then he asked it again: "Yes?"

"Yes!" I said, thinking perhaps he hadn't heard me.

"Yes?" he said one more time, and now I realized that he was asking me about something else here. We weren't talking about going out for dinner and a movie. He was asking me if I was *really* free tonight.

In an entirely different tone, I said, "*Yes.*"

W ithin a half hour, we were in his brother's bed.

I knew instantly that this was not going to be the same sort of sexual experience to which I was accustomed. First of all, I wasn't drunk and neither was he. And we weren't standing up in the cloakroom of a nightclub, or fumbling in the back of a cab. There was no fumbling to be had here. Anthony Roccella was not in a hurry. And he liked to talk as he worked, but not in a horrible way like Dr. Kellogg. He liked to ask me playful questions, which I loved. I think he just liked to hear me say *yes* again and again, and I was more than happy to oblige him.

"You know how pretty you are, don't you?" he asked, once he'd locked the door behind us.

"Yes," I said.

"You're gonna come sit on this bed with me now, right?"

"Yes."

"You know I'm gonna have to kiss you now, cuz of how pretty you are?"

"Yes."

And sweet mercy, could that boy *kiss*. One hand on each side of my face, with his long fingers reaching behind my skull, holding me still while he softly tested out my mouth. This part of sex—the kissing part, which I always loved—was usually over far too quickly in my experience, but Anthony didn't seem to be heading toward something more. This was the first time I'd been kissed by somebody who was getting as much pleasure out of kissing as I was.

After a long time—a very good long time—he pulled back. "Here's what we're gonna do now, Vivian Morris. I'm gonna sit here on this bed, and you're gonna stand right there, under the light, and take your dress off for me."

"Yes," I said. (Once you start saying it, it's so easy to keep going!)

I walked to the center of the room and stood—just as instructed— right under the lightbulb. I took my dress off, and stepped out of it, covering up my nervousness by throwing my hands up in the air. *Ta-da!* As soon as my dress came off, though, Anthony started laughing, and I was catapulted into shame—thinking of how thin I was, and how small my breasts were. When he saw the look on my face, he softened his laughter and said, "Oh, no, doll. I'm not laughing at you. I'm just laughing because I like you so much. You're a fast little operator, and it's cute."

He stood up and picked my dress up off the floor.

"Why don't you put this dress back on, doll?"

"Oh, I'm sorry," I said. "That's all right, I don't mind." I was making no sense, but I was thinking: *I blew it, it's over.*

"No, listen to me, baby. You're gonna put this dress back on for me, and then I'll ask you to take it off for me again. But this time, you're gonna slow it *way* down, okay? Don't be such a fast worker."

"You're crazy."

"I just want to see you do it again. Come on, doll. I've been waiting for this moment my whole life. Don't rush it."

"No, you have *not* been waiting for this moment your whole life!"

He grinned. "Nah, you're right. I haven't. But I sure do like it, now that it's here. So how 'bout you give it to me again? But real slow."

He sat back down on the bed, and I put my dress on. I came over and let him do up the buttons in the back, which he did, slowly and carefully. I could have reached the buttons myself, of course, and in just a few moments I would be unbuttoning them all over again, but I wanted to give him the task. Honestly, the experience of feeling this young man buttoning up my dress was the most erotic and intimate sensation I'd ever experienced—although it was soon to be surpassed.

I turned around and went back to the center of the room, fully dressed again. I fluffed my hair a bit. We were smiling at each other like fools.

"Now try it again," he said. "Go real slow for me. Make like I'm not even here."

This was my first experience of being *watched*. And while I'd had plenty of men put their hands all over me in the past few months, I'd not had nearly enough of them appraise me with their eyes. I turned my back to him, as if I were shy. Truthfully, I was a bit shy. I had never felt quite so nude, and I was still clothed! I reached back and unbuttoned the dress. I allowed it to drop from my shoulders, but it caught around my waist. I left it there. I unhooked my brassiere and slid it over my arms. I placed it on the chair next to me. Then I just stood there and let him look at my naked back. I could feel him looking at me, and it was like a current running up my spine. I stood there for a long time, waiting for him to say something, but he didn't speak. There was something thrilling about my not being able to see his face—not knowing what he was doing behind me on the bed. To this day, I can still feel the quality of air in the room. That cool, fresh, autumnal air.

Slowly I turned around, but kept my eyes down. My dress was still gathered loosely about my waist, but my breasts were bare. Still, he said nothing. I closed my eyes and allowed myself to be inspected and contemplated. The voltage I'd felt running up my spine had now circled to the front of me. My head felt light and spinny. The prospect of moving or speaking seemed impossible.

"That's right," he said finally. "That's what I'm talking about. *Now* you can come over here next to me."

He guided me down onto the bed and pushed my hair back away from my eyes. I expected him to more or less attack my breasts and mouth at this point, but he didn't go near them. His lack of urgency was driving me a bit wild. He didn't even kiss me again. He just smiled at me. "Hey, Vivian Morris. I've got a big idea. You wanna hear it?"

"Yes."

"So, here's what we're gonna do now. You're gonna lay back on this bed and let me take off the rest of your clothes. And then you're gonna shut your pretty little eyes. And then you know what I'm gonna do?"

"No," I said.

"I'm gonna show you what's what."

I t might be difficult for someone of your age, Angela, to understand how radical a concept oral sex was for a young woman of my generation. I knew about B.J.'s of course (that would've been our term for "blow jobs"—which I'd done a few times and wasn't sure I liked or even exactly understood), but the idea of a man putting his mouth on a *woman's* genitals? This was not done.

Let me amend that. Of course I'm sure it was done. Every generation likes to think that they discovered sex, but I'm sure that far more sophisticated people than me were experiencing cunnilingus in 1940, all over New York City—especially in the Village. But I'd never heard of it. God knows, I'd had everything else done to the flower of my femininity that summer, but not this. I'd been palmed and rubbed and penetrated, and certainly fingered and probed (my heavens, how the boys liked to *poke* about, and so vigorously, too)—but never *this*.

His mouth had ended up between my legs so fast, and the sudden realization of his destination and his intent had shocked me to the point that I said "Oh!" and started to sit up, but he reached up one of his long arms, placed his palm on my chest, and firmly pressed me back down again, without once stopping what he was doing.

"Oh!" I said again.

Then I felt it. There was a sensation occurring here that I didn't even know could occur. I took the sharpest inhale of my life, and I'm not sure I let my breath out for another ten minutes. I do feel that I lost the ability to see and hear for a while, and that something might have short-circuited in my brain—something that has probably never been fully fixed since. My whole being was astonished. I could hear myself making noises like an animal, and my legs were shaking uncontrollably (not that I was trying to control them), and my hands were gripping down so hard over my face that I left fingernail divots in my own skull.

Then it became *more*.

And after that, it became *even more still*.

Then I screamed as though I were being run over by a train, and that long arm of his was reaching up again to palm my mouth, and I bit into his hand the way a wounded soldier bites on a bullet.

And then it was the *most,* and I more or less died.

When it was all over, I was panting and crying and laughing and could not stop shuddering. But Anthony Roccella just smiled that same cocky smile as ever.

"Yeah, baby," said the skinny young man whom I now loved with all my heart. "That's what's what."

W ell, a girl is never really the same after something like that, now is she?

Here's the extraordinary thing, though: on that night of our remarkable first encounter, Anthony and I did not even have sex. By which I mean—we did not engage in literal intercourse. Nor did I do anything to Anthony that first night, to offer him pleasure in return for the potent revelation he had just delivered unto me. Nor did he seem to need me to do anything. He didn't seem to mind in the least if I just lay there, as immobilized as if I'd just fallen out of an airplane.

Again, this was part of the charm of Anthony Roccella—that incredible lack of urgency. The way that he could take it or leave it. I was beginning to understand the origins of Anthony Roccella's immense self-confidence. It now made perfect sense to me why this penniless young man strutted about as though he owned the whole town: because if you're a fellow who can do *that* to a woman without even needing anything in return, why wouldn't you think awfully highly of yourself?

After he'd held me for a while and teased me a bit for having screamed and cried in pleasure, he'd gone to the icebox and come back with a beer for each of us.

"You're gonna need a drink, Vivian Morris," he said, and he was right about that.

He never even took his clothes off that night.

That boy had ravaged me right to the point of unconsciousness without even removing the jacket of his cheap, cute suit!

Of course I was back there the next night to writhe around once more under the magnificent powers of his mouth. And the next night, too. Still, he stayed fully dressed, without asking for anything in reciprocation. On the third night, I finally dared to ask, "But what about you? Do you need . . . ?"

He grinned. "We'll get around to it, baby," he said. "Don't you worry."

And he was right about that, too. We got around to it—boy, did we ever—but he waited until I was famished for it.

I don't mind telling you, Angela—he waited until I was *begging* for it.

The begging bit was somewhat tricky on my part, because I didn't know how to beg for sex. What sort of language does a nicely bred young lady use to plead for access to that unnamable male organ, which she so dearly wants?

Could you kindly . . . ?

If it's not any trouble . . . ?

I just didn't have any of the terminology required for this sort of exchange. Sure, I'd been doing a lot of dirty, filthy things since my arrival in New York, but I was still a nice young lady at my core, and nice young ladies don't ask for things. For the most part, what I had been doing over the course of these past few months was *allowing* dirty, filthy things to happen to me, at the hands of men who were always in a big hurry to get it done. But this was different. I wanted Anthony, and he was in no hurry to give me what I wanted, which only made me want him more.

When it got to the point when I would stammer things like, "Do you think we might someday . . . ?" he would stop what he was doing, rise up on one elbow, grin at me, and say, "How's that, now?"

"If you ever wanted to . . ."

"If I ever wanted to *what*, baby? Just say it."

I would say nothing (because I could say nothing) and he would just grin wider and say, "Sorry, baby, I can't hear you. You gotta enunciate."

But I couldn't say it—at least not till he taught me how to say it.

"There are some words you need to learn, baby," he told me one night while he was toying with me in bed. "And we ain't doin' nothing more till I hear you say it."

Then he taught me the nastiest words I'd ever heard. Words that made me blush and burn. He made me repeat the words after him, and he relished how uncomfortable it made me. Then he went to work on my body again, leaving me splayed and flayed with longing. When I had reached such a peak of desire that I could scarcely draw a breath, he stopped what he was doing, and turned on the light.

"So, here's what we're gonna do now, Vivian Morris," he said. "You're gonna look me dead in the eye, and you're gonna tell me *exactly* what you want me to do to you—using the words I just taught you. And that's the only way it's ever gonna happen, baby doll."

And Angela, God help me, I did it.

I looked him dead in the eye, and I begged for it like a two-dollar hooker.

After that, it was Katy bar the door.

Now that I was infatuated with Anthony, the last thing I wanted to do anymore was go out on the town with Celia, picking up strangers for cheap, fast, pleasureless thrills. I didn't want to do anything anymore but be with *him*—pinned to his brother Lorenzo's bed—every moment that I could get. All of which is to say: I'm afraid I dropped Celia rather unceremoniously once Anthony showed up.

I don't know if Celia missed me. She never showed any indication of it. Nor did she pull away from me in any notable way. She just went about her life, and was friendly to me whenever we collided (which was usually in bed, when she would come stumbling in drunk at the usual hour). Looking back on it now, I feel that I wasn't a very loyal friend to Celia—in fact, I'd dumped her *twice:* first for Edna, and then for Anthony. But maybe the young are just feral animals in the way that they shift their affections and allegiances so capriciously. Celia could certainly be capricious, too. I realize now that I always needed somebody to be infatuated with when I was twenty years old, and it didn't really matter *who,* apparently. Anybody with more charisma than me would do the trick. (And New York was filled with people more charismatic than me.) I was so unformulated as a human being, so unsteady in myself, that I was constantly grasping for attachment to another person—constantly anchoring myself to someone else's allure. But evidently, I could only be infatuated with one person at a time.

And right now, it was Anthony.

I was glassy-eyed in love. I was dumbstruck with love. I was all but undone by him. I could barely concentrate on my duties at the theater, because honestly, who *cared*? I think the only reason I even went to the theater anymore is because Anthony was there every day, spending hours a day in rehearsal, and I got to see him. All I wanted was to be in his orbit. I would wait around for him after every rehearsal like the most absurd little twit, following him back and forth to his dressing room, running out to buy him a cold tongue sandwich on rye whenever he wanted one. I bragged to everyone who would listen that I had a boyfriend, and it was *forever.*

Like so many other dumb young girls throughout history, I was infected with love and lust—and moreover, I thought Anthony Roccella had invented the stuff.

But then there was the conversation I had with Edna one day, when I was fitting her with a new hat for the show.

She said, "You're distracted. That's not the color ribbon we'd agreed on."

"Is it not?"

She touched the ribbon in question, which was scarlet red, and asked, "Does this look emerald green to you?"

"I guess not," I said.

"It's that boy," Edna said. "He's commanding all your attention."

I couldn't help but grin. "He sure is," I said.

Edna smiled, but indulgently. "When you are around him, dear Vivian, you should know that you look exactly like a little dog in heat."

I rewarded her for her candor by accidentally stabbing her in the neck with a pin. "I'm so sorry!" I cried out—and whether it was about the pin-stabbing, or about looking like a little dog in heat, I could not have said.

Edna coolly dabbed at the spot of blood on her neck with her handkerchief and said, "Don't give it another thought. It's not the first time I've been stabbed, my dear, and it's probably richly deserved. But listen to me, darling, because I'm old enough to be an archaeological *relic*, and I know some things about life. It is not that I don't celebrate your affections for Anthony. It is delightful to watch a young person fall in love for the first time. Chasing your boy about, as you do—it's very sweet."

"Well, he's a dream, Edna," I said. "He's a living dream."

"Of course he is, darling. They always are. But I have a spot of

195

advice. By all means, take that racy young man to bed with you and put him in your memoirs when you get famous, but there is something you must *not* do."

I thought she was going to say, "Don't get married," or "Don't get pregnant."

But no. Edna had a different concern.

"Do *not* let it capsize the show," she said.

"I'm sorry?"

"At this point in a production, Vivian, we all must count on one another to sustain a certain degree of judiciousness and professionalism. It may seem as though we are just having some larks here—and we are having larks—but much is at stake. Your aunt is pouring everything she has into this play—heart, soul, and all her money, too—and we wouldn't want to drive her show over a cliff. Here is the solidarity of good theater people, Vivian: we try not to ruin each other's shows, and we try not to ruin each other's lives."

I didn't understand what she was on about, and my face must have showed it, because she tried again.

"What I'm trying to say, Vivian, is this: if you're going to be in love with Anthony, then be in love with him, and who could blame you for wanting your little exploit? But promise me that you will stay with him till the end of the run. He's a good actor—far better than average—and he's needed for this production. I don't want any disruptions. If one of you breaks the other's heart, I stand to lose not only a surprisingly excellent leading man, but also a damn good dresser. I need you both right now, and I need you to be in your right minds. Your aunt needs it, too."

I still must have looked awfully stupid, because she said, "Let me put it to you even more plainly, Vivian. As my worst ex-husband—that awful director—used to say to me, 'Live your life as you wish, my peach, but don't let it bitch up the bloody show.'"

FIFTEEN

C *ity of Girls* was now in the full swing of rehearsals, with the date set for the premiere of November 29, 1940. We would open the week after Thanksgiving, to try to snag the holiday crowd.

Mostly it was going well. The music was sensational and the costumes were *choice*, if I do say so myself. The best thing about the play, of course, was Anthony Roccella—or at least in my opinion. My boyfriend could sing, act, and dance up a storm. (I'd overheard Billy saying to Peg, "You can always find girls who can dance like angels, and some boys, too. But to get a man who can dance like a *man*—that's not easily found. This kid is everything I'd hoped he would be.")

Furthermore, Anthony was a natural comic, and he was absolutely convincing as a clever delinquent who could hustle a rich old lady into establishing a speakeasy and bordello in the great room of her mansion. And his scenes with Celia were fantastic. They were such a great-looking couple on stage. They had one particularly outstanding scene together, where they did the tango as Anthony seductively sang to Celia about "A Little Spot in Yonkers" that he wanted to show her. The way Anthony sang it, he made "A Little Spot in Yonkers" sound like an erogenous zone on a woman's body—and Celia certainly responded as though it were. It was the sexiest moment of the play. Any woman with a pulse would have agreed. Or at least I thought so.

Others, of course, would have claimed that the best thing about the play was Edna Parker Watson's performance—and I'm sure they were right. Even I, in my infatuated daze, could tell that Edna was brilliant. I'd seen a lot of theater in my life, but I'd never seen a real actress at work before. All the actresses I'd met so far were dolls with four or five different facial expressions to choose from—sadness, fear, anger, love, happiness—that they kept in rotation until the curtain went down. But Edna had access to every shade of human emotion. She was natural, she was warm, she was regal, and she could do a scene nine different ways in the space of an hour and somehow make each variation seem like the perfect one.

She was a generous actress, as well. She made everyone's performances look better, by her mere presence onstage. She coaxed the best out of everyone. She liked to step back a bit in rehearsal and let the light shine on another actor, beaming at them somewhat as they played their role. The great actresses are not often this kind. But Edna always thought of others. I remember Celia coming to rehearsal one day wearing false eyelashes. Edna took her aside to caution her not to wear them in performances, as they would cast shadows over her eye sockets and make her look "corpselike, darling, which is never what one wants."

A more jealous star would not have pointed out such a thing. But Edna was never jealous.

Over time, Edna made Mrs. Alabaster into a far more subtle character than what the script suggested. Edna transformed Mrs. Alabaster into a woman of *knowing*—a woman who knew how ridiculous her life was when she was rich, and then knew how ridiculous it was to be broke, and then knew how ridiculous it was to be running a casino in her drawing room. Yet she was a woman who bravely played the game of life anyhow—and allowed the game of life to somewhat play her. She was ironic, but not cold. The effect was a survivor who had not lost the ability to feel.

And when Edna sang her romantic solo—a simple ballad called "I'm Considering Falling in Love"—she brought the room to a state of silent awe, every single time. It didn't matter how many times we'd heard her sing it already; we all stopped whatever we were doing to listen. It's not that Edna had the best singing voice (she could be a tad chancy sometimes on the high notes), but she brought such poignancy to the moment that one couldn't help but sit up and pay attention.

The song was about an older woman who was deciding to give herself over to romance one more time, against her own better judgment. When Billy wrote the lyrics, he hadn't intended them to be quite so sad. The original point, I think, had been to create something light and amusing: *Look, how cute! Even older people can fall in love!* But Edna asked Benjamin to slow down the song and alter it to a darker key, and that changed everything. Now when she got to the last line ("I'm just an amateur / But what are we here for? / I'm considering falling in love") you could feel that this woman was *already* in love, and that it was terminal. You could feel her fear at what might happen to her heart, now that she had lost control of herself. But you could also feel her hope.

I don't think Edna ever sang that song in rehearsal that we didn't stop and applaud her at the end.

"She's the real deal, kiddo," Peg said to me one day from the wings. "Edna is the real blown-in-the-bottle deal. No matter how old you get, don't ever forget how lucky you were to see a master at work."

———

A more problematic actor, I'm afraid, was Arthur Watson. Edna's husband couldn't do anything. He couldn't act—he couldn't even remember his lines!—and he certainly couldn't sing. ("To listen to his singing," Billy diagnosed, "is to have the rare pleasure of envying the deaf.") His dancing had everything wrong with it that dancing can have and still be called dancing. And he couldn't move around the stage without looking as though he were about to knock something over. I wondered how he'd ever managed to be a carpenter without accidentally sawing his arm off. To his credit, Arthur did look awfully handsome in his costume of a morning suit, top hat, and tails, but that's about all I can say in his favor.

When it became evident that Arthur couldn't manage the role, Billy pared down the character's lines as much as possible, to make it simpler for the poor man to get through a sentence. (For instance, Billy had changed Arthur's opening line from "I'm your late husband's third cousin, Barchester Headley Wentworth, the fifth earl of Addington" to "I'm your cousin from England.") He also took away Arthur's solo. He even took away the dance number that Arthur was meant to have with Edna as he was attempting to seduce Mrs. Alabaster.

"Those two dance as though they've never been introduced," Billy said to Peg, before finally giving up on the idea of having them dance at all. "How is it possible that they are *married*?"

Edna tried to help out her husband, but he didn't take direction well and got sputteringly offended at any efforts to refine his performance.

"I never understand what you're talking about, my dear, and I always will!" he snapped at her once, insensibly, when she tried to explain the difference between stage right and stage left for the dozenth time.

The thing that drove us the craziest was that Arthur could not stop himself from whistling along with the music coming from the orchestra pit—even when he was on stage, and in character. Nobody could get him to stop.

One afternoon, Billy finally shouted, "Arthur! Your character can't *hear* that music! It's the theme from the goddamn overture!"

"Of course I can hear it!" Arthur protested. "The bloody musicians are right *there*!"

This had caused the exasperated Billy to go on a long rant about the difference in theater between *diagetic* music (which the characters onstage can hear), and *non-diagetic music* (which only the audience can hear).

"Talk English!" Arthur had demanded.

So Billy tried again: "Imagine, Arthur, that you are watching a western with John Wayne in it. There is John Wayne, riding his horse all alone across a mesa, and suddenly he starts *whistling along to the theme music*. Do you see how ridiculous that would be?"

"I just don't see why a man can't whistle these days without being *attacked*," sniffed Arthur.

(Later, I heard him ask one of the dancers, "What the devil is a *mesa*?")

used to look at Edna and Arthur Watson and try with all my might to imagine how she coped with him.

The only explanation I could come up with was that Edna genuinely loved beauty—and Arthur was undeniably beautiful. (He looked like Apollo, if Apollo were your neighborhood butcher—but, yes, he was beautiful.) This made a certain amount of sense, because there was nothing in Edna's life that wasn't beautiful. I never saw anybody who cared about aesthetics more than that woman did. I never once saw Edna that she wasn't exquisitely put together, and I saw her at all times of the day and night. (To be the kind of woman who is perfectly kempt even at the breakfast table or in the privacy of her own bedroom requires a certain amount of labor and commitment—but that was Edna for you, always ready to put in the hours.)

Her cosmetics were beautiful. The tiny silk drawstring purse in which she held her loose change was beautiful. The way she read her lines and sang onstage was beautiful. The way she folded her gloves was beautiful. She was both a connoisseur and a radiator of pure beauty, in all its forms.

In fact, I think part of the reason Edna liked to have me and Celia around her so much was that *we* were beautiful, too. Rather than being competitive with us—as many other older women might have been—she seemed enhanced and invigorated by us. I remember one day the three of us were walking down the street together, with Edna in the middle. She suddenly clasped us each by the arm, smiled up at us, and said, "When I walk around town with the two of you towering young ladies at my side, I feel like a perfect pearl, set between two gleaming rubies."

It was now a week before our opening and everyone was sick. We all had the same cold, and half the girls in the chorus line had pink eye from sharing the same infected cake of mascara. (The other half had crabs, from sharing their costume bottoms, *which I had told them a hundred times not to do*.) Peg wanted to give the performers a day off to rest up and heal, but Billy wouldn't hear of it. He still felt that the first ten minutes of the play were "spongy"—not moving along at a brisk enough clip.

"You haven't got a lot of time to win over an audience, kids," he said to the cast one afternoon as everyone was hacking their way through the opening number. "You've got to catch them right away. Doesn't matter if the second act is good, if the first act is slow. People don't come back for the second act if they hate the first one."

"They're just tired, Billy," said Peg.

And they *were* tired; most of our cast was still putting on two shows a night, keeping the regular schedule of the Lily running until our big new play opened.

"Well, comedy is hard," said Billy. "Keeping things light is heavy work. I can't start letting them sag now."

He made them do the opening number three more times that day—and each time it was a bit different and a bit worse. The chorus line braved it out, but some of the girls looked like they regretted ever having been cast.

The theater itself had become filthy during rehearsals—filled with folding camp chairs, cigarette smoke, and paper cups containing the remnants of cold coffee. Bernadette the maid tried to keep up with it all, but there was always trash everywhere. An impressive din and reek. Everybody was cranky, everybody was snapping at each other. There was no glamour in this for anyone. Even our prettiest dancers looked dowdy in their various snoods and turbans, their faces heavy with exhaustion, their lips and cheeks chafed from their colds.

One rainy afternoon during the final week of rehearsals, Billy ran out to pick up our sandwiches for lunch, and came back into the theater soaking wet, his arms full of soggy lunch bags.

"Christ, how I hate New York," he said, shaking the icy water off his jacket.

"Just out of curiosity, Billy," Edna said, "what would you be doing right now if you were back in Hollywood?"

"What is it, Tuesday?" Billy asked. He looked at his watch, sighed, and said, "Right now, I'd be playing tennis with Dolores del Rio."

"That's nice, but didja get my smokes?" Anthony asked Billy, just as Arthur Watson peeled opened one of the sandwiches and said, "What?

No bloody mustard?"—and for a moment there, I thought Billy might deck the both of them.

P eg had taken to drinking during the day—not to the point of visible intoxication, but I noticed that she kept a flask nearby, and she would take frequent nips. Careless as I was back then about drinking, I have to admit that this alarmed even me. And there were more instances now—a few times a week—when I would find Peg blacked out in the living room amid a tumble of bottles, never having made it upstairs to bed.

Worse, Peg's drinking did not serve to relax her, but made her more tense. She caught me and Anthony necking in the wings once in the middle of rehearsal, and snapped at me for the first time in our acquaintance.

"*Goddamn* it, Vivian, do you think you could manage for *ten minutes* to keep your lips off my leading man?"

(The honest answer? No. No, I couldn't. But still, it wasn't characteristic of Peg to be so critical, and my feelings were hurt.)

And then there was the day of the ticket blowout.

Peg and Billy wanted to buy rolls of new tickets for the Lily Playhouse, to reflect the new prices. They wanted the tickets to be big and brightly colored, and to read *City of Girls*. Olive wanted to use our old ticket rolls (which said nothing but ADMISSION), and she also wanted to use our old ticket prices. Peg dug in, insisting, "I'm not charging the same thing for people to see Edna Parker Watson onstage that I would charge them to see one of my stupid girlie shows."

Olive dug in harder: "Our audiences can't afford four dollars for an orchestra seat, and we can't afford to print new rolls of tickets."

Peg: "If they can't afford a four-dollar ticket, then they can buy a ticket in the balcony for three dollars."

"Our audience can't afford that, either."

"Then maybe they aren't our audience anymore, Olive. Maybe we'll get a new audience now. Maybe we'll get a better class of audience, just this once."

"We don't serve the carriage trade," Olive said. "We serve working people, or do I have to remind you?"

"Well maybe the *working people* of this neighborhood would like to see a quality show, Olive, for once in their lives. Maybe they don't like being treated like they are poor and tasteless. Maybe they think it would be worth it to pay a bit extra to see something good. Have you considered *that*?"

The two of them had been bickering about this for days, but it all came to a head when Olive burst in on a rehearsal one afternoon—interrupting Peg while she was talking to a dancer about some confusion over blocking—and announced, "I've just been to the printers. It's going to cost two hundred and fifty dollars to print the five thousand new tickets you want, and I refuse to pay it."

Peg spun on her heel and shouted: "Goddamn it, Olive—how much money do I have to pay you to *stop talking about fucking money?*"

The whole theater fell silent. Everybody iced over, right where they stood.

Maybe you remember, Angela, what a powerful impact the word "fuck" used to have in our society—back before everybody and their children started saying it ten times a day before breakfast. Indeed, it was once a *very* potent word. To hear it coming out of a respectable woman's mouth? This was never done. Not even Celia used that word. Billy didn't even use that word. (I used it, of course, but only in the privacy of Anthony's brother's bed, and only because Anthony made me say it before he would have sex with me—and I still blushed whenever I spoke it.)

But to hear it *shouted*?

I had never heard it shouted.

It did cross my mind for a moment to wonder where my nice old Aunt Peg had ever learned such a word—although I guess if you've taken care of wounded soldiers on the front lines of trench warfare, you've probably heard everything.

Olive stood there with the invoice in her hand. She had a distinctly slapped look about her, and it was something terrible to behold in one who was always so commanding. She put her other hand over her mouth, and her eyes filled with tears.

In the next moment, Peg's face went sodden with remorse.

"Olive, I'm sorry! I'm so sorry. I didn't mean it. I'm an ass."

She stepped toward her secretary, but Olive shook her head and skittered away backstage. Peg ran after her. The rest of us all looked around at each other in shock. The air itself felt dead and hard.

It was Edna who recovered first, perhaps not surprisingly.

"My suggestion, Billy," she said in a steady voice, "is that you ask the company to start the dance number again from the top. I believe Ruby knows where to stand now, don't you, my dear?"

The little dancer nodded quietly.

"From the top?" asked Billy, a bit uncertainly. He looked more uncomfortable than I'd ever seen him before.

"That's correct," Edna said, with her usual polish. "From the top. And Billy, if you could please remind the cast to keep their attention on their roles and the job at hand, that would be ideal. Let us be mindful to keep the tone light, as well. I know you are all tired, but we can do this. As you are discovering, my friends—making comedy can be hard."

The ticket incident might have dissolved from my memory, but for one thing.

That night, I went to Anthony's place as usual, ready for my standard evening fare of sensual debauchery. But his brother, Lorenzo, came home from work at the unforgivably early hour of midnight, so I had to beat it back to the Lily Playhouse, feeling more than a little frustrated and exiled. I was irritated, too, that Anthony wouldn't walk me home—but that was Anthony for you. That boy had many sterling qualities, but gentlemanliness was not among them.

Okay, maybe he only had one sterling quality.

In any case, I was flustered and distracted when I arrived back at the Lily, and it's likely that my blouse was on inside out, as well. As I climbed the stairs to the third floor, I could hear music playing. Benjamin was at the piano. He was playing "Stardust" in a melancholy way—more slowly and sweetly than I'd ever heard. Old and corny as that song was even back then, it has always been one of my favorites. I opened the door to the living room carefully, not wanting to interrupt. The only light in the room was the small lamp over the piano. There was Benjamin, playing so softly that his fingers barely touched the keys.

And there, standing in the middle of the darkened living room, were Peg and Olive. They were dancing with each other. It was a slow sort of dance—more of a rocking embrace than anything. Olive had her face pressed against Peg's bosom, and Peg was resting her cheek on the top of Olive's head. They both had their eyes closed tightly. They were clinging to each other, squeezed together in a silent grip of need. Whatever world they were in—whatever era of history they were in, whatever memories they were in, whatever story they were knitting back together in the tightness of their embrace—it was very much their own world. They were somewhere together, but they were not *here*.

I watched them, unable to move, and unable to comprehend what I was witnessing—while at the same time, unable to *not* comprehend what I was witnessing.

After a while, Benjamin glanced over to the doorway and saw me. I don't know how he sensed that I was there. He didn't stop playing, and his expression didn't change, but he kept his eyes on me. I kept my eyes on him, too—maybe looking for some kind of explanation or instruction, but none was offered. I felt pinned in the doorway by Benjamin's gaze. There was something in his eyes that said: "You do not take another step into this room."

I was afraid to move, for fear of making a sound and alerting Peg and Olive to my presence. I didn't want to embarrass them or humiliate myself. But when I could feel that the song was ending, I had no choice: I had to slip away, or be caught.

So I backed out and gently closed the door behind me—Benjamin's unblinking gaze on me as he finished playing the song, watching to make sure I was good and gone before he touched the final, wistful note.

I spent the next two hours in an all-night diner in Times Square, not sure when it would be safe to return home. I didn't know where else to go. I couldn't go back to Anthony's apartment, and I still felt the power of Benjamin's stare, warning me not to cross that threshold—*not now, Vivian.*

I had never been out alone at this hour in the city, and it frightened me more than I cared to acknowledge. I didn't know what to do, without Celia or Anthony or Peg as my guides. I still wasn't a real New Yorker, you see. I was still a tourist. You don't become a real New Yorker until you can manage the city alone.

So I had gone to the most brightly lit place I could find, where a tired old waitress kept refilling my coffee cup without comment or complaint. I watched a sailor and his girl arguing in the booth across from me. They were both drunk. Their fight was about somebody named Miriam. The girl was suspicious of Miriam; the sailor was defensive about Miriam. They were both making a strong case for their respective positions. I went back and forth between believing the sailor and believing the girl. I felt like I needed to see what Miriam looked like before rendering a verdict on whether the soldier had been untrue to his sweetheart.

Peg and Olive were *lesbians*?

It couldn't be, though. Peg was married. And Olive was . . . *Olive*. A sexless being if ever there was one. Olive was made of mothballs. But was there any other explanation for why those two middle-aged women were holding each other so tightly in the dark while Benjamin played the world's saddest love song for them?

I knew they had quarreled that day, but is this how you make up with your secretary after an argument? I hadn't been around a lot of business concerns in my life, but that embrace didn't seem professional. Nor did it seem like something that would happen between two friends. I slept in a bed with a woman every night—not just any woman, but one of the most beautiful women in New York—and we didn't embrace like that.

And if they were lesbians—well, since *when*? Olive had been working for Peg since the Great War. She'd met Peg before Billy did. Was this a new development or had it always been this way? Who knew about this? Did Edna know about this? Did my family know about this? Did Billy know about this?

Certainly Benjamin knew. The only thing that had rattled him about the scene was my presence in it. Did he play the piano for them often, so they could dance? What was going *on* in that theater behind closed doors? And was this the real source of the constant bickering and tension between Billy and Peg and Olive? Was their underlying argument not about money or drinking or control, but about sexual competition? (My mind raced back to that day at auditions when Billy had said to Olive, "How dull it would be if you and I always had the same taste in women.") Could Olive Thompson—she of the boxy woolen suits, and the moral sanctimony, and the thin line of a mouth—be a *rival* to Billy Buell?

Could *anybody* be a rival to the likes of Billy Buell?

I thought of Edna saying of Peg: "These days she wants loyalty more than fun."

Well, Olive was loyal. You had to give her that. And if you didn't need to have fun, you'd come to the right place, I suppose.

I could not parse what any of it meant.

I walked back home around two thirty.

I eased open the door to the living room, but nobody was there. All the lights were off. On one hand, it was as if the scene had never occurred—but at the same time, I felt that I could still see a shadow of the two women dancing in the middle of the room.

I slipped off to bed and was awoken a few hours later by Celia's familiar boozy warmth, crashing down next to me on the mattress.

"Celia," I whispered to her, once she'd settled in beside me. "I have to ask you something."

"Sleeping," she said, in a gluey voice.

I poked her, shook her, made her groan and turn over, and said louder, "Come *on*, Celia. This is important. Wake up. Listen to me. Is my Aunt Peg a lesbian?"

"Does a dog bark?" Celia replied, and she was sound asleep in the very next instant.

SIXTEEN

From Brooks Atkinson's review of *City of Girls* in *The New York Times*, November 30, 1940:

If the play is destitute of veracity, it is by no means destitute of charm. The writing is quick and sharp, and the cast is nearly universally excellent. . . . But the great pleasure of *City of Girls* lies in the rare opportunity to witness Edna Parker Watson at work. This lauded British actress possesses a flair for the comic that one might not have expected from so illustrious a tragedienne. Watching Mrs. Watson stand aside to appraise the clown show in which her character regularly finds herself is a marvel. Her reactions are so richly humorous and subtle as to make her walk away with this delightful little piece of lampoonery tucked tidily under one arm.

O pening night had been terrifying—and also contentious.

Billy had stocked the audience with old friends and loud-mouths, columnists and ex-girlfriends, and every publicist and critic and newspaperman he knew by name or reputation. (And he knew *everyone*.) Peg and Olive had both objected to this idea, and strongly.

"I don't know if we're ready for that," Peg said—sounding just like a woman who is panicked to learn that her husband has invited his boss over for dinner that night and expects a perfect meal on short notice.

"We'd better be ready," said Billy. "We're opening in a week."

"I don't want critics in this theater," Olive said. "I don't like critics. Critics can be so *unsympathetic*."

"Do you even believe in our play, Olive?" Billy asked. "Do you even like our play?"

"No," she replied. "Except in spots."

"I cannot resist asking, though I know I'll regret it—*which* spots?"

Olive thought carefully. "I might somewhat enjoy the overture."

Billy rolled his eyes. "You're a living tribulation, Olive." Then he turned his attention to Peg. "We've got to take the risk, honey. We've got to spread the word. I don't want the only important person in the audience that first night to be me."

"Give us a week at least to work out the kinks," said Peg.

"It doesn't make any difference, Pegsy. If the show is a bomb, it'll still be a bomb in a week, kinks or no. So let's find out right away whether we've wasted all our time and money, or not. We need big gravy people in the audience, or it'll never work. We need them to love it, and we need them to tell their friends to come and see it, and that's how the ball rolls. Olive won't let me spend money to advertise, so we need to ballyhoo the hell out of this thing. The sooner we start selling out every seat in the house, the sooner Olive will stop looking at me like I'm a murderer—and we can't sell out every seat in this house unless people know we're *here*."

"I think it's vulgar to invite one's social friends to one's place of work," said Olive, "and then expect them to provide free publicity."

"Then how do you aim for us to alert people to the fact that we have a show, Olive? Would you like me to stand on the street corner in a sandwich board?"

Olive looked as though she wouldn't be against it.

"As long as the sign doesn't say THE END IS NEAR," said Peg, who did not seem certain that it wasn't.

"Pegsy," said Billy, "where's your confidence? This mule kicks. You know it does. You *know* this show is good. You can feel it in your belly, just like I do."

But Peg was still uneasy. "So many times over the years you have told me that I was feeling something in my belly. And usually the only thing I was feeling was the unsettling sensation of having just lost my wallet."

"I'm about to *stuff* your wallet, lady," said Billy. "Just you watch me do it."

From Heywood Broun, writing in the *New York Post:*

Edna Parker Watson has long been a gem of the British stage, but after watching *City of Girls*, one wishes she had come to brighten our shores sooner. What might have been seen as a mere curio transforms into a memorable night of theater, thanks to Mrs. Watson's rare understanding and wit, as she portrays a down-on-her-luck society doyenne who must turn bordello madam in order to save the family mansion. . . . Benjamin Wilson's songs crackle with delight, and the dancers are brilliantly ascending. . . . Newcomer Anthony Roccella smolders as a flashy urban Romeo, and Celia Ray's distracting carnality gives the show an overall adult savor.

In the last few days before opening night, Billy spent money like crazy—even crazier than usual. He brought in two Norwegian masseuses for our dancers and stars. (Peg was appalled by the expense, but Billy said, "We do it in Hollywood all the time, with your jumpier stars. You'll see—it calms them right down.") He had a doctor come to the Lily Playhouse and give everyone vitamin shots. He told Bernadette to bring in every cousin she'd ever had—and their kids, too—to clean that theater until it was unrecognizable. He hired men from the neighborhood to hose down the façade of the Lily, and to make sure every lightbulb in the big electric sign was firing at full blaze, and he put new gels on all the stage lighting, as well.

For the final dress rehearsal, he brought in catering from Toots Shor's—caviar, smoked fish, finger sandwiches, the works. He hired a photographer to take publicity photos of the cast in full costume. He filled the lobby with large sprays of orchids, which probably cost more than my first semester at college (and was probably a better investment, too). He brought in a facialist, a manicurist, and a makeup artist for Edna and Celia.

On the day of our opening, he wrangled up some kids and unemployed men from the neighborhood, and hired them (at fifty cents a pop, which was a pretty good wage, for the kids, at least) to mill about outside the theater, giving the impression that something tremendously exciting was about to happen. He hired the kid with the loudest mouth to keep shouting, "Sold out! Sold out! Sold out!"

On the evening of opening night, Billy presented Edna, Peg, and Olive with surprise gifts—for good luck, he said. He gave Edna a slim gold bracelet from Cartier that was just to her taste. For Peg, there was a handsome new leather wallet from Mark Cross. ("You'll need it soon, Pegsy," he said with a wink. "Once the box office starts pouring in, your old wallet will bust at the seams.") As for Olive, he ceremoniously bestowed her with an overwrapped gift box, containing—once she had finally gotten all the paper and bows off it—a bottle of gin.

"Your own stash," he said. "To help you anesthetize yourself during the utter boredom that you apparently suffer from this production."

From Dwight Miller, in the *New York World-Telegram:*

Theatergoers are urged to ignore the saggy and worn seats of the Lily Playhouse, and to ignore the flakes of ceiling that may land in their hair as the hoofers dance onstage, and to ignore the ill-designed sets and the flickering lights. Yes, they are urged to ignore every discomfort and inconvenience, and get themselves over to Ninth Avenue to see Edna Parker Watson in *City of Girls!*

Then the audience was entering the theater, and we all crowded backstage—everyone in full costume and full makeup—listening to the glorious din of a packed house.

"Gather round," said Billy. "This is your moment."

The nervous, high-strung actors and dancers all formed a loose circle around Billy. I stood next to Anthony, as proud as I had ever been, holding his hand. He gave me a deep kiss, then dropped my hand and shifted back and forth on his feet lightly, jabbing the air with his fists, like a boxer about to fight.

Billy took a flask out of his pocket, helped himself to a generous swig, then passed it to Peg, who did the same.

"Now I'm not one for speeches," said Billy, "given that I'm unfamiliar with stringing words together and I don't enjoy being the center of attention." The cast laughed indulgently. "But I want to tell you people that what you've made here in a short amount of time and on a shoestring budget is just as good as theater can ever be. There is nothing playing on Broadway right now—or in London, too, I would wager—that's any better than the goods we've got to offer these folks tonight."

"I'm not sure there's anything playing in London at all right now, darling," corrected Edna dryly, "except maybe 'Bombs Away' . . ."

The cast laughed again.

"Thank you, Edna," said Billy. "You've reminded me to mention you. Listen to me, everyone. If you get nervous or unsettled onstage, look to Edna. From this moment on, she's your captain and you couldn't be in better hands. Edna is the coolest-headed performer with whom you will ever have the privilege of sharing a stage. Nothing can shake up this woman. So let her steadiness be your guide. Stay relaxed by seeing how relaxed she is. Remember that an audience will forgive a performer for anything except being uncomfortable. And if you forget your lines, just keep talking gibberish, and Edna will somehow fix it. Trust her—she's been doing this job since the Spanish Armada, haven't you, Edna?"

"Since somewhat before then, I should think," she said, smiling.

Edna looked incandescent in her vintage red Lanvin gown from the Lowtsky's bin. I had tailored the dress to her with such care. I was so proud of how well I'd dressed her for this role. Her makeup was exquisite, too. (But of course it was.) She still resembled herself, but this was a more vivid, regal version of herself. With her bobbed, glossy black hair and that lush red dress, she looked like a piece of Chinese lacquer—immaculate, varnished, and ever so valuable.

"One more thing before I turn it over to your trusty producer," said Billy. "Remember that this audience didn't come here tonight because they want to hate you. They came because they want to love you. Peg and I have put on thousands of shows over the years, in front of every kind of audience there is, and I know what an audience wants. They want to fall in love. So I've got an old vaudevillian's tip for you: If you love them first, they won't be able to help themselves from falling in love with you right back. So go out there and love them hard, is my advice."

He paused for a moment, wiped his eyes, and then spoke again.

"Now listen," he said. "I stopped believing in God during the Great War, and you would've too, if you'd seen what I saw. But sometimes I have relapses—usually when I get too drunk or overly emotional, and right now, I'm a little of both, so forgive me, but here goes. Let's bow our heads and have a prayer."

I couldn't believe it, but he was serious.

We bowed our heads. Anthony took my hand again, and I felt the thrill that I always got from his attentions, no matter how slight. Somebody took my other hand and gave it a squeeze. I could tell from her familiar touch that it was Celia.

I'm not sure I'd ever had a happier moment than this.

"Dear God of whatever nature you are," said Billy. "Shine your favor on these humble players. Shine your favor on this wretched old theater. Shine your favor on those bums out there and make them love us. Shine your favor on this useless little endeavor of ours. What we're doing here tonight doesn't matter a bit in the cruel scheme of the world, but we're doing it anyhow. Make it worth our while. We ask this in your name—whoever you are, and whether we believe in you or not, which most of us don't. Amen."

"Amen," we all said.

Billy took another swig off his flask. "Anything you'd like to add to that, Peg?"

My Aunt Peg grinned, and in that moment she looked about twenty years old.

"Just get out there, kids," she said, "and kick the living shit out of it."

From Walter Winchell, writing in the *New York Daily Mirror:*

I'm not bothered about whatever play Edna Parker Watson is in, just so long as she is in it! She stands head and shoulders above other actresses who think they know how! . . . She looks like royalty, but she can bring the ham! . . . *City of Girls* is a masterpiece of flapdoodle—and if that sounds like a complaint, folks, believe me, it is not. In these dark times, we could all use some more flapdoodle. . . . Celia Ray—and boo to whoever has been hiding *her* all these years—is an iridescent minx. You might not want to leave her alone with your boyfriend or your husband, but is that any way to judge a starlet? . . . Don't worry, chippies, there's something tasty for you in this show, too: I could hear all the ladies in the audience sighing for Anthony Roccella, who oughta be in pictures. . . . Donald Herbert is hilarious as a blind pickpocket—and that's what I call some politicians these days! . . . Now, as far as Arthur Watson goes, he's way too young for his wife, but she's way too good for him—so I bet that's how they make things work! I don't know if he's as wooden a fellow offstage as he is in the spotlight, but if he is, I feel sorry for his cutie-pie wife!

Edna got the first laugh of the show.

Act 1, scene 1: Mrs. Alabaster is at a tea party with a few other opulent ladies. Amidst the general chatter of idle gossip, she casually mentions that her husband was hit by a car the night before. The ladies all gasp in shock, and one of them asks, "Critical, my dear?"

"Always," replies Mrs. Alabaster.

There's a long beat. The ladies stare at her in arch confusion. Mrs. Alabaster stirs her tea calmly, with one pinky raised. Then she looks up in purest innocence: "I'm sorry, did you mean his condition? Oh, he's dead."

The audience roared.

Backstage, Billy grabbed my aunt's hand and said, "We got 'em, Pegsy."

From Thomas Lessig, in the *Morning Telegraph:*

The high-battery sex appeal of Miss Celia Ray will keep many a gentleman glued to his seat, but the wise audience member would do well to train his eyes on Edna Parker Watson—an international sensation who announces herself in *City of Girls* as a star whose big day in America has finally come.

Later in Act 1, Lucky Bobby is trying to convince Mrs. Alabaster to pawn her valuables in order to finance the speakeasy.

"I can't sell this watch!" she exclaims, holding up a large gold watch on a handsome chain. "I got this for my husband!"

"Good trade, lady." My boyfriend nods approvingly.

Edna and Anthony were hitting their punch lines like badminton birdies right over the footlights—and they did not miss a single shot.

"But my father taught me never to lie, cheat, or steal!" says Mrs. Alabaster.

"So did mine!" Lucky Bobby puts his hand over his heart. "My pops taught me that a man's honor is all he's got in this world—*unless* you get a chance for the big score, and then it's okay to fleece your brother and sell your sister to a whorehouse."

"But only if it were a *quality* whorehouse, one hopes," says Mrs. Alabaster.

"You and me come from the same kind of people, lady!" says Lucky Bobby, and then they launch into their duet, "Our Dastardly, Bastardly Ways"—and oh, how *hard* we had fought Olive for the right to use the word "bastardly" in a song!

This was my favorite moment of the show. Anthony had a tap-dance solo in the middle of the number, during which he lit up the place like an emergency flare. I can still see his predatory grin in that spotlight, dancing as though he aimed to tear a hole through the stage. The audience—the handpicked cream of New York City theatergoing society—was stomping their feet along with him like a bunch of apple-knockers. I felt like my own heart was going to explode. *They loved him.* Then, somewhere underneath my joy at his success, I felt a pinch of dread: *This guy is about to become a star, and I am about to lose him.*

But when the number was over, and Anthony rushed backstage, he tackled me in his sweaty costume, pushed me up against a wall, and kissed me with all his might and glory—and I forgot, for just a moment there, about my fears.

"I'm the *best*," he growled. "Did you see that out there, baby? I'm the best. I'm the *best* there ever was!"

"You are, you are! You are the very best there ever was!" I cried, for that is what twenty-year-old girls say to their boyfriends when they are desperately in love.

(To be fair to both Anthony and me, though, he *was* pretty damn electrifying.)

Then Celia did her striptease—singing plaintively in that gruff Bronx accent of hers about how bad she wanted to have a baby—and she had the audience simply *netted*. She somehow managed to look adorable and pornographic at the same time, which is not easily done. By the end of her dance, the audience was hooting and hollering like drunks at a burlesque show. And it wasn't just the men who had hot pants for her, either; I swear I heard some female voices in the cheers.

Then there was the pleasant hum of intermission—the men lighting cigarettes in the lobby, and the press of satiny women in the bathroom. Billy told me to go out and mingle among the crowd, to get a feeling for their reactions. "I would do it myself," he said, "but too many of them know me. I don't want their polite reactions; I want their real reactions. Look for *real* reactions."

"What am I looking for?" I asked.

"If they're talking about the play, that's good. If they're talking about where they parked their cars, that's bad. But mostly, watch for signs of pride. When an audience is happy with what they're watching, they always look so goddamn proud of themselves. As if they made the play themselves, the selfish bastards. Go out there and tell me if they're looking proud of themselves."

I pushed my way through the crowd and examined the happy, rosy faces all around me. Everyone looked rich, well fed, and deeply satisfied. They were chattering nonstop about the play—about Celia's figure, about

221

Edna's charm, about the dancers, about the songs. They were repeating bits of jokes to each other, and making each other laugh all over again.

"I've never seen so many people looking so proud of themselves," I reported back to Billy.

"Good," he said. "They damn well should be."

He gave another speech to the cast before the second curtain—a shorter speech this time.

"The only thing that matters now is what you leave 'em with," he said. "If you drop this thing in the middle of the second act, they'll forget that they ever loved you. You've gotta earn it all over again now. When you hit that finale, it can't just be good; it's got to be *stupendous*. Keep it zinging, kids."

Act 2, scene 1: The law-and-order mayor has come to Mrs. Alabaster's mansion, intent on shutting down the illegal gambling operation and bordello she is reputed to now be running. He comes in disguise, but Lucky Bobby is onto him, and gives warning. The showgirls quickly put maids' costumes over their spangled leotards, and the croupiers disguise themselves as butlers. The customers pretend to be visiting the mansion for a garden tour, and lace tablecloths are thrown over the gambling tables. Mr. Herbert, as the blind pickpocket, politely takes the mayor's coat and then helps himself to the man's wallet. Mrs. Alabaster invites the mayor to join her for a spot of tea in the solarium, discreetly dropping a stack of gambling chips down her bodice in the process.

"You've got yourself a pretty high-grade house here, Mrs. Alabaster," says the mayor while peering around the place, looking for signs of illegal activity. "Real fancy-like. Did your family come over on the *Mayflower*, or something?"

"Dear me, no," says Edna in her highest-tone accent while fanning herself elegantly with a deck of poker cards. "My family always had their own boats."

Toward the end of the show, when Edna sang her heartbreaking ballad, "I'm Considering Falling in Love," the theater was so silent it could have been empty. And when she finished the last wistful note, they got up out of their seats and cheered for her. They made Edna return to the stage for *four bows* after that song, before the play could continue. I'd heard the word "showstopper" before but had never really understood what it meant in actual practice.

Edna Parker Watson had literally stopped the show.

When it came time for the big-finish number of "Let's Make Ours a Double," I grew annoyed and distracted by watching Arthur Watson. He was trying to keep up with the dance steps of the other cast members, and making a poor job of it. Thankfully, his awfulness didn't seem to disturb the audience too much, and you couldn't hear his tuneless singing over the orchestra. Anyway, the audience was singing and clapping along with the chorus ("Sin babies, gin babies / Come right on in, babies!"). The Lily Playhouse glittered with a sheen of pure, shared joy.

Then it was over.

Curtain calls followed—so many curtain calls. Bows and more bows. Bouquets of flowers thrown upon the stage. Then finally the houselights came up, and the audience gathered their coats and were gone like smoke.

The whole exhausted lot of us, cast and crew, wandered out on that empty stage and just stood there for a moment in the dust of what we had just created—speechless in the staggering incredulity of what we had just seen ourselves do.

From Nichols T. Flint, in the *New York Daily News:*

Playwright and director William Buell has made a sly move to cast Edna Parker Watson in such a light role. Mrs. Watson throws herself into this candy-coated but clever play with the cheerful spirit of a natural-born good sport. In so doing, she has covered herself with glory while elevating the players around her. You cannot ask for a more entertaining spectacle than this—not in these dark times. Go see this play and forget your troubles. Mrs. Watson reminds us why we should import more actors from London to New York—and perhaps not let them leave!

We spent the rest of the night at Sardi's, waiting for the reviews to come in and drinking ourselves half blind in the process. Needless to say, the Lily Players were not a theater group normally accustomed to waiting for reviews at Sardi's—or to getting reviews at all—but this had not been a normal show.

"It all depends on what Atkinson and Winchell say," Billy told us. "If we can nail down both the high-end praise and the low-end praise, we'll have a hit."

"I don't even know who Atkinson is," Celia said.

"Well, babycakes, as of tonight he knows who *you* are—that much I can promise you. He couldn't keep his eyes off you."

"Is he famous? Does he have money?"

"He's a newspaperman. He's got no money. He's got nothing but power."

Then I watched a remarkable thing happen. Olive approached Billy, carrying two martinis in her hands. She offered one to him. He took it in surprise, but his surprise only deepened when she raised her glass to him in a toast.

"You've done ably well with this show, William," she said. "Very ably well."

He burst out laughing. *"Very ably well!* I will take that, coming from you, as the highest praise ever given to a director!"

Edna was the last cast member to arrive. She'd been mobbed at the stage door by admirers who wanted her autograph. She could have dodged them just by going upstairs to her apartment and waiting it out, but she'd indulged the populace with her presence. Then she must have taken a quick bath and changed clothes, because she walked in looking clean and fresh, and wearing the most expensive-looking little blue suit I'd ever seen (only expensive looking if you knew what you were looking for, which I did), with a fox stole thrown casually over one shoulder. On her arm was that good-looking idiot husband of hers, who had almost ruined our finale with his terrible dancing. He was beaming as though he were the star of the night.

"The much-praised Edna Parker Watson!" Billy cried, and we all cheered.

"Be careful, Billy," said Edna. "The praise hasn't come in yet. Arthur, darling, could you fetch me the most *icy* cocktail available?"

Arthur went wandering off in search of the bar, and I wondered if he would be smart enough to find his way back.

"You've made a wild success of things, Edna," said Peg.

"You did it all, my loves," said Edna, gazing up at both Billy and Peg. "You are the geniuses and the creators. I'm just a humble war refugee, grateful to have a job."

"I have the worst desire to get falling-down drunk just about now," said Peg. "I can't bear the wait for the notices. How do you remain so calm, Edna?"

"How do you know I'm not already falling-down drunk myself?"

"Tonight I should be sensible and mind my intake," said Peg. "No, never mind, I don't feel like it—Vivian, will you chase after Arthur and tell him to bring back about three times the number of drinks he had originally planned?"

If he can manage the math, I thought.

I headed to the bar. I was trying to wave down the bartender when a man's voice said, "Could I buy you a drink, miss?" I turned around with a flirty smile, and there was my brother, Walter.

It took me a moment to recognize him, because it was so incongruous to see him in New York City—in my world, surrounded by my people. Also, the family resemblance threw me for a loop. His face and mine were so similar that for a disorienting instant, I almost thought I'd bumped into a mirror.

What on earth was *Walter* doing here?

"You don't look too happy to see me," he said, with a careful smile.

I didn't know if I was happy or unhappy; I was just tremendously disoriented. All I could think was that I must be in trouble. Maybe my parents had gotten wind of my immoral behavior and sent my big brother to retrieve me. I found myself glancing over Walter's shoulder to see if my parents were with him, which definitely would have signaled the end of a good time.

"Don't be so jumpy, Vee," he said. "It's just me." It was as if he could read my mind. Which didn't serve to relax me any further. "I came by to see your little play. I liked it. You kids did a fine job."

"But why are you in New York City at all, Walter?" I was suddenly aware that my dress was revealing too much cleavage and that there was a hickey remnant on my neck.

"I quit school, Vee."

"You quit *Princeton*?"

"Yes, I did."

"Does Dad know?"

"Yes, he does."

None of this made any sense. I was the delinquent member of the family, not Walter. But now he had dropped out of Princeton? I suddenly got a vision of Walter breaking wild—throwing away all his years of good behavior to come to New York to join me in a carnival of drinking, carousing, and dancing himself to smithereens at the Stork Club. Maybe I'd inspired him to be bad!

"I'm joining the Navy," he said.

Ah. I should've known better.

"I start Officer Candidate School in three weeks, Vee. I'll be in training right here in New York City, just up the river, on the Upper West Side. The Navy's got a decommissioned battleship moored on the Hudson and they're using it as a school. Right now, they're short of officers, and they'll take anyone with two years of college. They'll train us in just three months, Vee. I start right after Christmas. When I graduate, I'll be an ensign. I'll ship out in the spring and go wherever they need to send me."

"What does Dad have to say about you quitting Princeton?" I asked.

My voice sounded weird and stilted in my ears. The awkwardness of this encounter was still throwing me off, but I was doing my best to make conversation, pretending as though everything was perfectly normal—pretending as though Walter and I chatted with each other at Sardi's every week.

"He hates it like gum," Walter said. "But it's not his call to make. I'm of age, and I can make my own choices. I called Peg and told her I was coming to the city. She said I could stay with her for a few weeks before OCS training begins. See a bit of New York, take in the sights."

Walter would be staying at the Lily? With us *degenerates*?

"But you didn't have to join the Navy," I said dumbly.

(To my mind, Angela, the only people who became sailors were working-class kids with no other options for advancement. I think I'd even heard my father say that, at some point.)

"There's a war on, Vee," said Walter. "America will be part of it sooner or later."

"But *you* don't have to be part of it," I said.

He looked at me with an expression that was both puzzled and disapproving. "It's my country, Vee. Of course I have to be part of it."

There was a wild cheer from the other side of the room. A newsboy had just walked in with a handful of early editions.

The raves were already coming in.

A nd look here, Angela, I've saved my favorite for last.
From Kit Yardley, in the *New York Sun*, November 30, 1940:

It is well worth seeing *City of Girls*, if only to enjoy Edna Parker Watson's costumes—which are delectable, from stem to stern.

SEVENTEEN

We had a hit on our hands.

Within the space of a week, we'd gone from begging people to come see our little play to turning them away at the gates. By Christmas, both Peg and Billy had made back all the money they'd invested, and now the shekels were really pouring in—or so Billy said.

You might have thought that with the success of our show, tensions would have tamped down between Peg and Olive and Billy, but it was not the case. Even with all the accolades and the sold-out house every night, Olive still managed to be anxious about money (her brief experiment with celebration apparently having ended the day after opening night).

Olive's concern—as she diligently reminded us every day—was that success is always fleeting. It is all well and good, she said, to have *City of Girls* bankrolling us now, but what will the Lily Playhouse do when the play closes? We had lost our neighborhood audience. The working-class folks whom we'd humbly entertained for so many years had been driven away by our new high ticket prices and our cosmopolitan comedy—and how could we be sure they would return once we went back to business as usual? Because certainly we *would* be getting back to business as usual sooner or later. It wasn't as though Billy would stay in New York forever, nor had he promised to write us any more hit shows. And once Edna was lured to a better theater company for a new production—which was bound to happen eventually—we would lose *City of Girls.* We couldn't very well expect somebody of Edna's prestige to stay in our slipshod little playhouse forever. And we couldn't afford to attract other actors of her caliber once she left. Really, all this abundance had been built on the talents of one woman alone, and that's an awfully shaky way to run a business.

And on and on it went from Olive—day after day. So much gloom. So much doom. She was a tireless Cassandra, constantly reminding us that ruin was right around the corner, even as we were all intoxicated with victory.

"Be careful, Olive," said Billy. "Make sure you don't enjoy a *minute* of this good fortune—and don't let anyone else enjoy it, either."

But even I could see that Olive was correct about one thing: our ongoing success with the show was all due to Edna, who never stopped being extraordinary. I watched that play every night, and I can report that she somehow managed to reinvent the role of Mrs. Alabaster each time. Some actors will get a character right and then freeze the performance, just repeating the same rote expressions and reactions. But Edna's Mrs. Alabaster never stopped feeling new. She was not delivering her lines, she was *inventing* them—or so it seemed. And because she was always playing with her delivery and changing the tone, the other players had to stay attentive and vibrant, too.

And New York City certainly rewarded Edna for her gifts.

Edna had been an actress forever, but with the wild success of *City of Girls,* she now became a star.

The term "star," Angela, is a vital but tricky designation that can only be bestowed upon a performer by the populace itself. Critics cannot make someone a star. Box-office receipts cannot make someone a star. Mere excellence cannot make someone a star. What makes someone a star is when the people decide to love you en masse. When people are willing to line up at the stage door for hours after a show just to catch a glimpse—that makes you a star. When Judy Garland releases a recording of "I'm Considering Falling in Love" but everyone who saw *City of Girls* says that your version was better—*that* makes you a star. When Walter Winchell starts writing gossip about you in his column every week, that makes you a star.

Then there was the table that came to be held for her at Sardi's every night after the show.

Then there was the announcement that Helena Rubinstein was naming an eye shadow after her ("Edna's Alabaster").

Then there was the thousand-word piece in *Woman's Day* about where Edna Parker Watson buys her hats.

Then there were the fans, deluging Edna with letters, asking questions like "My own attempt at a career on the stage was interrupted by the financial reversals of my husband—so would you consider taking me on as your protégée? I believe you will be surprised to find out that we have much the same style of acting."

And then there was this incredible (and very out of character) letter, from none less than Katharine Hepburn herself: "Darlingest Edna—I have just seen your performance, and it drove me insane, and of course I shall have to come and see it about four more times, and then I will jump in a river, because I shall *never* be as good as you!"

I know about all these letters because Edna asked me to read and respond to them for her, since I had such nice handwriting. This was an easy job for me, now that I didn't have any new costumes to design. Given that the Lily was running the same production now, week after week, there was no further need for my talents. Aside from mending and maintenance, my duties were over. For that reason, in the wake of our show's success, I more or less became Edna's private secretary.

I was the one who turned down all the invitations and pleas. I was the one who arranged the *Vogue* photo shoot. I was the one who gave a reporter from *Time* a tour of the Lily for an article called "How to Make a Hit." And I was the one who escorted around that terrifyingly acerbic theater critic Alexander Woollcott, when he profiled Edna for *The New Yorker*. We were all worried that he would savage Edna in print ("Alec never takes a nibble out of somebody when a chomp will do," said Peg), but we needn't have been concerned, as it turned out. For here was Woollcott on Watson:

Edna Parker Watson possesses the face of a woman who has lived her life in a state of upward dreaming. Enough of those dreams have come true, it appears, to have kept her forehead unlined by worry or sorrow, and her eyes are bright with the expectation of more good news to come. . . . What this actress now possesses is something beyond mere sincerity of feeling; she has an inexhaustible catalogue of *humanness* at her disposal. . . . Too spirited an artist to limit herself to Shakespeare and Shaw, she has recently donated her talents to *City of Girls*—the most dizzy-headed and heel-kicking show we have seen in New York for quite some time. . . . To watch her become Mrs. Alabaster is to watch comedy transmogrify into art. . . . When a breathless fan at the stage door thanked her for coming to New York City at last, Mrs. Watson replied, "Well, my dear, it is not as though I have *so* many claims on my time just now." If Broadway is wise, that situation shall soon be remedied.

———

Anthony was becoming a bit of a star, too, thanks to *City of Girls*. He'd got cast in some radio dramas, which he could record in the afternoons without interfering with his performance schedule. He'd also been hired as the new spokesman and model for the Miles Tobacco Company ("Why sweat, when you can smoke?"). So he had good money coming in now, for the first time in his life. But he still hadn't upgraded his living arrangements.

I'd started leaning on Anthony, trying to convince him to get his own place. Why would such a promising young star still be sharing quarters with his brother in a dank old tenement building that smelled of cooking oil and onions? I was pushing him to rent a nicer apartment, with an elevator and a doorman, and maybe even a garden in the back—and definitely not in Hell's Kitchen. But he wouldn't consider it. I don't know why he so resisted moving out of that filthy fourth-floor walk-up. All I can guess is that he suspected me of trying to make him look more *marriageable*.

Which was, of course, exactly what I was doing.

The problem was that my brother had now met Anthony—and needless to say, he did not approve.

If only there was a way to hide from Walter the fact I was dating Anthony Roccella at all! But Anthony and I were pretty obvious in our lust, and my brother was far too observant to have missed it. Plus, since Walter was now staying at the Lily, he was easily able to see what was going on in my life. He saw it all—the drinking, the back-and-forth flirtations, the rowdy repartee, the general depravity of theater folk. I'd hoped that Walter might get pulled into the fun (certainly the showgirls tried to lure my handsome brother into their embraces many times), but he was far too straitlaced to take the bait of pleasure. Sure, he'd have a cocktail or two, but he wasn't about to *cavort*. Instead of joining us, he seemed to monitor us.

I could have asked Anthony to tone down his carnal attentions to me so as not to stir up Walter's disfavor, but Anthony wasn't the sort of guy who was going to change his behavior to make anybody feel more comfortable. So my boyfriend still grabbed me, kissed me, and slapped my bottom just as much as ever—whether Walter was in the room or not.

My brother watched, judged, and then finally delivered this condemning analysis of my boyfriend: "Anthony doesn't seem very marriageable, Vee."

And now I couldn't get that weighty word—*marriageable*—out of my mind. I should say that I had never before even thought of marrying Anthony, nor was I sure that I would ever want to. But suddenly, with Walter's disapproval hanging over my head, it mattered that my boyfriend wasn't seen as *marriageable*. I felt insulted by the word, and maybe a little challenged by it. I felt that I should take this problem on and solve it.

You know—clean up my man a bit.

With this in mind, I had started making suggestions to Anthony—not too subtly, I'm afraid—about how he could boost his status in the world. Wouldn't he feel more grown-up if he didn't sleep on a couch? Wouldn't he be more attractive if he wore slightly less oil in his hair? Wouldn't he seem more refined if he wasn't always chewing gum? How about if his speech was somewhat less slangy? For instance, when my brother, Walter, had asked Anthony if he held any career aspirations outside of show business, Anthony had grinned, and said, "Not so's you'd notice." Might there have been a more cultivated way to answer this question?

Anthony knew exactly what I was doing—he was no dummy—and he hated it. He accused me of trying to get him to "turn square" in order to make my brother happy, and he wasn't having it. And it certainly didn't endear him to Walter.

In those few weeks Walter stayed at the Lily, the tension between my brother and my boyfriend grew so thick you could have busted it up with a sledgehammer. It was an issue of class, an issue of education, an issue of sexual threat, an issue of brother versus lover. But some of it, too, I suspect, was just a matter of unfettered, competitive young maleness. They each had a lot of pride and a lot of machismo, which made every room in New York City too small for the both of them.

Finally it all came to a head one night when a group of us had gone out for drinks at Sardi's after the show. Anthony had been manhandling me at the bar (to my delight and pleasure, of course) when he caught Walter giving him the stink-eye. Next thing I knew, the two young men were chest to chest.

"You want me to back outta this deal with your sister, dontcha?" Anthony demanded, pushing a little farther into Walter's space. "Well, just you try to make me do it, captain."

The way Anthony was grinning at Walter in that moment—leering, really—had an unmistakable edge of threat. For the first time, I could see the Hell's Kitchen street fighter in my boyfriend. It was also the first time I'd ever seen Anthony look like he cared about something. And in that moment, what he cared about was not me—but the pleasure of punching my brother in the face.

Walter held Anthony's gaze without blinking and replied in a low tone, "If you're trying to take a crack at me, son, don't do it with words."

I watched Anthony size up my brother—taking note of the football shoulders and the wrestling neck—and think better of it. Anthony dropped his eyes and backed down. He gave a careless laugh and said, "We got no beef here, captain. You're all right, you're all right."

Then he slid back into his customary air of nonchalance and stepped away.

Anthony had made the right call. My brother, Walter, was many things (an elitist, a puritan, and uptight as all hell), but he was not a weakling and he was not a coward.

My brother could've pounded my boyfriend straight into the pavement.

Anyone could see that.

The next day, Walter took me out to lunch at the Colony so that we could "have a talk."

I knew exactly what (or, rather, *whom*) this talk was going to be about, and I dreaded it.

"Please don't tell Mother and Dad about Anthony," I asked Walter as soon as we sat down at our table. I hated to even bring up the subject of my boyfriend, but I knew that Walter would, and I figured my best bet was to start off with a plea for my life. My biggest fear was that he was going to report my misdoings to my parents, and that they would barrel right down upon me and clip my wings.

It took awhile for him to answer.

"I want to be fair about this, Vee," he said.

Of course he did. Walter always wanted to be fair.

I waited, feeling the way I often did with Walter—like a child who has just been called before the headmaster. God, how I wished he was my ally! But he had never been. Even as a boy, he'd never kept a secret for me or conspired with me against the adults. He'd always been an extension of my parents. He'd always behaved more like a father than a peer. Moreover, I'd treated him as such.

Finally he said, "You can't fool around like this forever, you know."

"Oh, I know," I said—although my actual plan, in point of fact, was to fool around like this forever.

"There's a real world out there, Vee. You're going to have to put away the balloons and streamers at some point and grow up."

"Without a doubt," I agreed.

"You were raised right. I have to trust in that. When the time comes, your breeding will kick in. You're playing the bohemian now, but eventually you'll settle down and marry the correct kind of person."

"Of course I will." I nodded as though this were my plan precisely.

"If I didn't believe that you had good sense, I would send you back home to Clinton right now."

"I don't blame you!" I cried, in fullest agreement. "If I didn't believe that I had good sense, I would send *myself* back home to Clinton right now."

Which didn't particularly make sense, but seemed to mollify him. I knew my brother well enough, thank God, to know that my only hope for salvation was to agree with him completely.

"It's kind of like when I went to Delaware," he said, softening a bit, after another long silence.

This stopped me up. *Delaware?* Then I remembered that my brother had spent a few weeks the previous summer in Delaware. He'd been working at a power plant, if I recalled, learning something about electrical engineering.

"Of course!" I said. "Delaware!" I wanted to encourage this positive-sounding track—although I had no idea what he was referring to.

"Some of the people I spent time with in Delaware were pretty rough," he said. "But you know how that is. Sometimes you want to rub elbows with people who weren't raised the same way as you. Expand your horizons. Maybe it builds character."

Well, *that* was pretentious.

Encouragingly, though, he smiled.

I smiled, too. I tried to look like someone who was busy expanding her horizons and building her character through intentional fraternization with her social inferiors. A difficult look to master in a single facial expression, but I did my best.

"You're just having your kicks," he decided, sounding as though he were *almost* convinced of this diagnosis himself. "It's innocent enough."

"That's right, Walter. I'm just having my kicks. You don't have to worry about me."

His face darkened. I'd made a tactical error; I had contradicted him.

"Well, I *do* have to worry about you, Vee, because I'm starting Officer Candidate School in a few days. I'll be moving to the battleship uptown, and I won't be around to keep an eye on you anymore."

Hallelujah, I thought, while nodding gravely.

"I don't like the direction I see your life heading in," he said. "That's what I wanted to tell you today. I don't like it at all."

"I can certainly understand that!" I said, going back to my original strategy of absolute accordance.

"Tell me there's nothing serious for you about this Anthony fellow."

"Nothing," I lied.

"You haven't crossed the line with him?"

I could feel myself blush. It wasn't a blush of modesty, but of guilt. Still, it worked in my favor. I must have looked like an innocent girl, embarrassed that her brother had mentioned the subject of sex— however obliquely.

Walter flushed, too. "I'm sorry I had to ask," he said, protecting my perceived guilelessness. "But I need to know."

"I understand," I said. "But I would never . . . not with that kind of guy. Not with *anybody,* Walter."

"All right, then. If you say so, I trust you. I won't say anything to

Mother and Dad about Anthony," he said. (I took my first easy breath of the day.) "But you have to promise me something."

"Anything."

"If you get into *any* trouble with this fellow, you will call me."

"I will," I swore. "But I won't get into any trouble. I promise."

Suddenly, Walter looked old. It could not have been easy, being a twenty-two-year-old elder statesman on his way to war. Trying to uphold his familial duties and his patriotic duties all at the same time.

"I know you'll end this thing with Anthony soon, Vee. Just promise me you'll be smart. I know what a smart kid you are. You wouldn't do anything reckless. You've got too good a head on your shoulders for that."

My heart broke a little in that moment—watching my brother dig so deep into his pristine imagination, desperately searching for ways to think the best of me.

EIGHTEEN

Angela, I don't want to tell you this next part of the story.
I think I've been stalling.
It's painful, this next part.
Let me stall a little while longer.
No, let me get it over with.

Now it was the end of March 1941.

It had been a long winter. New York had been hit with a murderous snowstorm earlier in the month, and it took the city weeks to dig out from under it. We were all sick of being cold. The Lily was a drafty old building, you may be amazed to learn, and the dressing rooms were better suited to storing furs than warming human beings.

We all had chilblains and cold sores. All of us girls were longing to wear our cute spring frocks and to show our figures again, instead of being mummified in overcoats, galoshes, and scarves. I'd seen some of our dancers going out on the town with long underwear under their gowns—which they furtively took off in the bathrooms of nightclubs, and then just as furtively put back on again at the end of the evening, before braving the freezing night air. Believe me, there is nothing glamorous about a girl in a silk gown and long underwear. I'd been feverishly sewing new spring clothes for myself all winter—in the irrational hope that if my wardrobe was more summery, the weather would be, too.

Finally, toward the end of the month, the weather broke and the cold spell lifted a bit.

It was one of those bright, gladdening spring days in New York that tricks you into thinking that perhaps summer has come. I hadn't been in the city long enough not to fall for the trick (never trust the month of March in New York!), and so I allowed myself to feel a burst of joy at the appearance of the sun.

It was a Monday. The theater was dark. I got an invitation in the morning mail for Edna. An organization called the Ladies British-American Protection Alliance was hosting a fund-raiser that night at the Waldorf. All proceeds would go toward lobbying efforts to convince the United States to enter the war.

Late notice as it was, the organizers wrote, would Mrs. Watson consider gracing the event with her presence? Her name would bring such prestige to the occasion. Furthermore, would Mrs. Watson be kind enough to ask her young costar Anthony Roccella if he would join her at the event? And would the pair consider singing their celebrated duet from *City of Girls,* for the entertainment of the ladies gathered?

I turned down most of Edna's invitations without even running them by her. Her demanding performance schedule made most extra-curricular socializing impossible, and right now the world wanted more of Edna's energies than she had available to share. So I almost declined this invite, too. But then I gave it a second thought. If there was any cause that Edna cared about, it was the campaign to involve the United States in the war. Many nights, I had heard her talking with Olive about just that concern. And it looked like a modest enough request—a song, a dance, a supper. So I brought the invitation to her attention.

Edna instantly decided to attend. She'd been made so stir-crazy by the dreadful winter, she said, that she welcomed the chance to go out. And of course, she would do anything for poor England! Then she asked me to call Anthony and see if he would escort her to the benefit and sing their duet with her. Somewhat, but not entirely, to my surprise, he agreed. (Anthony could not have cared less about politics—he made even *me* look like Fiorello La Guardia by comparison—but he adored Edna. If I haven't mentioned before that Anthony adored Edna, please do forgive me. It would become tedious if I had to keep up a thorough list of everyone who adored Edna Parker Watson. Just assume they all did.)

"Sure, baby, I'll haul Edna over there," he said. "We'll have a gas."

"Thank you *awfully*, darling," Edna said to me, when I confirmed that Anthony would be her date for the evening. "Together we will defeat Hitler at last, and we'll be back at home in time for bed, no less."

That should have been the end of it.

This should have been a simple interaction—an innocent decision by two popular entertainers to attend an ultimately meaningless political event, hosted by a group of well-heeled, well-intentioned Manhattan women who could do absolutely nothing about winning the war in Europe.

But that wasn't the end of it. Because as I was helping Edna to get dressed for the evening, her husband, Arthur, walked in. Arthur saw Edna putting herself together so smashingly, and asked where she was going. She told him she was dropping by the Waldorf to perform a song at a small political benefit that some ladies were putting together for England. Arthur got sulky. He reminded her that he'd wanted them to go see a movie that night. ("We only get one night off a week, blast it!") She apologized ("But it's for *England*, darling!"), and that seemed to be all there was to this little marital tiff.

But when Anthony showed up an hour later to pick up Edna, and Arthur saw the young man standing there in his tuxedo (rather overdressed, if I may say so), Arthur became angry again.

"What's this one doing here?" he asked, eyeballing Anthony with naked suspicion.

"He's escorting me to the event, darling," said Edna.

"Why is *he* escorting you to the event?"

"Because he was *invited*, darling."

"You didn't say you were going on a *date*."

"It's not a date, darling. It's an *appearance*. The ladies want me and Anthony to perform our duet for them."

"Why don't *I* get to go to the event, then, and perform a duet with you?"

"Darling, because we don't *have* a duet."

Anthony made the mistake of laughing at this, and Arthur spun around to face him again. "You think it's funny to take a man's wife to the Waldorf?"

Always the diplomat, Anthony cracked his gum and responded, "I think it's *kinda* funny."

Arthur looked like he might lunge at him, but Edna spryly leapt between the two men and placed a petite, well-manicured hand on her husband's broad chest. "Arthur, darling, keep your wits. This is a professional engagement, and nothing more."

"Professional, is it? Are you being *paid*?"

"Darling, it's a *benefit*. Nobody is being paid."

"It doesn't benefit *me*!" Arthur cried, and Anthony—once more, with his native tact—laughed.

I asked, "Edna, would you like Anthony and me to wait outside?"

"Nah, I'm pretty comfortable right here, baby," Anthony said.

"No, you may stay," Edna said to both of us. "This is nothing of concern." She turned again to her husband. The patient, loving face she'd been showing him thus far was now replaced by an icier expression. "Arthur, I'm attending this event and Anthony is escorting me. We shall sing our duet for some harmless, pewter-haired old ladies, raise a spot of money for England, and I'll see you when I get home."

"I've about reached my limit with this!" he cried. "It's not enough that every newspaper in New York forgets I'm your husband, but now you forget it, too? You're not going, I say. I refuse!"

"Get a load of this guy," said Anthony helpfully.

"Get a load of *you*," retorted Arthur. "You look like a waiter in that tuxedo!"

Anthony shrugged. "I *am* a waiter, sometimes. At least I don't need my woman to buy my clothes for me."

"You get out of here right now!" Arthur shouted at Anthony.

"No dice, pal. The lady invited me. She decides."

"My wife goes *nowhere* without me!" said Arthur—somewhat ridiculously, because as I had witnessed over the past several months, she went to *many* places without him.

"You ain't in charge of her, bud," said Anthony.

"Anthony, please," I said, moving forward and putting my hand on his arm. "Let's step outside. There's no reason for us to be involved in this."

"And *you* ain't in charge of *me*, sister," Anthony said, shaking off my hand and throwing me a vicious look.

I recoiled as though I'd been kicked. He'd never snapped at me before.

Edna looked at each of us in turn.

"You're all infants," she pronounced mildly. Then she threw another rope of pearls around her neck, and collected her hat, her gloves, and her handbag. "Arthur, I'll see you at ten o'clock."

"No, you bloody well *won't!*" he shouted. "I won't be here! How will you like *that*, I wonder?"

She ignored him.

"Vivian, thank you for your assistance in dressing me," she said. "Enjoy your evening off. Anthony, come."

And Edna walked out with my boyfriend, leaving me alone with her husband—both of us shaken and cowed.

I honestly think that if Anthony had not snarled at me, I would have brushed off this entire incident, dismissing it as a meaningless squabble between Edna and her childish, jealous husband. I would have seen it for what it was: a problem that had nothing whatsoever to do with me. I probably would have left the room immediately and gone out for drinks with Peg and Billy.

But Anthony's reaction had shocked me, and I was rooted where I stood. What had I done to deserve such vitriol? *You ain't in charge of me, sister!* What had he meant by *that?* When had I ever tried to be in charge of Anthony? (Aside from constantly urging him to move to a new apartment, that is. And wanting him to dress and speak differently. And encouraging him to stop using so much slang. And asking him to style his hair in a more conservative manner. And trying to convince him to stop chewing gum all the time. And arguing with him whenever I saw him flirting with a dancer. But apart from that? Why, I gave the boy nothing *but* freedom.)

"That woman is destroying me," Arthur said, a few moments after Edna and Anthony had left. "She is a *destroyer* of men."

"I'm sorry?" I asked, once I'd found my voice.

"You should keep an eye on that greasy mutt of yours, if you like him. She'll make a meal out of him. She likes them young."

Again—if it hadn't been for Anthony's flare-up, I would not have paid attention to a word that Arthur Watson was saying. The world, as a collective habit, never paid attention to a word that Arthur Watson said. I should have known better.

"Oh, she wouldn't . . ." I didn't even know how to finish that sentence.

"Oh, yes she would," said Arthur. "You can be sure of it. She always does. You can be *sure* of it. She already *is,* you blind little ninny."

A cloud of black particles seemed to pass over my eyes.

Edna and *Anthony?*

I felt dizzy, and I reached for the chair behind me.

"I'm going out," Arthur declared. "Where's Celia?"

This question made no sense to me. What did Celia have to do with anything?

"Where's *Celia?*" I repeated.

"Is she in your room?"

"Probably."

"Let's bloody well go get her, then. We're clearing out of here. Come on, Vivian. Get your things."

And what did I do?

I followed that fool.

And why did I follow that fool?

Because I was an idiotic child, Angela, and at that age, I would have followed a stop sign.

So this is how it ended up that I spent that beautiful false-spring evening going out on the town with Celia Ray and Arthur Watson.

But not only with Celia and Arthur, as it turned out. We also shared the night with Celia's unlikely new pals—Brenda Frazier and Shipwreck Kelly.

Angela, you've probably never heard of Brenda Frazier and Shipwreck Kelly. At least I hope you haven't. They got far too much attention as it was, back when they were young and famous. They were a celebrated couple for a few minutes back in 1941. Brenda was an heiress and a debutante; Shipwreck was a star football player. The tabloids followed them everywhere. Walter Winchell invented the obnoxious word "celebutante" to describe Brenda.

If you're wondering what these sophisticates were doing hanging around my friend Celia Ray, so was I. But pretty soon into that evening, I figured it all out. Apparently New York's most famous couple had seen *City of Girls,* loved it, and had adopted Celia as their little accessory—much the same way they bought convertible cars and diamond necklaces on a whim. Evidently, they'd been gamboling about with each other for weeks. I'd missed all this, of course, because I was so entangled with Anthony. But it seemed Celia had found herself some new best friends, when I wasn't paying attention.

Not that I was jealous, of course.

I mean—not so's you'd notice.

We drove around that evening in Shipwreck Kelly's opulent, cream-colored, custom-made convertible Packard. Shipwreck drove, Brenda was in the passenger seat, and Arthur and Celia and I sat in the back. Celia was in the middle.

I disliked Brenda Frazier instantly. She was rumored to be the richest girl in the world—so just imagine how fascinating and intimidating I found that, will you? How does the richest girl in the world *dress?* I couldn't stop staring at her, to try to figure it all out—captivated by her, even as I was actively disliking her.

Brenda was a very pretty brunette, dressed in a pile of mink, wearing on her hand a diamond engagement ring approximately the size of a suppository. Underneath all those dead minks was a fairly staggering amount of black taffeta and bows. It looked as though she were going to a ball, or had just come from one. She had an overpowdered white face and bright red lips. Her tresses were styled in lush billows, and she was wearing a little black tricorn hat with a simple veil (the kind of thing that Edna used to disparagingly call "Tiny Bird's Nest Teetering Precariously on a Giant Mountain of Hair"). I didn't exactly embrace her style, but I had to hand it to her: she sure looked rich. Brenda didn't say much, but when she did speak, she had a starchy finishing school accent that grated on me. She kept trying to convince Shipwreck to put up the roof of the car, because the breeze was ruining her hairstyle. She didn't seem like fun.

I didn't like Shipwreck Kelly, either. I didn't like his nickname, and I didn't like his red, jowly cheeks. I didn't like his boisterous teasing. He was the kind of man who slaps you on the back. I have never liked a backslapper.

I *really* didn't like the fact that both Brenda and Shipwreck seemed to know Celia and Arthur so well. By which I mean—they seemed to know Celia and Arthur in tandem. As though Celia and Arthur were a couple. This was immediately evidenced by Shipwreck hollering to the backseat of the car: "You kids wanna go to that place in Harlem again?"

"We don't want to go to Harlem tonight," said Celia. "It's too cold."

"Well, you know what they say about the month of March!" said Arthur. "In like a lion, out like a lamb."

Idiot.

I couldn't help but notice that Arthur was in an awfully gladsome mood suddenly, with his arm securely around Celia.

Why did he have his arm securely around Celia?

What the hell was going on here?

"Let's just go to the Street," said Brenda. "I'm too cold to drive all the way to Harlem with the top down."

She meant Fifty-second Street, which everyone knew. Swing Street. Jazz Central.

"Jimmy Ryan's or the Famous Door? Or the Spotlite?" asked Shipwreck.

"The Spotlite," said Celia. "Louis Prima's playing."

And so it was decided. We drove that ridiculously expensive car a mere eleven blocks—which gave everyone in midtown enough time to see us and to spread the news that Brenda Frazier and Shipwreck Kelly were heading toward Fifty-second Street in their convertible Packard, which meant that there were a number of photographers waiting to snap photos of us as soon as we stepped out onto the curb in front of the nightclub.

(That part, I must admit, I enjoyed.)

I was drunk in a matter of minutes. If you think waiters back then were quick to bring cocktails to girls like Celia and me, you should've seen how fast drinks landed in front of the likes of Brenda Frazier.

I hadn't eaten dinner, and I was emotional from my fight with Anthony. (In my mind, it was the worst conflagration of modern times, and I'd been all but undone by it.) The alcohol went right to my head. The band was clobbering away, loud and hard. By the time Louis Prima came over to pay his respects to our table, I was blotto. I couldn't have cared less about meeting Louis Prima.

"What's going on between you and Arthur?" I asked Celia.

"Nothing that matters," she said.

"Are you fooling around with him?"

She shrugged.

"Don't you stonewall me, Celia!"

I watched her weigh her options, and then settle on the truth.

"Confidentially? Yeah. He's a bum, but yeah."

"But Celia, he's *married*. He's married to *Edna*." I said this a little too loud, and several people—who cared who?—turned to look at us.

"Let's go outside and get some air, just me and you," Celia said.

Moments later, we were standing in the frigid March wind. I didn't have a coat. This was not a warm spring day, after all. I'd even been duped by the weather. I'd been duped by *everything*.

"But what about Edna?" I asked.

"What about her?"

"She loves him."

"She loves young bucks, anyhow. She always has one on the side. A new one for every play. That's what he told me."

Young bucks. Young bucks like Anthony.

Seeing my face, Celia said, "Think smart! You think that marriage of theirs is legit? You don't think Edna is still in circulation? A big star like her, controlling all the money? Popular like she is? You think she sits around waiting for that hambone of hers to come home? I should hardly think so! It's not like she won the sweepstakes with that guy, anyway, cute as he is. So he doesn't sit around waiting for her, either. They're *continental*, Vivvie. That's how everyone does it over there."

"Over where?" I asked.

"Europe" was her full answer, as she vaguely waved toward a huge and distant place where all the rules were different.

I felt shocked past all reason. For months, I had suffered from petty envy whenever Anthony flirted with the cute little dancers, but it had never occurred to me to be suspicious of Edna. Edna Parker Watson was my friend—and moreover, she was *old*. Why would she take my Anthony? Why would he take her? And what would happen now to my precious drumbeat of love? My mind bent in sickening twists of hurt and worry. How could I have been so far off the mark about Edna? And about Anthony? I'd never seen the faintest sign of it. And how had I not noticed that my friend was sleeping with Arthur Watson? Why hadn't she told me earlier?

Then I had a flash of Peg and Olive dancing in the living room that night to "Stardust," and remembered how shocked I'd been. What *else* did I not know? When would I stop being surprised by people and their lust, and their sordid secrets?

Edna had called me an infant.

I felt like one.

"Ah, Vivvie, don't be a goose," Celia said when she saw my face. She pulled me into her long arms for a hug. Just when I was about to collapse into her bosom and unleash a river of fretful, drunken, pathetic tears, I heard a familiar and annoying voice at my side.

"I thought I'd pay a call on you two," said Arthur Watson. "If I'm going to squire two beauties like this around town, I can't leave you unattended, now, can I?"

I started to pull away from Celia's embrace, but Arthur said, "Say now, Vivian. No need to stop what you were doing just because I'm here."

He put his arms around both of us at the same time. Now our embrace was completely contained within his. We were tall women, but Arthur was a large and athletic man—and he easily got the two of us in quite a strong clasp. Celia laughed, and Arthur laughed, too.

"That's better," he murmured into my hair. "Isn't that better?"

In point of fact, something about it *was* better.

A good deal better.

For one thing, it was warm in their arms. I'd been freezing out there, standing on Fifty-second Street in the icy wind without a coat. The cold was pinching at my feet and hands. (Or maybe—poor me—all the blood had flowed to my lacerated, broken heart!) But now I was warm, or at least partially so. One side of me was pressed against

Arthur's monumentally dense body, and the front of me was glued to Celia's outrageously soft chest. My face was pressed into her familiar-smelling neck. I felt her move, as she lifted her face to Arthur and began kissing him.

Once I realized that they were kissing, I made a tiny effort—merely out of propriety—to remove myself from their embrace. But only a tiny effort. It was awfully cozy in there, and they felt good.

"Vivvie is a sad little kitten tonight," said Celia to Arthur, after they had kissed with considerable passion for a good long while, right in my ear.

"Who's a sad little kitten?" said Arthur. "This one?"

And then he kissed *me*—without letting go of either of us.

Now, this was a peculiar line of conduct.

I'd kissed Celia's boyfriends before, but not with her face an inch away from mine. And this wasn't just any random boyfriend—this was Arthur Watson, whom I rather detested. And whose wife I very much loved. But whose wife was right now quite likely having sex with my boyfriend—and if Anthony were using his talented mouth right now, doing to *Edna* what he could do to me . . .

I couldn't bear it.

I felt a sob rising in my throat. I pulled my mouth away from Arthur's to catch my breath, and in the next instant, Celia's lips were on mine.

"Now you're getting the idea," Arthur said.

In all my months of sensual adventures, I'd never yet kissed a girl—nor had I thought to. You'd think by this point in my journey I would have stopped being so easily surprised by the twists and vagaries of life—but Celia's kiss astonished me. Then it kept on astonishing me, as she dug in only deeper.

My first impression was that kissing Celia felt like such a frightful *extravagance*. There was so *much* to her. So much softness. So much in the way of lips. So much in the way of heat. Everything about her was pillowy and absorbing. Between Celia's enormously soft mouth, and the abundance of her breasts, and the familiar flowery smell of her—I felt subsumed by it all. It was nothing like kissing a man—not even like kissing Anthony, who knew how to kiss with rare tenderness. Even the gentlest kiss from a man would be rough compared to this experience with Celia's lips. This was velvet quicksand. I could not pull myself away from *this*. Who in their right mind would want to?

For a dreamy thousand years or so, I stood there under that streetlamp, letting her kiss me, and kissing her back. Gazing into each other's oh-so-beautiful and oh-so-similar eyes, kissing each other's oh-so-lovely and oh-so-similar lips, Celia Ray and I had finally reached the absolute zenith of our complete and mutual narcissism.

Then Arthur broke the trance.

"All right girls, I hate to interrupt, but it's time for us to nip on out of here and head to a nice hotel I know," he said.

He was grinning like a man who'd just won the trifecta, which I suppose he had done.

I t's not all it's cracked up to be, Angela.

I know that this would be a fantasy for many women—to find yourself in a big bed in a fancy hotel room with both a handsome man and a beautiful girl available for your enjoyment. But from a matter of sheer logistics, I quickly discovered that three people engaging in sexual exploits at the same time can be both a problematic and arduous situation. One never quite knows where to put one's attention, you see. There are so many limbs to organize! There can be a great deal of: *Oh, pardon me, I didn't see you there.* And just when you're getting settled into something nice, somebody new shows up to interrupt you. One also never quite knows when it is over. Just when you think you're done with your pleasure, you find that somebody out there isn't yet done with *theirs,* and back you go, into the fray.

Then again, maybe this triad would have been more satisfying if the man in question hadn't been Arthur Watson. He was practiced and vigorous in the sport of copulation, to be sure, but he was exactly as off-putting in bed as he was in the world—and for the same reasons. He was always looking at or thinking about himself, which was irritating. My sense was that Arthur had a deep and penetrating appreciation for his own physique, and thus he liked to arrange himself into tableaux that brought maximum attention to his own musculature and handsomeness. Never once did I get the feeling that he had stopped posing for us or admiring himself. (And imagine that ridiculousness, if you would! Imagine being in bed with the likes of Celia Ray and a twenty-year-old version of *me*—and not paying attention to anything but your own body! What a dumb man!)

As for Celia, I didn't know what to do with her. She was too much for me to manage—volcanic in her raptures, and labyrinthine in the secrets of her needs. She was forked lightning. I felt like I'd never met her before. Yes, I'd been sleeping and cuddling with Celia in the same bed for almost a year—but this was a very different kind of bed, and a very different kind of Celia. This Celia was a country I'd never visited, a language I could not speak. I could not find my *friend* hidden anywhere in this dark stranger of a woman, whose eyes never opened, and whose body never stopped moving—driven, it seemed, by some ferocious sexual incubus that was equal parts fever and wrath.

In the midst of all this—in fact, right at the white-hot center of it—I had never felt more lost or lonely.

I must say, Angela, that I had *almost* backed out of this arrangement at the door of the hotel room. Almost. But then I'd remembered the promise I'd made to myself months ago—that I would never again excuse myself from participating in something dangerous that Celia Ray was doing.

If she were engaged in wildness, then I would be, too.

While this promise now seemed stale and even confusing to me (so much had changed in the past few months, so why did it even matter to me anymore, to keep up with my friend's exploits?), I stuck with my vow anyway. I hung right in there. With no small amount of irony, I can say: consider it an expression of my immature honor.

I probably had other motives, as well.

I could still feel Anthony shoving my hand away from his arm, and saying that I wasn't in charge of him. Calling me *sister*, in that contemptuous tone.

I could still hear Celia talking about Edna and Arthur's marital arrangement—"They're *continental*, Vivvie"—and looking at me as if I were the most naïve and pitiable creature she'd ever encountered in all her days.

I could still hear Edna's voice, calling me an infant.

Who wants to be an infant?

So I proceeded. I rooted about that bed from one corner of the mattress to another—trying to be continental, trying not to be an *infant*—digging and pawing at Arthur and Celia's Olympian bodies for proof of something necessary about myself.

But all the while, somewhere in the only remaining corner of my brain that was not drunk or sorrowful or lusty or stupid, I perceived with unblurred clarity that this decision was going to bring me nothing but grief.

And boy, was I right.

NINETEEN

W hat befell me next is quickly told.

Eventually our activities ended. Arthur and Celia and I immediately fell asleep—or passed out. Awhile later (I had lost track of time) I got up and put on my clothes. I left the two of them sleeping in the hotel room and ran the eleven blocks home, clutching at my shaking, underdressed body, trying and failing to stay warm despite the cruel March wind.

It was well after midnight when I opened the door to the third floor of the Lily Playhouse and rushed in.

Instantly, I could see that something was wrong.

First of all, every light in the place was blazing.

Secondly, people were there—and they were all staring at me.

Olive and Peg and Billy were sitting in the living room, surrounded by a cumulus cloud of dense cigarette and pipe smoke. With them was a man I didn't recognize.

"There she is!" cried Olive, leaping up. "We've been waiting for you."

"Doesn't matter," said Peg. "It's too late." (This made no sense to me, but I didn't pay the comment much mind. I could tell by her voice that Peg was very drunk, so I didn't expect her to make sense. I was far more concerned about why Olive had been up waiting for me, and who was this strange man?)

"Hello," I said. (Because what else do you say? Always helpful to start with the preliminaries.)

"We have an emergency, Vivian," Olive said.

I could tell by how calm Olive was that something truly terrible had happened. She only became hysterical over insignificant matters. Whenever she was this composed, it had to be a real crisis.

I could only assume that somebody had died.

My parents? My brother? Anthony?

I stood there on my shaky legs, reeking of sex, waiting for the bottom to fall out of my world—which it subsequently did, but not in the manner I was expecting.

"This is Stan Weinberg," said Olive, introducing me to the stranger. "He's an old friend of Peg's."

Nice girl that I was, I made a polite move to approach the gentleman and shake his hand. But Mr. Weinberg blushed as he saw me nearing him, and turned his face away. His obvious discomfort at my presence stopped me in my tracks.

"Stan is an editor on the night desk at the *Mirror*," Olive continued, in that same disconcertingly flat tone. "He came over a few hours ago with some bad news. Stan has offered us the courtesy of letting us know that Walter Winchell will be publishing an exposé tomorrow afternoon in his column."

She looked at me plainly, as though that should explain everything.

"An exposé about what?" I asked.

"About what happened this evening between you and Arthur and Celia."

"But . . ." I stammered around a bit, and then said, "But what *did* happen?"

I promise you, Angela, I was not being coy. For a moment, I truly didn't know what had happened. It was as though I had just shown up on this scene—a stranger to myself, and a stranger to the story that was being told here. Who were these people, anyhow, that everyone was talking about? Arthur and Vivian and Celia? What did they have to do with me?

"Vivian, they've got photos."

That sobered me up.

In a panic, I thought: *There was a photographer in the hotel room?!* But then I remembered the kisses that Celia and Arthur and I had shared on Fifty-second Street. Right underneath the streetlamp. Beautifully lit. In full view of the tabloid photographers who had been crawling outside the Spotlite earlier this evening, waiting for glimpses of Brenda Frazier and Shipwreck Kelly.

We must have given them quite a show.

That's when I saw the large manila folder in Mr. Weinberg's lap. Presumably, it contained these photos. Oh, God help me.

"We've been trying to figure out how to stop this from happening, Vivian," said Olive.

"It can't be stopped." Billy spoke up for the first time—and proved by the slur in his voice that he, too, was drunk. "Edna is famous, and Arthur Watson is her husband. Which makes this *news*, girlie, fair and square. And what news it is! Here's a man—a semistar, married to a real star—caught kissing what looks like two showgirls outside a nightclub. Then we see this man—this semistar, married to a real star—checking into a hotel with not one, but *two* women not his wife. It's *news*, baby. Nothing this juicy can be stopped. Winchell dines out on this kind of ruin. Christ, that Winchell is a *reptile*! I can't bear him.

I've hated him since I knew him on the vaudeville circuit. I never should've let him come see our show. Oh, poor Edna."

Edna. The sound of her name hurt me all the way down to my bowels.

"Does Edna know?" I asked.

"Yes, Vivian," said Olive. "Edna knows. She was here when Stan arrived with the photos. She's gone to bed now."

I thought I might throw up. "And Anthony—?"

"He knows, too, Vivian. He's gone home for the evening."

Everyone knew. So there was no hope of salvation in any direction.

Olive went on, "But Anthony and Edna are the least of your worries right now, if I may say. You have a far bigger problem to contend with, Vivian. Stan has told us that you've been identified."

"Identified?"

"Yes, identified. They know who you are, at the newspaper. Somebody at the nightclub recognized you. This means that your name—your full name—will be printed in Winchell's column. My objective tonight is to stop that from happening."

Desperately, I looked at Peg—for what, I could not have said. Maybe I wanted comfort or guidance from my aunt. But Peg was leaning back on the couch with her eyes closed. I wanted to go shake her, and beg her to take care of me, to save me.

"Can't be stopped," Peg slurred again.

Stan Weinberg nodded in agreement solemnly. He didn't look up from his hands, which were clasped over the hideously innocuous manila folder. He looked like a man who operated a funeral parlor, trying to keep his dignity and reserve as he was surrounded by a collapsing, grieving family.

"We can't stop Winchell from reporting on Arthur's dalliance, no," said Olive. "And of course he will gossip about Edna, because she's a star. But Vivian is your *niece*, Peg. We cannot allow her name to be in the papers in a scandal like this. Her name is not necessary to the story. It would be ruinous for the poor girl's life. If you would just call your people at the studio, Billy, and ask them to intervene . . ."

"I've told you ten times already that the studio can't do anything about this," Billy said. "First of all, this is New York gossip, not Hollywood gossip. They don't have that kind of clout over here. And even if they *could* fix it, I can't play that card. Who do you want me to call? Zanuck himself? Wake him up at this hour, and say, 'Hey, Darryl— can you get my wife's niece out of trouble?' I might need a favor of my own from Zanuck someday. So, no, I've got no pull here. Stop being such a mother hen, Olive. Let the chips fall. It'll be ugly for a few weeks, but it will pass. It always does. Everyone will survive it. Just a little squib in the papers. What do you care?"

"I'll fix things, I promise," I said, like an idiot.

"Can't be fixed," said Billy. "And maybe for now you should keep your mouth shut. You've done enough damage for one night, girlie."

"Peg," said Olive, walking over to the couch to shake my aunt awake. "*Think*. You must have an idea. You know people."

But Peg just repeated, "Can't be stopped."

I found my way to a chair and sat down. I had done something very bad, and tomorrow it would be splashed across the gossip pages, and it could not be stopped. My family would know. My brother would know. Everyone I'd grown up with and gone to school with would know. All of New York City would know.

As Olive had said: my life would be ruined.

I hadn't tended to my life very carefully thus far, to be sure, but I still cared about it enough that I didn't want it *ruined*. No matter how recklessly I'd been behaving for the past year, I guess I'd always had a distant thought that someday I would probably clean myself up and become respectable again (that my "breeding" would kick in, as my brother had said). But this level of scandal, with this level of publicity, would preclude respectability forever.

And then there was Edna. *She already knew.* Here came another wave of nausea.

"How did Edna take it?" I dared to ask, in a hazardously shaky voice.

Olive looked at me with something like pity, but did not answer.

"How do you think she took it?" said Billy, who was not so pitying. "That woman's tough as nails, but her heart is constructed of the more typically flimsy composite materials—so, yeah, she's pretty broken up about it, Vivian. If it had been just one bimbo chomping at her husband's face, she might have been able to handle it—but two? And one of those girls was *you*? So what do you think, Vivian? How do you *think* she feels?"

I put my hands over my face.

The best thing for me to do right now, I thought, would be to never have been born.

"You're taking an awfully self-righteous position on this, William," I heard Olive say in a low, warning voice. "For a man with your particular history."

"Christ, how I hate that Winchell." Billy ignored Olive's comment. "And he hates me just as much. I think he would light a match to me if he thought he could get insurance money for it."

"Just call the studio, Billy," Olive pleaded again. "Just call them and ask them to intervene. They can do anything."

"No the studio *can't* do anything, Olive," said Billy. "Not with something as red hot as this. This is 1941, not 1931. Nobody has that kind of weight anymore. Winchell's got more power than the goddamn president. You and I can fight about this till next Christmas, but the answer will always be the same—I can't do anything to help, and the studio can't do anything to help, either."

"Can't be stopped," said Peg again, and sighed—a deep, sickly sigh.

I rocked in the chair with my eyes closed, nauseated by self-disgust and alcohol.

M inutes passed, I guess. They always do.

When next I looked up, Olive was coming back into the room wearing her coat and hat and carrying her purse. I suppose she'd stepped out for a moment, but I hadn't taken notice. Stan Weinberg had gone, leaving his horrible news behind like a stench. Peg was still slumped on the couch with her head knocked back against the upholstery, muttering something insensible every once in a while.

"Vivian," said Olive, "I need you to go change into something more modest. Do it quickly, please. Put on one of those flowery dresses you brought with you from Clinton. And get yourself a coat and a hat. It's cold out there. We're going out. I don't know when we'll be back."

"We're going *out?*" *Christ, would this night of horrors never end?*

"We're going to the Stork Club. I'm going to find Walter Winchell and talk to him about this myself."

Billy laughed. "Olive's going to the Stork Club! To demand an audience with the great Winchell! Ain't that a tickle! I didn't know you'd ever *heard* of the Stork Club, Olive! I would've guessed you thought it was a maternity ward!"

Olive ignored this, other than to say, "Don't let Peg drink any more tonight, Billy, please. We will need her clearheadedness to help us manage all this mess, just as soon as we can get her back to her senses."

"She *can't* drink any more," exclaimed Billy, waving to his wife's prostrate form. "Look at her!"

"Vivian, hurry," said Olive. "Go get ready. Remember—you are a modest girl, so dress like one. And tidy up your hair while you're in there. Take off some of that makeup, too. Clean up as best you can.

And wash your hands with a generous amount of soap. You smell like a brothel, and that won't do."

It's incredible to me, Angela, to realize that so many people these days have forgotten Walter Winchell's name. He was once the most powerful man in American media, and that made him one of the most powerful men in the world. He wrote about the rich and famous, to be sure, but he was just as rich and famous as they were. (More, in most cases.) He was loved by his audience and feared by his prey. He built up and tore down other people's reputations at will—like a kid toying about with sandcastles. Some even claimed that Winchell was the reason FDR got reelected—because Winchell (who was passionate about America joining the war and defeating Hitler) outright commanded his followers to vote for Roosevelt. And millions obeyed.

Winchell had been famous for a long time by doing nothing more than selling dirt on people, and for being a pretty snappy writer. My grandmother and I used to read his columns together, of course. We hung on his every word. He knew everything about everyone. He had tentacles everywhere.

Back in 1941, the Stork Club was essentially Winchell's office. The whole world knew this. I certainly knew it because I'd seen him there dozens of times when I was out on the town with Celia. I would see him holding court from the throne that was always reserved for him: Table 50. He could be found there every night between 11:00 P.M. and 5:00 A.M. This is where he did his dirty work. This is where the denizens of his kingdom would come slithering forth like Kublai Khan's ambassadors, from every corner of the empire—to ask for favors, or to bring him the gossip he needed to feed the monstrous belly of his newspaper column.

Winchell liked to be around pretty showgirls (who doesn't?), so

Celia had sat at his table a few times. He knew her by name. They danced together often—I'd seen it. (No matter what else Billy said about him, the man was a good dancer.) But despite all the nights I'd been at the Stork, I'd never dared to go sit at Winchell's table myself. For one thing, I wasn't a showgirl, an actress, or an heiress, so I wouldn't have been of interest to him. For another thing, the man scared me to death—and I didn't even have a reason back then to be scared of him.

Well, I had a reason now.

Olive and I didn't talk in the cab. I was too consumed by fear and shame to make conversation, and she was never one for casual chitchat. I will say that her demeanor toward me was not degrading. She was not giving me a dose of schoolmarm disapproval—although she had cause. No, Olive's attitude that night was all business. She was a woman on a mission, and her focus was solely upon the task at hand. If I'd had my wits about me, I might have been touched and amazed that it was Olive—not Peg, or even Billy—who was putting her neck on the line for me. But I was too distraught to register this act of grace. All I could feel was doom.

The only thing Olive said to me as we were getting out of the taxi was, "I don't want you saying a *word* to Winchell. Not a word. Be pretty and be quiet. That's your only task. Follow me."

When we reached the entrance to the Stork, we were stopped by two doormen whom I knew well. James and Nick. They knew me, too, although they didn't realize it right away. They knew me as a glamour girl who was always hanging around Celia Ray, and that's not even close to how I looked this evening. I wasn't dressed to go dancing at the Stork. I wasn't wearing an evening gown or furs, or jewels that I'd borrowed from Celia. On the contrary—as per Olive's directions for

sartorial modesty, which, thankfully, I'd had the good sense to obey—
I was wearing the same simple frock I'd worn on the train to New York
City all those many months ago. And I had on my good school coat.
My face was scrubbed clean of makeup. I probably looked about fifteen
years old.

What's more, I was keeping a different sort of company that night
(to say the least) than what the doormen were used to. Instead of being
on the arm of the luscious showgirl Celia Ray, I was in the company of
one Miss Olive Thompson—a dour lady in steel-rimmed spectacles
and an old brown overcoat. She looked like a school librarian. She
looked like a school librarian's *mother*. We certainly did not look like
the sort of guests who would elevate the tone of a place like the Stork,
and so both James and Nick put up their hands to stop us, just as Olive
was marching in.

"We need to see Mr. Winchell, please," she announced, briskly.
"It's rather an emergency."

"I'm sorry, madam, but the nightclub is full, and we are not accept-
ing any more guests for the evening."

He was lying, of course. If Celia and I had been trying to get in—
dressed in all our glory—those doors would have flung open so fast
they might have lost their hinges.

"Is Mr. Sherman Billingsley here this evening?" Olive asked, un-
deterred.

The doormen exchanged glances. What did this homely librarian
know of Sherman Billingsley, the club's owner?

Taking advantage of their hesitation, Olive pressed on.

"Please tell Mr. Billingsley that the manager of the Lily Playhouse
has come to speak with Mr. Winchell, and that it's a grave emergency.
Tell him that I come on behalf of his good friend Peg Buell. We
haven't much time. It's regarding the potential publication of these
photographs."

Olive reached into her unassuming plaid satchel and pulled out the ruination of my life—that manila folder. She handed it to the doormen. This was a bold tactic, but desperate times call for desperate measures. Nick took the folder, opened it, looked at the photos, and let out a low whistle. Then he looked from the photos to me, and back to the photos. Something changed in his face. *Now* he knew me.

He gave me a raised eyebrow and a lewd grin. He said, "We haven't seen you around here in a while, Vivian. But now I see why. I guess you've been busy, huh?"

I seared in shame—while at the same time understanding: *This is just the beginning of it.*

"I will ask you to take care with how you speak to my niece, sir," said Olive, in a voice so steely it could have drilled a hole through a bank safe.

My niece?

Since when did Olive call me her niece?

Nick apologized, cowed. But Olive wasn't done. She said, "Young man, you can either bring us to see Mr. Billingsley—who will not appreciate your rude treatment of two people he essentially considers to be family members—or you can bring us directly to Mr. Winchell's table. You will do one, or you will do the other, but I will not be leaving. My suggestion is that you bring us directly to Mr. Winchell's table because that's where I'll be ending up this evening—regardless of what it takes me to get there, or who has to lose their job along the way for trying to stop me."

It's amazing how frightened young men will always be of dowdy, middle-aged women with stern voices—but it's true: they are *terrified* of them. (Too much like their own mothers, or nuns, or Sunday-school teachers, I suppose. The trauma from those old scoldings and beatings must run very deep.)

James and Nick exchanged a glance, looked at Olive one more time, and then decided as one: *Give the old bird whatever she wants.*

We were delivered straight to Mr. Winchell's table.

Olive sat down with the great man, but gestured at me to remain standing behind her. It was as though she were using her squatty little body as a shield between me and the world's most dangerous newspaperman. Or maybe she just wanted to put me at a far enough remove from the conversation that I wouldn't speak and ruin her strategy.

She pushed Winchell's ashtray aside and placed the folder in front of him. "I've come to discuss *these.*"

Winchell opened the folder and fanned out the photos in front of him. For the first time, I could see the photos—though I wasn't close enough to make out the details. But there it was. Two girls and a man, all entwined in each other. You didn't need the details to understand what was going on.

He shrugged. "I've seen these. Already bought them. Can't help you."

"I know," said Olive. "I understand you'll be publishing them tomorrow in the afternoon edition."

"Say, lady, who the hell are you, anyhow?"

"My name is Olive Thompson. I'm the manager of the Lily Playhouse."

You could see the abacus of his mind doing a quick calculation, and then he landed on it. "That dump where *City of Girls* is playing," he said, lighting a new cigarette off the still-burning ember of his last one.

"That's correct," confirmed Olive. (She took no issue with the word "dump" as applied to our theater—though, honestly, who could have debated it?)

"It's a good show," Winchell said. "I gave it a rave."

He seemed to want credit for this, but Olive wasn't the sort of woman to hand out free credit—not even in this situation, when she was essentially coming before Winchell on bended knee.

"Who's the little rabbit hiding behind you?" he asked.

"She's my niece."

So I guess we were sticking to *that* story.

"A bit past her bedtime, ain't it?" said Winchell, giving me the once-over.

I'd never been this close to him before, and I didn't like it one bit. He was a tall and hawkish man in his midforties, with baby-smooth pink skin and a twitchy jaw. He was wearing a navy blue suit (pressed to lacerating creases), with a sky blue Oxford shirt, brown wingtips, and a snappy gray felt fedora. He was wealthy and powerful, and he looked wealthy and powerful. His hands never stopped fidgeting, but his eyes were disconcertingly still as he took me in. His was a predator's stare. You might have said he was good-looking, if you could release your concerns about when he was going to eviscerate you.

A moment later, though, he had dropped his gaze from me. I'd failed to keep his interest. He'd quickly browsed me and analyzed me— *female, young, unconnected, inconsequential*—and then dismissed me as useless to his needs.

Olive tapped one of the photos in front of her. "The gentleman in these photographs is married to our star."

"I know exactly who that guy is, lady. Arthur Watson. Talentless sop. Dumb as a bag of hair. Better at chasing girls than he is at acting, by the looks of this evidence. And he's gonna take one hell of a pasting from his wife when she sees these photos."

"She's seen them already," said Olive.

Now Winchell was openly irritated. "How'd *you* see them, is what I want to know. These pictures are my property. And what are you doing, showing them all over town? What are you—selling tickets to these pictures?"

Olive didn't answer this, but just fixed Winchell with her firmest stare.

A waiter approached and asked if the ladies would like a drink.

"No thank you," said Olive. "We're temperates." (A claim that would have been soundly refuted, had anyone been close enough to smell my breath.)

"If you're asking me to kill the story, you can forget about it," said Winchell. "It's news, and I'm a newsman. If it's true or interesting, I got no choice but to publish it. And this item here is both true *and* interesting. Edna Parker Watson's husband, running around like that, with two loose women? What do you want me to do, lady? Look down at my shoes demurely while famous people make whoopee with showgirls right there in the middle of the Street? As everyone knows, I don't like to publish items on married couples, but if people are gonna be this indiscreet about their indiscretions, whaddaya want me to do about it?"

Olive continued to level him with her iceberg stare. "I expect you to have some decency."

"You know, you're really something, lady. You don't scare easy, do you? I'm beginning to piece you together. You work for Billy and Peg Buell."

"That's correct."

"It's a miracle that junky theater of yours is still operating. How do you keep your audience, year after year? Do you pay them to come? Bribe them?"

"We coerce them," said Olive. "We coerce them by providing excellent entertainment, and they, in return, reward us by buying tickets."

Winchell laughed, drummed his fingers on the table, and cocked his head. "I like you. Despite the fact that you work for that arrogant louse Billy Buell, I like you. You got some nerve. You could be a good secretary for me."

"You already have an excellent secretary, sir, in the figure of Miss Rose Bigman—a woman whom I consider a friend. I doubt she'd appreciate you hiring me."

Winchell laughed again. "You know more about everybody than I do!" Then his laughter vanished—never having reached his eyes. "Look, I got nothing for you, lady. Sorry about your star and her feelings, but I'm not killing the story."

"I'm not asking you to kill the story."

"Then whaddaya want from me? I already offered you a job. I already offered you a drink."

"It is important that you do not print the name of *this girl* in your newspaper." Olive pointed at one of the photographs again. And there I was—in a picture taken just a few hours (and a few centuries) earlier—with my head thrown back in rapture.

"Why shouldn't I name that girl?"

"Because she's an innocent."

"Got a funny way of showing it." There was that cold, wet laugh again.

"Nothing about this story is further served by putting this poor girl's name in your newspaper," said Olive. "The other people involved in this kerfuffle are public figures—an actor and a showgirl. They are known by name already to the general public. To be exposed to public scrutiny was the risk they took when they entered a life of show business. They will be hurt by your story, to be sure, but they'll survive the wound. It all comes with the territory of fame. But this youngster here"—again, she tapped the photo of my ecstatic face—"is naught but a college girl, from a good family. She will be laid low by this. If you publish her name, you doom her future."

"Wait a minute, is she *this* kid?" Winchell was pointing at me now.

To have his finger aimed at me felt something like being singled out of a crowd by an executioner.

"That's correct," said Olive. "She's my niece. She's a nice young girl. She's attending Vassar."

(Here, Olive was reaching: I had *been to* Vassar, yes, but I don't think anyone could accuse me of ever having *attended* Vassar.)

He was still staring at me. "Then why the hell ain't you in *school*, kid?"

Right about then, I wished I were. My legs and my lungs felt about to collapse. I was never happier to keep my mouth shut. I tried to look as much as possible like a nice girl who was studying literature at a respectable college, and who was not drunk—a role for which I was uniquely ill-equipped that night.

"She's just a visitor to the city," said Olive. "She's from a small town, from a nice family. She took up with some dubious company recently. It's the sort of thing that happens all the time to nice young girls. She made a mistake, that's all."

"And you don't want me sending her to the glue factory for it."

"That's correct. That's what I'm asking you to consider. Print the story if you must—even print the photos. But leave an innocent young girl's name out of the papers."

Winchell riffled through the photos again. He pointed to a picture of me with my mouth devouring Celia's face, and my arm wrapped—serpentlike—around Arthur Watson's neck.

"Real innocent," he pronounced.

"She was seduced," said Olive. "She made a mistake. It could happen to any girl."

"And how do you propose that I keep my wife and daughter in mink coats if I stop publishing gossip, just because innocent people make mistakes?"

"I like your daughter's name," I blurted out right then, without thinking.

The sound of my voice shocked me. I truly hadn't planned to speak. It just came flying out of my mouth. My voice startled Winchell and Olive, too. Olive spun around and stared daggers at me while Winchell drew back a bit in puzzlement.

"How's that?" he said.

"We don't need to hear from you now, Vivian," said Olive.

"Zip it," Winchell said to Olive. "What'd you say, girl?"

"I like your daughter's name," I repeated, unable to break his stare. "Walda."

"What do you know about my Walda?" he demanded.

If I'd had my wits about me, or if I'd been capable of making up an interesting story, I might have given a different answer—but as it was, all I could manage in my terrified state was the truth.

"I've always liked her name. You see, my brother's name is Walter, just like yours. My grandmother's father's name was Walter, too. My grandmother was the one who named my brother. She wanted the name to carry on. She started listening to your radio broadcasts a long time ago because she liked your name. She read all your columns, too. We read them together, in the *Graphic*. Walter was my grandmother's favorite name. She was so happy when you named your children Walter and Walda. She made my parents name me Vivian, because the letter *V* is half a *W*, and that was close to Walter. But after you named your daughter Walda, she said she wished that Walda were my name, too. It was a clever name, she said, and a good omen. We used to listen to you all the time on the *Lucky Strike Dance Hour*. She always liked your name. I wished my name was Walda, too. That would have made my grandmother happy."

I was running out of steam—running out of tattered sentences—and also, what the hell was I talking about?

"Who invited *that* compendium?" Winchell joked, pointing at me again.

"You needn't pay any mind to her," said Olive. "She's nervous."

"I needn't pay any mind to *you*, lady," he said to Olive, and turned his chilling attention to me again. "I feel like I've seen you before, kid. You've been in this room before, haven't you? You used to hang around with Celia Ray, didn't you?"

I nodded, defeated. I could see Olive's shoulders deflate.

"Yeah, I thought so. You come in here tonight, dressed all sweet and pretty like Little Mary Cotton Socks, but that's not how I remember you. I've seen you up to all sorts of hanky-panky in this room. So I think it's pretty rich—*you* trying to convince *me* that you're a decent young lady. Listen, you two, I'm on to your racket. I know what you're doing here—you're campaigning me—and I hate like hell to be campaigned." Then he pointed at Olive. "Only thing I can't figure out is why you're making all the effort to save this girl. Every soul in this club could testify that she's no fainting virgin, and I know for a fact that she ain't your niece. Hell, you're not even from the same country. You don't even talk the same."

"She *is* my niece," insisted Olive.

"Kid, are you this lady's niece?" Winchell asked me directly.

I was terrified to lie to him, but equally terrified not to. My solution was to cry out, "I'm sorry!" and to burst into tears.

"Ack! You two are giving me a headache," he said. But then he passed me his handkerchief and instructed, "Sit down, kid. You're making me look bad. The only girls I ever want crying around me are showgirls and starlets whose hearts I just broke."

He lit two cigarettes and offered me one. "Unless you're *temperate*?" he said, with a cynical smile.

I gratefully took the cigarette and gulped down the smoke in a few deep, shaky breaths.

"How old are you?" he asked.

"Twenty."

"Old enough to know better. Not that they ever know better. Now, listen—you say you used to read me in the *Graphic*? You're a little young for that, aren't you?"

I nodded. "You were my grandmother's favorite. She read your columns to me when I was little."

"I was her favorite, was I? What'd she like about me? I mean, aside from my beautiful name, about which you've already given us quite a memorable monologue."

This wasn't a difficult question. I knew my grandmother's tastes. "She liked your slang. She liked it when you called married people *welded*, instead of *wedded*. She liked the fights you picked. She liked your theater reviews. She said you really watched the shows, and cared about them, and that most critics don't."

"She said all that, your old grandma? Good for her. Where is this genius of a woman now?"

"She died," I said, and I almost started crying again.

"Too bad. I hate losing a loyal reader. What about that brother of yours—the one they named after me. Walter. What's his story?"

I don't know how Walter Winchell had gotten the idea that my family had named my brother after *him*, but I wasn't about to dispute it.

"My brother Walter is in the Navy, sir. He's training to be an officer."

"Signed up of his own accord?"

"Yes, sir," I said. "He dropped out of Princeton."

"That's what we need right now," said Winchell. "More boys like that. More boys brave enough to volunteer to fight Hitler before somebody tells them they have to. Is he a good-looking kid?"

"Yes, sir."

"Of course he is, with a name like that."

The waiter came over to ask if we needed anything, and I came *this close* to ordering a gin fizz double, purely out of habit—but had the presence of mind to stop myself just in time. The waiter's name was

Louie. I'd kissed him before. He didn't appear to recognize me, thank goodness.

"Look," said Winchell. "I need you two to scram. You're making this table look low rent. I don't even know how you shoehorned yourselves in here in the first place, looking the way you do."

"We will leave after I get an assurance from you that you won't put Vivian's name in the newspaper tomorrow," said Olive, who always knew how to push people *just a little bit further.*

"Hey, you don't come to Table 50 at the Stork Club and tell *me* what *you* need, lady," snapped Winchell. "I don't owe you anything. That's the only assurance you're getting."

Then he turned to me. "I would tell you to keep your nose clean from now on, but I know you won't. The indictment stands—you did a lousy thing, little girl, and you got caught. You've probably done a bunch of other lousy things, too, only you've been lucky so far not to get busted. Well, your luck ended tonight. Getting tangled up with somebody's bum husband and a hot-to-trot lezzie—that's no way for a girl from a good family to live. You'll do more stupid things in the future, if I know people. So all I can tell you is this: if a so-called nice girl like you is gonna keep rummaging around with rough trade like Celia Ray, you're gonna have to learn how to fight your own corner. This old hag here is a pain in my neck, but she's got a lot of fortitude, going to bat for you like this. Not sure why she cares about you, or why you deserve it. But from now on, little girl, fight your own battles. Now get the hell out of here, you two, and stop ruining my night. You're scaring away all the important people."

TWENTY

The next day, I hid in my room for as long as I could. I kept waiting for Celia to come home so we could talk all this over, but she never showed up. I hadn't slept and my nerves were a jangling nightmare. It was like I had thousands of doorbells attached to my brain, and they were all buzzing at the same time. I was too afraid of running into anyone—but most especially Edna—to risk going to the kitchen for breakfast, or for lunch.

In the afternoon, I slipped out of the theater to go buy the paper so I could read Winchell's column. I opened it up right there at the newsstand, fighting the March wind that wanted to blow my bad news away.

There was the photo of Arthur and Celia and me, in our embrace. You could vaguely make out my profile, but there was no way to be sure it was me. (In low light, all pretty brunettes look the same.) Arthur's and Celia's faces, however, could be seen clear as day. They were the important ones, I suppose.

I swallowed hard, and made myself read it.

———

From Walter Winchell, in the *New York Daily Mirror,* afternoon edition, March 25, 1941:

> Here's some conduct ungentlemanly and improper from one "Mr. Edna Parker Watson." How 'bout two American showgirls to keep you warm, you greedy limey, if one ain't enough? . . . That's right, we caught Arthur Watson pashing it outside the Spotlite with his *City of Girls* costar Celia Ray and another leggy denizen of Lesbos. . . . I call that a nice way to spend your time, mister, while your countrymen are fighting and dying against Hitler. . . . What a commotion out there on the sidewalk last night! . . . Let's hope these three stupid cupids had fun playing for the cameras, because anyone with brains can see it: Here's another showbiz marriage about to get Reno-vated! . . . Arthur Watson probably got a number nine spanking from his wife last night. . . . What a lousy day for the Watsons! They shoulda stood in bed! . . . That's the word from the bird!

A leggy denizen of Lesbos."
  But no name.
Olive had saved me.

Around six that evening, there was a knock on my door. It was Peg, looking just as green and grisly as I felt.

She sat down on my clothes-strewn bed.

"Shit," she said, and it sounded like she meant every word of it.

We sat in silence for a long while.

"Well, kiddo, you sure did foul things up," she said at last.

"I'm so sorry, Peg."

"Save it. I won't queen it over you. But this sure has brought down trouble upon our heads—trouble of every variety. I've been up with Olive since dawn, trying to bring order to the wrack and ruin."

"I'm *so* sorry," I said again.

"You should really save it. You'll need those sorries for other people. Don't waste them on me. But we do have some items to discuss. First off, I want you to know that Celia has been fired."

Fired! I'd never heard of anyone getting fired from the Lily.

"But where will she go?" I asked.

"She will go elsewhere. She's done. She's in the ash can. I told her to come get her things tonight while the show is on. I'm going to ask you not to be in this room when she arrives. I don't want any further agitation."

Celia was leaving and I wouldn't even get a chance to say goodbye! But where was she going *to*? I knew for a fact that she didn't have a dime to her name. Nowhere to stay. No family. She'd be laid to waste.

"I had to do it," Peg said. "I wasn't going to make Edna share the stage with that girl again. And if I didn't get rid of Celia after this mess, we would've had a palace revolt from the rest of the cast. Everyone is too angry. We can't risk that. So I've replaced Celia with Gladys. She's not as good, but she'll do fine. Wish I could fire Arthur, too, but Edna won't have that. She may end up firing him herself down the line, but that's her call. The man's a bad hat—but what can you do? She loves him."

"Is Edna going onstage tonight?" I asked, in wonder.

"Of course she is. Why wouldn't she? She's not the one who did anything wrong."

I winced. But truly, I was shocked to hear she would be performing. I thought maybe Edna would be in hiding—checked into a sanatorium somewhere, or at least crying behind a locked door. I thought maybe the whole play would have been canceled.

"It won't be a pleasant evening for her," said Peg. "Everyone's read Winchell, of course. There will be a lot of whispers. The audience will be staring at her with bloodlust, wanting to see her flounder and flail. But she's a trouper, and she'll face it. Better to get it over with, is her feeling. Show must go on, and all that. We're lucky for her strength. If she wasn't this resolute, or such a good friend, she probably would have quit the show—and then where would we be? Thankfully, she knows how to prevail—and she will."

She lit a cigarette and went on: "I also had a talk today with your boyfriend, Anthony. He wanted to leave the show. Said he wasn't having fun anymore. Said we were 'bugging' him, whatever that means. Specifically said that you are bugging him. I managed to convince him to stay, but we have to pay him more, and he stipulated he doesn't want you 'messing' with him anymore. Because you 'did him dirt.' Says he's done with you. Doesn't even want to hear you 'jawing' at him. I'm just quoting here, Vivvie. I think I've conveyed the fullness of his message. I don't know whether he'll be able to put on a good show tonight, but we'll find out soon enough. Olive had a long talk with him this morning, trying to keep the boy on track. It would be best if you steered clear of him. For now on, pretend he doesn't exist."

I felt like throwing up. Celia was banished. Anthony never wanted to talk to me again. And because of me, Edna would have to face an audience tonight that wanted to see her twist on a rope.

Peg said, "I'm going to ask it straight from the shoulder, Vivvie. How long have you been dallying around with Arthur Watson?"

"I haven't been. It was just last night. It was just the one time."

My aunt studied me, as though determining if that were true or not. Ultimately, she shrugged it off. She may have believed me, she

279

may not have. Maybe she came to the conclusion that it didn't matter, one way or another. As for me, I didn't have the energy to fight my case. It wasn't much of a case, anyhow.

"Why'd you do it?" Her tone was more puzzled than judgmental. When I didn't answer right away, she said, "Never mind. People always do it for the same reason."

"I thought Edna was fooling around with Anthony," I said lamely.

"Well, that's not true. I know Edna, and I can promise you it's not true. She's never operated that way, and never will. And even if it *had* been true—it's not a good enough reason, Vivian."

"I'm so sorry, Peg," I said again.

"This story's going to be picked up by every rag in town, you know. In every town. *Variety* will run it. All the tabloids in Hollywood. In London, too. Olive's had reporters calling all afternoon, asking for statements. There are photographers at the stage door. Such a comedown for a woman like Edna—someone of her dignity."

"Peg. Tell me what I can do. *Please*."

"You can't," she said. "You can't do anything other than be humble and keep your mouth shut, and hope everyone will be charitable with you. Meanwhile, I hear you and Olive went to the Stork last night."

I nodded.

"I don't mean to be melodramatic, Vivvie, but you do understand that Olive has saved you from ruin, don't you?"

"I understand."

"Can you imagine what your parents would say about this? In a community like yours? To have this sort of reputation? And with photos, to boot?"

I could imagine. I *had* imagined.

"It's not entirely fair, Vivvie. Everyone else will have to take it on the chin—not least of all Edna—but you're getting away with it, scot-free."

"I know," I said. "I'm sorry."

Peg sighed. "Well. Once again, Olive saves the day. I've lost track of the number of times she's rescued us—rescued *me*—over the years. She is the most remarkable and honorable woman I've ever known. I do hope you thanked her."

"I did," I said, though I wasn't sure I had.

"I wish I'd gone with you and Olive last night, Vivvie. But apparently I wasn't in good enough shape. I've been having too many nights like that, lately. Drinking gin like it's soda water. I don't even remember coming home. But let's face it—it should've been me, petitioning Winchell on your behalf. Not Olive. I am your aunt, after all. Family duty. Would've been nice if Billy had lent a hand, as well, but you never can count on Billy to stick his neck out for anyone. Not that it was his responsibility. No, it was my job, and I dropped it. I feel sick about all this, kiddo. I should've been keeping a better eye on you all this time."

"It's not your fault," I said, and I meant it. "It's all my fault."

"Well, there's nothing to be done for it now. Looks like my bout with the bottle has run its course once more. It always ends the same way, you know, when Billy comes around, bringing the fun and the confetti. I always start out by having a big old time with him, and then one morning I wake up to learn that the world has gone smacko while I was blacked out, and meanwhile Olive's been struggling to fix everything behind my back. I don't know why I never can learn."

I didn't even know what to say to that.

"Well, try to keep up some spirits, Vivvie. It's not the end of the world, as the man says. Hard to believe on a day like this, but it really isn't the end of the world. There are worse things. Some people have no legs."

"Am I fired?"

She laughed. "Fired from what? You don't even have a job!" She looked at her watch and stood up. "One more thing. Edna doesn't want to see you tonight before the show. Gladys will help dress her this evening. But Edna does wish to see you after the show. She's asked me to tell you to meet her in her dressing room."

"Oh, God, Peg," I said. There was the nausea again.

"You'll have to face her eventually. Might as well be now. She won't be gentle with you, I dare say. But she deserves her chance to lay into you—and you deserve whatever's coming. Go in there and apologize, if she'll let you. Admit what you did. Take your lumps. The sooner you get flattened to the ground, the sooner you can begin to rebuild your life again. That's always been my experience, anyway. Take it from an old pro."

I stood in the back of the theater and watched the show from the shadows, where I belonged.

If the audience had come to the Lily Playhouse that night to watch Edna Parker Watson squirm in discomfort, then they left disappointed. Because she didn't squirm for a moment. Pinned to the stage like a butterfly by that hot, white spotlight—scrutinized by hundreds of eyes, whispered about, giggled over—she played her role for all it was worth. Not a *flinch* of nerves did that woman reveal for the satisfaction of a bloodthirsty mob. Her Mrs. Alabaster was humorous, she was charming, she was relaxed. If anything, Edna moved across the stage that night with more economy and grace than ever. She carried herself with undented self-assurance, her face revealing nothing except how pleasant it was to be the star of this light, joyful show.

The rest of the company, on the other hand, was visibly squirrelly at first—missing their marks and stammering over their lines, until Edna's steadfast performance eventually righted theirs. She was the gravitational force who kept everyone stabilized that night. What was stabilizing *her*, I could not tell you.

I don't think it was my imagination that Anthony's performance in the first act had an angrier edge to it than usual—he was less Lucky Bobby than Ferocious Bobby—but Edna managed to pull even him into line, eventually.

My friend Gladys—stepping into Celia's role and Celia's costume—looked perfectly good and danced without flaw. She lacked the comic, languid delivery that had made Celia such a hit. But she did the job ably, and that's all that was needed.

Arthur was dreadful, but of course he was always dreadful. The only difference tonight was that he also *looked* dreadful. He had sickly gray circles under his eyes, and he spent most of his performance mopping sweat off the back of his neck, and staring at his wife across the stage with the most pathetic hound-dog eyes. He didn't even try to pretend he wasn't upset. The only saving grace was that his part had been so trimmed down that he didn't have too many minutes onstage in which to ruin everything.

Edna made one significant alteration to the show that night. When she sang her ballad, she spontaneously changed the blocking. Instead of aiming her face and voice up to the heavens, which is how she usually did it, she took herself straight to the edge of the stage. She sang directly to the audience, peering out at them, picking people out of the crowd and singing to them—singing *at* them, really. She held eye contact, staring them down as she sang her heart out. Her voice was never richer, never more defiant. ("It'll surely do me in this time / I'll probably be left behind / But I'm considering falling in love.")

The way she sang that night, it was as though she were challenging the audience, person by person. It was as if she were demanding: *And you've never been hurt? And you've never had your heart broken? And you've never taken a risk for love?*

By the end, she had them weeping—while she stood dry-eyed in their ovations.

To this day, I have never seen a mightier woman.

I knocked on the dressing-room door with a hand that felt, itself, like a piece of wood.

"Come in," she said.

My head had a cottony feel. My ears were stuffed up and numbed. My mouth tasted like cigarette-flavored cornmeal. My eyes were dry and sore—both from lack of sleep and from crying. I had not eaten for twenty-four hours and I couldn't imagine ever eating again. I was still wearing the same dress I'd worn to the Stork Club. My hair, I'd left unattended all day. (I hadn't been able to confront a mirror.) My legs felt curiously unattached to the rest of my body; I didn't understand how my legs knew how to walk. For a minute there, they didn't. Then I pushed myself into the room like a person jumping off a cliff into the cold ocean below.

Edna was standing in front of her dressing-room mirror, haloed in its blazing lights. Her arms were folded, her posture relaxed. She'd been waiting for me. She was still in her costume—the showstopping evening gown I'd made for her finale so many months ago. Shimmering blue silk and rhinestones.

I stood before her, head bowed. I was a good foot taller than this woman—but at that moment, I was a rodent at her feet.

"Why don't you speak first?" she said.

Well, I hadn't exactly prepared any remarks. . . .

But her invitation was not really an *invitation;* it was a command. So I opened my mouth and began pouring out ragged, hapless, directionless sentences. Mine was a liturgy of excuses, contained within a flood of pathetic apologies. There were pleas to be forgiven. There were grasping offerings to make things better. But there was also cowardliness and denial. ("It was just the one time, Edna!") And I'm very sorry to report that—at some point in my messy speech—I quoted Arthur Watson as having said of his wife, "She likes them young."

I spun through all the stupid words I had, and Edna let me twist without interrupting or responding. Finally, I stuttered to a stop, coughing up my last bit of verbal trash. Then I stood silent once more, sickly under her blinkless gaze.

At last Edna said in a disturbingly mild tone, "The thing that you don't understand about yourself, Vivian, is that you're not an interesting person. You are pretty, yes—but that's only because you are young. The prettiness will soon fade. But you will never be an interesting person. I'm telling you this, Vivian, because I believe you've been laboring under the misconception that you *are* interesting, or that your life has significance. But you are not, and it doesn't. I once thought you had the potential to become an interesting person, but I was incorrect. Your Aunt Peg is an interesting person. Olive Thompson is an interesting person. I am an interesting person. But you are not an interesting person. Do you understand me?"

I nodded.

"What you are, Vivian, is a *type* of person. To be more specific, you are a *type* of woman. A tediously common type of a woman. Do you think I've not encountered your type before? Your sort will always be slinking around, playing your boring and vulgar little games, causing your boring and vulgar little problems. You are the type of woman who cannot be a friend to another woman, Vivian, because you will always be playing with toys that are not your own. A woman of your type often believes she is a person of significance because she can make trouble and spoil things for others. But she is neither important nor interesting."

I opened my mouth to talk, ready to spurt out some more disconnected garbage, but Edna put up her hand. "You may want to consider preserving whatever dignity you have remaining to you, my dear, by not speaking anymore."

The fact that she said this with a trace of a smile—even with the slightest hint of fondness—is what destroyed me.

"There's something else you should know, Vivian. Your friend Celia spent so much time with you because she thought you were an aristocrat—but you're not one. And you spent so much time with Celia because you thought she was a star—but she's not one. She will never be a star, just as you will never be an aristocrat. The two of you are just a pair of dreadfully average girls. *Types* of girls. There are a million more just like you."

I felt my heart collapsing down to its smallest possible dimension—until it became a crumpled cube of foil, crushed in her dainty fist.

"Would you like to know what you must do now, Vivian, in order to stop being a *type* of person—and become, instead, a real person?"

I must have nodded.

"Then I shall tell you. There is nothing you can do. No matter how hard you may try to gain substance throughout your life, it will never work. You will never be *anything*, Vivian. You will never be a person of the slightest significance."

She smiled tenderly.

"And unless I miss my bet," she concluded, "you'll probably be going back home to your parents very soon now. Back to where you belong. Won't you, darling?"

TWENTY-ONE

I spent the next hour in a small telephone booth in the back corner of a nearby all-night drugstore, trying to reach my brother.

I was berserk with distress.

I could have called Walter from the phone at the Lily, but I didn't want anyone hearing me, and I was too ashamed to show my face around the playhouse, anyhow. So out to the drugstore I ran.

I had in my possession a general phone number for Walter's OCS barracks on the Upper West Side. He'd given it to me in case of an emergency. Well, this was an emergency. But it was also eleven o'clock at night and nobody was picking up the phone. This didn't deter me. I kept dropping my nickel into the slot, and listening to the phone ring endlessly on the other end. I would let the phone ring twenty-five times, then hang up and start over again with the same phone number and the same nickel. Sobbing and hiccupping all the while.

It became hypnotic—dialing, counting the rings, hanging up, hearing the nickel drop, putting the nickel back in the slot, dialing, counting the rings, hanging up. Sobbing, wailing.

Then suddenly there was a voice on the other end. A furious voice. "WHAT?!" someone was shouting in my ear. "Goddamn *WHAT*?!"

I almost dropped the phone. I'd fallen into such a trance, I'd forgotten what telephones are *for.*

"I need to talk to Walter Morris," I said, when I recovered my senses. "Please, sir. It's a family emergency."

The man on the other end sputtered out a litany of curses ("You Christless, piss-soaked eight ball!"), as well as the expected lecture about *do you have any idea what time it is?* But his anger was no match for my desperation. I was doing an excellent rendition of a hysterical relative—which, in point of fact, is exactly what I was. My sobs easily overpowered this stranger's outrage. His shouts about protocol meant nothing to me. Eventually he must've realized that his rules were no match for my mayhem, and he went searching for my brother.

I waited for a long while, dropping more nickels into the phone, trying to collect myself, listening to the sound of my own ragged breath in the little booth.

And then at last, Walter. "What happened, Vee?" he asked.

At the sound of my brother's voice, I disintegrated all over again, into a thousand pieces of lost little girl. And then—through my waves of sobbing heaves—I told him absolutely everything.

"You have to get me out of here," I begged, when he'd finally heard it all. "You have to take me home."

didn't know how Walter managed to arrange it all so fast—and in the middle of the night, no less. I didn't know how these things worked in the military—taking leave, and such. But my brother was the most resourceful person I knew, so he'd solved it somehow. I knew he would solve it. Walter could fix anything.

While Walter was pulling together his part of my escape plan (gaining leave and finding a car to borrow), I was packing—stuffing my clothes and shoes into my luggage, and putting away my sewing machine with shaking fingers. Then I wrote Peg and Olive a long, tear-stained, self-lacerating letter, and left it on the kitchen table. I don't remember everything the letter said, but it was full of hysteria. In hindsight, I wish I'd just written, "Thank you for taking care of me, I'm sorry I was an idiot," and left it at that. Peg and Olive had enough to deal with. They didn't need a stupid twenty-page confessional from me, in addition to everything else.

But they got one, anyhow.

Just before dawn, Walter pulled up to the Lily Playhouse to collect me and to take me home.

He wasn't alone. My brother had been able to borrow a car, yes, but it came with a catch. To be more specific, it came with a driver. There was a tall, skinny young man at the wheel, wearing the same uniform as Walter. An OCS classmate. An Italian-looking kid with a thick Brooklyn accent. He would be taking the drive with us. Apparently the beat-up old Ford was his.

I didn't care. I didn't care who was there, or who saw me in my fragmented state. All I felt was desperate. I just needed to leave the Lily Playhouse *right now,* before anybody there woke up and saw my face. I could not live in the same building as Edna, not for another minute. She had, in her own cool way, effectively commanded me to leave, and I had heard her loud and clear. I had to go.

Right now.

Just get me out of here was all I cared about.

———

We crossed the George Washington Bridge as the sun was coming up. I couldn't even look at the view of New York City retreating behind me. I couldn't bear it. Even though I was taking myself away from the city, I experienced the exact opposite sensation—that the city was being taken away from *me*. I'd proven that I couldn't be trusted with it, so New York was being removed from my reach, the way you take a valuable object out of a child's hands.

Once we were on the other side of the bridge, safely out of the city, Walter tore into me. I had never seen him so angry. He was not a guy to show his temper, but he damn sure showed it now. He let me know what a disgrace I was to the family name. He reminded me how much I'd been given in life and how recklessly I'd squandered it. He pointed out what a waste it had been for my parents to have invested any money whatsoever in my education and upbringing, when I was so unworthy of their gifts. He told me what happens to girls like me over time— that we get used, then we get used up, then we get thrown away. He said I was lucky not to be in jail, pregnant, or dead in the gutter, the way I'd been behaving. He said I'd never find a respectable husband now: who would have me, if they knew even part of my story? After all the mutts I had been with, I was now part mutt myself. He informed me that I must never tell our parents what I had done in New York, or what level of calamity I had caused. This was not to protect *me* (I didn't de- serve protection), but to protect *them*. Mother and Dad would never get over the blow, if they knew how degraded their daughter had become. He made it clear that this was the last time he would ever rescue me. He said, "You're lucky I'm not taking you straight to reformatory school."

All this he said right in front of the young man driving the car—as if the guy were invisible, deaf, or inconsequential.

Or as if I were so disgusting, Walter didn't care who found out about it.

So Walter poured vitriol upon me, and our driver got to hear all the details, and I just sat there in the backseat and braved it out in silence. It was bad, yes. But I have to say, in comparison to my recent confrontation with Edna, it wasn't *that* bad. (At least Walter was giving me the respect of being angry; Edna's unshakable sangfroid had been so *minimizing*. I'd take his fire over her ice any day.)

What's more, by this point, I was pretty much numb to all pain. I'd been awake for over thirty-six hours. In the past day and a half, I'd been drunk and screwed and scared and debased and dumped and reproached. I'd lost my best friend, my boyfriend, my community, my fun job, my self-respect, and New York City. I'd just been informed by Edna, a woman whom I loved and admired, that I was a nothing of a human being—and moreover that I would always be a nothing. I'd been forced to beg my older brother to save me, and to let him know what a shitheel I was. I'd been exposed, carved out, and thoroughly scoured. There wasn't much more that Walter could say to add to my shame or to further wound me.

But—as it turns out—there was something our *driver* could say.

Because about an hour into the ride, when Walter had stopped lecturing me for just a moment (just to catch his breath, I guess), the skinny kid at the wheel spoke up for the first time. He said, "Must be pretty disappointing for a stand-up guy like you, Walt, to end up with a sister who's such a dirty little whore."

Now, *that* I felt.

Those words did more than just sting; they burned me all the way to the center of my being, as though I'd swallowed acid.

It's not only that I couldn't believe the kid said it; it's that he said it *right in front of my brother*. Had he ever *seen* my brother? All six foot two inches of Walter Morris? All that muscle and command?

With my breath caught in my throat, I waited for Walter to deck this guy—or at the very least to reprimand him.

But Walter said nothing.

Apparently, my brother would let the indictment stand. Because he agreed.

As we drove on, those brutal words echoed and ricocheted throughout the small, enclosed space of the car—and through the even smaller, even more enclosed space of my mind.

Dirty little whore, dirty little whore, dirty little whore . . .

The words melted at last into an even more brutal silence that pooled around us all like dark water.

I closed my eyes and let it drown me.

My parents—who'd had no warning that we were coming—were at first overjoyed to see Walter, and then baffled and concerned by what he was doing there, and why he was with *me*. But Walter offered nothing much by means of explanation. He said that Vivian had gotten homesick, so he'd decided to drive her back upstate. He left it at that, and I added nothing to the story. We didn't even make an effort at acting normal around our confused parents.

"But how long are you staying, Walter?" my mother wanted to know.

"Not even for dinner," he answered. He had to turn right around and get back to the city, he explained, so he wouldn't miss another day of training.

"And how long is Vivian staying?"

"Up to you," said Walter, shrugging as if he couldn't care less what happened to me, or where I stayed, or for how long.

In a different sort of family, more probing questions might have followed. But let me explain my culture of origin to you, Angela, in case you have never been around White Anglo-Saxon Protestants. You need to understand that we have only one central rule of engagement, and here it is:

This matter must never be spoken of again.

We WASPs can apply that rule to anything—from a moment of awkwardness at the dinner table to a relative's suicide.

Asking no further questions is the song of my people.

So when my parents got the message that neither Walter nor I was going to share any information about this mysterious visit—this mysterious drop-off, really—they pursued the matter no further.

As for my brother, he deposited me in my house of birth, unpacked my belongings from the car, kissed my mother goodbye, shook my father's hand, and—without saying another word to me—drove straight back to the city, to prepare for another, more important war.

TWENTY-TWO

What followed was a time of murky and contourless un-happiness.

Some engine within me had now stalled, and as a result I went limp. My actions had failed me, so I stopped taking action. Now that I was living at home, I allowed my parents to set my routine for me, and I dumbly went along with whatever they proposed.

I breakfasted with them over newspapers and coffee, and helped my mother make sandwiches for lunch. Dinner (cooked by our maid, of course) was at five thirty, followed by the reading of the evening papers, card games, and listening to the radio.

My father suggested that I work at his company, and I agreed to it. He put me in the front office, where I shuffled around papers for seven hours a day and answered phones when nobody else was free to do so. I learned how to file, more or less. I should have been arrested for impersonating a secretary, but at least it gave me something to do with the bulk of my days, and my father paid me a small salary for my "work."

Dad and I drove to work together every morning, and we drove home together every evening. His conversation during those car rides was more like a collection of rants about how America needed to stay out of the war, and how FDR was a tool of the labor unions, and how the communists would soon be taking over our country. (Always more fearful of communists than fascists, was dear old Dad.) I heard his words, but I can't say I was listening.

I felt distracted all the time. Something awful was clomping around inside my head in heavy shoes, always reminding me that I was a dirty little whore.

I felt the smallness of everything. My childhood bedroom with its little, girlish bed. The rafters that were too low. The tinny sound of my parents' conversation in the mornings. The sparse number of cars in the church parking lot on Sundays. The old local grocery store with its limited collection of familiar foods. The luncheonette that closed at two o'clock in the afternoon. My closet full of adolescent clothing. My childhood dolls. It all cramped me, and filled me with gloom.

Every word coming out of the radio sounded ghostly and haunted to me. The uplifting songs and the sorrowful ones alike filled me with disheartenment. The radio dramas could barely hold my attention. Sometimes I would hear Walter Winchell's voice on the air, bellowing out his gossip, or sending forth his urgent calls for intervention in Europe. My belly clenched at the sound of his voice, but my father would snap off the radio, saying, "That man won't rest until every good American boy is sent overseas to be killed by the Huns!"

When our copy of *Life* magazine arrived in the middle of August, there was an article about the hit New York play *City of Girls,* that included photos of famed British actress Edna Parker Watson. She looked fantastic. For her primary portrait, she wore one of the suits I'd made for her the previous year—a deep gray number with a tiny, tucked waist and a fiercely chic bloodred taffeta collar. There was also a photo of Edna and Arthur walking through Central Park, hand in hand. ("Mrs. Watson, despite all her success, still praises marriage as her favorite role of all. 'Many actresses will say that they are married to their work,' says the stylish star. 'But I prefer being married to a man, if given the choice!'")

At the time, reading that article made my conscience feel like a rotting little rowboat sinking into a pond of mud. But thinking about it today, I have to say that it enrages me. Arthur Watson had completely gotten away with his misdeeds and lies. Celia had been banished by Peg, and I had been banished by Edna—but Arthur had been allowed to carry on with his lovely life and his lovely wife, as though nothing had ever happened.

The dirty little whores had been disposed of; the man was allowed to remain.

Of course, I didn't recognize the hypocrisy back then.

But Lord, I recognize it now.

On Saturday nights, my parents and I went to our local country-club dances. I could see that what we had always so grandly called the "ballroom" was merely a medium-sized dining room with the tables pushed to one side. The musicians weren't terrific, either. Meanwhile, I knew that down in New York City, the Viennese Roof was open for summer at the St. Regis, and I would never dance there again.

At the country-club dances, I talked to old friends and neighbors. I did my best. Some of them knew I'd been living in New York City and they tried to make conversation about it. ("I can't imagine why people would want to live all boxed up on top of each other like that!") I tried to make conversation with these people, too, about their lake houses, or their dahlias, or their coffee-cake recipes—or whatever seemed to matter to them. I couldn't work out why anything mattered to anyone.

The music dragged on. I danced with anyone who asked while noticing none of my partners with any specificity.

On weekends, my mother went to her horse shows. I went with her when she asked me to go. I would sit in the bleachers with cold hands and muddy boots, watching the horses go round and round the ring, and wondering why anybody would want to do that with their time.

My mother got regular letters from Walter, who was now stationed on an aircraft carrier out of Norfolk, Virginia. He said the food was better than you'd expect, and that he was getting along with all the guys. He sent best wishes to his friends back home. He never mentioned my name.

There was a rather headachy number of weddings to attend that spring, as well. Girls whom I'd gone to school with were getting married and pregnant—and in that order, too, can you imagine? I ran into a childhood friend of mine one day on the sidewalk. Her name was Bess Farmer, and she'd also gone to Emma Willard. She already had a one-year-old child whom she was pushing in a pram and she was pregnant again. Bess was a sweetheart—a genuinely intelligent girl with a hearty laugh and a talent for swimming. She'd been quite gifted in the sciences. It would be insulting and demeaning to say of Bess that she was nothing but a housewife now. But seeing her pregnant body gave me the sweats.

Girls whom I used to swim with naked in the creeks behind our houses back when we were all children (so skinny and energetic and sexless) were now plump matrons, leaking breast milk, bursting with babies. I couldn't fathom it.

But Bess looked happy.

As for me, I was a dirty little whore.

I had done *such* a rotten thing to Edna Parker Watson. To betray a person who has helped you and been kind to you—this is the furthest reach of shame.

I walked through more agitated days, and slept fitfully through even worse nights.

I did everything I was told to do, and caused no trouble to anyone, but I still could not solve the problem of how to bear myself.

I met Jim Larsen through my father.

Jim was a serious, respectable, twenty-seven-year-old man who worked for Dad's mining company. He was a freight clerk. If you want to know what that means, it means that he was in charge of manifests, invoices, and orders. He also managed outgoing shipments. He was good at mathematics, and he used his skill with numbers to handle the complexities of route rates, storage costs, and the tracking of freight. (I just wrote down all those words, Angela, but I myself am not sure what any of them actually mean. I memorized those sentences back when I was courting Jim Larsen so that I could explain his job to people.)

My father thought highly of Jim despite his humble roots. My father saw Jim as a purposeful young man on the rise—a sort of working-class version of his own son. He liked that Jim had started out as a machinist, but through steadfastness and merit had quickly worked his way up to a position of authority. My father intended to make Jim the general manager of his entire operation one day, saying, "That boy is a better accountant than most of my accountants, and he's a better fore-man than most of my foremen."

Dad said, "Jim Larsen is not a leader, but he's the reliable sort of man that a leader wants to have beside him."

Jim was so polite, he asked my father if he could take me out on a date before he'd ever spoken to me. My father agreed. In fact, it was my father who told me that Jim Larsen would be taking me on a date. This was before I even knew who Jim Larsen was. But the two men had already worked it all out without consulting me, so I just went along with their plan.

On our first date, Jim took me out for a sundae at the local fountain shop. He watched me carefully as I ate it, to check that I was satisfied. He cared about my satisfaction, which is something. Not every man is like that.

The next weekend, he drove me to the lake, where we walked around and looked at ducks.

The weekend after that, we went to a small county fair, and he bought me a little painting of a sunflower after I'd admired it. ("For you to hang on your wall," he said.)

I'm making him sound more boring than he was.

No, I'm not.

Jim was such a nice man. I had to give him that. (But be careful here, Angela: whenever a woman says about her suitor, "He's such a nice man," you can be sure she is not in love.) But Jim *was* nice. And to be fair, he was more than merely nice. He possessed deep mathematical intelligence, honesty, and resourcefulness. He was not shrewd, but he was smart. And he was good-looking in what they call the "all-American" way—sandy-haired, blue-eyed, and fit. Blond and sincere is not how I prefer my men, given a choice, but there was certainly nothing wrong with his face. Any woman would have identified him as handsome.

Help me! I'm trying to describe him, and I can barely remember him.

What else can I tell you about Jim Larsen? He could play the banjo and he sang in the church choir. He worked part time as a census taker and was a volunteer fireman. He could fix anything, from a screen door to the industrial tracks at the hematite mine.

Jim drove a Buick—a Buick that would someday be traded in for a Cadillac, but not before he had earned it, and not before he had first purchased a bigger home for his mother, with whom he lived. Jim's sainted mother was a forlorn widow who smelled of medicinal balms and who kept her Bible tucked by her side at all times. She spent her days peering out the windows at her neighbors, waiting for them to slip up and sin. Jim instructed me to call her "Mother," and so I did, even though I never felt comfortable around the woman for a moment.

Jim's father had been dead for years, so Jim had been taking care of his mother since he was in high school. His father was a Norwegian immigrant, a blacksmith who had not so much sired a son as *forged* him—shaping this boy into somebody unerringly responsible and decent. He'd done a good job making this kid into a man by a young age. And then the father had died, leaving his son to become a full adult at the age of fourteen.

Jim seemed to like me. He thought I was funny. He'd not been exposed to much irony in his life, but my little jokes and jabs amused him.

After a few weeks of courtship, he began kissing me. That was pleasant, but he did not take further liberties with my body. I didn't ask for anything more, either. I didn't reach for him in a hungry way, but only because I felt no hunger for him. I felt no hunger for anything anymore. I had no access anymore to my appetites. It was as if all my passion and my urges were stored up in a locker somewhere else—somewhere very far away. Maybe at Grand Central Station. All I could do was go along with whatever Jim was doing. Whatever he wanted was fine.

He was solicitous. He asked if I was comfortable with various temperatures in various rooms. He affectionately started calling me "Vee"—but only after asking permission to give me a nickname. (It made me uncomfortable that he inadvertently settled on the same nickname my brother had always called me, but I said nothing, and allowed it.) He helped my mother repair a broken horse jump, and she appreciated him for it. He helped my father transplant some rosebushes.

Jim started coming around in the evenings to play cards with my family. It was not unpleasant. His visits provided a nice break from listening to the radio or reading the evening papers. I was aware that my parents were breaking a social taboo on my behalf—namely: consorting with an employee in their home. But they received him graciously. There was something warm and safe about those evenings.

My father came to like him more and more.

"That Jim Larsen," he would say, "has the best head on his shoulders in this whole town."

As for my mother, she probably wished that Jim had more social standing, but what could you do? My mother herself had married neither above nor below her class, but at exact eye level to it—finding in my father a man of the same age, education, wealth, and breeding as herself. I'm sure she wished I would do the same. But she accepted Jim, and for my mother, acceptance would always have to be a stand-in for enthusiasm.

Jim wasn't dashing, but he could be romantic in his own way. One day when we were driving around town, he said, "With you in my car, I feel that I am the envy of all eyes."

Where did he come up with a line like that? I wonder. That was sweet, wasn't it?

Next thing you know, we were engaged.

I don't know why I agreed to marry Jim Larsen, Angela.

No, that's not true.

I do know why I agreed to marry Jim Larsen—because I felt sordid and vile, and he was clean and honorable. I thought maybe I could erase my bad deeds with his good name. (A strategy that has never worked for anyone, by the way—not that people don't keep trying it.)

And I liked Jim, in some ways. I liked him because he wasn't like anybody from the previous year. He didn't remind me of New York City. He didn't remind me of the Stork Club, or Harlem, or a smoky bar down in Greenwich Village. He didn't remind me of Billy Buell, or Celia Ray, or Edna Parker Watson. He damn sure didn't remind me of Anthony Roccella. (*Sigh.*) Best of all, he didn't remind me of *myself*—a dirty little whore.

When I spent time with Jim, I could be just who I was pretending to be—a nice girl who worked in her father's office, and who had no past history worth mentioning. All I had to do was follow Jim's lead and act like him, and I became the last person in the world I had to think about—and that's exactly how I wanted it.

And so I slid toward marriage, like a car sliding off the road on a scree of loose gravel.

B y now, it was the autumn of 1941. Our plan was to get married the following spring, when Jim would have enough money saved to buy us a house we could share comfortably with his mother. He had purchased a small engagement ring that was pretty enough, but that made my hand look like a stranger's.

Now that we were engaged, our sensual activities escalated. Now when we parked the Buick out by the lake, he would take off my shirt, and delight himself with my breasts—making sure at every turn, of course, that I was comfortable with this arrangement. We would lie together across that big backseat and grind against each other—or, rather, he would grind against me, and I would allow it. (I didn't dare to be so forward as to grind back. I also didn't really *want* to grind back.)

"Oh, Vee," he would say, with simple rapture. "You are the prettiest girl in the whole wide world."

Then one night the grinding got more heated, until he pulled back from me with considerable effort and scrubbed his hands over his face, collecting himself.

"I don't want to do anything more with you until we're married," he said, once he could speak again.

I was lying there with my skirt up around my waist, and my breasts naked to the cool autumn air. I could sense that his pulse was racing wildly, but mine was not.

"I would never be able to look your father in the face if I took your virginity before you were my wife," he said.

I gasped. It was an honest and unfettered reaction. I *audibly* gasped. Just the mention of the word "virginity" gave me a shock. I hadn't thought of this! Even though I had been playing the role of an unsullied girl, I hadn't thought he truly *imagined* I was one, all the way through. But why wouldn't he have imagined it? What sign had I ever given him that I was anything less than pure?

This was a problem. He would know. We were getting married, and he would want to take me on our wedding night—and then he would *know*. The moment we had sex for the first time, he would *know* that he was not my first visitor.

"What is it, Vee?" he asked. "What's wrong?"

Angela, I was not one for telling the truth back then. Truth telling was not my first instinct in any situation—especially in stressful situations. It took me many years to become an honest person, and I know why: because the truth is often terrifying. Once you introduce truth into a room, the room may never be the same again.

Nonetheless, I said it.

"I'm not a virgin, Jim."

I don't know why I said it. Maybe because I was panicking. Maybe because I wasn't smart enough to make up a plausible lie. Or maybe because there's only so long a person can endure wearing a mask of falseness before a trace of one's true self starts to gleam through.

He stared at me for a long while before asking, "What do you mean by that?"

Jesus Christ, what did he *think* I meant by it?

"I'm not a virgin, Jim," I repeated—as though the problem had been that he hadn't heard me correctly the first time.

He sat up and stared ahead for a long time, collecting himself.

Quietly, I put my shirt back on. This is not the sort of conversation that you want to be having while your boobs are hanging out.

"Why?" he asked finally, his face hard with pain and betrayal. "Why aren't you a virgin, Vee?"

That's when I started crying.

Angela, I must pause here for a moment to tell you something.

I am an old woman now. As such, I have reached an age where I cannot *stand* the tears of young girls. It exasperates me to no end. I especially cannot stand the tears of pretty young girls—pretty young affluent girls, worst of all—who have never had to struggle or work for anything in their lives, and who thus fall apart at the slightest disturbance. When I see pretty young girls crying at the drop of a hat these days, it makes me want to strangle them.

But falling apart is something that all pretty young girls seem to know how to do instinctively—and they do it because it *works*. It works for the same reason that an octopus is able to escape in a cloud of ink: because tears provide a distracting screen. Buckets of tears can divert difficult conversations and alter the flow of natural consequences. The reason for this is that most people (men especially) hate to see a pretty young girl crying, and they will automatically rush to comfort her—forgetting what they were talking about only a moment before. At the very least, a thick showering of tears can create a *pause*—and in that pause, a pretty young girl can buy herself some time.

I want you to know, Angela, that there came a point in my life when I stopped doing this—when I stopped responding to life's challenges with floods of tears. Because really, there is no dignity in it. These days, I am the sort of tough-skinned old battle-ax who would rather stand dry-eyed and undefended in the most hostile underbrush of truth than degrade herself and everyone else by collapsing into a swamp of manipulative tears.

But in the autumn of 1941, I had not yet become that woman.

So I wept and wept, in the backseat of Jim Larsen's Buick—the prettiest and most copious tears you ever saw.

"What is it, Vee?" Jim's voice betrayed an undertow of desperation. He had never before seen me cry. Instantly, his attention turned from his own shock to my care. "Why are you crying, dear?"

His solicitousness only made me sob harder.

He was so good, and I was such trash!

He gathered me in his arms, begging me to stop. And because I could not speak in that moment, and because I could not stop crying, he just went right ahead and made up a story for himself about why I was not a virgin.

He said, "Somebody did something horrible to you, didn't they, Vee? Somebody in New York City?"

Well, Jim, lots of people did lots of things to me in New York City—but I can't say that any of it was particularly horrible.

That would have been the correct and honest answer. But I couldn't very well give that answer, so I said nothing, and just sobbed away in his competent arms—my heaving voicelessness giving him plenty of time to embellish his own details.

"That's why you came home from the city, isn't it?" he said, as though it were all dawning on him now. "Because somebody violated you, didn't they? That's why you're always so meek. Oh, Vee. You poor, poor girl."

I heaved some more.

"Just nod if it's true," he said.

Oh, Jesus. How do you get out of *this* one?

You don't. You can't get out of this one. Unless you're able to be honest, which of course I could not do. By admitting that I wasn't a virgin, I had already played my one card of truthfulness for the year; I didn't have another one in the deck. His story was preferable, anyway.

God forgive me, I nodded.

(I know. It was awful of me. And it feels just as awful for me to write that sentence as it did for you to read it. But I didn't come here to lie to you, Angela. I want you to know exactly who I was back then—and that's what happened.)

"I won't make you talk about it," he said, petting my head and staring off into the middle distance.

I nodded through my tears: *Yes, please don't make me talk about it.*

If anything, he seemed relieved not to hear the details.

He held me for a long time, until my crying had subsided. Then he smiled at me valiantly (if a little shakily) and said, "It's all going to be all right, Vee. You're safe now. I want you to know that I will *never* treat you like you are tainted. And you needn't worry—I'll never tell anyone. I love you, Vee. I will marry you despite this."

His words were noble, but his face said: *Somehow I will learn to bear this repugnant hunk of awfulness.*

"I love you, too, Jim," I lied, and I kissed him with something that might have been interpreted as gratitude and relief.

But if you would like to know when—in all my years of life—I felt the most sordid and vile, it was right then.

———

Winter came.

The days got shorter and colder. My commute to work with my father was executed both morning and night in pitch darkness.

I was working on knitting Jim a sweater for Christmas. I had not unpacked my sewing machine since returning home nine months earlier—even looking at its case made me feel sad and grim—but I had recently taken up knitting. I was good with my hands, and handling the thick wool came easily. I'd ordered a pattern through the mail for a classic Norwegian sweater—blue and white, with a snowflake pattern—and I worked on it whenever I was alone. Jim was proud of his Norwegian heritage, and I thought he might like a gift that reminded him of his father's country. In making this sweater, I pushed myself to the same level of excellence my grandmother would have demanded of me, ripping back whole rows of stitches when they were not perfect, and trying them again and again. It would be my first sweater, yes, but its excellence would be beyond reproach.

Other than that, I was doing nothing with myself but going where I was told, filing whatever needed to be filed (more or less alphabetically), and doing whatever anyone else did.

It was a Sunday. Jim and I had gone to church together, and then we went off to see a matinee of *Dumbo*. When we came out of the movie theater, the news was already all over town: The Japanese had just attacked the American fleet at Pearl Harbor.

By the next day, we were at war.

Jim didn't need to enlist.

He could have dodged the war for so many reasons. For one thing, he was old enough that the draft would not necessarily have caught him. For another, he was the sole financial provider of a widowed mother. And lastly, he worked in a position of authority at the hematite mine, which was an industry essential to the war effort. There would have been deferments available in all directions, should he have wished to reach for them.

But you can't be a man with the constitution of Jim Larsen and let other boys go to war on your behalf. That's not how he was *forged*. And on December 9, he sat me down for a conversation about it. We were alone at Jim's house—his mother was at lunch with her sister in another town—and he asked if he could have a serious talk. He was determined to join up, he said. This was his duty, he said. He would never be able to live with himself if he didn't help his country in its hour of need, he said.

I think he expected me to try to talk him out of it, but I didn't.

"I understand," I said.

"And there's something else we should discuss." Jim took a deep breath. "I don't want to upset you, Vee. But I've given the matter a great deal of thought. Given the circumstances of the war, I think we should cancel our engagement."

Again, he looked at me carefully, waiting for me to protest.

"Go on," I said.

"I can't ask you to wait for me, Vee. It's not right. I don't know how long this war will last, or what will become of me. I could come back injured, or not come back at all. You're a young girl. You shouldn't put your life away on my account."

Now, let me point out a few things here.

For one thing, I wasn't a young girl. I was twenty-one—which by the standards of the day practically made me a crone. (Back in 1941, it was no joke for a twenty-one-year-old woman to lose her wedding engagement, believe me.) For another thing, a lot of young couples across America that week were in exactly the straits as Jim and I.

Millions of American boys were shipping off to war in the aftermath of Pearl Harbor. Vast numbers of them, though, *hastened* to get married before they departed. Some of this rush to the altar surely had to do with romance, or with fear, or with the desire to have sex before facing possible death. Or maybe it was driven by an anxiety about pregnancy, for couples who'd already begun having sex. Some of it probably had to do with an urgent push to pack as much life as possible into a short amount of time. (Your father, Angela, was one of the many young American men who sealed himself up in swift matrimony to his neighborhood sweetheart before being thrown into battle. But of course you would know that.)

And there were millions of American girls eager to nail down their sweethearts before the war took all the boys away. There were even girls who angled to marry soldiers whom they barely knew, anticipating that the boy might be killed in battle and his widow would receive a ten-thousand-dollar allotment for his death. (These kinds of girls were called "Allotment Annies"—and when I heard about them, I felt some relief in knowing that there were actually worse people out there than me.)

What I'm saying is this: the general trend among people in these circumstances was to hurry up and get married already—not to call off their damn engagements. All over America that week, dreamy-eyed boys and girls were following the same romantic script, saying, "I'll always love you! I'll prove my love by marrying you right now! I'll love you forever, come what may!"

This isn't what Jim was saying, though. He wasn't following the script. And neither was I.

I asked, "Would you like your ring back, Jim?"

Unless I was dreaming—and I do not believe I was dreaming—an expression of enormous relief flickered across his face. In that moment, I knew what I was seeing. I was seeing a man who'd just realized he had an *out*—that he did not have to marry the frighteningly tainted girl now. *And* he could keep his honor. He looked so nakedly grateful. The reaction lasted only for an instant, but I saw it.

Then he pulled himself back together. "You know I will always love you, Vee."

"And I will always love you, too, Jim," I dutifully replied.

Now we were back on script.

I slid that ring off my finger and placed it firmly in his waiting palm. I do believe to this day that it felt just as good for him to get that ring back as it felt for me to shed it.

And thus we were saved from each other.

You see, Angela, history is not so busy shaping nations that it cannot take the time to shape the lives of two insignificant people. Among the many revisions and transformations that the Second World War would bring to the planet was this tiny plot twist: Jim Larsen and Vivian Morris were mercifully spared from matrimony.

An hour after we had broken off our engagement, the two of us were having the most outrageous, memorable, backbreaking sex you could ever imagine.

I suppose I had initiated it.

All right, I'll admit it: categorically, I had initiated it.

Once I'd returned the ring, Jim had offered me a tender kiss and a warm embrace. There's a way that a man can hold a woman that says, "I don't want to hurt your gentle feelings, darling," and that's how he was holding me. But my gentle feelings had not been hurt. If anything, it felt like a cork had been yanked from my skull and I was now exploding with an intoxicating rush of freedom. Jim was going to be *gone*— and of his own volition, better still! I would come out of this situation looking blameless, and so would he. (But more important: me!) The threat had been lifted. There was nothing more to be pretended, nothing more to be disguised. From this moment onward—ring off my hand, engagement canceled, reputation intact—I had nothing more to lose.

He gave me another one of those tender "I'm sorry if you're hurting, baby" kisses, and I don't mind saying that I responded by sticking my tongue so far down that man's throat, it's a miracle I didn't lick the bottommost quadrant of his heart.

Now, Jim was a good man. He was a churchgoing man. He was a respectful man. But he was still a *man*—and once I switched that toggle over to complete sexual permission, he responded. (I don't know any man who *wouldn't* have responded, she says modestly.) And who knows? Maybe he was drunk on the same spirit of freedom as I was. All I know is that within a few minutes, I had managed to push and pull him through his house to his bedroom, and gotten him situated on his narrow pine bed, where I could now tear off both his clothes and mine with unfettered abandon.

I will say that I knew a good deal more about the act of love than Jim did. This was immediately obvious. If he'd ever had sex at all, he clearly hadn't had much of it. He was navigating around my body the way you drive a car around an unfamiliar neighborhood—slowly and carefully while nervously looking for street signs and landmarks. This would not do. Swiftly it became evident that I would need to be the one driving this car, so to speak. I had learned some things back in New York, and in no time at all, I employed my rusty old skills and took over the whole operation. I did this quickly and wordlessly—too quickly for him to have a chance to question what I was up to.

I drove that man like a mule, Angela, is what I'm saying. I didn't want to give him the slightest opportunity to reconsider, or to slow me down. He was breathless, he was carried away, he was fully consumed—and I kept him that way for as long as I could. And I will give him this—he had the most beautiful shoulders I'd ever seen.

Christ, but I had missed having sex!

What I will never forget about that occasion was glancing down at Jim's all-American face as I rode him into oblivion, and seeing—almost lost amid his other expressions of passion and abandon—a look of baffled terror, as he stared up at me in excited, but panicked, wonderment. His guileless blue eyes, in that moment, seemed to be asking, "Who *are* you?"

If I had to guess, I suppose my eyes were responding: "I don't know, pal, but it's none of your business."

When we were done, he could barely even look at me or speak to me.

It's incredible how much I didn't mind.

Jim departed the following day for basic training.

As for me, I was delighted to learn three weeks down the line that I had not gotten pregnant. It had been quite a gamble I'd taken there—having sex with no precautions whatsoever—but I do believe it was worth it.

As for the Norwegian sweater I'd been knitting, I finished it up and mailed it to my brother for Christmas. Walter was stationed in the South Pacific, so I'm not sure what use he had for a heavy wool sweater, but he wrote me a polite note of thanks. That was the first time he'd communicated with me directly since our dreadful drive home to Clinton. So that was a welcome development. A softening of relations, you could say.

Years later, I found out that Jim Larsen had won the Distinguished Service Cross for extreme valor and risk of life in actual combat with an armed enemy force. He eventually settled in New Mexico, married a wealthy woman, and served in the state senate. So much for my father saying he would never be a leader.

Good for Jim.

We both turned out fine in the end.

See that, Angela? Wars are not necessarily bad for everyone.

TWENTY-THREE

After Jim left, I became the recipient of much sympathy from my family and neighbors. They all assumed I was heartbroken to have lost my fiancé. I hadn't earned their sympathy, but of course I took it anyway. It was better than condemnation and suspicion. It was certainly better than trying to explain anything.

My father was furious that Jim Larsen had abandoned both his hematite mine and his daughter (in that order of fury, without a doubt). My mother was mildly disappointed that I wouldn't be getting married in April, after all, but she looked as though she would survive the blow. She had other things to do that weekend, she told me. April is a big time for horse shows in upstate New York.

As for me, I felt as though I had just woken from a drugged slumber. Now my only desire was to find something interesting to do with myself. I gave the briefest consideration to asking my parents if I could return to college, but my heart wasn't in it. I wanted to get out of Clinton, though. I knew I couldn't go back to New York City, having burned all my bridges, but I also knew that there were other cities to be considered. Philadelphia and Boston were rumored to be nice; maybe I could settle in one of those places.

I had just enough sense to realize that if I wanted to move, I would need money, so I got my sewing machine out of its crate at last and set up shop as a seamstress in our guest bedroom. I let word spread that I was now available for custom tailoring and alterations. Soon I had plenty to do. Wedding season was coming again. People needed dresses, but that need brought problems—namely, fabric shortages. You couldn't get good lace and silk anymore from France, and moreover it was considered unpatriotic to spend a good deal of money on such a wild luxury as a wedding gown. So I used the scavenging skills I'd honed at the Lily Playhouse to create works of beauty out of precious little.

One of my friends from childhood—a bright girl named Madeleine—was getting married in late May. Her family had fallen on hard times since her father's coronary the year before. She couldn't have afforded a good dress in peacetime, much less now. So we scoured her family's attic together, and I constructed Madeleine the most romantic concoction you ever saw—made from *both* of her grandmothers' old wedding gowns, disassembled and put back together in a brand-new arrangement, with a long, antique lace train and everything. It was not an easy dress to make (the old silk was so fragile, I had to handle it like nitroglycerine), but it worked.

Madeleine was so grateful, she named me as her maid of honor. For the occasion of her wedding, I sewed myself a snazzy little kelly green suit with a peplum jacket, using some raw silk I'd inherited from my grandmother and had stored under my bed years earlier. (Ever since I'd met Edna Parker Watson, I tried to wear suits whenever possible. Among other lessons, that woman had taught me that a suit will always make you look more chic and important than a dress. And not too much jewelry! "A majority of the time," Edna said, "jewelry is an attempt to cover up a badly chosen or ill-fitting garment." And yes, it is true—I still could not stop thinking about Edna.)

Madeleine and I both looked splendid. She was a popular girl, and a lot of people came to her wedding. I got all kinds of customers after that. I also got to kiss one of Madeleine's cousins at the reception—outside, against a honeysuckle-covered fence.

I was beginning to feel a bit more like myself.

Longing for a bit of frippery one afternoon, I put on a pair of sunglasses I'd purchased many months earlier in New York City, purely because Celia had swooned over them. The glasses were dark, with giant black frames, and they were studded with tiny seashells. They made me look like an enormous insect on a beach vacation, but I was mad for them.

Finding these sunglasses made me miss Celia. I missed the glorious spectacle of her. I missed dressing up together, and putting on makeup together, and conquering New York together. I missed the sensation of walking into a nightclub with her, and setting every man in the place panting at our arrival. (Hell, Angela—maybe I still miss that sensation, seventy years later!) Dear God, I wondered, what had become of Celia? Had she landed on her feet somehow? I hoped so, but I feared the worst. I feared she was scraping and struggling, broke and abandoned.

I came downstairs wearing my absurd glasses. My mother stopped in her tracks when she saw me. "For the love of mud, Vivian, what is *that?*"

"That's called fashion," I told her. "These sorts of frames are very much in style just now in New York City."

"I'm not sure I'm glad I lived to see the day," she said.

I kept them on anyhow.

How could I have explained that I wore them in honor of a fallen comrade, lost behind enemy lines?

In June, I asked my father if I could stop working in his office. I was making as much money sewing as I could make pretending to file papers and answer phones, and it was more satisfying, too. Best yet, as I told my father, my customers were paying me in cash, so I didn't have to report my earnings to the government. That sealed the deal; he let me go. My father would do anything to hornswoggle the government.

For the first time in my life, I had some money saved.

I didn't know what to do with it, but I had it.

Having money saved is not quite the same thing as having a plan, mind you—but it does start to make a girl feel as though a plan could someday be possible.

The days got longer.

In mid-July, I was sitting down to dinner with my parents when we heard a car pull into the driveway. My mother and father looked up, startled—the way they were always startled when something even slightly disturbed their routine.

"Dinner hour," my father said, managing to form those two words into a grim lecture about the inevitable collapse of civilization.

I answered the door. It was Aunt Peg. She was red-faced and sweaty in the summer heat, she was wearing the most deranged getup (an oversized men's plaid Oxford shirt, a pair of baggy dungaree culottes, and an old straw farm hat with a turkey feather in its brim), and I don't think I've ever been more surprised or more happy to see anyone in my life. I was so surprised and happy, in fact, that I actually forgot at first to be ashamed of myself in her presence. I threw my arms around her in flagrant joy.

"Kiddo!" she said with a grin. "You're looking choice!"

My parents had a less enthusiastic response to Peg's arrival, but they adjusted themselves as best they could to this unexpected circumstance. Our maid dutifully set another place. My father offered Peg a cocktail, but to my surprise she said she would rather have iced tea, if it wasn't too much trouble.

Peg plunked herself down at our dining-room table, mopped at her damp forehead with one of our fine Irish linen napkins, looked around at the lot of us, and smiled. "So! How's everyone faring up here in the hinterlands?"

"I didn't know you had a car," my father said by means of a reply.

"I don't. It belongs to a choreographer I know. He's gone off to the Vineyard in his boyfriend's Cadillac, so he let me borrow this one. It's a Chrysler. It's not so bad, for an old clunker. I'm sure he'd let you take it for a spin, if you'd like."

"How'd you get the gas rations?" my father asked the sister whom he had not seen in over two years. (You might wonder why this was his preferred line of questioning, in lieu of a more standard salutation, but Dad had his motives. Gas rationing had just been mandated in New York State a few months earlier, and my father was in fits about it: *He didn't work as hard as he did in order to live in a totalitarian government! What would come next? Telling a man what time of night he might go to sleep?* I prayed that the subject of gas rations would quickly change.)

"I cobbled together some stamps with a bit of bribery here and a bit of black-market elbow grease there. It's not so hard in the city to get gas stamps. People don't need their cars as much as they do out here." Then Peg turned to my mother and asked warmly, "Louise, how are you?"

"I'm well, Peg," said my mother, who was looking at her sister-in-law with an expression I would not call suspicious as much as cautious. (I couldn't blame her. It didn't make sense for Peg to be in Clinton. It wasn't Christmas, and nobody had died.) "And how are you?"

"Disreputable as always. But it's nice to escape the general mayhem of the city and come up here. I should do this more often. I'm sorry I didn't let you folks know I was coming. It was a sudden decision. Your horses are well, Louise?"

"Well enough. There haven't been as many shows since the war started, of course. They haven't liked this heat, either. But they're well."

"What brings you here, anyhow?" my father asked.

My father didn't *hate* his sister, but he did hold her in rather violent contempt. He thought she'd done nothing but revel about recklessly with her life (not unlike the way Walter perceived me, now that I think of it), and I suppose he had a point. Still, you'd think he could have ginned up a slightly more hospitable welcome.

"Well, Douglas, I'll tell you. I've come to ask Vivian if she'll return to New York City with me."

At the sound of these words, a dusty old doorway in the center of my heart blew open, and a thousand white doves flew out. I didn't even dare to speak. I was afraid that if I opened my mouth, the invitation would evaporate.

"Why?" my father asked.

"I need her. I've been commissioned by the military to put on a series of lunchtime shows for workers at the Brooklyn Navy Yard. Some propaganda, some song-and-dance numbers, some romantic dramas and such. To keep up morale. That sort of thing. I don't have enough help anymore to run the playhouse and also handle the Navy commission. I could really use Vivian."

"But what does Vivian know about romantic dramas and such?" my mother asked.

"More than you might think," said Peg.

Thankfully, Peg didn't look at me when she said this. I could feel my neck turning red all the same.

"But she's only just settled back here," said my mother. "And she got so homesick last year in New York. The city didn't suit her."

"You were *homesick*?" Now Peg was looking me straight in the eye, with the faintest trace of a smile. "That's what happened, was it?"

My blush spread farther up my neck. But again, I didn't dare speak.

"Look," said Peg, "it doesn't have to be forever. Vivian could come back to Clinton if she gets homesick again. But I'm in a spot of trouble. It's awful hard to find workers these days. The men are all gone. Even my showgirls have gone to work in factories. Everyone can pay better than I can. I just need hands on deck. Hands I can trust."

She said it. She said the word "trust."

"It's hard for me to find workers, too," said my father.

"What, is Vivian working for you?" Peg asked.

"No, but she did work for me for some time, and I might need her at some point. I think she could learn a great deal from working for me again."

"Oh, does Vivian have a particular bent for the mining industry?"

"It just seems to me that you've driven a long distance to find a menial laborer. It seems to me you could've filled the position in the city. But then I've never understood why you always resist everything that might make your life easier."

"Vivian's not menial labor," Peg said. "She's a sensational costumer."

"What makes you say that?"

"Years of exhaustive research in the field of theater, Douglas."

"Ha. The *field* of theater."

"I'd like to go," I said, finding my voice at last.

"Why?" my father asked me. "Why would you want to go back to that city, where people live on top of each other, and you can't even see the daylight?"

"Says the man who has spent the better part of his life in a *mine*," retorted Peg.

Honestly, they were like a couple of children. It wouldn't have surprised me if they started kicking each other under the table.

But now they were all looking at me, waiting for my answer. Why did I want to go to New York? How could I explain it? How could I explain what this proposal felt like, compared to the marriage proposal Jim Larsen had recently offered me? It was merely the difference between cough syrup and champagne.

"I would like to go to New York City again," I announced, "because I wish to expand the prospects of my life."

I delivered this line with a certain amount of authority, I felt, and it got everyone's attention. (I must confess that I'd heard the phrase "I wish to expand the prospects of my life" on a radio soap opera recently, and it had stayed with me. But no matter. In this situation, it worked. Also it was true.)

"If you go," said my mother, "we won't be supporting you. We can't keep giving you an allowance. Not at your age."

"I don't need an allowance. I'll earn my own way."

Even the word "allowance" embarrassed me. I never wanted to hear it again.

"You'll have to find employment," my father said.

Peg stared at her brother in astonishment. "It's incredible, Douglas, how you never listen to me. Only moments ago—at this very table—I told you that I had a job for Vivian."

"She'll need *proper* employment," said my father.

"She'll *have* proper employment. She'll be working for the United States Navy, just like her brother. The Navy's given me enough of a budget to hire another person. She'll be a government employee."

Now it was I who wanted to kick Peg under the table. For my father, there was scarcely a worse combination of two words in the English language than "government employee." It would have been better if Peg had said I'd be working as a "money thief."

"You can't keep going back and forth between here and New York City eternally, you know," said my mother.

"I won't," I promised. And boy, did I mean it.

"I don't want my daughter spending a lifetime working in the theater," said my father.

Peg rolled her eyes. "Yes, that would be *appalling*."

"I don't like New York," he said. "It's a city full of second-place winners."

"Yes, famously," shot back Peg. "Nobody who has ever been successful at anything has ever lived in Manhattan."

My father must not have cared that much about his argument, though, because he didn't dig in.

In all honesty, I think my parents were willing to consider allowing me to leave because they were weary of me. In their eyes, I shouldn't have been inhabiting their home anyway—and it was *their* home. I should have been out of the house a long time ago—ideally through the portal of college, followed by a finalizing shunt into matrimony. I didn't come from a culture where children are welcome to remain in the family household after childhood. (My parents hadn't even wanted me around that much during childhood, for that matter, if you consider the amount of time I'd spent at boarding school and summer camps.)

My father just had to razz Aunt Peg a little more before he could finally agree to it.

"I'm unconvinced that New York would be a good influence on Vivian," he said. "I would hate to see a daughter of mine becoming a Democrat."

"I wouldn't worry about that," said Peg, with a fat smile of satisfaction. "I've been into the matter. Turns out, they don't allow registered Democrats into the Anarchist Party."

That line actually made my mother laugh—to her credit.

"I'm going," I pronounced. "I'm nearly twenty-two years old. There's nothing here for me in Clinton. From this point forward, where I live should be my decision."

"That's laying it on a bit thick, Vivian," said my mother. "You won't be twenty-two until October, and you've never paid for a thing in your life. You don't have the faintest notion of how anything in the world functions."

Still, I could tell she was pleased by the tone of resolve in my voice. My mother, after all, was a woman who had spent her life on horseback, hurling herself at ditches and fences. Perhaps she was of the opinion that when faced with the challenges and obstacles of life, a woman should *leap*.

"If you take on this commitment," said my father, "at the very least, we expect you to see it through. One cannot afford in life to do less than one promises."

My heart quickened.

That last, limp lecture was his way of saying yes.

Peg and I left for New York City the following morning.

It took us forever to get there, as she insisted on driving her borrowed car at a patriotic, gas-preserving thirty-five miles an hour. I didn't care how long it took, though. The sensation of being pulled back toward a place I loved—a place that I had not imagined would ever welcome me again—was such a delightful one that I didn't mind stretching it out. For me, the ride was as thrilling as a Coney Island roller coaster. I was more keyed up than I'd felt in over a year. Keyed up, yes, but also nervous.

What would I find, back in New York?

Who would I find?

"You've made a hefty choice," said Peg, as soon as we got on the road. "Good for you, kiddo."

"Do you really need me back in the city, Peg?" It was a question I had not dared to pose in the presence of my parents.

She shrugged. "I can find a use for you." But then she smiled. "No, Vivian—it's quite true. I've bitten off more than I can chew with this Navy Yard commission. I might have come for you sooner, but I wanted to give you more time to cool your heels. In my experience, it's always important to take a break between catastrophes. You took a bad knock in the city last year. I figured you'd need some time to recover."

This reference to my *catastrophe* made my stomach flip.

"About that, Peg—" I started.

"It is no more to be mentioned."

"I'm so sorry for what I did."

"Of course you are. I'm sorry for many of the things I've done, too. Everyone is sorry. It's good to be sorry—but don't make a fetish of it. The one good thing about being Protestant is that we are not expected to cringe forever in contrition. Yours was a venial sin, Vivian, but not a mortal one."

"I don't know what that means."

"I'm not sure I do, either. It's just something I read once. Here is what I do know, however: sins of the flesh will not get you punished in the afterlife. They will only get you punished in *this* life. As you've now learned."

"I only wish I hadn't caused so much trouble for everyone."

"It's easy to be wise after the event. But what's the use of being twenty years old, if not to make gross errors?"

"Did you make gross errors when you were twenty?"

"Of course I did. Not nearly so bad as yours, but I had my days."

She smiled to show she was teasing. Or maybe she wasn't teasing. It didn't matter. She was taking me back.

"Thank you for coming to get me, Peg."

"Well, I missed you. I like you, kiddo, and once I like a person, I can only like them always. That's a rule of my life."

This was the most wonderful thing anyone had ever said to me. I marinated in it for a while. And then slowly the marinade turned sour, as I recalled that not everyone was as forgiving as Aunt Peg.

"I'm nervous about seeing Edna," I said at last.

Peg looked surprised. "Why would you see Edna?"

"Why would I *not* see Edna? I'll see her at the Lily."

"Kiddo, Edna's not at the Lily anymore. She's in rehearsals right now for *As You Like It,* over at the Mansfield. She and Arthur moved out of the Lily in the spring. They're living at the Savoy now. You didn't hear?"

"But what about *City of Girls*?"

"Oh, boy. You really haven't heard anything, have you?"

"Heard anything about what?"

"Back in March, Billy got an offer to move *City of Girls* to the Morosco Theatre. He took the offer, packed up the show, and went."

"He packed up the *show*?"

"Yes, indeed."

"He *took* it? He took it from the Lily?"

"Well, he wrote that play and he directed it—so technically it was his to take. That was his argument, anyway. Not that I argued with him about it. Wasn't gonna win that one."

"But what about—?" I couldn't finish the question.

What about *everything* and *everyone*, is what I might have asked.

"Yes," said Peg. "What about it? Well, that's how Billy operates, kiddo. It was a good deal for him. You know the Morosco. It has a thousand seats, so the money is better. Edna went with him, of course. They did the show for a few months, same as always, until Edna got tired of it. Now she's gone back to her Shakespeare. They've replaced her with Helen Hayes, which isn't working, as far as I can see. I like Helen, don't get me wrong. She's got everything Edna's got—except that *thing* that Edna's got. Nobody's got that *thing*. Gertrude Lawrence might have been able to do it justice—she's got her own version of that *thing*—but she's not in town. Really, nobody can do what Edna can do. But they're still packing the house night after night over there, and it's like Billy's got a license to print money."

I didn't even know what to say to all this. I was appalled.

"Pick up your jaw, kiddo," Peg said. "You look like you just fell off a turnip truck."

"But what about the Lily? What about you and Olive?"

"Business as usual. Scrambling along. Putting on our dumb little productions again. Trying to lure back our humble neighborhood audience. It's harder now that the war is on, and half our audience is off fighting it. It's mostly grandmothers and children these days. That's why I took the commission at the Navy Yard—we need the income. Olive was right all along, of course. She knew we'd be left holding the bag after Billy took his playthings and went away. I guess I knew it, too. That's always the way it goes with Billy. Of course, he took our best performers with him, too. Gladys went with him. Jennie and Roland, too."

She said all this so mildly. As though betrayal and ruin were the most mundane happenings you could ever imagine.

"What about Benjamin?" I asked.

"Unfortunately, Benjamin got drafted. Can't blame Billy for that. But can you imagine Benjamin in the military? Putting a gun in those gifted hands? Such a waste. I hate it for him."

"What about Mr. Herbert?"

"Still with me. Mr. Herbert and Olive will never leave me."

"No sign of Celia, though?"

It wasn't really a question. I already knew the answer.

"No sign of Celia," Peg confirmed. "But I'm sure she's fine. That cat has about six more lives in her, believe me. I'll tell you what is interesting, though," Peg went on, clearly not concerning herself with the fate of Celia Ray. "Billy was right, too. Billy said we could create a hit play together, and we actually did it. We pulled it off! Olive never believed in *City of Girls*. She thought it would bomb, but she was dead wrong. It was a terrific show. I was right, I believe, to take the risk with Billy. It was an awful lot of fun while it lasted."

As she told me all this, I stared at her profile, searching for signs of disturbance or suffering—but there were none.

She turned her head, saw me staring at her, and laughed. "Try not to look so shocked, Vivian. It makes you look simple."

"But Billy promised you the rights to the play! I was there! I heard him say it in the kitchen, the first morning he came to the Lily."

"Billy promises a lot of things. Somehow, he never got around to putting it in writing."

"I just can't believe he did that to you," I said.

"Look, kiddo, I've always known how Billy is, and I invited him in anyway. I don't regret it. It was an adventure. You must learn in life to take things more lightly, my dear. The world is always changing. Learn how to allow for it. Someone makes a promise, and then they break it. A play gets good notices, and then it folds. A marriage looks strong, and then they divorce. For a while there's no war, and then there's another war. If you get too upset about it all, you become a stupid, unhappy person—and where's the good in that? Now enough about Billy—how was your year? Where were you when Pearl Harbor happened?"

"At the movies. Watching *Dumbo*. Where were you?"

"Up at the Polo Grounds, watching football. Last Giants game of the season. Then suddenly, late in the second quarter, they start making these strange announcements, asking all active military personnel to report immediately to the main office. I knew right then something bad was afoot. Then Sonny Franck got injured. That distracted me. Not that Sonny Franck has anything to do with it. Hell of a player, though. What a tragic day. Were you at the movies with that fellow you got engaged to? What was his name?"

"Jim Larsen. How did you know I'd gotten engaged?"

"Your mother told me about it last night while you were packing. Sounds like you escaped by the skin of your teeth. Sounds like even your mother was relieved, though she's tough to read. She was of the opinion that you didn't much like him."

This surprised me. My mother and I had never once had an intimate conversation about Jim—or about anything, really. How had she known?

"He was a nice man," I said lamely.

"Good for him. Give him a trophy for it, but don't marry a man just because he's nice. And try not to make a habit of getting engaged in the first place, Vivvie. It can lead to marriage if you're not careful. Why'd you say yes to him, anyhow?"

"I didn't know what else to do with myself. Like I say, he was nice."

"So many girls get married for that same reason. Find something else to do with yourself, I say. Gosh, ladies, take up a hobby!"

"Why did *you* get married?" I asked.

"Because I liked him, Vivvie. I liked Billy very much. That's the only reason to ever marry somebody—if you love them or like them. I still like him, you know. I had dinner with him only last week."

"You *did*?"

"Of course I did. Look, I can understand that you're upset with Billy right now—a lot of people are—but what did I tell you earlier, about my rule in life?"

When I didn't answer, because I couldn't remember, she reminded me: "Once I like a person, I can only like them always."

"Oh, that's right." But I still wasn't convinced.

She smiled at me again. "What's the matter, Vivvie? You think that rule should only apply to you?"

I t was evening by the time we arrived in New York City.

It was July 15, 1942.

The town was perched proud and solid on its nest of granite, tucked between its two dark rivers. Its stacks of skyscrapers glittered like columns of fireflies in the velvety summer air. We crossed over the silent, commanding bridge—broad and long as a condor's wing—and entered the city. This dense place. This meaningful place. The greatest metropolis the world has ever known—or at least that's what I've always thought.

I was overcome with reverence.

I would plant my little life there and never abandon it again.

TWENTY-FOUR

The next morning, I woke up in Billy's old room all over again. It was just me in the bed this time. No Celia, no hangover, no disasters.

I had to admit: it felt good to have the bed to myself.

For a while I listened to the sounds of the Lily Playhouse coming to life. Sounds I never thought I would hear again. Someone must have been running a bath, because the pipes were banging in protest. Two telephones were already ringing—one upstairs, and one in the offices below. I felt so happy, it made me light-headed.

I put on my robe and wandered forth to make myself some coffee. I found Mr. Herbert sitting at the kitchen table just like always—wearing his undershirt, staring at his notebook, drinking his Sanka, and composing his jokes for an upcoming show.

"Good morning, Mr. Herbert!" I said.

He looked up at me and—to my amazement—he actually smiled.

"I see you've been reinstated, Miss Morris," he said. "*Good.*"

———

By noon that day, I was at the Brooklyn Navy Yard with Peg and Olive, getting oriented to the job at hand.

We'd taken the subway from midtown to the York Street station, then transferred to a streetcar. Over the next three years, I would make this commute nearly every day and in every kind of weather. I would share that commute with tens of thousands of other workers, all changing shifts like clockwork. The commute would become tedious, and sometimes spirit-breakingly exhausting. But on that day, it was all new and I was excited. I was outfitted in a snazzy lilac suit (although never again would I wear something so nice to that filthy, greasy destination) and my hair was clean and bouncy. I had my paperwork in order so that I could be officially inducted as a Navy employee (Bureau of Yards and Docks, Classification: Skilled Laborer). The job came with a salary of seventy cents an hour, which was a fortune for a girl my age. They even issued me my own pair of safety glasses—although my eyes were never in danger from anything more serious than Peg's cigarette embers flying up in my face.

This would be my first real job—if you don't count the work I did in my father's office back in Clinton, which you shouldn't.

I'd been nervous to see Olive again. I still felt so ashamed of myself for my shenanigans, and for having needed her to rescue me from the talons of Walter Winchell. I was afraid she might chastise me, or look upon me with contempt. I had my first moment alone with her that morning. She and Peg and I were walking downstairs, on our way out the door to Brooklyn. Peg had to run back up to get her thermos, so for a minute it had just been Olive and me standing there on the landing between the second and third floors of the playhouse. I decided this would be my opportunity to apologize, and to thank her for having gallantly saved me.

"Olive," I began. "I owe you a great debt—"

"Oh, Vivian," she interrupted, "don't be so *grasping*."

And that was the end of that.

We had a job to do, and there wasn't any time for flimflam.

S pecifically, our job was this:

We were assigned by the military to put on two shows a day at the Brooklyn Navy Yard, in a bustling cafeteria located right on Wallabout Bay. You have to understand, Angela, that the Navy Yard was *huge*—the busiest in the world—with over two hundred acres of buildings and almost a hundred thousand employees working around the clock throughout the war years. There were over forty active cafeterias at the Yard and we were in charge of "entertainment and education" for just one of them. Our cafeteria was number 24, but everyone called it "Sammy." (I was never clear on why. Maybe because they served so many sandwiches? Or maybe because our head cook was named Mr. Samuelson?) Sammy fed thousands of people a day—serving enormous piles of limp and tired food to equally limp and tired laborers.

It was our task to entertain these weary workers while they ate. But we were more than entertainers; we were also propagandists. The Navy filtered information and inspiration through us. We had to keep everyone angry and fired up at Hitler and Hirohito at all times (we killed Hitler so many times, in so many different skits, that I can't believe the man wasn't having nightmares about us all the way over there in Germany). But we also had to keep our workers concerned about the welfare of our boys overseas—reminding them that whenever they slacked off on the job, they put American sailors at risk. We had to issue warnings that spies were everywhere, and that loose lips sink ships. We had to give safety lessons and news updates. And in addition to all that, we had to deal with military censors who often sat in the front row of our performances to make sure we were not deviating from the party line. (My favorite censor was a genial man named Mr. Gershon. I spent so much time with him, we became like a family. I attended his son's bar mitzvah.)

We had to communicate all this information to our workers in thirty minutes, twice a day.

For three years.

And we had to keep our material fresh and fun, or the audience might start throwing food at us. ("It's good to be back in the field," Peg said happily, the first time our audience started booing—and I think she truly meant it.) It was an impossible, thankless, exhausting job, and the Navy gave us precious little to work with, in terms of our "theater." At the front of the cafeteria was a small stage—a platform, really, built of rough pine. We didn't have a curtain or stage lighting, and our "orchestra" amounted to a honky-tonk stand-up piano played by a tiny old local named Mrs. Levinson who (incongruously) could pound those keys so hard you could hear the music all the way from Sands Street. Our props were vegetable crates, and our "dressing room" was the back corner of the kitchen, right next to the dishwasher's station. As for our actors, they were not exactly the cream of the crop. Most of New York's showbiz community had either gone off to battle or gotten good industrial jobs since the advent of the war. This meant that the only people left for us to recruit were the sorts of folks whom Olive, not very kindly, called "the lost and the lame." (To which Peg replied, also not very kindly, "How does that differ from any other theater company?")

So we improvised. We had men in their sixties playing young swains. We had hefty middle-aged women playing the parts of ingénues, or boys. We couldn't pay our players nearly as much as they could earn working on the line, so we were constantly losing our actors and dancers to the Navy Yard itself. Some pretty young girl would be singing a song on our stage one day, and the next day you'd see her eating at

Sammy on her lunch break, with her hair up in a bandanna and cover-alls on. She'd have a wrench in her pocket and a hearty paycheck on its way. It's tough to get a girl back in the spotlight once she's seen a hearty paycheck—and we didn't even *have* a spotlight.

Putting together costumes was, of course, my primary job, although I also wrote the occasional script, and even sometimes penned a song lyric or two. My work had never been more difficult. I had virtually no budget, and, because of the war, there was a nationwide shortage of all the materials I needed. It wasn't just fabrics that were scarce; you couldn't get buttons, zippers, or hooks and eyes, either. I became ferociously inventive. In my most shining moment, I created a vest for the character of King Victor Emmanuel III of Italy using some two-toned jacquard damask I'd ripped from a rotting, overstuffed couch I'd found on the corner of Tenth Avenue and Forty-fourth Street one morning, awaiting removal to the dump. (I won't pretend that the costume smelled good, but our king really looked like a king—and that's saying something, given the fact that he was portrayed by a sunken-chested old man who only one hour before showtime had been cooking beans in the Sammy kitchen.)

Needless to say, I became a fixture at Lowtsky's Used Emporium and Notions—even more than before the war. Marjorie Lowtsky, who was now in high school, became my partner in costuming. She was my fixer, really. Lowtsky's now had a contract to sell textiles and rags to the military, so even they didn't have as much volume or variety to choose from anymore—but they were still the best game in town. So I gave Marjorie a small cut of my salary and she culled and saved the choicest materials for me. Truly, I could not have done my job without her help. Despite our age difference, the two of us grew genuinely fond of each other as the war dragged on, and I soon came to think of her as a friend—although an odd one.

I can still remember the first time I ever shared a cigarette with

Marjorie. I was standing on the loading dock of her parents' warehouse in the dead of winter, taking a break from sorting through the bins in order to have a quiet smoke.

"Let me have a drag of that?" came a voice next to me.

I looked down, and there was little Marjorie Lowtsky—all ninety-five pounds of her—wrapped up in one of those absurdly giant raccoon fur coats that fraternity boys used to wear to football games in the 1920s. On her head, a Canadian Mountie's hat.

"I'm not giving you a cigarette," I said. "You're only sixteen!"

"Exactly," she said. "I've already been smoking for ten years."

Charmed, I caved in to her demands and handed over the smoke. She inhaled it with impressive expertise, and said, "This war isn't satisfying me, Vivian." She was gazing out at the alleyway with an air of world-weariness that I couldn't help but find comical. "I'm displeased with it."

"Displeased with it, are you?" I was trying not to smile. "Well, then, you should do something about it! Write a strongly worded letter to your congressman. Go talk to the president. Put this thing to an end."

"It's only that I've waited so long to grow up, but now there's nothing worth growing up for," she said. "Just all this fighting, fighting, fighting, and working, working, working. It makes a person weary."

"It'll all end soon enough," I said—although I was not sure of that fact myself.

She took another deep drag off the cigarette and said in a very different tone, "All my relatives in Europe are in big trouble, you know. Hitler won't rest till he's gotten rid of every last one of them. Mama doesn't even know where her sisters are anymore, or their kids. My father's on the phone with embassies all day, trying to get his family over here. I have to translate for him a lot of the time. It doesn't look like there's any way for them to get through, though."

"Oh, Marjorie. I'm so sorry. That's terrible."

I didn't know what else to say. This seemed like too serious a situation for a high school student to be facing. I wanted to hug her, but she wasn't the sort of person who cared for hugs.

"I'm disappointed in everybody," she said after a long silence.

"In who, exactly?" I was thinking she would say the Nazis.

"The adults," she said. "All of them. How did they let the world get so out of control?"

"I don't know, honey. But I'm not sure anybody out there really knows what they're doing."

"*Apparently not*," she pronounced with theatrical disdain, flicking the spent cigarette into the alley. "And this is why I'm so eager to grow up, you see. So I won't be at the mercy anymore of people who have no idea what they're doing. I figure the sooner I can get full control of things, the better my life will be."

"That sounds like an excellent plan, Marjorie," I said. "Of course, I've never had a plan for my own life, so I wouldn't know. But it sounds as though you've got it all sorted out."

"You've never had a *plan*?" Marjorie looked up at me in horror. "How do you *get by*?"

"Gosh, Marjorie—you sound just like my mother!"

"Well, if you can't make a plan for your own life, Vivian, then *somebody* needs to be your mother!"

I couldn't help but laugh. "Stop lecturing me, kid. I'm old enough to be your babysitter."

"Ha! My parents would never leave me with somebody as irresponsible as you."

"Well, your parents would probably be right about that."

"I'm just teasing you," she said. "You know that, right? You know that I've always liked you."

"*Really?* You've always liked me, have you? Since you were what— in eighth grade?"

"Hey, give me another cigarette, would you?" she asked. "For later?"

"I shouldn't," I said, but I handed her a few of them, anyhow. "Just don't let your mother know I'm supplying you."

"Since when do my parents need to know what I'm up to?" asked this strange little teenager. She hid the cigarettes in the folds of her enormous fur coat, and gave me a wink. "Now tell me what kind of costumes you came in for today, Vivian, and I'll set you up with whatever you need."

New York was a different place now than it had been my first time around.

Frivolity was dead—unless it was useful and patriotic frivolity, like dancing with soldiers and sailors at the Stage Door Canteen. The city was weighted with seriousness. At every moment, we were expecting to be attacked or invaded—certain that the Germans would bomb us into dust, just as they'd done to London. There were mandatory blackouts. There were a few nights when the authorities even turned off all the lights in Times Square, and the Great White Way became a dark clot—shining rich and black in the night, like pooled mercury. Everyone was in uniform, or ready to serve. Our own Mr. Herbert volunteered as an air-raid warden, wandering around our neighborhood in the evenings with his official city-issued white helmet and red armband. (As he headed out the door, Peg would say, "Dear Mr. Hitler: Please don't bomb us until Mr. Herbert has finished alerting all the neighbors. Sincerely, Pegsy Buell.")

What I most remember about the war years was an overriding sense of *coarseness*. We didn't suffer in New York City like so many people across the world were suffering, but nothing was *fine* anymore—no butter, no pricey cuts of meat, no quality makeup, no fashions from Europe. Nothing was soft. Nothing was a delicacy. The war was a vast, starving colossus that needed everything from us—not just our time and labor, but also our cooking oil, our rubber, our metals, our paper, our coal. We were left with mere scraps. I brushed my teeth with baking soda. I treated my last pair of nylons with such care, you would have thought they were premature babies. (And when those nylons finally died in the middle of 1943, I gave up and started wearing trousers all the time.) I got so busy—and shampoo became so difficult to acquire—that I cut my hair short (very much in the style of Edna Parker Watson's sleek bob, I must admit) and I've never grown it long again.

It was during the war that I became a New Yorker at last. I finally learned my way around the city. I opened a bank account and got my own library card. I had a favorite cobbler now (and I needed one, because of leather rations) and I also had my own dentist. I made friends with my coworkers at the Yard, and we would eat together at the Cumberland Diner after our shift. (I was proud to be able to chip in at the end of those meals, when Mr. Gershon would say, "Folks, let's pass the hat.") It was during the war, too, that I learned how to be comfortable sitting alone in a bar or restaurant. For many women, this is a strangely difficult thing to do, but eventually I mastered it. (The trick is to bring a book or newspaper, to ask for the best table nearest to the window, and to order your drink just as soon as you sit down.) Once I got the hang of it, I found that eating alone by the window in a quiet restaurant is one of life's greatest secret pleasures.

I bought myself a bicycle for three dollars from a kid in Hell's Kitchen, and this acquisition opened up my world considerably. Freedom of movement was everything, I was learning. I wanted to know that I could get out of New York quickly, in case of an attack. I rode my bike all over the city—it was cheap and effective for running errands—but somewhere in the back of my mind I believed that I could outride the Luftwaffe if I had to. This brought me a certain delusional sense of safety.

I became an explorer of my vast urban surroundings. I prowled the city extensively, and at such odd hours. I especially loved to walk around at night and catch glimpses through windows of strangers living their lives. So many different dinnertimes, so many different work hours. Everyone was different ages, different races. Some people were resting, some laboring, some all alone, some celebrating in boisterous company. I never tired of moving through these scenes. I relished the sensation of being one small dot of humanity in a larger ocean of souls.

When I was younger, I had wanted to be at the very center of all the action in New York, but I slowly came to realize that there *is* no one center. The center is everywhere—wherever people are living out their lives. It's a city with a million centers.

Somehow that was even more magical to know.

I didn't pursue any men during the war.

For one thing, they were difficult to come by; most everyone was overseas. For another thing, I didn't feel like playing around. In keeping with the new spirit of seriousness and sacrifice that blanketed New York, I more or less put my sexual desire away from 1942 until 1945— the way you might cover your good furniture with sheets while you go off on vacation. (Except I wasn't on vacation; all I did was work.) Soon I grew accustomed to moving about town without a male companion. I forgot that you were supposed to be on a man's arm at night, if you were a nice girl. This was a rule that seemed archaic now, and furthermore impossible to execute.

There simply weren't enough men, Angela.

There weren't enough arms.

One afternoon in early 1944, I was riding my bicycle through midtown when I saw my old boyfriend Anthony Roccella stepping out of an arcade. Seeing his face was a shocker, but I should have known I'd run into him someday. As any New Yorker can tell you, you will eventually run into *everyone* on the sidewalks of this city. For that reason, New York is a terrible town in which to have an enemy.

Anthony looked exactly the same. Hair pomaded, gum in his mouth, cocky smile on his face. He wasn't in uniform, which was unusual for a man of his age in good health. He must have weaseled his way out of service. (Of course.) He was with a girl—short, cute, blond. My heart did a quick rumba at the sight of him. He was the first man I'd laid eyes on in years who made me feel a rush of desire—but of course, that would make sense. I screeched to a stop just a few feet from him, and stared right at him. Something in me wanted to be seen by him. But he didn't see me. Alternatively, he saw me, but didn't recognize me. (With my short hair and trousers, I didn't look any more like the girl he used to know.) The final possibility, of course, is that he recognized me and elected not to pay me any mind.

That night, I burned with loneliness. I also burned with sexual longing—I will not lie about this. I took care of it myself, though. Thankfully, I had learned how to do that. (Every woman should learn how to do that.)

As for Anthony, I never saw him or heard his name again. Walter Winchell had predicted that the kid would be a movie star. But he never made it.

Or who knows. Maybe he never even bothered to try.

Only a few weeks later, I was invited by one of our actors to a benefit at the Savoy Hotel to raise money for war orphans. Harry James and His Orchestra would be playing, which was a fun enticement, so I beat down my tiredness and went to the party. I stayed for just a short while as I didn't know anybody there, and there weren't any interesting-looking men to dance with. I decided it would be more fun to go home and sleep. But as I was walking out of the ballroom, I bumped straight into Edna Parker Watson.

"Excuse me," I mumbled—but in the next instant, my mind calculated that it was *her*.

I'd forgotten that she lived at the Savoy. I never would have gone there that night had I remembered.

She looked up at me and held my gaze. She was wearing a soft brown gabardine suit with a pert little tangerine blouse. Casually tossed over her shoulder was a gray rabbit stole. As ever, she looked immaculate.

"You are very excused," she said, with a polite smile.

This time there could be no pretending that I had not been identified. She knew exactly who I was. I was familiar enough with Edna's face to have caught that quick shimmer of disturbance behind her mask of adamant calm.

For almost four years, I had pondered what I would say to her, if our paths ever crossed. But now all I could do was say, "Edna," and reach for her arm.

"I'm terribly sorry," she said, "but I don't believe you're somebody I know."

Then she walked away.

When we are young, Angela, we may fall victim to the misconception that time will heal all wounds and that eventually everything will shake itself out. But as we get older, we learn this sad truth: some things can never be fixed. Some mistakes can never be put right—not by the passage of time, and not by our most fervent wishes, either.

In my experience, this is the hardest lesson of them all.

After a certain age, we are all walking around this world in bodies made of secrets and shame and sorrow and old, unhealed injuries. Our hearts grow sore and misshapen around all this pain—yet somehow, still, we carry on.

TWENTY-FIVE

Now it was late 1944. I had turned twenty-four years old.

I kept working around the clock at the Navy Yard. I can't remember ever taking a day off. I was squirreling away good money from my wartime wages, but I was exhausted, and there was nothing to spend it on anyway. I barely had the energy to play gin rummy with Peg and Olive in the evenings anymore. More than once, I fell asleep during my evening commute and woke up in Harlem.

Everyone was bone weary.

Sleep became a golden commodity that everyone longed for but nobody had.

We knew we were winning the war—there was a lot of big talk about what a bruising we were giving the Germans and the Japanese— but we didn't know when it would all be over. Not knowing, of course, didn't stop anyone from running their mouths nonstop, spreading fruitless gossip and speculation.

The war would end by Thanksgiving, they all said.

By Christmas, they all said.

But then 1945 rolled in, and the war wasn't done yet.

Over at the Sammy cafeteria theater, we were still killing Hitler a dozen times a week in our propaganda shows, but it didn't seem to be slowing him down any.

Don't worry, everyone said—it'll all be sewn up by the end of February.

In early March, my parents got a letter from my brother on his aircraft carrier somewhere in the South Pacific, saying, "You'll be hearing talk of surrender soon. I'm sure of it."

That was the last we ever heard from him.

Angela, I know that you—of all people—know about the USS *Franklin*. But I'm ashamed to admit that I didn't even know the name of my brother's ship before we got word that it had been hit by a kamikaze pilot on March 19, 1945, killing Walter and over eight hundred other men. Always the responsible one, Walter had never mentioned the name of the ship in his correspondence, in case his letters fell into enemy hands and state secrets were revealed. I knew only that he was on a large aircraft carrier somewhere in Asia, and that he had promised the war would end soon.

My mother was the one who got the notice of his death. She was riding her horse in a field next to our house when she saw an old black car with one white, non-matching door come speeding up our driveway. It raced right past her, driving far too fast for the gravel road. This was unusual; country people know better than to speed down gravel roads next to grazing horses. But the car was one she recognized. It belonged to Mike Roemer, the telegraph operator at Western Union. My mother stopped what she was doing and watched as both Mike and his wife stepped out of the car and knocked on her door.

The Roemers were not the sort of people with whom my mother

socialized. There was no reason they should be knocking on the Morrises' door except one: a telegram must have come in, and its contents were dire enough that the operator thought he should deliver the news himself—along with his wife, who had presumably come to offer womanly comfort to the grieving family.

My mother saw all of this, and she *knew*.

I have always wondered if Mother had an impulse in that moment to turn the horse around and ride like hell in the opposite direction—just to run straight away from that horrible news. But my mother wasn't that sort of person. What she did, instead, was to dismount and walk very slowly toward the house, leading her horse behind her. She told me later that she didn't think it was prudent for her to be on top of an animal at an emotional moment like this. I can just see her—choosing her steps with care, handling her horse with her typical sense of conscientiousness. She knew exactly what was waiting for her on the doorstep, and she was in no hurry to meet it. Until that telegram was handed over, her son was still alive.

The Roemers could wait for her. And they did.

By the time my mother reached the doorstep of our house, Mrs. Roemer—tears streaming down her face—had her arms open for an embrace.

Which my mother, needless to say, refused.

My parents didn't even have a funeral for Walter.

First of all, there was no body to be buried. The telegram notified us that Lieutenant Walter Morris had been buried at sea with full military honors. The telegram also requested that we not divulge the name of Walter's ship or his station to our friends and family, so as not to accidentally "give aid to the enemy"—as though our neighbors in Clinton, New York, were saboteurs and spies.

My mother didn't want a funeral service without a body. She found it too grisly. And my father was too shattered by rage and sorrow to face his community in a state of mourning. He had railed so bitterly against America's involvement in this war, and had fought against Walter's enlistment, too. Now he refused to have a ceremony to honor the fact that the government had stolen from him his greatest treasure.

I went home and spent a week with them. I did what I could for my parents, but they barely spoke to me. I asked if they wanted me to stay with them in Clinton—and I would have, too—but they looked at me as though I were a stranger. *What possible use could I be to them, if I stayed in Clinton?* If anything, I got the sense they wanted me to leave, so I wouldn't be staring at them all day in their grief. My presence seemed only to remind them that their son was dead.

If they ever thought that the wrong child had been taken from them—that the better and nobler child was gone while the less worthy one remained—I would forgive them for it. I sometimes had that thought myself.

Once I left, they were able to collapse back into their silence.

I probably don't need to tell you that they were never the same again.

W alter's death utterly shocked me.

I swear to you, Angela, I'd never considered for a minute that my brother could be harmed or killed in this war. This may seem stupid and naïve of me, but if you knew Walter, you'd have understood my confidence. He had always been so competent, so powerful. He had brilliant instincts. He'd never even been injured, in all his years of athletics. Even among his peers, he was seen as semimythical. What harm could ever befall him?

Not only that, I never worried about anybody who served under

Walter—although he did. (The one worrying subject my brother mentioned in his letters home was concern for his men's safety and morale.) I figured anybody who was serving with Walter Morris was safe. He would see to it.

But the problem, of course, was that Walter wasn't in charge. He was a full lieutenant by then, yes, but the ship wasn't in his hands. At the helm was Captain Leslie Gehres. The captain was the problem.

But you know all this already—don't you, Angela?

At least I assume you do?

I'm sorry, sweetheart, but I really don't know how much your father told you about any of this.

Peg and I held our own ceremony for Walter in New York City, at the small Methodist church next to the Lily Playhouse. The minister had become a friend of Peg's over the years, and he agreed to conduct a small service for my brother, remains or no remains. There were just a handful of us, but it was important for me that something be done in Walter's name, and Peg had recognized that.

Peg and Olive were there, of course, flanking me like the pillars they were. Mr. Herbert was there. Billy didn't come, having moved back to Hollywood a year earlier when his Broadway production of *City of Girls* finally closed. Mr. Gershon, my Navy censor, came. My pianist from the Sammy cafeteria, Mrs. Levinson, also came. The entire Lowtsky family was there. ("Never saw so many Jews at a Methodist funeral," said Marjorie, scanning the room. This brought me a laugh. Thank you, Marjorie.) A few of Peg's old friends came. Edna and Arthur Watson were not there. I suppose that should not have been a surprise, although I must admit I'd thought Edna might show up in support of Peg, at least.

The choir sang "His Eye Is on the Sparrow," and I could not stop crying. I felt a stunned sense of bereavement for Walter—not so much for the brother I lost, but for the brother I'd never had. Aside from a few sweet, sun-dappled, early childhood memories of the two of us riding ponies together (and who knew if those memories were even accurate?), I had no tender recollections of this imposing figure with whom I'd allegedly shared my youth. Perhaps if my parents had expected less of him—if they'd allowed him to be a regular little boy, instead of a *scion*—he and I could've become friends over the years, or confidants. But it was never to be. And now he was gone.

I cried all night but went back to work the next day.

A lot of people had to do that kind of thing during those years.

We cried, Angela, and then we worked.

On April 12, 1945, FDR died.

To me, this felt like another family member gone. I could barely remember there ever having been another president. Whatever my father thought of the man, I loved him. Many loved him. Certainly in New York City, all of us did.

The mood the next day at the Yard was somber. At the Sammy cafeteria, I hung the stage with bunting (blackout curtains, actually) and had our actors read from years of Roosevelt's speeches. At the end of the show, one of the steel workers—a Caribbean man, with dark skin and a white beard—rose spontaneously from his seat and began to sing "The Battle Hymn of the Republic." He had a voice like Paul Robeson's. The rest of us stood in silence while this man's song shook the walls in doleful sorrow.

President Truman was quickly and quietly ushered in, with no majesty.

We all worked harder.

Still the war did not end.

———

On April 28, 1945, the burned-out, twisted hulk of my brother's aircraft carrier sailed into the Brooklyn Navy Yard on her own steam. The USS *Franklin* had somehow managed to limp and list half-way across the world, and through the Panama Canal—piloted by a skeleton crew—to arrive now at our "hospital." Two thirds of her crew were dead, missing, or injured.

The *Franklin* was met at the docks by a Navy band playing a dirge-ful hymn, and also by Peg and me.

We stood on the dock and saluted as we watched this wounded ship—which I thought of as my brother's coffin—sailing home to be repaired, as best she could. But even I could tell, just by looking at that blackened, gutted pile of steel, that nobody would ever be able to fix *this*.

On May 7, 1945, Germany finally surrendered.

But the Japanese were still holding out, and they were hold-ing out hard.

That week, Mrs. Levinson and I wrote a song for our workers called "One Down, One to Go."

We kept working.

On June 20, 1945, the *Queen Mary* sailed into New York Harbor carrying fourteen thousand U.S. servicemen returning home from Europe. Peg and I went to meet them at Pier 90, on the Upper West Side. Peg had painted a sign on the back of an old piece of scen-ery that said: "Hey, YOU! Welcome HOME!"

"Who are you welcoming home, specifically?" I asked.

"Every last one of them," she said.

I initially hesitated to join her. The thought of seeing thousands of young men coming home—but none of them Walter—seemed too sad to bear. But she had insisted on it.

"It will be good for you," she predicted. "More important, it will be good for *them*. They need to see our faces."

I was glad I went, in the end. Very glad.

It was a delicious early summer day. I'd been living in New York for more than three years at that point, but I still wasn't immune to the beauty of my city on a perfect blue-sky afternoon like this—one of those soft, warm days, when you can't help but feel that the whole town loves you, and wants nothing but your happiness.

The sailors and soldiers (and nurses!) came streaming down the wharf in a delirious wave of celebration. They were met by a large cheering crowd, of which Peg and I constituted a small but enthusiastic delegation. She and I took turns waving her sign, and we cheered till our throats were hoarse. A band on the docks pounded out loud versions of the year's popular songs. The servicemen were tossing balloons in the air, which I quickly realized were not balloons at all, but blown-up condoms. (I wasn't the only one who realized this; I couldn't help laughing as the mothers around me tried to stop their children from picking them up.)

One lanky, sleepy-eyed sailor paused to take a long look at me as he was walking by.

He grinned, and said in a broad southern accent, "Say, honey—what's the name of this town anyhow?"

I grinned back. "We call it New York City, sailor."

He pointed to some construction cranes on the other side of the wharf. He said, "Looks like it'll be a nice enough place, once it's finished."

Then he slung his arm around my waist and kissed me—just like you've seen in that famous photo from Times Square, on VJ Day. (There was a lot of that going on that year.) But what you never saw in that photo was the girl's reaction. I've always wondered how she felt about her kiss. We will never know, I suppose. But I can tell you how I felt about *my* kiss—which was long, expert, and considerably passionate.

Well, Angela, I liked it.

I *really* liked it. I kissed him right back, but then—out of the blue—I started weeping and I couldn't stop. I buried my face in his neck, clung to him, and bathed him with tears. I cried for my brother, and for all the young men who would never come back. I cried for all the girls who had lost their sweethearts and their youth. I cried because we had given so many years to this infernal, eternal war. I cried because I was so goddamned tired. I cried because I *missed* kissing boys—and I wanted to kiss so many more of them!—but now I was an ancient hag of twenty-four, and what would become of me? I cried because it was such a beautiful day, and the sun was shining, and all of it was glorious, and none of it was fair.

This was not quite what the sailor had expected, I'm sure, when he'd initially grabbed me. But he rose to the occasion admirably.

"Honey," he said in my ear, "you ain't gotta cry no more. We're the lucky ones."

He held me tight, and let me boil forth my tears, until finally I got control of myself. Then he pulled back from the embrace, smiled, and said, "Now, how 'bout you let me have another?"

And we kissed again.

It would be three more months before the Japanese surrendered.

But in my mind—in my hazy, peach-colored, summer-day memory—the war ended in that very moment.

TWENTY-SIX

A s swiftly as I can, Angela, let me tell you about the next twenty years of my life.

I stayed in New York City (of course I did—where else would I go?), but it was not the same town anymore. So much changed, and so fast. Aunt Peg had warned me about this inevitability back in 1945. She'd said, "Everything is always different after a war ends. I've seen it before. If we are wise, we should all be prepared for adjustments."

Well, she was certainly correct about *that*.

Postwar New York was a rich, hungry, impatient, and growing beast—especially in midtown, where whole neighborhoods of old brownstones and businesses were knocked down in order to make room for new office complexes and modern apartment buildings. You had to pick through rubble everywhere you walked—almost as though the city *had* been bombed, after all. Over the next few years, so many of the glamorous places I used to frequent with Celia Ray closed down and were replaced by twenty-story corporate towers. The Spotlite closed. The Downbeat Club closed. The Stork Club closed. Countless theaters closed. Those once-glimmering neighborhoods now looked like weird, broken mouths—with half the old teeth knocked out, and some shiny new false ones randomly stuck in.

But the biggest change happened in 1950—at least in our little circle. That's when the Lily Playhouse closed.

Mind you, the Lily didn't simply close: she was demolished. Our beautiful, crooked, bumbling fortress of a theater was destroyed by the city that year in order to make room for the Port Authority Bus Terminal. In fact, our entire neighborhood was torn down. Within the doomed radius of what would eventually become the world's ugliest bus terminal, every single theater, church, row house, restaurant, bar, Chinese laundry, penny arcade, florist, tattoo parlor, and school—it all came down. Even Lowtsky's Used Emporium and Notions—*gone.*

Turned to dust right before our eyes.

At least the city did right by Peg. They offered her fifty-five thousand dollars for the building—which was pretty good cheese back in a time when most folks in our neighborhood were living on four thousand dollars a year. I wanted her to fight it, but she said, "There's nothing to fight here."

"I just can't believe you can walk away from all this!" I wailed.

"You have no idea what I'm capable of walking away from, kiddo."

Peg was dead right, by the way, about the fact that there was "nothing to fight here." In taking over the neighborhood, the city was exercising a civic right called "the power of condemnation"—which is every bit as sinister and inescapable as it sounds. I had myself a good sulk over it, but Peg said, "Resist change at your own peril, Vivian. When something ends, let it end. The Lily has outlasted her glory, anyway."

"That's not true, Peg," corrected Olive. "The Lily never had any glory."

Both of them were right, in their way. We had been limping along since the war ended—barely making a living out of the building. Our shows were more sparsely attended than ever and our best talent had never returned to us after the war. (For instance: Benjamin, our composer, had elected to stay in Europe, settling down in Lyon with a Frenchwoman who owned a nightclub. We loved reading his letters—he was absolutely thriving as an impresario and bandleader—but we sure did miss his music.) What's more, our neighborhood audience had outgrown us. People were more sophisticated now—even in Hell's Kitchen. The war had blown the world wide open and filled the air with new ideas and tastes. Our shows had seemed dated even back when I first came to the city, but now they were like something out of the Pleistocene. Nobody wanted to watch cornball, vaudevillelike song-and-dance numbers anymore.

So, yes: whatever slight glory our theater had ever possessed, it was long gone by 1950.

Still, it was painful for me.

I only wish I loved bus terminals as much as I'd loved the Lily Playhouse.

When the day came for the actual demolition, Peg insisted on being present for it. ("You can't be afraid of these things, Vivian," she said. "You have to see it through.") So I stood alongside Peg and Olive on that fateful day, watching as the Lily came down. I was not nearly as stoic as they were. To see a wrecking ball take aim at your home and history—at the place that really *birthed* you—well, that takes a degree of spinal fortitude that I did not yet possess. I couldn't help but tear up.

The worst part was not when the façade of the building came crashing down, but when the interior lobby wall was demolished. Suddenly you could see the old stage as it was never meant to be seen—naked and exposed under the cruel, unsentimental winter sun. All its shabbiness was dragged into the light for everyone to witness.

Peg had the strength to bear it, though. She didn't even flinch. She was made of awfully stern stuff, that woman. When the wrecking ball had done all the damage it could do for the day, she smiled at me and said, "I'll tell you something, Vivian. I have no regrets. When I was a young girl, I honestly believed that a life spent in the theater would be nothing but fun. And God help me, kiddo—it *was*."

U sing the money from the settlement with the city, Peg and Olive bought a nice little apartment on Sutton Place. Peg even had enough money left over after the purchase of the apartment to give a sort of retirement subsidy to Mr. Herbert, who moved down to Virginia to live with his daughter.

Peg and Olive liked their new life. Olive got a job at a local high school working as the principal's secretary—a position she was born to hold. Peg was hired at the same school to help run their theater department. The women didn't seem unhappy about the changes. Their new apartment building (brand new, I should say) even had an elevator, which was easier for them, as they were getting older. They also had a doorman with whom Peg could gossip about baseball. ("The only doormen I ever had before were the bums sleeping under the Lily's proscenium!" she joked.)

Troupers that they were, the two women adapted. They certainly didn't complain. Still, there is poignancy for me in the fact that the Lily Playhouse was destroyed in 1950—the same year that Peg and Olive purchased their first television set for their modern new apartment. Clearly, the golden age of theater was now over. But Peg had seen that development coming, too.

"Television will run us all out of town in the end," she'd predicted the first time she ever saw one in action.

"How do you know?" I asked.

"Because even *I* like it better than theater" was her honest response.

As for me, with the death of the Lily Playhouse I no longer had a home or a job—or for that matter, a family with whom to share my daily life. I couldn't exactly move in with Peg and Olive. Not at my age. It would have been embarrassing. I needed to create my own life. But I was a twenty-nine-year-old woman now—unmarried, no college education—so what could that life *be*?

I wasn't too worried about how I would support myself. I had a decent amount of money saved and I knew how to work. By that point, I'd learned that as long as I had my sewing machine, my nine-inch shears, a tape measure around my neck, and a pincushion at my wrist, I could always make a living somehow. But the question was: what sort of existence would I now lead?

In the end, I was saved by Marjorie Lowtsky.

By 1950, Marjorie Lowtsky and I had become best friends.

It was an unlikely match, but she had never stopped looking out for me—in terms of salvaging treasures from the bottomless Lowtsky's bins—and I, in turn, had delighted in watching this kid grow up into a charismatic and fascinating young woman. There was something quite special about her. Of course, Marjorie had always been special, but after the war years, she blossomed into an atomically energetic creative force. She still dressed wildly—looking like a Mexican bandito one day, and a Japanese geisha the next—but she had come into her own, as a person. She'd gone to art school at Parsons while still living at home with her parents and running the family business— while at the same time making money on the side as a sketch artist. She'd worked for years at Bonwit Teller, drawing romantic fashion illustrations for their newspaper ads. She also did diagrams for medical journals, and once—quite memorably—was hired by a travel company to illustrate a guidebook to Baltimore with the tragic title: *So You're Coming to Baltimore!* So really, Marjorie could do anything and she was always on the hustle.

Marjorie had grown into a young woman who was not only creative, eccentric, and hardworking, but also bold and astute. And when the city announced that it was going to knock down our neighborhood, and Marjorie's parents decided to take the buyout and retire to Queens, suddenly dear Marjorie Lowtsky was in the same position I was in—out of a home and out of work. Instead of crying about it, Marjorie came to me with a simple and well-thought-out proposal. She suggested that we join forces in the world, by living together and working together.

Her plan—and I must give her every bit of credit for it—was: *wedding gowns.*

H er exact proposal was this: "Everyone is getting married, Vivian, and we have to do something about it."

She had taken me out to lunch at the Automat to talk about her idea. It was the summer of 1950, the Port Authority Bus Terminal was inevitable, and our whole little world was about to come tumbling down. But Marjorie (dressed today like a Peruvian peasant, wearing about five different kinds of embroidered vests and skirts at the same time) was shining with purpose and excitement.

"What do you want *me* to do about everyone getting married?" I asked. "Stop them?"

"No. *Help* them. If we can help them, we can profit from them. Look, I've been at Bonwit Teller all week doing sketches in the bridal suite. I've been *listening.* The salesclerks say they can't keep up with orders. And all week I've been hearing customers complain about the lack of variety. Nobody wants the same dress as anyone else, but there aren't that many dresses to choose from. I overheard a girl the other day saying that she would sew her own wedding dress, just to make it unique, if only she knew how."

"Do you want me to teach girls how to sew their own wedding dresses?" I asked. "Most of those girls couldn't sew a potholder."

"No. I think *we* should make wedding dresses."

"Too many people make wedding dresses already, Marjorie. It's an industry of its own."

"Yeah, but we can make nicer ones. I could sketch the designs and you could sew them. We know materials better than anyone else, don't we? And our gimmick would be to create new gowns out of old ones. You and I both know that the old silk and satin is better than anything that's being imported. With my contacts, I can find old silk and satin all over town—hell, I can even buy it in bulk from France; they're selling everything right now, they're so hungry over there—and you can use that material to make gowns that are finer than anything at Bonwit Teller. I've seen you take good lace off old tablecloths before, to make costumes. Couldn't you make trims and veils the same way? We could create one-of-a-kind wedding dresses for girls who don't want to look like everyone else in the department stores. Our dresses wouldn't be *industry;* they would be custom tailored. Classic. You could do that, couldn't you?"

"Nobody wants to wear a used, old wedding dress," I said.

But as soon as I spoke these words, I remembered my friend Madeleine, back in Clinton at the beginning of the war. Madeleine, whose gown I had created by tearing up both of her grandmothers' old silk wedding dresses and combining them into one concoction. That gown had been stunning.

Seeing that I was beginning to catch on, Marjorie said, "What I'm picturing is this—we open a boutique. We'll use your classiness to make the place seem high tone and exclusive. We'll play up the fact that we import our materials from Paris. People love that. They'll buy anything if you tell them it came from Paris. It won't be a total lie—some of the stuff *will* come from France. Sure, it will come from France in barrels stuffed full of rags, but nobody needs to know this. I'll sort out the treasures, and you'll make the treasures into better treasures."

"Are you talking about having a *store?*"

"A boutique, Vivian. God, honey, get used to saying the word. Jews have *stores;* we shall have a *boutique.*"

"But you are Jewish."

"Boutique, Vivian. Boutique. Practice saying it with me. *Boutique.* Let it roll off your tongue."

"Where do you want to do this?" I asked.

"Down around Gramercy Park," she said. "That neighborhood will always be fancy. I'd like to see the city try to tear *those* town houses down! That's what we're selling to people—the idea of *fancy.* The idea of *classic.* I want to call it L'Atelier. There's a building down there I've been eyeing. My parents told me they'll give me half the payment from the city when Lowtsky's gets demolished—as well they *should,* having worked me like a stevedore ever since I was a babe in arms. My cut will be just enough to buy the place I'm looking at."

I was watching her mind work and whip—and honestly, it was a little scary. She was moving awfully fast.

"The building I want is on Eighteenth Street, one block from the park," she went on. "Three stories, with a storefront. Two apartments upstairs. It's small, but it's got charm. You could fake that it's a little boutique on a quaint street in Paris. That's the feeling we're looking to create. It's not in bad shape. I can find people to fix it up. You can live on the top floor. You know how I hate climbing stairs. You'll like it—there's a skylight in your apartment. Two skylights, actually."

"You want us to buy a *building*, Marjorie?"

"No, honey, I want *me* to buy a building. I know how much money you've got in the bank—and no offense, Vivian, but you couldn't afford Paramus, much less Manhattan. Although you *can* afford to buy into the business, so we'll go halfsies on that. But I'll be the one who buys the building. It will cost me every dime I have, but I'm willing to shoot the whole works at it. I'm damn sure not going to rent a place—what am I, an *immigrant*?"

"Yes," I said. "You are an immigrant."

"Immigrant or no, the only way people make money in retail in this city is by owning property, not by selling clothes. Ask the Saks family—they know. Ask the Gimbel family—they know. Although we *will* make money selling clothes, too, because our wedding gowns will be simply lovely, thanks to your considerable talents, and mine. So, yes, Vivian, in conclusion: I want *me* to buy a building. I want *you* to design wedding dresses, I want *us* to run a boutique, and I want *both of us* to live upstairs. That's the plan. Let's live together, and let's work together. It's not as though we've got anything else going on, right? Just say you'll do it."

I gave her proposal deep and serious consideration for about three seconds, and then said, "Sure. Let's do it."

If you're wondering whether this decision turned out to be a giant mistake, Angela, it didn't. In fact, I can tell you right now how it all turned out: Marjorie and I made sublime wedding gowns together for decades; we earned enough money to support ourselves comfortably; we took care of each other like family; and I live in that same building to this day. (I know I'm old, but don't worry—I can still climb those stairs.)

I never made a better choice than to throw in my lot with Marjorie Lowtsky and to follow her into business.

Sometimes it's just true that other people have better ideas for your life than you do.

All that said, it was not easy work.
As with costumes, wedding gowns are not sewn but *built*. They are intended to be monumental, and so it takes a monumental amount of effort to make one. My gowns were especially time-consuming because I wasn't starting with bolts of clean, fresh fabrics. It's harder to make a new dress from an old dress (or from several old dresses, as in my case), because you must disassemble the old dress first, and then your options will be limited by how much material you are able to glean from it. Besides which, I was working with aging and fragile textiles—antique silks and satins, and ancient spiderwebs of lace—which meant that I had to use an especially careful hand.

Marjorie would bring me sacks of old wedding and christening gowns that she scavenged from God knows where, and I would pick through them judiciously, to see what I could work with. Often the materials were yellowed with age or stained down the bodice. (Never give a bride a glass of red wine!) So my first task would be to soak the garment in ice water and vinegar to clean it. If there was a stain that I couldn't remove, I'd have to cut around it, and figure out how much I could salvage of the old fabric. Or maybe I would turn that piece inside out, or use it as a lining. I often felt like a diamond cutter—trying to keep as much of the value of the original material as I could while shaving away what was flawed.

Then it was a question of how to create a dress that was unique. At some level, a wedding gown is just a *dress*—and like all dresses, it's made of three simple ingredients: a bodice, a skirt, and sleeves. But over the years, with those three limited ingredients, I made thousands of dresses that were not at all alike. I had to do this, because no bride wants to look like another bride.

So it was challenging work, yes—both physically and creatively. I had assistants over the years, and that helped a bit, but I never found anyone who could do what I could do. And since I couldn't bear to create a L'Atelier dress that was anything less than impeccable, I put in the long hours myself to make sure that each gown was a piece of perfection. If a bride said—on the evening before her wedding—that she wanted more pearls on her bodice, or less lace, then I would be the one up after midnight making those changes. It takes the patience of a monk to do this kind of detail work. You have to believe that what you are creating is sacred.

Fortunately, I happened to believe that.

Of course, the greatest challenge in building wedding dresses is learning how to handle the customers themselves.

In offering my service to so many brides over the years, I became delicately attuned to the subtleties of family, money, and power—but mostly, I had to learn how to understand *fear.* I learned that girls who are about to get married are always afraid. They're afraid that they don't love their fiancés enough or that they love them too much. They're afraid of the sex that is coming to them or the sex that they are leaving behind. They're afraid of the wedding day going awry. They're afraid of being looked at by hundreds of eyes—and they're afraid of *not* being looked at, in case their dress is all wrong or their maid of honor is more beautiful.

I recognize, Angela, that in the great scale of things, these are not monumental concerns. We had just come through a world war in which millions died and millions more saw their lives destroyed; clearly the anxiety of a nervous bride is not a cataclysmic matter, in comparison. But fears are fears, nonetheless, and they bring strain upon the troubled minds who bear them. I came to see it as my task to alleviate as much fear and strain as I could for these girls. More than anything, then, what I learned over the years at L'Atelier was how to help frightened women—how to humble myself before their needs, and how to lend myself to their wishes.

For me, this education started as soon as we opened for business.

The first week of our boutique's existence, a young woman wandered in, clutching our advertisement from *The New York Times*. (This was Marjorie's sketch of two guests at a wedding admiring a willowy bride. One woman says, "That gown is so poetical! Did she bring it home from Paris?" The second woman replies, "Why, almost! It comes from L'Atelier, and their gowns are the fairest!")

I could see the girl was nervous. I got her a glass of water and showed her samples of the gowns I was currently working on. Very quickly, she gravitated toward a great big pile of meringue—a dress that resembled a puffy summer cloud. In fact, it looked exactly like the wedding gown that the swan-thin model in our advertisement was wearing. The girl touched her dream dress and her face grew soft with longing. My heart sank. I knew this garment was not right for her. She was so small and roundish; she would look like a marshmallow in it.

"May I try it on?" she asked.

But I couldn't allow her to do that. If she saw herself in the mirror wearing that dress, she would recognize how farcical she looked, and she would leave my boutique and never come back. But it was worse than that. I didn't so much mind losing the sale. What I minded was this: I knew that this girl's feelings would be wounded by seeing herself in that dress—deeply wounded—and I wanted to spare her the pain.

"Sweetheart," I said, as gently as I could, "you're a beautiful girl. And I think that particular gown will be a bitter disappointment for you."

Her face fell. Then she squared her little shoulders and bravely said, "I know why. It's because I'm too short, isn't it? And because I'm too plump. I knew it. I'm going to look like a fool on my wedding day."

There was something about this moment that went straight through the heart of me. There is nothing like the vulnerability of an insecure girl in a bridal shop to make you feel the small but horrible pains of life. I instantly felt nothing but concern for this girl, and I didn't want her to suffer for another moment.

Also—please remember that up until this time, Angela, I hadn't worked with civilians. For years, I'd been sewing clothing for professional dancers and actresses. I wasn't accustomed to normal-looking, regular girls, with all their self-consciousness and perceived flaws. Many of the women whom I had been serving thus far had been passionately in love with their own figures (and for good reason) and were eager to be seen. I was accustomed to women who would shed their clothes and dance around in front of a mirror with joy—not to women who would flinch at their own reflections.

I had forgotten that girls could be anything *but* vain.

What this girl taught me in my own boutique that day was that the wedding-gown business was going to be considerably different from show business. Because this little human being standing before my eyes was not some sumptuous showgirl; she was just a regular person who wanted to look sumptuous on her wedding day, and who did not know how to get there.

But I knew how to get her there.

I knew she needed a dress that was snug and simple, so she wouldn't vanish in it. I knew that her dress needed to be made of crepe-backed satin, so it would drape but not cling. Nor could it be a vivid white, because of her somewhat ruddy complexion. No, her gown needed to be a softer, creamier color—which would make her skin look smoother. I knew that she needed a simple crown of flowers, rather than a long veil that would—again—hide her from view. I knew that she needed three-quarter sleeves to show off her pretty wrists and hands. No gloves for this one! Also, I could tell just by looking at her in her street clothes where her natural waist was located (and it was *not* where her current dress was belted) and I knew that her gown would need to fall from the natural waist, in order to give the illusion of an hourglass figure. And I could feel that she was so modest—so mercilessly self-conscious and self-critical—that she would not be able to bear it if the slightest hint of cleavage was revealed. But her ankles—those, we could show and so we would. I knew *exactly* how to dress her.

"Oh, sweetheart," I said, and I quite literally tucked her under my wing. "Don't you fret. We're going to take good care of you. You will be a spectacularly beautiful bride, I promise it."

And so she was.

Angela, I will tell you this: I came to love all the girls I ever served at L'Atelier. Every last one of them. This was one of the biggest surprises of my life—the upwelling of love and protectiveness that I felt toward every girl I ever dressed for her wedding. Even when they were demanding and hysterical, I loved them. Even when they were not so beautiful, I saw them as beautiful.

Marjorie and I had gone into this business primarily to make money. My secondary motive had been to practice my craft, which had always brought me fulfillment. A tertiary reason had been that I really didn't know what else to do with my life. But I never could have anticipated the greatest benefit this business would bestow: the powerful rush of warmth and tenderness that I felt *every single time* another nervous bride-to-be crossed my threshold and entrusted me with her precious life.

In other words—L'Atelier gave me *love*.

I could not help it, you see.

They were all young, they were all so afraid, and they were all so dear.

TWENTY-SEVEN

The great irony, of course, is that neither Marjorie nor I was married.

Over the years that we ran L'Atelier, we were up to our eyeballs in wedding gowns, helping thousands of girls prepare for their nuptials—but nobody ever married us, and we never married anybody. There's that old expression: *Always a bridesmaid, never a bride*. But we weren't even bridesmaids!! If anything, Marjorie and I were bride tenders.

We were both too weird, was the problem. That's how we diagnosed ourselves, anyhow: too weird to wed. (Perhaps that would be the slogan of our next business, we often joked.)

Marjorie's weirdness was not hard to see. She was just such a kook. It wasn't only the way she dressed (although her sartorial choices were indeed patently strange); it was also the interests that she had. She was always taking lessons in things like Eastern penmanship and *breathing* up at the Buddhist temple on Ninety-fourth Street. Or she was learning how to make her own yogurt—and causing our entire building to smell like yogurt in the process. She appreciated avant-garde art, and listened to challenging (to my ear, anyway) music from the Andes. She signed up to be hypnotized by graduate students in psychology, and underwent analysis. She read the Tarot and the I Ching, and she threw runes. She went to a Chinese healer who worked on her feet, which she never stopped talking about to people, no matter how many times I begged her to stop talking to people about her *feet*. She was always on some kind of fad diet—not to lose weight necessarily, but to become healthier or more transcendent. She spent one summer, as I recall, eating nothing but tinned peaches, which she had read were good for respiration. Then it was on to bean-sprout and wheat-germ sandwiches.

Nobody wants to marry an odd girl who eats bean-sprout and wheat-germ sandwiches.

And I was odd, too. I may as well admit it.

For instance: I had my own bizarre way of dressing. I'd grown so accustomed to wearing trousers during the war that now I wore them all the time. I liked being able to ride my bicycle about town with liberty, but it was more than that—I *liked* wearing clothing that looked like menswear. I thought (and still think) that there is no better way for a woman to look smart and chic than to wear a man's suit. Good woolens were still difficult to come by in the immediate postwar period, but I discovered that if I bought quality used suits—I'm talking about Savile Row designs from the 1920s and 1930s—I could trim them down for myself and put together outfits that made me look, I liked to imagine, like Greta Garbo.

It was not in style after the war, I should say, for a woman to dress like this. Sure, back in the 1940s a woman could wear a mannish suit. It was considered patriotic, almost. But once the hostilities had ended, femininity came back with a vengeance. Around 1947, the fashion world was taken hostage by Christian Dior and his decadent "New Look" dresses—with the nipped waists, and the voluminous skirts, and the upwardly striving breasts, and the soft shoulder line. The New Look was meant to prove to the world that wartime shortages were over, and now we could squander all the silk and netting we wanted, just to be pretty and feminine and flouncy. It could take up to twenty-five yards of fabric just to make one New Look dress. Try getting out of a taxicab in *that*.

I hated it. I didn't have the kind of va-va-voom figure for that sort of dress, for one thing. My long legs, lanky torso, and small breasts were always better suited to slacks and blouses. Also, there was the matter of practicality. I couldn't work in a billowing dress like that. I spent much of my workday on the floor—kneeling over patterns, and crawling around the women whom I was outfitting. I needed pants and flats in order to be free.

So I rejected the fashion trends of the moment and did my own thing—just as Edna Parker Watson had taught me. This made me a bit of an oddball for the times. Not as odd as Marjorie, of course, but still rather unusual. I did find, however, that my uniform of trousers and a jacket worked well, in terms of serving my female customers. My short hair was also psychologically advantageous. By defeminizing my look, I telegraphed to the young brides (and their mothers) that I was not any sort of threat or rival. This was important because I was an attractive woman, and for the purposes of my profession it was best not to be *too* attractive. Even in the privacy of the dressing room, one must never outshine the bride. Those girls didn't want to see a sexy woman standing behind them while they chose the most important dress of their lives; they wanted to see a quiet and respectful tailor, all dressed in black, standing at their service. So I became that quiet and respectful tailor—gladly.

The other thing that was odd about me was how much I had come to love my independence. There was never a time in America when marriage was more of a fetish than in the 1950s, but I found that I simply wasn't interested. This made me quite the aberration—almost even a deviant. But the trials of the war years had turned me into someone both resourceful and confident, and opening up a business with Marjorie had filled me with a sense of self-determination—so maybe I just didn't believe anymore that I *needed* a man for very many purposes. (For one purpose only, really, if I am being honest.)

I had discovered that I rather liked living alone in my charming apartment above the bridal boutique. I liked my little place, with its two happy skylights, with its infinitesimally small bedroom (overlooking a magnolia tree in the alleyway behind me), and with its cherry-red kitchenette that I had painted myself. Once I'd laid claim to my own space, I quickly became accustomed to my own weird habits—like ashing my cigarettes into the flower box outside the kitchen window, or getting up in the middle of the night to turn on all the lights so I could read a mystery novel, or eating cold spaghetti for breakfast. I liked to pad about my home softly in my house slippers—never once touching shoes to the carpet. I liked to keep my fruit not randomly cast about in a bowl, but lined up neatly on my gleaming kitchen counter in a satisfying row. If you had told me that a man was going to move into my pretty little apartment, it would have felt like a home invasion.

Moreover, I had started to think that perhaps marriage wasn't such a great bargain for women, after all. When I looked around at all the women I knew who'd been married for more than five or ten years, I didn't see anybody whose lives I envied. Once the romance had faded, these women all seemed to be living in constant service to their husbands. (They either served their men happily or with resentment—but they all *served*.)

Their husbands didn't look ecstatically happy about the arrangement, either, I must say.

I would not have traded places with any of them.

———

All right, all right—to be fair, also nobody *asked* me to marry him. Not since Jim Larsen, anyhow.

I do think I narrowly escaped a marriage proposal in 1957 from a senior financier at Brown Brothers Harriman, which was a private Wall Street bank, cloaked in hushed discretion and thunderous wealth. It was a temple of money, and Roger Alderman was one of its high priests. He owned a seaplane, if you can imagine it. (What possible use does a person have for a seaplane? Was he a *spy*? Did he have to drop provisions to his troops on an *island*? It was ludicrous.) I will say of him that he had the most divine suits, and there has always been something about a good-looking man in a freshly pressed and well-fitted suit that makes me feel a bit faint with desire.

His suits made me feel so faint, in fact, that I convinced myself to romance this man for over a year—despite the fact that, whenever I gazed into my heart for signs of love toward Roger Alderman, I could find no trace of love's existence. Then one day he started talking about what kind of house we might like to inhabit in New Rochelle, should we someday decide to get out of this god-awful city. That's when I woke up. (There is nothing intrinsically wrong with New Rochelle, mind you—except that I know for a fact that I could not live in New Rochelle for even a single day without wanting to break my own neck with my own two hands.)

Soon after this, I gently excused myself from our arrangement.

But I enjoyed the sex that I had with Roger while it lasted. It wasn't the world's most electrifying or creative lovemaking, but it did the trick. It took me "over the top," as Celia and I used to say. It has always astonished me, Angela, how easily I can convince my body to become free and *unstuck* during sex—even with the most unappealing man. Roger was not unappealing in terms of handsomeness, of course. He

371

was quite becoming, actually (and although I wish sometimes that I were not *quite* so susceptible to handsomeness, there's no way around it: I just am). But he did not stir my heart. Yet still, my body was grateful for its encounters with him. Indeed, I had found over the years that I could always rise to a grand finale in bed—not only with Roger Alderman, but with just about anybody. No matter how indifferent my mind and heart might have been toward a man, my body could always respond with enthusiasm and delight.

And after we were done? I always wanted the man to go home.

Perhaps I should back up here a bit and explain that I had recommenced my sexual activities after the war ended—and with considerable enthusiasm, too. Despite the picture I may be painting of myself in the 1950s as a cross-dressing, short-haired, solitary-dwelling spinster, let me make one thing clear: just because I didn't want to get married doesn't mean I didn't want to have sex.

Also, I was still quite pretty. (I've always looked terrific with short hair, Angela. I didn't come here to lie to you.)

The truth is, I emerged from the war with a hunger for sex that was deeper than ever. I was tired of deprivation, you see. Those three coarse years of hard work in the Navy Yard (and, by extension, three dry years of celibacy) had left my body not only tired, but dissatisfied. There was a sense I had after the war that this is not what my body was *for*. I was not built only to labor, and then to sleep, and then to labor again the next day—with no pleasure or excitement. There had to be more to life than toil and travail.

So my appetites returned, right along with the global peace. Moreover, I found that as I matured, my appetites had grown more specific, more curious, and more confident. I wanted to *explore*. I was fascinated by the differences in men's lust—by the curious ways that they each expressed themselves in bed. I never tired of the profound intimacy of finding out who is bashful in the sexual act and who is not. (Hint: It's never what you expect.) I was touched by the surprising noises that men made in their moments of abandon. I was curious about the endless variation in their fantasies. I was thrilled by the ways a man could rush me in one moment, all guns blazing, only to be overcome in the next moment by tenderness and uncertainty.

But I also had different rules of conduct now. Or, rather, I had one rule: I refused to engage in sexual activity with a married man. I am certain, Angela, that I do not need to tell you why. (But in case I do need to tell you, here's why: because after the catastrophe with Edna Parker Watson, I refused to ever again harm another woman as a result of my sexual activity.)

I would not even engage in sexual congress with a man who claimed to be going through a divorce—because who really knows? I've met a lot of men who always seemed to be going through a divorce, but who never quite managed to complete one. I once went on a dinner date with a man who confessed to me during the dessert course that he was married, but claimed that it didn't count, because he was on his fourth wife—and can you honestly even call that *married*?

I could see his point, to a certain extent. But still: no.

If you're wondering where I found my men, Angela, I shall inform you that never in human history has it been difficult for a woman to find a man who will have sex with her, if that woman is *easy*.

So, generally speaking, I found my men everywhere. But if you want the specifics: I most often found them at the bar at the Grosvenor Hotel, on the corner of Fifth Avenue and Tenth Street. I had always appreciated the Grosvenor. It was old and staid and unassuming— elegant, but not off-puttingly elegant. The barroom had a few tables with white tablecloths set near the window. I liked to go there in the late afternoons, after my long days of sewing, and sit at one of those window-side tables, reading a novel and enjoying a martini.

Nine times out of ten, all I did was read and sip my drink and relax. But every so often, a male guest at the bar would send over a drink. And then something might or might not transpire between us—depending on how things went.

I usually knew fairly quickly if this gentleman was somebody with whom I wished to engage. Once I knew, I liked to move things right along. I've never been one to game a man, or pretend to be coy. Also, if I'm being honest, I often found the conversations tiring. The postwar period in America was a terrible time, Angela, when it came to the problem of men talking boastfully about themselves. American men had not only won the war; they had won the *world,* and they were feeling pretty damn proud of themselves about it. And they liked to talk about it. I became quite good at cutting short all the chitchat by being sexually direct. ("I find you attractive. Shall we go someplace where we can be alone together?") Also, I liked to witness the man's surprise and joy at being propositioned so blatantly by a good-looking woman. They would light up every time. I have always loved that moment. It is as though you have brought Christmas to an orphanage.

The bartender at the Grosvenor was named Bobby, and he was so gracious to me. Whenever he saw me leaving the bar with one of his hotel guests—heading to the elevators with a man I'd met only an hour earlier—Bobby would ever so discreetly bow his head over his newspaper, not noticing a thing. Behind his spiffy uniform and professional demeanor, you see, Bobby was quite the bohemian himself. He lived in the Village, and went away to the Catskills for two weeks every summer to paint watercolors and wander about in the nude at an art retreat for "naturists." Needless to say, Bobby was not the sort to cast judgments. And if a man ever gave me unwelcome attention, Bobby would intervene and ask the gentleman to please leave the lady alone. I adored Bobby, and I probably would have had an affair with him at some point over the years, but I needed him as my sentry more than I needed him as my lover.

As for the men in the hotel rooms, we would have our adventure together, and then I would usually never see them again.

I liked to leave their beds before they started telling me things about themselves that I didn't want to know.

If you are wondering whether I ever fell in love with any of those gentlemen, Angela, the answer is no. I had lovers, but not *loves*. Some of those lovers turned into boyfriends, and a precious handful of those boyfriends turned into friends (the best outcome of all). But nothing advanced into the realm of what you might call true love. Maybe I just wasn't looking for it. Or maybe I was being spared from it. Nothing will uproot your life more violently than true love—at least as far as I've always witnessed.

I was often quite fond of them, though. For a while, I had a fun affair with a young—*very* young—Hungarian painter, whom I met at an art exhibition at the Park Avenue Armory. His name was Botond and he was an absolute lamb. I brought him home to my apartment the night I met him, and—right on the brink of sex—he told me that he didn't need to use a prophylactic because "you are a nice woman, and I'm sure you are clean." I sat up in bed, turned on the light, and said to this boy who was practically young enough to be my son, "Botond, now listen to me. I *am* a nice woman. But I need to tell you something important that you must never forget: if a woman is willing to go home and have sex with you after she's only known you for an hour, *she has done it before*. Always, always, *always* use a prophylactic."

Sweet Botond, with his round cheeks and his terrible haircut!

And then there was Hugh—a quiet, kind-faced widower who came in with his daughter one day to buy her a wedding dress. I found him to be so dear and attractive that after our business was completed, I slipped him my private phone number, saying, "Please call me any time you would like to spend a night together."

I could tell that I'd embarrassed him, but I didn't want to let him get away!

About two years later, I received a phone call one Saturday afternoon. It was Hugh! Once he had reintroduced himself—stammering nervously—he clearly had no idea how to continue the conversation. Smiling into the phone, I rescued him as quickly as I could. "Hugh," I said, "it's wonderful to hear from you. And you needn't be embarrassed. I did say *any time*. Why don't you come right on over?"

If you're wondering if any of those men ever fell in love with me—well, sometimes they did. But I always managed to talk them out of it. It's easy for a man who has just experienced good sex to believe that he is now in love. And I *was* good at sex, Angela, by this point. I'd certainly had enough practice at it. (As I said once to Marjorie, "The only two things I've ever been good at in this world are sex and sewing." To which she responded: "Well, honey—at least you chose the right one to monetize.") When men became too dewy-eyed with me, I merely explained to them that they were not in love with *me*, but with the sexual act itself, and they would usually calm down.

If you're wondering whether I was ever in any physical danger from my nocturnal encounters with all these strange and unknown men, the only honest answer is *yes*. But it did not stop me. I was as careful as I could be, but I had nothing to go on but my instincts when choosing my men. Sometimes, I chose wrong. This is bound to happen. There were times, behind closed doors, when things got rougher and more dicey than I might have preferred. Not often, but sometimes. When that happened, I rode it out like an experienced sailor in a bad squall.

I don't know how else to explain it. And while I did have an unpleasant night every so often, I never felt *enduringly* harmed. Nor did the threat of danger ever deter me. These were risks I was willing to take. It was more important for me to feel free than safe.

And if you're wondering whether I ever had crises of conscience about my promiscuity, I can honestly tell you: no. I did believe that my behavior made me *unusual*—because it didn't seem to match the behavior of other women—but I didn't believe that it made me *bad*.

I used to think that I was bad, mind you. During the dry years of the war, I still carried such a burden of shame about the incident with Edna Parker Watson, and the words "dirty little whore" never fully left my consciousness. But by the time the war ended, I was finished with all that. I think it had something to do with my brother being killed, and the painful belief that Walter had died without ever having enjoyed his life. The war had invested me with an understanding that life is both dangerous and fleeting, and thus there is no point in denying yourself pleasure or adventure while you are here.

I could have spent the rest of my life trying to prove that I was a *good girl*—but that would have been unfaithful to who I really was. I believed that I was a good person, if not a *good girl*. But my appetites were what they were. So I gave up on the idea of denying myself what I truly wanted. Then I sought ways to delight myself. As long as I stayed away from married men, I felt that I was doing no harm.

Anyway, at some point in a woman's life, she just gets tired of being ashamed all the time.

After that, she is free to become whoever she truly is.

TWENTY-EIGHT

As for female friends, I had many.

Of course, Marjorie was my best friend, and Peg and Olive would always be my family. But Marjorie and I had a lot of other women around, too.

There was Marty—a doctoral candidate in literature at NYU, brilliant and funny, whom we'd met one day at a free concert on Rutherford Place. There was Karen—a receptionist at the Museum of Modern Art, who wanted to be a painter, and who had attended Parsons with Marjorie. There was Rowan, who was a gynecologist—which we all found terribly impressive, and also useful. There was Susan—a grade-school teacher with a passion for modern dance. There was Callie, who owned the flower shop around the corner. There was Anita, who came from money and never did anything at all—but she did get us a pirated key to Gramercy Park, so we appreciated her forever.

There were more women, too, who came and went out of my life. Sometimes Marjorie and I would lose a friend to marriage; other times we would gain a friend after a divorce. Sometimes a woman would move out of the city, sometimes she would move back. The tides of life came in and out. The circles of friendship grew, then shrank, then grew again.

But the gathering place for us women was always the same—our rooftop on Eighteenth Street, which we could access from the fire escape outside my bedroom window. Marjorie and I dragged a bunch of cheap folding chairs up there, and we would spend our evenings on the roof with our friends, anytime the weather was fine. Summer after summer, our little group of females would sit together under what passes for starlight in New York City, smoking our cigarettes, drinking our rotgut wine, listening to music on a transistor radio, and sharing with each other our big and small concerns of life.

During one brutally airless August heat wave, Marjorie managed to haul a big stand-up fan up onto our roof. This she plugged into my kitchen outlet, using a long industrial extension cord. As far as the rest of us were concerned, this made her a genius at the level of Leonardo da Vinci. We would sit in the artificial breeze of the fan, lifting our shirts to cool our breasts, and pretending that we were at a beach somewhere exotic.

Those are some of my happiest memories of the 1950s.

It was on the rooftop of our little bridal boutique that I learned this truth: when women are gathered together with no men around, they don't have to be anything in particular; they can just *be*.

Then in 1955, Marjorie got pregnant.

I'd always feared it was going to be me who ended up pregnant—the smart bet would have been on me, obviously—but poor Marjorie was the one who got hit.

The culprit was an old married art professor, with whom she'd been having an affair for years. (Although Marjorie would have said that the culprit was herself, for wasting so much of her life with a married man who kept promising that he would leave his wife for her, if only Marjorie would "stop acting so Jewish.")

A bunch of us were on the rooftop one night when she told us the news.

"Are you sure?" asked Rowan, the gynecologist. "Do you want to come into my office for a test?"

"I don't need a test," said Marjorie. "My period is gone, gone, gone."

"Gone, how long?" said Rowan.

"Well, I've never been regular, but maybe three months?"

There's a tense silence that women fall into when they hear that one of their own has become accidentally pregnant. This is a matter of highest gravity. I could feel that none of us wanted to say another word until Marjorie had told us more. We wanted to know what her plan was, so that we could support it, whatever the plan may have been. But she just sat there in silence, after dropping this bomb, and added no further information.

Finally, I asked, "What does George have to say about this?" George, of course, being the anti-Semitic married art professor who apparently loved having sex with Jewish girls.

"Why do you assume it's George?" she joked.

We all knew it was George. It was always George. Of course it was George. She had been infatuated with George since she was a wide-eyed student in his Sculpture of Modern Europe class, so many years earlier.

Then she said, "No, I haven't told him. I think I won't tell him. I just won't see him anymore. I'll cut it off from here. If nothing else, this is finally a good excuse to stop sleeping with George."

Rowan cut right to the chase: "Have you considered a termination?"

"No. I wouldn't do that. Or, rather, maybe I would do that. But it's too late."

She lit another cigarette and took another drink of wine—because that's what pregnancy looked like in the 1950s.

She said, "I found out about a place in Canada. It's sort of a home for unwed mothers, but more deluxe than the usual fare. You get your own room, and all that. My understanding is that the clientele is a bit older. Women with some money. I can go there toward the end, when I can't hide it anymore. Tell people I'm on vacation—even though I've never taken a vacation in my life, so nobody will believe me, but that's all I can do. They even said they could place the baby in a Jewish family—although where they aim to find a Jewish family in Canada, who knows? Anyway, I don't care about religion, you all know that. As long as it's a good home. It seems like a nice enough facility. Plenty expensive, but I can swing it. I'll use the Paris money."

It was typical of Marjorie to have solved a problem on her own before reaching out to her friends for help, and certainly her plan was sound. Still, my heart hurt. Marjorie didn't want any of this. She and I had been saving our money for years, planning to take a trip to Paris together. As soon as we had enough cash gathered, our plan was to close the boutique for the entire month of August, get on the *Queen Elizabeth*, and sail to France. This was our shared dream. We were almost there with our savings, too. We had worked for years without so much as a weekend off. And now this.

I knew right then that I would go to Canada with her. We would close down L'Atelier for however long was necessary. Wherever she was going, I would go with her. I would stay with her through the birth of her baby. I would spend my share of the Paris money to buy a car. Whatever she needed.

I scooted my chair over next to Marjorie's and took her hand. "That all sounds wise, honey," I said. "I'll be right there with you."

"It does sound wise, doesn't it?" Marjorie took another drag off her cigarette, and looked around at the circle of her friends. We all had the same loving, pitying, and somewhat panicked expressions on our faces.

Then the most unexpected thing happened. Suddenly Marjorie grinned at me, in a slightly crazed-looking, lopsided manner. She said, "Goddamn it to hell, but I don't think I'll go to Canada. Oh, Christ, Vivian, I must be out of my mind. But I just decided it right now. I have a better plan. No, not a better plan. But a different plan. I'll keep it."

"You're going to keep the *baby*?" Karen asked, in open shock.

"What about George?" Anita asked.

Marjorie stuck her chin up in the air like the tough little bantamweight fighter she'd always been. "I don't need stinkin' George. Vivian and I are gonna raise this kid ourselves. Aren't we, Vivian?"

I gave it only a moment's thought. I knew my friend. Once she had decided something, that was it. She would somehow make it work. And I would make it work with her, like always.

So once again I said to Marjorie Lowtsky: "Sure. Let's do it."

And once again, my life completely changed.

So that's what we did, Angela.

We had a kid.

And that kid was our beautiful, difficult, tender little Nathan.

Everything about it was hard.

Her pregnancy wasn't so bad, but the delivery itself was something from a horror movie. They ended up doing a cesarian, but not before she'd suffered through eighteen hours of labor. They really hacked her up during the procedure, too. Then she didn't stop bleeding, and there was a concern they would lose her. They nicked the baby's face with the scalpel during the cesarian, and very nearly took out his eye. Then Marjorie got an infection and was in the hospital for almost four weeks.

I still maintain that all this carelessness at the hospital was due to the fact that Nathan was what they called a "non-marital infant" (politely sinister 1950s terminology for "bastard"). As a result, the doctors weren't especially attentive to Marjorie during her labor, and the nurses weren't particularly kind, either.

It was Marjorie's and my girlfriends who took care of her when she was recovering. Marjorie's family—for the same reason as the nurses—didn't want much to do with her and the baby. That may sound extremely unkind (and it was), but you can't imagine what a stigma it was for a woman at that time to bear a child out of wedlock—even in liberal New York. Even for a mature woman like Marjorie, who ran her own business and owned her own building, undergoing a pregnancy without a husband attached was *disgraceful*.

So she was brave, is what I'm driving at. And she was on her own. Thus it came down to our circle of friends to take care of Marjorie and Nathan as best we could. It was good that we had so much backup. I couldn't be with Marjorie all the time at the hospital, because I was the one taking care of the baby while she was recovering. This was like its own horror movie as I had no idea what I was doing. I hadn't grown up with babies, nor had I ever longed for a child myself. I had no instinct or aptitude for it. Moreover, I hadn't bothered to learn much about babies while Marjorie was pregnant. I didn't even really know what they ate. The plan had never been that Nathan would be my baby, anyhow; the plan had been that he would be Marjorie's baby, and that I would work doubly hard to support all three of us. But for that first month, he was my baby, and he was not in the most expert hands, I'm sorry to say.

Moreover, Nathan was not easy. He was colicky and underweight, and it was a struggle to get him to take the bottle. He had rampant cradle cap and diaper rash ("catastrophes at both ends," as Marjorie said) and I couldn't seem to get any of it to go away. Our assistants at L'Atelier managed the boutique as best they could, but it was June—wedding season—and I had to be at work at least sometimes or the business wouldn't function at all. I had to do Marjorie's work for her, as well, while she was absent. But every time I set Nathan down so I could attend to my duties, he would scream until I picked him back up again.

The mother of one of my brides-to-be saw me struggling with the infant one morning, and gave me the name of an older Italian woman who had helped out her own daughter, when her twin grandchildren were born. That older nursemaid's name was Palma, and she turned out to be St. Michael and all the angels. We kept Palma on as Nathan's nanny for years, and she truly saved us—especially during that brutal first year. But Palma was expensive. In fact, everything about Nathan was expensive. He was a sickly baby, and then he was a sickly toddler, and then he was a sickly little boy. I swear he spent more time in the doctor's office during those first five years of his life than he did at home. If there was anything a child could come down with, he came down with it. He always had trouble with his breathing, and he was constantly on penicillin, which upset his stomach, and then you couldn't feed him—which led to its own problems.

Marjorie and I had to work harder than ever to pay the bills, now that there were three of us—and one of us was always sick. So work harder, we did.

You wouldn't believe the number of wedding gowns we churned out during those years. Thank God people were getting married in higher numbers than ever.

Neither of us talked about going to Paris anymore.

———

Time passed and Nathan grew older but not much bigger. He was such a squirt of a thing—so dear in his affections, so tenderhearted and gentle, but also so nervous and easily frightened. And *always* sick.

We loved him so. It was impossible *not* to love him; he was such a sweetheart. You never met a more kind little person. He never got into trouble, or was disobedient. The problem was only that he was so fragile. Maybe we babied him too much. Almost certainly we babied him too much. Let's be clear: this child grew up in a bridal boutique surrounded by hordes of women (customers and employees alike) who were more than willing to indulge his fears and his clinginess. ("Oh, God, Vivian, he's gonna be such a *queer*," Marjorie said to me once, when she saw her son twirling in a wedding veil in front of a mirror. That may sound harsh, but to be fair to Marjorie, it was difficult to imagine how Nathan could grow up to be anything else. We used to joke that Olive was the only masculine figure in his life.)

As Nathan approached the age of five, we realized that we could not possibly enroll this kid in public school. He weighed in at about twenty-five pounds dripping wet, and the presence of other children alarmed him. He wasn't a stickball-playing, tree-climbing, rock-throwing, knee-skinning sort of boy. He liked puzzles. He liked to look at books, but nothing too scary. (*Swiss Family Robinson:* too scary. *Snow White:* too scary. *Make Way for Ducklings:* just about right.) Nathan was the kind of child who would have been brutalized at a public school in New York City. We pictured him being pounded like bread dough by tough city bullies, and we couldn't bear the thought. So we enrolled him in Friends Seminary (at two thousand dollars a year tuition, thank you very much) so that the gentle Quakers could take all our hard-earned money and teach our boy how to be non-violent, which was never going to be a problem anyhow.

385

When the other children asked Nathan where his daddy was, we taught him to say, "My daddy was killed in the war"—which didn't even make sense, because Nathan was born in 1956. But we figured kindergartners were too dumb to do the math, so his answer would keep them at bay for a while. As Nathan got older, we'd come up with a better story.

One bright winter's day, when Nathan was around six years old, Marjorie and I were sitting in Gramercy Park with him. I was doing beadwork on a bodice and Marjorie was trying to read *The New York Review of Books,* despite the wind that kept whipping at her pages. Marjorie was wearing a poncho (in a puzzling plaid of violet and mustard) and some kind of crazy Turkish shoes with curled-up toes. Wrapped around her head was a white silk pilot's scarf. She looked like a medieval guildsman with a toothache.

At one point, we both paused what we were doing to watch Nathan. He was carefully drawing stick figures in chalk on the pathway. But then he became scared of some pigeons—some very innocuous pigeons, which were minding their own business and pecking at the ground a few feet away from where Nathan sat. He stopped drawing and froze. We watched as the boy grew wide-eyed with terror at the sight of the birds.

Under her breath, Marjorie said, "Look at him. He's afraid of everything."

"That's right," I agreed, because it was true. He really was.

She said, "I can't even give him a bath without him thinking I'm trying to drown him. Where did he even hear of mothers drowning their children? Why would that idea even be in his head? You never tried to drown him in the bath, did you, Vivian?"

"I'm almost certain I didn't. But you know how I get when I'm angry. . . ."

I was trying to make her laugh but it didn't work.

"I don't know about this child," she said, her face overcome by worry. "He's even afraid of his red hat. I think it's the color. I tried to put it on him this morning, and he burst into tears. I had to let him have the blue one. Do you know something, Vivian? He has utterly ruined my life."

"Oh, Marjorie, don't say that," I said, laughing.

"No, it's true, Vivian. He's ruined everything. Let's just admit it. I should've gone to Canada and given him up for adoption. Then we would still have money, and I would have some freedom. I'd be able to sleep through the night, without listening for his coughing. I wouldn't be seen as a fallen woman with a bastard child. I wouldn't be so tired. Maybe I would have time to paint. I would still have a figure. Maybe I could even have a boyfriend. Let's just call a spade a spade: I never should've had this kid."

"Marjorie! Stop it. You don't mean that."

But she wasn't done. "No, I *do* mean it, Vivian. He was the worst decision I ever made in my life. You can't deny that. Nobody could deny that."

I was starting to get terribly worried, but then she said, "The only problem is, I love him so much, I can't even bear it. I mean—*look at him.*"

And there he was. There was that touching little broken figurine of a boy, trying to get as far away as possible from any and all pigeons (which is not easy in a New York City park). There was our little Nathan, in his snowsuit, with his chapped lips and his cheeks all red with eczema. There was his sweet, peaked face—glancing around in panic for somebody to protect him from some nine-ounce birds who were completely ignoring him. He was perfect. He was made of spun glass. He was a reedy little disaster and I adored him.

I glanced over at Marjorie, and could see that she was now crying. This was significant because Marjorie never cried. (That had always been my department.) I'd never seen her looking so rueful and so tired.

Marjorie said, "Do you think Nathan's father might claim him someday, if he ever stops acting so Jewish?"

I punched her in the arm. "Stop it, Marjorie!"

"I'm just so *weary*, Vivian. But I love this kid so much, sometimes I think it will break me in half. Is that the dirty trick? Is this how they get mothers to ruin their lives for their children? By tricking them into loving them so much?"

"Maybe. It's not a bad strategy."

We watched Nathan for a while longer, as he braved the specter of the harmless, oblivious, retreating pigeons.

"Hey, don't forget that my son ruined *your* life, too," Marjorie said, after a long silence.

I shrugged. "A little bit, sure. But I wouldn't worry about it. It's not as though I had anything more important to attend to."

The years passed.

The city continued to change. Midtown Manhattan became wilted and moldy and sinister and vile. We never went near Times Square anymore. It was a latrine.

In 1963, Walter Winchell lost his newspaper column.

Death started to pick at my community.

In 1964, Uncle Billy died in Hollywood of a sudden heart attack while dining with a starlet at the Beverly Hills Hotel. We all had to admit that this was just *exactly* the death Billy Buell would've wanted. ("He floated away on a river of champagne" was Peg's take.)

Only ten months later, my father died. His was not such a peaceful death, I'm afraid. Driving home from the country club one afternoon, he hit black ice and crashed into a tree. He lived for a few days, but succumbed to complications after emergency spine surgery.

My father died an angry man. He was no longer a captain of

industry—hadn't been one for years. He had lost his hematite mine after the war. He got into such a ferocious battle against union activists that he drove the company into the ground—spending nearly all his fortune on legal battles against his workers. His had become a scorched-earth policy of negotiation: *If I cannot control this business, then nobody can.* He died never having forgiven the American government for having taken his son in the war, or the unions for having taken his business, or the modern world itself for having chipped away over the decades at every last one of his cherished, narrow, old-fashioned beliefs.

We all drove up to Clinton for the funeral: me, Peg, Olive, Marjorie, and Nathan. My mother was silently appalled by the spectacle of my friend Marjorie in her strange clothes with her strange child. My mother had become a deeply unhappy woman over the years, and she responded to no gestures of kindness from anyone. She didn't want us there.

We stayed only one night, and hustled back to the city just as fast as we could.

Home was New York City now, anyway. It had been for years.

M ore time passed.

After a certain age, Angela, time just drizzles down upon your head like rain in the month of March: you're always surprised at how much of it can accumulate, and how fast.

One night in 1964, I was watching Jack Paar on television. I was only halfway paying attention, as I was working on disassembling an old Belgian wedding gown without destroying its ancient fibers in the process. Then the ads came on, and I heard a familiar female voice— gruff, tough, and sarcastic. The cigarette-roughened voice of a real old New York City broad. Before I could even register it in my mind, that voice set off a depth charge in my gut.

I looked up at the screen and caught a glimpse of a thickset, chestnut-haired woman with a great prow of a bosom, shouting in a funny Bronx accent about all her problems with floor wax. ("It's not enough that I gotta deal with these crazy kids of mine, but now it's sticky floors, too?!") She could have been any middle-aged brunette, by the sight of her. But I would've known that voice anywhere: it was Celia Ray!

I had thought of Celia so many times over the years—with guilt, with curiosity, with anxiety. All I could ever imagine for her life were bad outcomes. In my darkest fantasies, the story was this: After being exiled from the Lily Playhouse, Celia had lived a life of doom and ruin. Perhaps she had died in the streets somewhere along the way, brutalized by the kind of man she had once so effortlessly controlled. Other times, I imagined her as an old prostitute. Sometimes I would pass by a drunken, middle-aged woman on the street who looked (there is no other word for it) *trashy,* and I would wonder if it was Celia. Had she dyed her hair so blond that it had turned brittle and orange? Was she that woman over there in the tottering heels, with the bare, veined legs? Was that her, with the bruised circles under the eyes? Was that her, picking through the garbage can? Was that her red lipstick on that collapsing mouth?

But I'd been wrong: Celia was fine. Better than fine—she was selling floor wax on TV! Oh, that stubborn, determined, little survivor. Still fighting her way into the spotlight.

I never saw the ad again, and I never tried to track Celia down. I didn't want to interfere with her life, and I knew better than to assume that she and I would have anything in common anymore. We'd never really had anything in common in the first place. Scandal or no scandal, I believe that our friendship was always destined to have been momentary—a collision of two vain young girls who intersected at the zenith of their beauty and the nadir of their intelligence, and who had blatantly used each other to acquire status and turn men's heads. That's all it had ever been, really, and that was perfect. That's all it had ever needed to be. I'd found deeper and richer female friendships later on in life, and I hoped that Celia had, too.

So, no, I never sought her out.

But it is impossible for me to convey the amount of delight and pride that it gave me to hear her voice blasting out of my television set that evening.

It made me want to cheer.

A quarter of a century later, folks, and Celia Ray was still in show business!

TWENTY-NINE

I n the late summer of 1965, my Aunt Peg received a curious letter in the mail.

It was from the commissioner of the Brooklyn Navy Yard. The letter explained that the Navy Yard would soon be closing down forever. The city was transforming, and the Navy had decided that it was no longer feasible to maintain a shipbuilding industry in such an expensive urban area. Before it closed, however, the Yard would host a ceremonial reunion—throwing open the gates once more, in celebration of all the Brooklyn workers who had labored there so heroically during World War II. Since it was the twentieth anniversary of the end of the war, this kind of celebration seemed particularly appropriate.

The commissioner's office had gone through their files and found Peg's name on some old paperwork, listing her as having been an "independent entertainment contractor." They'd managed to track her down through city tax records and now they were wondering whether Mrs. Buell might consider producing a small commemorative show on the day of the Navy Yard reunion, to celebrate the accomplishments of the wartime laborers? They were looking for something of a nostalgia piece—just twenty minutes or so of old-time singing and dancing, in the style of the war days.

Now, Peg would have enjoyed nothing more than to take on this job. The only problem was, she was no longer in good health. That big, tall body of hers was starting to break down. She was suffering from emphysema—not surprising after her lifetime of chain-smoking—and she also had arthritis, and her eyes were starting to go. As she explained it: "The doctor says that there's nothing much wrong with me, kiddo, but there's nothing much right with me, either."

She had retired from her job at the high school a few years earlier, due to her failing health, and she didn't get around easily anymore. Marjorie and Nathan and I had dinner with Peg and Olive a few nights a week, but that was about all Peg could handle in terms of excitement. Most evenings, she would just stretch across the couch with her eyes closed, trying to catch her breath, while Olive read to her from the sports pages. So, no, unfortunately, it wasn't going to be possible for Peg to produce a commemorative show at the Brooklyn Navy Yard.

But I could do it.

It turned out to be easier than I thought—and far more fun.

I'd helped to create so many hundreds of skits back in the day, and I guess I never lost the knack for it. I hired some of the drama students from Olive's high school as my actors and dancers. Susan (my friend with the passion for modern dance) said she would handle the choreography, though it didn't need to be anything complex. I borrowed the organist from the church down the street, and worked with him on writing some elementary, corny songs. And of course, I created the costumes, which were simple enough: just a bunch of dungarees and overalls for both the boys and the girls. I threw some red kerchiefs around the girls' heads and the same red kerchiefs around the boys' necks, and *voilà*—now they were industrial workers from the 1940s.

On September 18, 1965, we hauled all of our theatrical gear over to the ratty old Navy Yard and got ready for our show. It was a bright and windy morning on the waterfront, and gusts kept rising off the bay and knocking people's hats off. But a fairly decent-sized crowd had shown up, and there was a carnival-type feeling to the festivities. There was a Navy band playing old songs and a women's auxiliary group serving cookies and refreshments. A few high-ranking Navy officials spoke about how we had won that war, and how we would win all the wars to come until the end of days. The first woman ever licensed to work as a welder at the Yard during World War II gave a short, nervous speech in a voice much meeker than you might expect from a lady of such accomplishment. And a ten-year-old girl with chapped knees sang the National Anthem, wearing a dress that was not going to fit her next summer, and was not keeping her warm right now.

Then it was time for our little show.

I had been asked by the commissioner of the Navy Yard to introduce myself and to explain our skit. I'm not crazy about public speaking, but I managed to pull through it without bringing down ruin upon my head. I told the audience who I was, and what my role had been at the Yard during the war. I made a joke about the poor quality of food at the Sammy cafeteria, which earned a few scattered laughs from those who remembered. I thanked the veterans in the audience for their service, and the families of Brooklyn for their sacrifice. I said that my own brother had been a naval officer who lost his life in the final days of the war. (I was afraid I wouldn't be able to get through that section of my remarks without losing my composure, but I managed it.) Then I explained that we were going to be re-creating a typical propaganda skit, which I hoped would boost the morale of the current audience just as much as it used to cheer on the workers during their lunch breaks.

The show I had written was about a typical day on the line at the Navy Yard, building battleships in Brooklyn. The high school kids in their overalls played the workers who sang and danced with joy as they did their part to make the world safe for democracy. Pandering to my constituency, I'd peppered the script with slangy dialogue that I hoped the old Navy Yard workers would remember.

"Coming through with the general's car!" shouted one of my young actresses, pushing a wheelbarrow.

"No carping!" shouted another girl to a character who was complaining about the long hours and the dirty conditions.

I named the factory manager Mr. Goldbricker, which I knew all the old laborers would appreciate ("goldbricker" being the favorite old Yard term for "one who slacks off at work").

Look, it wasn't exactly Tennessee Williams, but the audience seemed to like it. What's more, the high school drama club was having fun performing it. For me, though, the best part was seeing little Nathan—my ten-year-old sweetheart, my dear boy—sitting in the front row with his mother, watching the production with such wonder and amazement, you would've thought he was at the circus.

Our big finale was a number called "No Time for Coffee!" about how important it was at the Navy Yard to keep on schedule at all costs. The song contained the ever-so-catchy line: "Even if we had coffee, we wouldn't have had the milk! / War rations made coffee just as valuable as silk!" (I don't like to boast, but I did write that snazzy bit of brilliance all by myself—so move over, Cole Porter.)

Then we killed Hitler, and the show was over, and everyone was happy.

As we were packing up our cast and our props into the school bus we had borrowed for the day, a uniformed patrolman approached me.

"May I have a word with you, ma'am?" he asked.

"Of course," I said. "I'm sorry we're parked here but it will just be a moment."

"Could you step away from the vehicle, please?"

He looked terribly serious, and now I was concerned. What had we done wrong? Should we not have set up a stage? I'd assumed there were permits for all this.

I followed him over to his patrol car, where he leaned against the door and fixed me with a grave stare.

"I heard you speaking earlier," he said. "Did I hear you correctly when you said your name is Vivian Morris?" His accent identified him as pure Brooklyn. He could have been born right on this very spot of dirt, by the sound of that voice.

"That's right, sir."

"You said your brother was killed in the war?"

"That's correct."

The patrolman took off his hat and ran a hand through his hair. His hands were trembling. I wondered if perhaps he was a veteran himself. He was the right age for it. Sometimes they were shaky like this. I studied him more closely. He was a tall man in his middle forties. Painfully thin. Olive skin and large, dark-brown eyes—further darkened by the circles beneath them and by the lines of worry above. Then I saw what looked like burn scars, running up the right side of his neck. Ropes of scars, twisted in red, pink, and yellowish flesh. Now I knew he was a veteran. I had a feeling I was about to hear a war story, and that it would be a tough one.

But then he shocked me.

"Your brother was Walter Morris, wasn't he?" he asked.

Now *I* was the one who felt shaky. My knees almost went out of business. I had not mentioned Walter by name during my speech.

Before I could speak, the patrolman said, "I knew your brother, ma'am. I served with him on the *Franklin*."

I put my hand over my mouth to stop the involuntary little sob that had risen in my throat.

"You knew *Walter*?" Despite my effort to control my voice, the words came out choked. "You were *there*?"

I didn't elaborate upon my question, but clearly he knew what I meant. I was asking him: *You were there on March 19, 1945? You were there when a kamikaze pilot crashed right through the flight deck of the USS* Franklin, *detonating the fuel storages, igniting the onboard aircraft, and turning the ship itself into a bomb? You were there when my brother and over eight hundred other men died? You were there, when my brother was buried at sea?*

He nodded several times—a nervous, jerky bobbing of the head.

Yes. He was there.

I told my eyes not to glance again at the burn marks on this man's neck.

My eyes glanced there anyhow, goddamn it.

I looked away. Now I didn't know where to look.

Seeing me so uncomfortable, the man himself became only more nervous. His face looked almost panic-stricken. He seemed legitimately distraught. He was either terrified of upsetting me, or he was reliving his own nightmare. Maybe both. Witnessing this, I gathered my senses about me, took a deep breath, and set myself to the task of trying to put this poor man at ease. What was my pain, after all, compared to what he had lived through?

"Thank you for telling me," I said, in a slightly more steady voice. "I'm sorry for my reaction. It's just a shock to hear my brother's name after all these years. But it's an honor to meet you."

I put my hand on his arm, to give him a little squeeze of gratitude. He cringed as though I had attacked him. I pulled back my hand, but slowly. He reminded me of the sort of horses my mother was always good with—the jumpy ones, the agitated ones. The timorous and troubled ones that nobody but she could handle. I instinctively took the tiniest step back, and dropped my arms to my sides. I wanted to show him that I was no threat.

I tried a different tack.

"What's your name, sailor?" I asked in a more gentle voice—almost a teasing voice.

"I'm Frank Grecco."

He didn't reach out for a handshake, so I didn't, either.

"How well did you know my brother, Frank?"

He nodded once more. Again, with that nervous bobbing. "We were officers together on the flight deck. Walter was my division commander. We'd been ninety-day wonders together, too. Went in different directions at first, but ended up on the same ship at the end of the war. By then, he outranked me."

"Oh. All right."

I wasn't sure what any of those words meant, but I didn't want him to stop talking. There was somebody standing right in front of me who had known my *brother*. I wanted to find out everything about this man.

"Did you grow up around here, Frank?" I asked, already knowing the answer from his accent. But I was trying to make things as easy for him as I could. I would give him the simple questions first.

Again, the twitchy nod. "South Brooklyn." "And were you and my brother good friends?"

He winced.

"Miss Morris, I need to tell you something." The patrolman took off his hat once more and jammed his trembling fingers through his hair. "You don't recognize me, do you?"

"Why would I recognize you?"

"Because I already know you, and you already know me. Please don't walk away, ma'am."

"Why on earth would I walk away?"

"Because I met you back in 1941," he said. "I was the guy who drove you home to your parents' house."

The past came roaring up at me like a dragon woken from a deep slumber. I felt dizzy with the heat and the force of it. In a vertiginous series of flashes, I saw Edna's face, Arthur's face, Celia's face, Winchell's face. I saw my own young face in the back of that beat-up Ford—shamed and shattered.

This was the *driver.*

This was the guy who had called me a dirty little whore, right in front of my brother.

"Ma'am," he said—and now he was the one grabbing *my* arm. "Please don't walk away."

"Stop saying that." My voice came out ragged. Why did he keep saying that, when I wasn't going anywhere? I just wanted him to stop saying that.

But he did it again: "Please don't walk away, ma'am. I need to talk to you."

I shook my head. "I can't—"

"You need to understand—I'm so sorry," he said.

"Could you let go of my arm, please?"

"I'm sorry," he repeated, but he dropped my arm.

What did I feel?

Repulsion. Pure repulsion.

I couldn't tell, though, if it was repulsion for him or for me. Whatever it was, it was growing out of a trove of shame that I thought I'd buried long ago.

I hated this guy. That's what I felt: *hate.*

"I was a stupid kid," he said. "I didn't know how to act."

"I really must go now."

"Please don't walk away, Vivian."

His voice was rising, which disturbed me. But hearing him call me by my name was even worse. I hated it, that he knew my name. I hated that he'd watched me onstage today, and knew who I was the whole time—that he knew this much about me. I hated that he'd seen me get choked up about my brother. I hated that he probably knew my brother better than I did. I hated that Walter had attacked me in front of him. I hated that this man had once called me a dirty little whore. Who did he think he was, approaching me now, after all these years? This sense of rage and disgust compounded, and it strengthened something in my spine: I needed to leave *right now.*

"I have a bus full of kids waiting for me," I said.

I started walking away.

"I need to talk to you, Vivian!" he cried out after me. "*Please.*"

But I got on the bus and left him standing there by his patrol car—hat in hand, like a man begging for alms.

And that, Angela, is how I officially met your father.

Somehow, I managed to do all the things I needed to get done that day.

I dropped the kids back at the high school and helped unload the props. We returned the bus to its parking space. Marjorie and I walked home with Nathan, who could not stop chattering on about how much he had loved the show, and how when he grew up *he* wanted to work in the Brooklyn Navy Yard.

Of course, Marjorie could tell I was upset. She kept casting glances at me, over Nathan's head. But I just nodded at her, to indicate that I was fine. Which I decidedly was not.

Then—just as soon as I was free—I ran straight to Aunt Peg's house.

had never before told anybody about that car ride home to Clinton back in 1941.

Nobody knew how my brother had savaged me up one side and down the other—eviscerating me with rebuke, and allowing his disgust to rain down upon me in buckets. I had certainly never told anyone about the double disgrace of having this attack occur in front of a witness—a *stranger*—who had then added his own coup de grâce to my punishment by calling me a dirty little whore. Nobody knew that Walter had not so much rescued me from New York City as dumped me like a bag of garbage on my parents' doorstep—too sickened by my behavior to even look at my face for a moment longer than he had to.

But now I rushed over to Sutton Place, to bring the story to Peg.

I found my aunt stretched out on her couch, as she was wont to do those days—alternating between smoking and coughing. She was listening to radio coverage of the Yankees. As soon as I walked in, she told me that it was Mickey Mantle Day over at Yankee Stadium—that they were honoring his stellar fifteen-year career in baseball. In fact, when I burst into the apartment and started talking, Peg put up her hand: Joe DiMaggio was speaking, and she didn't want him interrupted.

"Have some respect, Vivvie," she said, all business.

So I shut my mouth and let her have her moment. I knew she would have liked to be there at the stadium in person, but she wasn't strong enough anymore for such a strenuous excursion. But Peg's face was awash with rapture and emotion as she listened to DiMaggio honoring Mantle. By the end of his speech, she had fat tears running down her cheeks. (Peg could handle anything—war, catastrophe, failure, death of a relative, a cheating husband, the demolition of her beloved theater— without shedding a tear, but great moments in sports history always made her weepy.)

I've often wondered if our conversation would have gone differently, had she not been so saturated with emotion for the Yankees that day. There's no way of telling. I did sense that it was frustrating for her to turn off the radio once DiMaggio was done talking and give her full attention to me—but she was a generous person, so she did it anyhow. She wiped her eyes and blew her nose. Coughed some more. Lit another cigarette. Then she listened to me with full absorption, as I began to tell her my tale of woe.

Midway through my saga, Olive came in. She had been out shopping at the market. I stopped talking in order to help her put away groceries, and then Peg said, "Vivvie, start from the beginning again. Tell Olive everything you've been telling me."

This wouldn't have been my preference. I had learned to love Olive Thompson over the years, but she would not be the first candidate I would run to if I needed a shoulder to cry on. Olive wasn't exactly a soft bosom of overflowing sympathy. Still, she was *there*, and she and Peg—as they had gotten older—had increasingly become my parental figures.

Seeing my hesitation, Peg said, "Just tell her about it, Vivvie. Trust me—Olive is better at this kind of stuff than any of us."

So I backed up, and started my saga all over again. The car ride in 1941, Walter's disgracing of me, the driver calling me a dirty little whore, my dark time of shame and banishment in upstate New York, and now the return of the driver—a patrolman with burn scars who had been on the *Franklin*. Who knew my brother. Who knew *everything*.

The women listened to me attentively. And when I got to the end they stayed attentive—as though they were waiting for more of the story.

"And then what happened?" asked Peg when she realized I wasn't talking anymore.

"Nothing. After that, I left."

"You *left*?"

"I didn't want to talk to him. I didn't want to see him."

"Vivian, he knew your *brother*. He was on the *Franklin*. From your description, it sounds as though he was gravely wounded in that attack. And you didn't want to talk to him?"

"He hurt me," I said.

"He hurt you? He hurt your feelings twenty-five years ago, and you just walked away from him? This person who knew your brother? This *veteran*?"

I said, "That car ride was the worst thing that ever happened to me, Peg."

"Oh, was it?" snapped Peg. "Did you think to ask the man about the worst thing that ever happened to *him*?"

She was becoming agitated, in a manner that was not at all in character. This was not what I had come for. I wanted comfort, but I was being scolded. I was starting to feel foolish and embarrassed.

"Never mind," I said. "It's nothing. I shouldn't have bothered you today."

"Don't be stupid—it's not nothing."

She had never spoken to me this sharply.

"I should never have brought it up," I said. "I interrupted your game—you're just irritated with me about that. I'm sorry I burst in here."

"I don't give a rat's ass about the goddamn baseball game, Vivian."

"I'm sorry. I'm just upset and I wanted to talk to someone."

"*You're* upset? You walked away from that wounded veteran and then came here to me, because you wanted to talk about *your difficult life?*"

"Jesus, Peg—don't come down on me like this. Just forget it. Forget I said anything."

"How *can* I?"

Then she started coughing—one of her awful, jagged, coughing fits. Her lungs sounded barbed and brittle. She sat up, and Olive pounded on her back for a bit. Then Olive lit another cigarette for Peg, who took the deepest drags she could, interspersed with more fits of coughing.

Peg composed herself. Dummy that I was, I was hoping she was about to apologize for having been so mean to me. Instead she said, "Look, kiddo, I give up here. I don't understand what you want out of this situation. I don't understand you at all right now. I'm just very disappointed in you."

She had *never* said that. Not even all those years ago, when I had betrayed her friend and nearly capsized her hit show.

Then she turned to Olive, and said, "I don't know. What do *you* think, boss?"

Olive sat quietly with her hands folded over her lap, looking down at the floor. I listened to Peg's labored breathing, and to the sound of a window shade on the other side of the room, tapping in the breeze. I wasn't sure I wanted to know what Olive thought. But there we were.

Finally Olive looked up at me. Her expression was stern, as always. But as she chose her words, I could sense that she was choosing them carefully, so as to not do unnecessary harm.

"The field of honor is a painful field, Vivian," she said.

I waited for her to say more, but she didn't.

Peg started laughing—and again coughing. "Well, thank you for your contribution, Olive. That settles everything."

We sat there quietly for a long time. I got up and helped myself to one of Peg's cigarettes, even though I'd quit a few weeks earlier. Or had sort of quit.

"The field of honor is a painful field," Olive went on at last, as though Peg had not spoken. "That's what my father taught me when I was young. He taught me that the field of honor is not a place where children can play. Children don't have any honor, you see, and they aren't expected to, because it's too difficult for them. It's too painful. But to become an adult, one must step into the field of honor. Everything will be expected of you now. You will need to be vigilant in your principles. Sacrifices will be demanded. You will be judged. If you make mistakes, you must account for them. There will be instances when you must cast aside your impulses and take a higher stance than another person—a person without honor—might take. Such instances may hurt, but that's why honor is a painful field. Do you understand?"

I nodded. The words, I understood. What this had to do with Walter and Frank Grecco and me, I had no clue. But I was listening. I had a feeling her words would make more sense to me later, once I had time to give them more consideration. But as I say—I was listening. This was the longest speech I'd ever heard Olive make, so I knew this was an important moment. Actually, I don't think I'd ever listened more carefully to anyone.

"Of course, nobody is required to stand in the field of honor," Olive continued. "If you find it too challenging, you may always exit, and then you can remain a child. But if you wish to be a person of character, I'm afraid this is the only way. But it may be painful."

Olive turned her hands over on her lap, exposing her palms.

"All this, my father taught me when I was young. It constitutes everything I know. I try to apply it to my life. I'm not always successful, but I try. If any of this is helpful to you, Vivian, you are welcome to put it to use."

———————

It took me over a week to contact him.

The difficulty wasn't in finding him—that part had been easy. Peg's doorman's older brother was a police captain, and it took him no time at all to confirm that, yes, there was a Francis Grecco stationed as a patrolman in the 76th Precinct in Brooklyn. They gave me the phone number for the precinct desk, and that was that.

Picking up the phone was the hard part.

It always is.

I will admit that the first few times I called, I hung up just as soon as somebody answered. The next day, I talked myself out of calling back. The next few days, too. When I found my courage to try again, and to actually stay on the line, I was told that Patrolman Grecco was not there. He was out on the job. Did I want to leave a message? *No.*

I tried a couple more times over the next few days and always got the same message: he was out on patrol. Patrolman Grecco clearly did not have a desk job. Finally I agreed to leave a message. I gave my name, and left the number for L'Atelier. (Let his fellow officers wonder why a nervous broad from a bridal shop was calling him so insistently.)

Not one hour later, the phone rang and it was him.

We exchanged awkward greetings. I told him that I would like to meet him in person, if he would be amenable to that idea? He said he would. I asked if it would be easier for me to go out to Brooklyn, or for him to come to Manhattan. He said Manhattan would be fine; he had a car and he liked to drive. I asked when he was free. He said he would be free later that very afternoon. I suggested that he meet me at Pete's Tavern at five o'clock. He hesitated, then said, "I'm sorry, Vivian, but I'm not good at restaurants."

I wasn't sure what that meant, but I didn't want to put him on the spot.

I said, "How about we meet in Stuyvesant Square, then? On the west side of the park. Would that be better?"

He allowed that this would be better.

"By the fountain," I said, and he agreed—yes, by the fountain.

I didn't know how to go about any of this. I really didn't want to see him again, Angela. But I kept hearing what Olive had said to me: *You can remain a child. . . .*

Children run away from problems. Children hide.

I didn't want to remain a child.

I couldn't help but think back to the time when Olive had rescued me from Walter Winchell. I could see now that she'd saved me in 1941 precisely because she had known that I was still a child. She could tell that I was not yet somebody who was accountable for her own actions. When Olive had told Winchell that I was an innocent who'd been seduced, it had not been a ploy. She had really meant it. Olive had seen me for what I was—an immature and unformed girl, who could not yet be expected to stand in the painful field of honor. I had needed a wise and caring adult to save me, and Olive had been that champion. She had stood in the field of honor on my behalf.

But I had been young then. I wasn't young anymore. I would have to do this myself. But what would an adult—a *formed* person, a person of honor—do in this circumstance?

Face the music, I suppose. Fight her own corner, as Winchell had said. Forgive somebody, perhaps.

But how?

Then I remembered what Peg had told me years earlier, about the British army engineers during the Great War, who used to say: "We can do it, whether it can be done or not."

Eventually, all of us will be called upon to do the thing that cannot be done.

That is the painful field, Angela.

That is what caused me to reach for the phone.

Your father was already at the park when I arrived, Angela—and I was early, and had only three blocks to walk.

He was pacing before the fountain. I'm sure you remember the way he used to pace. He was dressed in civilian clothes: brown wool pants, a light blue nylon sports shirt, and a dark green Harrington jacket. The clothing hung loosely on his frame. He was awfully thin.

I approached him. "Hi, there."

"Hello," he said.

I wasn't certain if I should shake his hand. He didn't seem sure of protocol, either, so we did nothing but stand with our hands in our pockets. I'd never seen a man more uncomfortable.

I gestured to a bench and asked, "Would you care to sit down and talk with me for a moment?"

I felt stupid—as though I were offering him a chair in my own home, rather than a seat in a public park.

He said, "I'm not good at sitting down. If you don't mind, can we walk?"

"I don't mind at all."

We started walking the perimeter of the park, under the lindens and the elms. He had a long stride, but that was fine—so do I.

"Frank," I said, "I apologize for running off the other day."

"No, I apologize to you."

"No, I should have stayed and heard you out. That would've been the mature thing to do. But you have to understand—meeting you again after all these years gave me quite a start."

"I knew you would walk away when you found out who I was. You should have."

"Look, Frank—all that was long ago."

"I was a *stupid* kid," he said. He stopped and turned to face me. "Who the hell did I think I was, talking to you like that?"

"It doesn't matter anymore."

"I had no right. I was such a stupid goddamn kid."

"If we're going to get down to brass tacks about it," I said, "I was just a stupid kid, too. I was surely the stupidest kid in New York City that week. You may recall the details of the situation in which I had found myself?"

I was attempting to introduce a little levity, but Frank was all business.

"All I was trying to do was impress your brother, Vivian—you gotta believe that. He'd never talked to me before that day—never took notice of me at all. And why would he talk to me—a popular guy like him? Then all of a sudden, there he is waking me up in the middle of the night. *Frank, I need your car.* I was the only guy at OCS with a car. He knew that. Everyone knew that. Guys were always wanting to borrow my car. Well, the thing is—it wasn't my car, Vivian. It was my old man's car. I was allowed to use it, but I couldn't give it to anyone. Here I am, middle of the night, talking to Walter Morris for the first time—a guy I admire with all my heart—telling him that I can't give him my old man's car. I'm trying to explain all this from a dead sleep, and I don't even know what it's all about."

As Frank spoke, his native accent thickened. It was as if, by going back in time, he was going back deeper into himself—even deeper into his Brooklyn-ness.

"It's all right, Frank," I said. "It's over."

"Vivian, you gotta let me say this. You gotta let me tell you how sorry I am. For years, I wanted to find you, tell you I was sorry. But I didn't have the courage to look for you. Please, you gotta let me tell you how it happened. See, I told Walter, *I can't help you, buddy.* Then he deals me the facts. Tells me his sister's gone and got herself in trouble. He needs to get her out of the city, pronto. He says I gotta help him save his sister. What was I gonna do, Vivian? Say no? It was *Walter Morris.* You know how he was."

I did. I knew how he was.

Nobody ever said no to my brother.

"So I tell him the only way I can lend him the car is if I drive. Thinking to myself, *How am I gonna explain the mileage to my old man.* Thinking to myself, *Maybe me and Walter will be friends after this.* Thinking, *How are we gonna just walk away from OCS like this, in the middle of the night?* But Walter sorted it all out. Got permission from the commander for both of us to leave for a day—for twenty-four hours only. No one but Walter who could've gotten that permission in the middle of the night, but he did it. I don't know what he had to say, or promise, to get that leave, but he got it. Next thing I know, we're in midtown, and I'm throwing your suitcases in my old man's car, getting ready to drive six hours, to a town I've never heard of, for what reason I don't even know. I don't even know who you are, but you're the prettiest-looking girl I ever saw in my life."

There was nothing flirtatious in the way he said this. He was just relaying the facts, cop that he was.

"Now we're in the car, I'm driving, and then Walter starts giving you the fifth degree. I never heard anyone go at someone as hard as that. What am I supposed to do while he's reaming you out? Where am I supposed to go? I can't be hearing all this. I've never been in a situation like this. I'm from South Brooklyn, Vivian, and it can be a tough neighborhood, but you gotta understand—I'm a bookish kid, I'm a shy kid. I don't get involved in fights. I'm the kind of kid who keeps his head down. Something goes on, people start yelling, I leave

410

the scene. But I can't leave this scene, 'cause I'm *driving*. And he wasn't yelling—even though I think it might've been better if he was yelling. He was just taking you apart, so cold. Do you remember that?"

Oh, I remembered.

"Add to it all, I don't know anything about women. The things he was talking about, the things he said you were up to? I don't know anything about all that. And your picture is in the papers, he says—a picture of you messing around with *two* people? One of them is a movie star of some kind? Another one is a *showgirl*? I never heard of anything like that. But he just keeps going at you and going at you—and you're just there in the backseat, smoking cigarettes and taking it. I look in the rearview mirror, you aren't even blinking. It's like water off a duck's back, everything he's saying to you. I could see it was making Walter crazy, that you weren't responding. That was just firing him up more. But I swear to God, I never saw anyone looking so cool-headed as you."

"I wasn't coolheaded, Frank," I said. "I was in shock."

"Well, whatever it was, you kept your cool. Like you didn't even care. Meanwhile, I'm sweating bullets, wondering, is this how you people talk all the time? Is this what rich people are like?"

Rich people, I thought. *How had Frank been able to tell that Walter and I were rich people?* And then I realized: *Oh, yes, of course. The same way we'd been able to tell that he was a poor person. Someone not even worth acknowledging.*

Frank kept going: "And I'm thinking, they don't even know I'm here. I'm nothing to these people. Walter Morris isn't my friend. He's just using me. And you—you hadn't even looked at me. Back at the theater, you told me, 'Take down those two suitcases.' Like I was a porter, or something. Walter, he didn't even introduce me. I mean, I know you were all under duress, but it's like, in his eyes, I'm nobody, you know? I'm just a tool that he needs—just somebody to drive the machine. And I'm trying to figure out how to stop being so invisible, you know? So then I think, *Hey, I'll jump on the bandwagon.* Join the conversation. Try to act like *him*—talk the way he's talking, the way he's going after you. So that's when I said it. That's when I called you what I called you. Then I see how it lands. I look in the rearview mirror and I see your face. I see what my words just did to you. It was like I killed you. Then I see his face—it's like he just got hit by a baseball bat. I thought it was gonna be nothing, me saying that. I thought it was gonna make me seem cool, too—but, no, it was like mustard gas. Because no matter how bad it was, the way your brother was reaming you out, he hadn't used a word like *that.* I see him try to figure out what to do about it. Then I see him decide to do nothing. That was the worst part."

"That was the worst part," I agreed.

"I gotta tell you, Vivian—hand on the Bible—I never used a word like that to anybody in my life. Never in my *life.* Not before, not since. I'm not that guy. Where did it come from, that day? Over the years, I've watched that scene a thousand times in my mind. I watch myself say it, and I think—Frank, what's the *matter* with you? But those words, I swear to God, they just came flying out of my mouth. Then Walter clams up. Remember that?"

"I do."

"He doesn't defend you, doesn't tell me to shut my hole. Now we gotta drive for hours in that silence. And I can't tell anyone I'm sorry, 'cause I feel like I'm never supposed to open my mouth around the two of you again. Like I wasn't hired to open my mouth around you in the first place—not that I was *hired,* but you know what I mean. Then we get to your family's house—and I never saw a house like that in my life—and Walter doesn't even introduce me to your parents. Like I don't exist. Back in the car, all the way back to OCS, he doesn't say a word to me. Doesn't say a word to me the whole rest of training. Acts like it never happened. Looks at me like he never saw me before. Then we graduate, and thank God I never have to see him again. But still, I gotta think about this thing forever, and there's nothing I can ever do to put it right. Then two years later, I end up transferred to the same ship as him. Of all the luck. Now he outranks me, no surprise there. He acts like he doesn't know me. And I gotta sit with it. I gotta live with it all over again, every day."

At that point, Frank seemed to run out of words.

There was somebody that he'd reminded me of, as he was spinning out his story and struggling to explain himself. Then I realized: it was *myself.* He reminded me of myself that night in Edna Parker Watson's dressing room, when I had desperately tried to talk my way out of something that could never be put right. He was doing the same thing I had done. He was trying to talk his way into absolution.

In that moment, I felt overcome by a sense of mercy—not only for Frank, but also for that younger version of myself. I even felt mercy for Walter, with all his pride and condemnation. How humiliated Walter must have felt by me, and how dreadful it must have been for him to feel exposed like that in front of someone he considered a subordinate— and Walter considered everyone a subordinate. How angry he must have been, to have to clean up my mess in the middle of the night. Then my mercy swelled, and for just a moment I felt mercy for everyone who has ever gotten involved in an impossibly messy story. All those predicaments that we humans find ourselves in—predicaments that we never see coming, do not know how to handle, and then cannot fix.

"Have you really been thinking about this forever, Frank?" I asked.

"Always."

"Well, I'm sorry to hear that," I said—and I meant it.

"You're not the one who needs to be sorry, Vivian."

"In some ways I am. There's a great deal that I'm very sorry about, surrounding that incident. Even more so now that I've heard all this."

"Have *you* thought about it forever?" he asked.

"I thought about that car ride for a long time," I admitted. "Your words especially. It was hard on me. I won't pretend it wasn't. But I put it away some years ago, and I haven't thought about it in a long time. So don't worry, Frank Grecco—you didn't ruin my life, or anything. How about we just agree to strike this whole sad event from the books?"

Abruptly, he stopped walking. He spun and looked at me, wide-eyed. "I don't know if that's possible."

"Of course it is," I said. "Let's chalk it up to people being young, and not knowing how to behave."

I put my hand on his arm, wanting him to feel that it was all going to be all right now—that it was over.

Again, just as he had done on the first day we met, he yanked his arm away, almost violently.

This time, I must have been the one who flinched.

He still finds me repulsive was how I read it. *Once a dirty little whore, always a dirty little whore.*

Seeing my expression, Frank grimaced, and said, "Oh, Jesus, Vivian, I'm sorry. I gotta tell you. It's not you. I just can't . . ." He trailed off, looking around the park hopelessly, as though searching for someone who was going to rescue him from this moment, or explain him to me. Bravely, he tried again. "I don't know how to say this. I hate like heck to talk about it. But I can't be touched, Vivian. It's a problem I have."

"Oh." I took a step back.

"It's not you," he said. "It's everybody. I can't be touched by anybody. It's been that way ever since *this*." He waved his hand in a general way over the right side of his body—where the burn scars came crawling up his neck.

"You were injured," I said, like an idiot. Of course he was injured. "I'm sorry. I didn't understand."

"Yeah, that's okay, why would you?"

"No, I'm *very* sorry, Frank."

"You know what? You didn't do it to me."

"Nonetheless."

"Other guys, they were injured that day, too. I woke up on a hospital ship with hundreds of guys—some of them burned even as bad as me. We were the ones they pulled out of the burning water. But a lot of those guys are fine now. I don't understand it. They don't have this thing I have."

"This thing," I said.

"This thing of not being able to be touched. Not being able to sit still. That thing I have about enclosed spaces. I can't do it. I'm okay in a car as long as I'm the one in the driver's seat, but anything else, if I have to sit still too long, I can't do it. I have to stay on my feet, all the time."

This was why he hadn't wanted to meet me in a restaurant, or even sit with me on a park bench. He couldn't be in an enclosed space, and he couldn't sit still. And he couldn't be touched. This was probably why he was so thin—from needing to pace all the time.

Dear God, this poor man.

I could see that he was getting agitated so I asked, "Would you like to walk around the park with me some more? It's a nice evening, and I enjoy walking."

"Please," he said.

So that's what we did, Angela.

We just walked and walked and walked.

THIRTY

Of course I fell in love with your father, Angela.

I fell in love with him, and it made no sense for me to fall in love with him. We could not possibly have been more different. But maybe that's where love grows best—in the deep space that exists between polarities.

I was a woman who had always lived in privilege and comfort, and thus I had always been fortunate enough to skate quite lightly across life. During the most violent century of human history, I had never really suffered any harm—aside from the small troubles that I brought down upon my own head through my own carelessness. (Lucky is the soul whose only troubles are self-inflicted.) Yes, I had worked hard, but so do a lot of people—and my job was the relatively inconsequential task of sewing pretty dresses for pretty girls. And in addition to all that, I was a freethinking, unbridled sensualist who had made the pursuit of sexual pleasure one of the guiding forces in her life.

And then there was Frank.

He was such a *weighty* person—by which I mean, heavy in his very essence. He was a person whose life had been hard from the beginning. He was a man who did nothing casually, thoughtlessly, or carelessly. He was from a poor immigrant family; he couldn't afford to make mistakes. He was a devout Catholic, a police officer, and a veteran who had been through hell in service to his country. There was nothing of the sensualist about him. He could not bear to be touched, yes—but it was not only that. He had no hedonic traces within him whatsoever. He dressed in clothing that was purely utilitarian. He ate food merely in order to fuel his body. He didn't socialize; he didn't go out for entertainment; he had never been to a play in his life. He didn't drink. He didn't dance. He didn't smoke. He'd never been in a fight. He was frugal and responsible. He didn't engage in irony, teasing, or tomfoolery. He only ever told the truth.

And, of course, he was faithfully married—with a beautiful daughter whom he'd named after God's angels.

In a sane or reasonable world, how would a serious man like Frank Grecco ever have crossed paths with a lightweight individual like me? What had brought us together? Aside from our shared connection to my brother, Walter—a person who had made both of us feel intimidated and minimized—we had no other commonalities. And our only shared history was a sad one. We had spent one dreadful day together, back in 1941—a day that had left the both of us shamed and scarred.

Why would that day have led us to falling in love, twenty years later? I don't know.

I only know that we don't live in a sane or reasonable world, Angela.

So here is what happened.

Patrolman Frank Grecco called me a few days after our first meeting and asked if we could go for another walk.

The call came in to L'Atelier rather late at night—well after nine o'clock. It had startled me to hear the boutique's phone ringing. I happened to be there, because I had just finished up some alterations. I was feeling stagnant and bleary-eyed. My plan had been to go upstairs and watch television with Marjorie and Nathan, and then call it a night. I had almost ignored the ringing phone. But then I picked it up, and there was Frank on the line, asking me if I would go walking with him.

"Right now?" I asked. "You want to go for a walk *now*?"

"If you would. I'm feeling restless tonight. I'll be out walking, anyway, and I hoped maybe you would join me."

Something about this intrigued me, and touched me, too. I'd gotten plenty of calls from men at this hour of the night—but not because they wanted to go for a walk.

"Sure," I said. "Why not?"

"I'll be there in twenty minutes. I'll take the streets, not the expressway."

We ended up walking all the way over to the East River that night—through some neighborhoods that were not so safe back then, by the way—and then we kept on walking along the deteriorating waterfront until we got to the Brooklyn Bridge. Once we got to the bridge, we walked right over it. It was cold out, but there was no breeze, and our exercise kept us warm. There was a new moon, and you could almost see some stars.

That was the night when we told each other everything about ourselves.

That was the night I found out that Frank had become a patrolman expressly because of his inability to sit still. Walking a beat for eight hours a day was exactly what he needed, he said, in order not to crawl out of his own skin. This is also why he took so many extra shifts—always volunteering to fill in for the other cops who needed a day off. If he was lucky enough to get a double shift, he might be able to walk a beat for sixteen straight hours. Only then might he be sufficiently tired to sleep through the night. Every time he was offered a promotion on the force, he turned it down. A promotion would have meant a desk job, and he couldn't manage that.

He told me, "Being a patrolman is the only job beyond street sweeper that I'm qualified to do."

But it was a job that was far below his mental capacities. Your father was a brilliant man, Angela. I don't know if you are aware of this, because he was so modest. But he was something close to a genius. He'd been born to illiterate parents, sure, and he'd been neglected in a tumble of siblings, but he was a mathematical prodigy. As a child, he may have looked like a thousand other kids in Sacred Heart parish— all children of dockworkers and bricklayers, born to be dockworkers and bricklayers, themselves—but Frank was different. Frank was *exceptionally* smart.

From an early age, he'd been singled out by the nuns as something special. His own mother and father believed that school was a waste of time—*why study, when you could work?*—and when they did send him to school, they were superstitious enough to tie a knot of garlic around his neck, to keep away the evil spirits. But Frank bloomed in school. And the Irish nuns who taught him—distracted and tough though they were, and often viciously discriminatory against Italian children— could not help but notice the brains on this kid. They skipped him a few grades ahead, gave him extra assignments, and marveled at his skill with numbers. He excelled at every level.

He got placed in Brooklyn Technical High School, easily. He finished at the top of his class. Then he put in two years at Cooper Union studying aeronautical engineering before he enrolled in Officer Candidate School and joined the Navy. Why did he even join the Navy? He was fascinated by airplanes and was studying them; you would've thought he'd have wanted to be a flier. But he went into the Navy, because he wanted to see the ocean.

Imagine that, Angela. Imagine being a kid from Brooklyn—a place that is almost entirely surrounded by ocean—and growing up with the dream of someday *seeing* the ocean. But the thing was, he never had seen it. Not properly, anyhow. All he'd seen of Brooklyn were dirty streets and tenements, and the filthy docks of Red Hook, where his father worked in a longshoreman's gang. But Frank had romantic dreams of ships and naval heroes. So he quit college and signed up for the Navy, just like my brother had done, before the war had even been declared.

"What a waste," he told me that night. "If I'd wanted to see the ocean, I could have just walked to Coney Island. I had no idea it was so close."

His intention had always been to return to school after the war, finish that degree, and get a good job. But then came the attack on his ship, and he had very nearly been burned alive. And the physical pain was the least of it, to hear him tell it. While recovering in Pearl Harbor at the Navy hospital with third-degree burns over half his body, he had been served with a court-martial order. Captain Gehres, the captain of the USS *Franklin,* had court-martialed every single man who'd ended up in the water on the day of the attack. The captain claimed that those men had deserted, against direct orders. Those men—many of whom, like Frank, had been blown off the ship in flames—were accused of being cowards.

This was the worst of it for Frank. The branding of "coward" burned him more deeply than the branding of fire. And even though the Navy eventually dropped the case, recognizing it for what it was (an attempt by an incompetent captain to shift attention from his many errors that fateful day, by blaming innocent men), the psychological damage had been done. Frank knew that many of the men who had stayed aboard the ship during the attack still considered the men in the water to have been deserters. The other survivors were given medals of valor. The dead were called heroes. But not the guys in the water—not the guys who had gone overboard in flames. They were the cowards. The shame had never left him.

He came home to Brooklyn after the war. But because of his injuries and his trauma (they called it a "neuro-psychopathic condition" back then, and had no treatment for it), he was never the same. There was no way he could go back to college now. He couldn't sit in a classroom anymore. He tried to finish his degree, but he constantly had to leave the building, run outside, and hyperventilate. ("I can't be in rooms with people," as he put it.) And even if he had been able to complete his degree, what kind of job could he have gotten? The man couldn't sit in an office. He couldn't sit through a meeting. He could barely sit through a telephone call without feeling like his chest was going to implode from agitation and dread.

How could I—in my easy, comfortable life—understand pain like that?

I couldn't.

But I could listen.

'm telling you all this now, Angela, because I promised myself I would tell you everything. But I'm also telling you all this because I'm fairly certain that Frank never told you any of it.

Your father was proud of you and he loved you. But he did not want you to know the details of his life. He was ashamed that he had never made good on his early academic promise. He was embarrassed to be working in a job that was so far below his intellectual capacities. He was sick in the heart about the fact that he had never finished his education. And he felt constantly humiliated by his psychological condition. He was disgusted with himself that he couldn't sit still, or sleep through the night, or be touched, or have a proper career.

He kept all this from you as much as possible because he wanted you to be able to establish your own life—free from his bleak history. He saw you as a fresh and unsullied creation. He thought it was best if he stayed somewhat distant from you so that you would not be infected by his shadows. That's what he told me, in any case, and I don't have any reason not to believe it. He didn't want you to know him very well, Angela, because he didn't want his life to hurt *your* life.

I've often wondered what it felt like for you, to have a father who cared so much about you, but who deliberately removed himself from your day-to-day existence. When I asked him if perhaps you longed for more attention from him, he said that you probably did. But he didn't want to come close enough to damage you. He thought of himself as a person who damaged things.

That's what he told me, anyway.

He thought it was better just to leave you in the care of your mother.

I haven't mentioned your mother yet, Angela.

I want you to know that this hasn't been out of disrespect, but quite the opposite. I'm not sure how to talk about your mother or about your parents' marriage. I will tread carefully here so as to not offend or hurt you. But I will also try to be thorough in my report. At the least, you deserve to know everything I know.

I must start off by saying that I never met your mother—I never even saw a photo of her—and so I know nothing about her, beyond what Frank told me. I tend to believe that his descriptions of her were truthful, only because *he* was so truthful. But just because he described your mother truthfully doesn't necessarily mean he described her *accurately*. I can only assume that she was like all of us—a complicated being, composed of more than one man's impressions.

You may have known a completely different woman than the person whom your father described to me, is what I'm saying. I'm sorry if my story, then, clashes with what you perceived.

But I will convey it to you, nonetheless.

I learned from Frank that his wife's name was Rosella, that she was from the neighborhood, and that her parents (also Sicilian immigrants) owned the grocery store down the street from where Frank grew up. As such, Rosella's family was of higher social stature than Frank's family, who were mere manual laborers.

I know that Frank started working for Rosella's parents when he was in eighth grade, as a delivery boy. He always liked your grandparents, and admired them. They were more gentle and refined people than his own family. And that's where he met your mother—at the grocery store. She was three years younger. A hard worker. A serious girl. They got married when he was twenty and she was seventeen.

When I asked if he and Rosella had been in love at the time of their marriage, he said, "Everyone in my neighborhood was born on the same block, raised on the same block, and married someone from the same block. It's just what you did. She was a good person, and I liked her family."

"But did you love her?" I repeated.

"She was the right sort of person to marry. I trusted her. She knew I would be a good provider. We didn't go in for luxuries like love."

They were married right after Pearl Harbor, like so many other couples, and for the same reasons as everyone else.

And of course you, Angela, were born in 1942.

I know that Frank was unable to get much leave during the last few years of the war, so he didn't see you and Rosella for quite a long time. (It wasn't easy for the Navy to ship people home from the South Pacific all the way to Brooklyn; a lot of those guys didn't see their families for years.) Frank spent three Christmases in a row on an aircraft carrier. He wrote letters home but Rosella rarely replied. She had not finished school, and was self-conscious about her handwriting and her spelling. Because Frank's family was also barely literate, he was one of the sailors on the aircraft carrier who never got mail.

"Was that painful for you?" I asked him. "Never to hear news from home?"

"I didn't hold it against anyone," he said. "My people weren't the kind to write letters. But even though Rosella never wrote to me, I knew she was faithful, and that she was taking good care of Angela. She was never the type to go around with other boys. That was more than a lot of men on the ship could say about their wives."

Then there was the kamikaze attack, and Frank was burned over 60 percent of his body. (For all his talk of how other guys on his ship had been just as badly injured as him, the truth is that nobody else with burns as severe as Frank's had ended up surviving. People didn't survive burns over 60 percent of their bodies back then, Angela—but your father did.) Then there were the long months of torturous recovery at the naval hospital. When Frank finally came home, it was 1946. He was a changed man. A broken man. You were now four years old, and you didn't know him except from a photo. He told me that when he met you again after all those years, you were so pretty and bright and kind that he could not believe you belonged to him. He could not believe that anything associated with him could be as pure as you. But you were also a little bit afraid of him. Not nearly so afraid, though, as he was of you.

His wife also felt like a stranger. Over those missing years, Rosella had transformed from a pretty young girl to a matron—heavyset and serious, dressed always in black. She was the sort of woman who went to Mass every morning, and prayed to her saints all day long. She wanted to have more children. But of course that was now impossible, because Frank could not bear to be touched.

That night as we walked all the way to Brooklyn, Frank told me, "After the war, I started sleeping in a cot out in the shed behind our house. Made a room for myself there, with a coal stove. I've been sleeping there for years. It's better that way. I don't keep anyone awake with my strange hours. Sometimes I wake up screaming, that sort of thing. My wife and kid, they didn't need to be hearing that. For me, with sleeping, the whole procedure is a disaster. Better that I do it alone."

He respected your mother, Angela. I want you to know that.

He never once said a bad word about her. On the contrary—he approved entirely of the way she raised you, and he admired her stoicism in the face of her life's many disappointments. They never bickered. They were never at each other's throats. But after the war, they barely ever spoke other than to make arrangements about the family. He deferred to her on all matters, and turned over his paychecks to her without question. She had taken over management of her parents' greengrocer business, and had inherited the building that housed the shop. She was a good businesswoman, he said. He was happy that you, Angela, had grown up in the store, chatting with everyone. ("The light of the neighborhood," he called you.) He was always eyeing you for signs that you, too, might someday be an oddball recluse (which is how he saw himself), but you seemed normal and social. Anyway, Frank trusted your mother's choices around you completely. But he was always at work on patrol, or walking the city at night. Rosella was always working at the greengrocer, or taking care of you. They were married in name only.

At one point, he told me, he had offered her a divorce, so she might have the chance to find a more suitable man. With his inability to uphold his duties of marital consortium and companionship, he felt certain they could secure an annulment. She was still young. With another man, she might still have the big family she had always wanted. But even if the Catholic Church had allowed her to divorce, Rosella would never have gone ahead with it.

"She's more church than the Church itself," he said. "She's not the kind of person who would ever break a vow. And nobody in our neighborhood gets divorced, Vivian, even if things are bad. And with me and Rosella—things were never *bad*. We just lived separate lives. What you gotta understand about South Brooklyn, is that the neighborhood itself is a family. You can't break up that family. Really, my wife is married to the neighborhood. It was the neighborhood who took care of her while I was in the service. The neighborhood still takes care of her now—and Angela, too."

"But do you like the neighborhood?" I asked.

He gave a rueful smile. "It's not a choice, Vivian. The neighborhood is what I am. I'll always be part of it. But I'm also *not* part of it anymore, since the war. You come back, everyone expects you to be the same guy you were before you got blown up. I used to have enthusiasms like everyone else—baseball, movies, what have you. The Church feasts on Fourth Street, the big holidays. But I don't have enthusiasms anymore. I don't fit there anymore. It's not the neighborhood's fault. They're good people. They wanted to take care of us guys who came back from the war. Guys like me, if you had a Purple Heart, everyone wants to buy you a beer, give you a salute, give you free tickets to a show. But I can't do anything with all that. After a while, people learned to leave me alone. Now it's like I'm a ghost, when I walk down those streets. Still, though, I belong to that place. It's hard to explain, if you're not from there."

I asked him, "Do you ever think about moving away from Brooklyn?"

He said, "Only every day for the last twenty years. But that wouldn't be fair to Rosella and Angela. Anyhow, I'm not sure I'd be better off anywhere else."

A s we walked back over the Brooklyn Bridge that night, he said to me, "What about you, Vivian? You never got married?"

"Almost. But I was saved by the war."

"What does that mean?"

"Pearl Harbor came, my guy enlisted, we broke off the engagement."

"I'm sorry to hear that."

"Don't be. He wasn't right for me, and I would have been a disaster for him. He was a fine person, and he deserved better."

"And you never found another man?"

I was quiet for a while, trying to think how to answer that. Finally, I decided to just answer it with the truth.

"I've found many other men, Frank. More than you could count."

"Oh," he said.

He was quiet after that, and I wasn't sure how that information had landed on him. This was a moment where another sort of woman might have chosen to be discreet. But something stubborn in me insisted that I be even more clear.

"I've slept with a lot of men, Frank, is what I'm saying."

"No, I get it," he said.

"And I will be sleeping with a lot more men in the future, I expect. Sleeping with men—lots of men—that's more or less my way of life."

"Okay," he said. "I understand."

He didn't seem agitated by it. Just thoughtful. But I felt nervous, sharing this truth about myself. And for some reason, I couldn't stop talking about it.

"I just wanted to tell you this about me," I said, "because you should know what kind of woman I am. If we're going to be friends, I don't want to run into any judgment from you. If this aspect of my life is going to be a problem . . ."

He stopped suddenly in his tracks. "Why would I judge you?"

"Think about where I'm coming from here, Frank. Think about how we first met."

"Yeah, I see," he said. "I get it. But you don't need to worry about that."

"Good."

"I'm not that guy, Vivian. I never was."

"Thank you. I just wanted to be honest."

"Thank you for the tribute of your honesty," he said—which I thought then, and still think, was one of the most elegant things I'd ever heard anyone say.

"I'm too old to hide who I am, Frank. And I'm too old to be made to feel ashamed of myself by anyone—do you understand that?"

"I do."

"But what do you think of it, though?" I asked. I couldn't believe I was pushing this issue. But I couldn't help but ask. His poise—his lack of shocked response on the matter—was puzzling.

"What do I think about you sleeping with a lot of men?"

"Yeah."

He thought for a moment, then said, "There's something that I know about the world now, Vivian, that I didn't know when I was young."

"And what's that?"

"The world ain't straight. You grow up thinking things are a certain way. You think there are rules. You think there's a way that things have to be. You try to live straight. But the world doesn't care about your rules, or what you believe. The world ain't straight, Vivian. Never will be. Our rules, they don't mean a thing. The world just *happens* to you sometimes, is what I think. And people just gotta keep moving through it, best they can."

"I don't think I ever believed that the world was straight," I said.

"Well, I did. And I was wrong."

We walked on. Below us, the East River—dark and cold—progressed steadily toward the sea, carrying away the pollution of the whole city with its currents.

"Can I ask you something, Vivian?" he said after a while.

"Certainly."

"Does it make you happy?"

"Being with all those men, you mean?"

"Yes."

I gave this question real consideration. He hadn't asked it in an accusing way. I think he genuinely wished to comprehend me. And I'm not sure I'd ever pondered it before. I didn't want to take the question lightly.

"It makes me *satisfied,* Frank," I finally replied. "It's like this: I believe I have a certain darkness within me, that nobody can see. It's always in there, far out of reach. And being with all those different men—it satisfies that darkness."

"Okay," Frank said. "I think I can maybe understand that."

I had never before spoken this vulnerably about myself. I had never before tried to put words to my experience. But still, I felt that my words fell short. How could I explain that by "darkness" I didn't mean "sin" or "evil"—I only meant that there was a place within my imagination so fathomlessly deep that the light of the real world could never touch it. Nothing but sex had ever been able to reach it. This place within me was prehuman, almost. Certainly, it was precivilization. It was a place beyond language. Friendship could not reach it. My creative endeavors could not reach it. Awe and joy could not reach it. This hidden part of me could only be reached through sexual intercourse. And when a man went to that darkest, secret place within me, I felt as though I had landed in the very beginning of myself.

Curiously, it was in that place of dark abandon where I felt the least sullied and most true.

"But as for *happy*?" I went on. "You asked if it makes me happy. I don't think so. Other things in my life make me happy. My work makes me happy. My friendships and the family that I've created, they make me happy. New York City makes me happy. Walking over this bridge with you right now makes me happy. But being with all those men, that makes me *satisfied*, Frank. And I've come to learn that this kind of satisfaction is something I need, or else I will become unhappy. I'm not saying that it's right. I'm just saying—that's how it is with me, and it's not something that's ever going to change. I'm at peace with it. The world ain't straight, as you say."

Frank nodded, listening. Wanting to understand. Able to understand.

After another long silence, Frank said, "Well, I think you're fortunate, then."

"Why's that?" I asked.

"Because not many people know how to be satisfied."

THIRTY-ONE

I have never loved the people I was supposed to love, Angela.

Nothing that was ever arranged for me worked out the way it was planned. My parents had pointed me in a specific direction—toward a respectable boarding school and an elite college—such that I could meet the community I was meant to belong to. But apparently, I didn't belong there, because to this day, I don't have a single friend from those worlds. Nor did I meet a husband for myself at one of my many school proms.

Nor did I ever really feel like I belonged to my parents, or that I was meant to reside in the small town where I grew up. I still don't keep in touch with anybody from Clinton. My mother and I had only the most superficial of relationships, right up until her death. And my father, of course, was never much more than a grumbling political commentator at the far end of the dinner table.

But then I moved to New York City, and I came to know my Aunt Peg, an unconventional and irresponsible lesbian, who drank too much and spent too much money, and who only wanted to cavort through life with a sort of *hop-skip-tralala*—and *I loved her*. She gave me nothing less than my entire world.

And I also met Olive, who didn't seem lovable—but whom I came to love, nonetheless. Far more than I loved my own mother or father. Olive was not warm or affectionate, but she was loyal and good. She was something of a bodyguard to me. She was our anchoress. She taught me whatever morality I possess.

Then I met Marjorie Lowtsky—an eccentric Hell's Kitchen teenager whose immigrant parents were in the rag trade. She was not at all the sort of person I was supposed to befriend. But she became not only my business partner, but my sister. I loved her, Angela, with all my heart. I would do anything for her, and she for me.

Then came Marjorie's son, Nathan—this weak little boy who was allergic to life itself. He was Marjorie's child, but he was my child, too. If my parents' vision for my life had gone according to plan, I would surely have had my own children—big, strong, horseback-riding future captains of industry—but instead I got Nathan, and that was better. I chose Nathan and he chose me. I loved him, too.

These random-seeming people were my family, Angela. These people were my *real* family. I'm telling you all this because I want you to understand that—over the next few years—I came to love your father just as much as I loved any of them.

My heart cannot offer him higher praise than that. He became as close to me as my own, beautiful, random, and *real* family.

Love like that is a deep well, with steep sides.

Once you fall in, that's it—you will love that person always.

A few nights a week, for years on end, your father would call me at some odd hour and say, "Do you want to get out? I can't sleep."
I'd say, "You can never sleep, Frank."

And he'd say, "Yeah, but tonight I can't sleep worse than usual."

It didn't matter what the season was, or the time of night. I always said yes. I've always enjoyed exploring this city, and I have always liked the nighttime. What's more, I've never been a person who needed much sleep. But most of all, I just loved being with Frank. So he would call me, and I would agree to see him, and he would drive over from Brooklyn to pick me up, and we would go someplace together and walk.

It didn't take us long to walk every neighborhood in Manhattan, and so pretty soon we started exploring the outer boroughs, as well. I never met anybody who knew the city better. He took me to neighborhoods I'd never even heard of, and we would explore them on foot in the wee hours of the morning, talking all the while. We walked all the cemeteries and all the industrial yards. We walked the waterfronts. We walked by the row houses and through the projects. We eventually walked over every single bridge in the greater New York metropolitan area—and there are a lot of them.

Nobody ever bothered us. It was the strangest thing. The city was not a safe place back then, but we walked through it as though we were untouchable. We were often so deep in our own conversations that we often didn't even notice our surroundings. Miraculously, the streets kept us safe and the people let us be. I wondered at times if people could even see us at all. But then sometimes the police would stop us and ask what we were doing, and Frank would show his badge. He would say, "I'm walking this lady home"—even if we were in a Jamaican neighborhood in Crown Heights. He was always walking me home. That was always the story.

Sometimes, late at night, he would drive me to Long Island to buy fried clams at a place he knew—a twenty-four-hour diner where you could pull right up to the window and order your food from the car. Or we'd go to Sheepshead Bay for littlenecks. We'd eat them while parked on the dock, watching the fishing boats head out to sea. In the spring, he would drive me out to the countryside in New Jersey to pick dandelion leaves in the moonlight, for making bitter salads. It's something Sicilians enjoy, he taught me.

Driving and walking—those were the things that he could do, without getting too anxious.

He always listened to me. He became the most trusted confidant of my life. There was a clarity about Frank—a deep and unshakable integrity. It was soothing to be with a man who never boasted about himself (so rare, in men of that generation!) and who did not impose himself on the world in any way. If he ever had a fault, or made a mistake, he would tell you before you could find out for yourself. And there was nothing I could ever tell him about myself that he would judge or criticize. My own glints of darkness did not frighten him; he had such darkness of his own that nobody else's shadows scared him.

Most of all, though, he *listened.*

I told him everything. When I had a new lover, I told him. When I had a fear, I told him. When I had a victory, I told him. I was not accustomed, Angela, to having men listen to me.

And as for your father, he was not accustomed to being with a woman who would walk five miles with him in the middle of the night, in the rain, in Queens, just to keep him company when he could not sleep.

He was never going to leave his wife and daughter. I knew that, Angela. That's not who he was. And I was never going to lure him into bed. Aside from the fact that his injuries and his trauma made a sexual life impossible for him, I was not a woman who could have an affair with a married man. That's not who I was. Not anymore.

Moreover, I can't say I ever fantasized about marrying him. In general, of course, the thought of marriage gave me a hemmed-in feeling, and I didn't long for it with anyone. But certainly not with Frank. I couldn't imagine us sitting at a breakfast table, talking over a newspaper. Planning vacations. That picture didn't look like either of us.

Lastly, I can't be certain that Frank and I would have shared the same depth of love and tenderness for each other, had sex ever been part of our story. Sex is so often a cheat—a shortcut of intimacy. A way to skip over knowing somebody's heart by knowing, instead, their mere body.

So we were devoted to each other, in our own way, but we kept our lives separate. The one New York City neighborhood that we never explored together on foot was his—South Brooklyn. (Or Carroll Gardens, as the realtors eventually named it, although your father never called it that.) This was the neighborhood that belonged to his family—to his tribe, really. Out of respect, we left it quietly untouched by our footsteps.

He never came to know my people and I never came to know his.

I introduced him briefly to Marjorie—and certainly my friends knew *about* him—but Frank was not somebody who could socialize. (What was I going to do—have a dinner party, and show him off? Expect a man with his nervous condition to stand in a crowded room and make idle chitchat with strangers while holding a cocktail? No.) To my friends, Frank was just the walking phantom. They accepted that he was important to me because I said that he was important to me. But they never understood him. How could they have?

For a while, I'll admit, I'd indulged a fantasy that he and Nathan might meet someday, and that he could become a father figure to that dear little boy. But that wasn't going to work, either. He could barely be a father figure to *you*, Angela—his actual child, whom he loved with all his heart. Why would I ask him to take on another child to feel guilty about?

I asked nothing of him, Angela. And he asked nothing of me. (Other than, "Do you want to go for a walk?")

So what were we to each other? What would you call it? We were something more than friends—that was certain. Was he my boyfriend? Was I his mistress?

Those words all fall short.

Those words all describe something that we were not.

Yet I can tell you that there was a lonely and untenanted corner of my heart that I'd never known was there—and Frank moved right into it. Holding him in my heart made me feel like I belonged to love itself. Although we never lived together or shared a bed, he was always a part of me. I saved stories for him all week, so I would have good things to tell him. I asked for his opinions, because I respected his ethics. I came to cherish his face precisely because it was his. Even his burn scars became beautiful to my eye. (His skin looked like the weathered binding of some ancient, sacred book.) I was enchanted by the hours that we kept and the mysterious places we went—both in the course of our conversations, and in the city itself.

The time we spent together happened outside of the world, is how it felt.

Nothing about us was normal.

We always ate in the car.

What *were* we?

We were Frank and Vivian, walking through New York City together, while everyone else slept.

Frank normally reached out to me at night, but on one roastingly hot day in the summer of 1966, I got a call from him in the middle of the afternoon, asking if he could please see me immediately. He sounded frantic, and when he arrived at L'Atelier, he leapt out of the car and started pacing in front of the boutique with more nervousness than I'd ever before witnessed. I quickly handed over my work to an assistant, and hopped into the car, saying, "Let's go, Frank. Come, now. Just drive."

He drove all the way out to Floyd Bennett Field in Brooklyn—speeding the entire time, and not saying a word. He parked in a patch of dirt at the end of a runway, where we could watch the Naval Air Reserve planes come in for landings. I knew that he must have been profoundly agitated: he always went to Floyd Bennett Field to watch the planes land when nothing else would calm him. The roar of the engines settled his nerves.

I knew better than to ask him what was wrong. Eventually, once he had caught his breath, I knew he would tell me.

So we sat in the crushing July heat with the car off, listening to the engine tick and cool. Silence, then a landing plane, then silence again. I cranked down my window, to bring in some air, but Frank didn't seem to notice. He hadn't yet taken his white-knuckled hands off the steering wheel. He was wearing his patrolman's uniform, which must've been sweltering. But again, he didn't appear to notice. Another plane landed and shook the ground.

"I went to court today," he said.

"All right," I said—just to let him know that I was listening.

"I had to testify about a break-in last year. A hardware store. Some kids on dope, looking for things to fence. They beat up the owner, so there were assault charges. I was the first officer on the scene, so."

"I understand."

Your father often had to appear in court, Angela, on some police matter or another. He never liked it (sitting in a crowded courtroom was hell for him, of course), but it had never caused him to have a panicked reaction like this. Something more troubling must have occurred.

I waited for it.

"I saw somebody I used to know today, Vivian," he said at last. His hands were still not off the wheel, and he was still staring straight ahead. "A guy from the Navy. Southern guy. He was on the *Franklin* with me. Tom Denno. I haven't thought of that name in years. He was a guy who came from Tennessee. I didn't even know he lived up here. Those southern guys, you'd think they would've all gone back home after the war, right? But he didn't, I guess. Moved here to New York. Lives way the hell up on West End Avenue. He's a lawyer now. He was in court today, representing one of the kids who broke into the hardware store. I guess that kid's parents must have some money. They got a lawyer. Tom Denno. Of all people."

"That must have surprised you." Again, just letting him know I was there.

"I can still remember Tom when he was brand new on the ship," Frank went on. "I don't know the date—don't own me to it—but he come on in something like early forty-four. He came straight off the farm. Country boy. You think city kids are tough, but you should see those country boys. Most of them, they came from such poverty, you never saw anything like it. I thought *I* grew up poor, but it was nothing compared to these kids. They never saw food before, like the amounts of food on the ship. They ate like they were starving, I remember. First time in their lives they hadn't shared dinner with ten brothers. Some of them had hardly ever worn shoes. Accents like you never heard. You could barely understand them. But they were tough as hell in battle. Even when we weren't under fire, they were tough. Fighting with one another all the time, or mouthing off to the marines who were guarding the admiral, when the admiral was onboard. They didn't know how to do anything except come at life hard, you know? Tom Denno was the hardest of them all."

I nodded. Frank rarely talked in such detail about life onboard the ship, or about anyone he'd known in the war. I didn't know where this was all going, but I knew it was important.

"Vivian, I was never tough like those guys." He was still gripping that steering wheel like it was a life preserver—like it was the only thing in the world keeping him afloat. "One day on the flight deck, one of my men—young kid from Maryland—stopped paying attention for a second. He took a step in the wrong direction, and his head got sucked right off his body, right into a plane propeller. Just pulled his head right off him, right in front of me. We weren't even under fire—just a routine day on the deck. Now we have a headless body on the deck, and you better hurry and clean it up, because more planes are coming in, landing every two minutes. You gotta keep the flight deck clear at all times. But I just freeze. Now here comes Tom Denno, and he grabs the body by its feet and drags it away—probably the way he used to drag pig carcasses back on the farm. He doesn't even flinch, just knows what to do. Meanwhile, I can't even move. And then Tom's gotta come and pull me out of the way, too, so I won't be the next one killed. Me—an officer! Him, an enlisted kid. This was a kid who'd never been to a *dentist,* Vivian. How the hell did he end up as a Manhattan lawyer?"

"Are you sure it was him that you saw today?" I asked.

"It was *him.* He knew me. He came over and talked to me. Vivian, he's one of the 704 Club. Jesus Christ!" Frank threw me a tortured look.

"I don't know what that means," I said as gently as I could.

"The men who stayed on the *Franklin* when we were hit that day— there were seven hundred and four of them. Captain Gehres named those guys the 704 Club. He built them up as heroes. Hell, maybe they *were* heroes. The Heroic Living, Gehres called them. The ones who didn't desert the ship. They get together every year and have reunions. Relive the glories."

"You didn't desert the ship, Frank. Even the Navy knew that. You were blown overboard in flames."

"Vivian, it doesn't matter," he said. "I was already a coward long before that."

The panic had drained from his voice. Now he spoke with dreadful calm.

"No, you weren't," I said.

"It's not an argument, Vivian. I was. We'd been under fire already for months before that day. I couldn't handle it. I could *never* handle it. Guam in July of forty-four—bombing the hell out of Guam. I couldn't imagine how there was even a single blade of grass left standing on that island when we were done with it, we rained such hell on that place. But when our troops landed at the end of July, out come all these Japanese soldiers and tanks. How did they even survive it? I can't imagine. Our marines were brave, the Japanese soldiers were brave, but I wasn't brave. I couldn't bear the noise of the guns, Vivian—and they weren't even being fired *at* me. That's when I started being like *this*. The nerves, the shakes. The men started calling me Twitchy."

"Shame on them," I said.

"They were right, though. I was a pile of nerves. One day, we had a bomb fail to release from one of our planes—a hundred-pound bomb, just got jammed in the open bomb bay. The pilot radios in that he's got a bomb stuck in the bay, and he has to land like that, can you imagine? Then, during the landing, the bomb kind of shudders lose and falls *out*, and now we have a hundred-pound bomb skittering across the flight deck. Your brother and some other guys just ran right at it and pushed that thing over the edge of the ship like it's nothing—and again, I'm frozen. Can't help, can't act, can't do anything."

"It doesn't matter, Frank." But again, it was like he couldn't hear me.

"Then it's August 1944," he went on. "We're in the middle of a typhoon, but we're still running sorties, landing planes even while the waves are breaking over the flight deck. And those pilots, landing on a postage stamp in the middle of the Pacific, in the teeth of the gale—they never even *flinch*. Here I am, my hands can't stop shaking, and I'm not even *piloting* the goddamn planes, Vivian. They called our convoy 'Murderers' Row.' We were supposed to be the toughest guys around. But I wasn't tough."

"Frank," I said, "it's all right."

"Then the Japanese start suicide-bombing us in October. They know they're gonna lose the war, so they decide to go down in glory. Take out as many of us as they can, by any means necessary. They just kept coming at us, Vivian. One day in October, there were *fifty* of them that came at us. Fifty kamikaze planes in one day. Can you imagine it?"

"No," I said, "I cannot."

"Our guys knocked them out of the air, one after another, but they sent more planes the next day. I knew it was just a matter of time before one of them would hit us. Everyone knew we were sitting ducks, not more than fifty miles off the coast of Japan, but our guys were so cavalier about it. Strutting around like it was nothing. And there was Tokyo Rose on the radio every night, telling the world that the *Franklin* was already sunk. That's when I stopped sleeping. Couldn't eat, couldn't sleep. Terrified, every minute. I've never slept right since then. Some of those kamikaze pilots, when they got shot down, we fished them out of the water as prisoners. One of those Japanese pilots, he was being marched across our flight deck to the brig, but then he broke away and ran right to the edge of the ship. Jumped off and killed himself, rather than be taken prisoner. Death with honor, right in front of me. I looked at his face as he was running to the edge, Vivian—and I swear to God, he didn't look anything near as scared as I felt."

I could feel Frank spinning back into the past now, hard and fast, and it wasn't good. I needed to bring him back home—back to himself. Back to now.

"What happened today, Frank?" I asked. "What happened with Tom Denno in that courtroom today?"

Frank exhaled, but gripped the steering wheel even harder.

"He comes up to me, Vivian, right before I'm supposed to testify. Remembers me by name. Asks how I'm doing. Tells me about how he's a lawyer now, where he lives on the Upper West Side, where he went to college, where his kids go to school. Gave me a speech about how well he's done. He was one of the skeleton crew that sailed the *Franklin* back to the Brooklyn Navy Yard after the attack, you know, and I guess he never left New York after that. Still has that accent from right off the farm, though. But wearing a suit that probably costs more than my house. Then he looks me up and down in my uniform, and says, 'A beat cop? That's what naval officers become these days?' Christ, Vivian, what am I supposed to say? I just nod. Then he asks me, 'Do they even let you carry a gun?' And I say something stupid, like, 'Yeah, but I've never used it,' and he says, 'Well, you always were a soft apple, Twitchy,' and he walks away."

"He can go straight to hell," I said. I felt my own fists balling up. A wave of rage overcame me so fiercely that the noise of it in my ears—a roar of rushing blood—was, for a moment, louder than the roar of the plane landing in front of us. I wanted to hunt down Tom Denno and slit his neck. *How dare he?* I also wanted to gather up Frank in my arms and rock him and comfort him—but I couldn't, because the war had bunged up his mind and his body so badly that he couldn't even be held in the arms of a woman who loved him.

It was all so vicious and it was all so *wrong*.

I thought of how Frank had once told me that—when he came up in the water after being blown off the ship—he emerged into a world that was completely on fire. Even the seawater around him was on fire, blanketed with burning fuel. And the engines of the stricken aircraft carrier were only fanning the flames. Burning the men in the water even more severely. Frank found that if he splashed hard, he could push the fire away and create a small spot in the Pacific that was not on fire. So that's what he did for two hours—him, with burns over most of his body—until he was rescued. He just kept pushing the flames away, trying to keep one small area of his world free from the inferno. All these years later, I felt like he was *still* trying to do that. Still trying to find a safe radius somewhere in the world. Someplace where he could stop burning.

"Tom Denno is right, Vivian," he said. "I've always been a soft apple."

I wanted so badly to comfort him, Angela, but how? Aside from my presence in the car that day—as somebody who would listen to his awful story—what could I give him? I wanted to tell him that he was heroic, strong, and brave, and that Tom Denno and the rest of the 704 Club were *wrong*. But I knew this wouldn't work. He wouldn't have been able to hear those words. He wouldn't have believed them. I had to say something, though, because he was in such pain. I closed my eyes and begged my mind for something useful to offer. Then I opened my mouth and just spoke—blindly trusting that fate and love would grant me the right words.

"So what if it's true?" I asked.

My voice came out harder than I'd expected. Frank turned to look at me in surprise.

"What if it's true, Frank, that you're a soft apple? What if it's true, that you were never made for combat, and you couldn't handle the war?"

"It *is* true."

"Okay, then. Let's agree that it's true, just for the sake of argument. But what would that mean?"

He said nothing.

"What would it *mean*, Frank?" I demanded. "Answer me. And take your hands off the goddamn steering wheel. We're not going anywhere."

He took his hands off the wheel, set them gently in his lap, and stared down at them.

"What would it mean, Frank? If you were a soft apple. Tell me."

"It would mean I'm a coward."

"And what would *that* mean?" I demanded.

"It would mean I'm a failure as a man." His voice was so quiet I could barely hear him.

"No, you're *wrong*," I said, and I had never been more fiercely sure of anything in my life. "You're wrong, Frank. It would not mean that you're a failure as a man. Do you want to know what it actually means? It means *nothing*."

He blinked at me, confused. He'd never heard me speak as sharply as this.

"You listen to me, Frank Grecco," I said. "If you're a coward—and let's just say that you are, for the sake of argument—it means nothing. My Aunt Peg, she's an alcoholic. She can't handle drinking. It ruins her life and turns her into a mess—and do you know what that means? It means *nothing*. Do you think it makes her a bad person, that she has no control over booze? A failure of a person? Of course not—it's just the way she is. Alcoholism just happened to her, Frank. Things happen to people. We are the way we are—there's nothing to be done for it. My Uncle Billy—he couldn't keep a promise or stay faithful to a woman. It meant *nothing*. He was a wonderful person, Frank, and he was completely untrustworthy. It's just how he *was*. It didn't mean anything. We all still loved him."

"But men are supposed to be brave," said Frank.

"So what!" I nearly shouted it. "Women are supposed to be *pure*, and look at me. I've had sex with countless men, Frank—and do you know what it means about me? *Nothing*. It's just how it is. You said it yourself, Frank—*the world ain't straight*. That's what you told me, our first night. Use your own words to understand your own life. The world ain't straight. People have a certain nature, and that's just how it goes. And things happen to people—things that are beyond their control. The war *happened* to you. And you weren't made for battle—so what? None of it means a damn thing. Stop doing this to yourself."

"But tough guys like Tom Denno—"

"You know nothing about Tom Denno. Something happened to him, too, I guarantee it. For a grown man to come at you like that? With such cruelty? Oh, I promise you—life has happened to him, too. Something left him wrecked as a person. Not that I care about that asshole, but his world ain't straight, either, Frank. You can bet on it."

Frank started crying. When I saw this, I nearly wept, too. But I held back my tears because his were far more important, far more rare. At that moment, I would have given years off my life to be able to hold him, Angela—in that moment, more than any other. But it wasn't possible.

"It's not *fair*," he said, through body-wracking sobs.

"No, it's not, sweetheart," I said. "It's not fair. But it's what *happened*. It's just the way things are, Frank, and it means *nothing*. You're a wonderful man. You're no failure. You're the best man I've ever known. That's the only thing that matters."

He kept on crying—separated from me by a safe distance, as always. But at least he'd taken his hands off the wheel. At least he had been able to tell me what had happened. Here in the privacy of his swelteringly hot car—in the one corner of his world that was not on fire at this moment—at least he'd been able to tell the truth.

I would sit with him until he was all right again. I knew that I would sit with him for as long as it took. That's all I could do. That was my only job in the world that day—to sit with this good man. To watch over him from the other side of the car until he was steadied.

When he finally got control of himself again, he stared out the window with the saddest expression I ever saw. He said, "What are we gonna do about it all?"

"I don't know, Frank. Maybe nothing. But I'm right here."

That's when he turned to look at me. "I can't live without you, Vivian," he said.

"Good. You'll never have to."

And that, Angela, was the closest your father and I ever came to saying *I love you*.

THIRTY-TWO

The years passed like they always do.

My Aunt Peg died in 1969, from emphysema. She smoked cigarettes right up until the end. It was a hard death. Emphysema is a brutal way to die. Nobody can fully remain themselves when they are in such pain and discomfort, but Peg tried her best to stay *Peg*—optimistic, uncomplaining, enthusiastic. But slowly, she lost the ability to breathe. It's a horrible thing to watch someone struggling for air. It's like witnessing a slow drowning. By the end, sorrowful though it was, we were glad that she could go in peace. We couldn't bear to see her suffer any longer.

There is a limit, I have found, to how much you can mourn as "tragic" the death of an older person who has lived a rich life, and who is privileged enough to die surrounded by loved ones. There are so many worse ways to live, after all, and so many worse ways to die. From birth to death, Peg was one of life's fortunate ones—and nobody knew it more than her. ("We are the luckies," she used to say.) But still,

Angela, she had been the most important and influential figure in my life, and it hurt to lose her. Even to this day, even all these years later, I still believe that the world is a poorer place without Peg Buell in it.

The only upside of her death was that it got me to finally quit smoking for good—and that's probably why I'm still alive today.

Yet another generous offering from that good woman to me.

After Peg's death, I was mostly concerned about what would become of Olive. She had spent so many years tending to my aunt—how would she fill her hours now? But I needn't have worried. There was a Presbyterian church over near Sutton Place that always needed volunteers, and so Olive found a use for herself running the Sunday school, organizing fund drives, and generally telling people what to do. She was *fine*.

Nathan got older, but still not much bigger. We kept him in Quaker schools for his whole education. It was the only environment gentle enough for him. Marjorie and I kept trying to find him a passion (music, art, theater, literature), but he was not a person made for passion. What he liked more than anything was to feel safe and cozy. So we kept his world gentle, cocooning him within our peaceful little universe. We never asked much of Nathan. We thought he was good enough, just the way he was. We were proud of him sometimes just for getting through the day.

As Marjorie said, "Not everyone is meant to charge through the world, carrying a spear."

"That's right, Marjorie," I told her. "We shall leave the spear charging to you."

L'Atelier continued to do steady business even as society changed during the 1960s, and fewer people were getting married. We were fortunate in one regard: we had never been a "traditional" bridal shop, so when tradition went out of style, we remained au courant. We had always sold vintage-inspired gowns—long before the word "vintage" was fashionable. So when the counterculture arrived, and all the hippies were dressing in crazy old clothing, we did not get rejected. In fact, we found a new clientele. I became the seamstress to many a well-heeled flower child. I made gowns for all the affluent bankers' hippie daughters who wanted wedding dresses that would make them look as though they had sprung fully grown from some rural meadow, rather than having been born on the Upper East Side and educated at the Brearley School.

I loved the 1960s, Angela.

By all rights, I should not have loved that moment in history. At my age, I should have been one of those stodgy old bitches bemoaning the breakdown of society. But I had never been an ardent fan of society, so I didn't object to seeing it challenged. In fact, I delighted in all the mutiny and rebellion and creative expression. And of course, I loved the clothes. How fabulous, that those hippies turned our city streets into a circus! It was all so freeing and playful.

But the 1960s made me feel proud, too, because there was a level at which my community had already foretold all these transformations and upheavals.

The sexual revolution? I'd been doing that all along.

Homosexual couples, living together as spouses? Peg and Olive had practically invented it.

Feminism and single motherhood? Marjorie had walked that beat for ages.

A hatred of conflict and a passion for non-violence? Well, I'd like to introduce you to a sweet little boy named Nathan Lowtsky.

With the greatest of pride, I was able to look out across all the cultural upheavals and transformations of the 1960s, and know this:

My people got there first.

Then, in 1971, Frank asked me for a favor.

He asked me, Angela, if I would make your wedding dress for you.

This startled me on several levels.

For one thing, I was genuinely surprised to hear that you were getting married. It didn't seem to be in keeping with what your father had always told me about you. He'd been so proud of you as you finished your master's degree at Brooklyn College, and your doctoral degree at Columbia—and in psychology, of course. (With a family history like ours, he used to say, what else could she study?) Your father was fascinated by your decision not to open a private practice, but instead to work at Bellevue—exposing yourself every day to the most severe and grinding cases of mental illness.

Your work had become your life, he said. He fully approved. He was glad that you hadn't married young, like him. He knew that you were not a traditional person, and that you were an intellectual. He was so proud of your mind. He was thrilled when you started doing postdoctoral research on the trauma of suppressed memories. He said the two of you had finally found something you could talk about, and that sometimes he would help you to sort data.

He used to say, "Angela is too good and too thoughtful for any man I've ever met."

But then one day he told me you'd acquired a boyfriend.

Frank had not been expecting this. You were twenty-nine years old by then, and perhaps he'd thought you would remain single forever. Don't laugh, but I think he may have believed you to be a lesbian! But you had met somebody you liked, and you wanted to bring him home for Sunday dinner. Your boyfriend turned out to be the head of security at Bellevue. A recently returned veteran of Vietnam. A native of

Brownsville, Brooklyn, who was going back to school at City College to study law. A black man by the name of Winston.

Frank was not upset that you were dating a black man, Angela. Not for a minute. I hope you know that. More than anything, he was awed by your courage and confidence, to bring Winston to South Brooklyn. He saw the looks on the neighbors' faces. It brought him satisfaction to see how uncomfortable you had made the neighborhood—and to see that other people's judgments would not stop you. But most of all, he liked and respected Winston.

"Good for her," he said. "Angela's always known what she wanted, and she's never been afraid to take her own path. She's chosen well."

From what I understand, your mother was less happy about you and Winston.

According to your father, Winston was the only subject upon which he and Rosella ever argued. Frank had always deferred to your mother's opinion about what was best for you. Here, though, they parted ways. I don't know the details of their argument. It's not important. In the end, though, your mother came around. Or at least that's what I was told.

(Again, Angela—I apologize if anything I'm telling you here is incorrect. I'm aware that I'm relaying your own history to you at this point, and it makes me self-conscious. You surely know what happened better than anyone—or maybe you don't. Again, I don't know how much you were shown of your parents' dispute. I just don't want to leave out anything that you might not be aware of.)

And then, in early spring of 1971, Frank told me that you were getting married to Winston in a small private ceremony, and he asked me to create your dress.

"Is this what Angela wants?" I asked.

"She doesn't know yet," he said. "I'm going to talk to her about it. I'm going to ask her to come and see you."

"You want Angela to meet me?"

"I have only one daughter, Vivian. And knowing Angela, she will have only one marriage. I want you to make her wedding dress. It would mean a lot to me. So yeah, I want Angela to meet you."

You came into the boutique on a Tuesday morning—early, because you had to be at work by nine. Your father's car pulled up in front of my shop, and the two of you entered together.

"Angela," said Frank, "this is my old friend Vivian that I was telling you about. Vivian, this is my daughter. Well, I'll leave you both to it."

And he walked out.

I had never been more nervous to meet a client.

What's worse, I could instantly see your reluctance. You were more than reluctant: I could see that you were deeply impatient. I could see your confusion about why your father—who had never interfered with a minute of your life—had insisted on bringing you here. I could see that you didn't want to be here. And I could tell (because I have an instinct for these things) that you didn't even *want* a wedding dress. I was willing to bet that you found wedding gowns corny and old-fashioned and demeaning to women. I would have wagered a million to one odds that you were planning to wear the exact same thing on your wedding day that you were wearing now: a peasant blouse, a wraparound denim skirt, and clogs.

"Dr. Grecco," I said, "it's a pleasure to meet you."

I hoped you were glad that I had called you by your title. (Forgive me, but having heard so many stories about you over the years, I was a bit proud of your title myself!)

Your manners were impeccable. "It's a pleasure to meet you, too, Vivian," you said—smiling as warmly as you were able to, given that you obviously wished you were anywhere but here.

I found you to be such a striking woman, Angela. You didn't have your father's height, but you had his intensity. You had those same dark, searching eyes that signaled both curiosity and suspicion. You nearly vibrated with intelligence. Your eyebrows were thick and serious, and I liked the fact that you appeared never to have tweezed them. And you had restless energy, just like your dad. (Not so restless as his, of course—lucky for you!—but still, it was notable.)

"I hear you're getting married," I said. "Congratulations to you."

You cut right to the chase. "I'm not much of a wedding person. . . ."

"I understand completely," I said. "Believe it or not, I'm not really one for weddings, either."

"You've chosen a funny line of work, then," you said, and we both laughed.

"Listen, Angela. You don't have to be here. It won't hurt my feelings in the least if you're not interested in buying a wedding dress."

Now you seemed to backtrack, perhaps fearing that you'd offended me.

"No, I'm happy to be here," you said. "It's important to my father."

"That's true," I agreed. "And your father is a good friend of mine and the best man I know. But in my business, I'm not so interested in what fathers have to say. Or mothers, either, for that matter. I care only about the bride."

You winced slightly at the word "bride." In my experience, there are only two kinds of women who ever get married—women who love the idea of being a bride, and women who hate it but are doing it anyway. It was obvious what kind of woman I was working with here.

"Angela, let me tell you something," I said. "And is it all right with you, that I call you Angela?"

It felt so strange to say the name to your face—that most intimate name, the name I had been hearing for years!

"That's fine," you said.

"May I assume that everything about a traditional wedding is repugnant and off-putting to you?"

"That's correct."

"And if it were up to you, it would be a quick trip to the county clerk's office, on your lunch break? Or maybe not even marriage vows at all, but just an ongoing relationship, without getting the government involved?"

You smiled. Again, I caught that flash of intelligence. You said, "You must be reading my mail, Vivian."

"Somebody else in your life wants a proper-looking marriage ceremony for you, then. Who is it? Your mother?"

"It's Winston."

"Ah. Your fiancé." Again, the wince. I had chosen the wrong word. "Your partner, perhaps I should say."

"Thank you," you said. "Yes, it's Winston. He wants a ceremony. He wants us to stand before the whole world, he says, and declare our love."

"That's sweet."

"I suppose so. I do love him. I only wish that I could send a stand-in that day, to do the job for me."

"You hate being the center of attention," I said. "Your father always told me that about you."

"I despise it. I don't even want to wear white. It seems ridiculous, at my age. But Winston wants to see me in a white gown."

"Most grooms do. There's something about a white gown—setting aside the obnoxious question of virginity—that signals to a man that this day is not like any other day. It shows him that he's been *chosen*. It means a lot to men, I have learned over the years, to see their brides walking toward them in white. Helps to quiet their insecurities. And you'd be surprised how insecure the men can be."

"That's interesting," you said.

"Well, I've seen a lot of it."

At this point, you relaxed enough to start taking in your surroundings. You drifted over to one of my sample racks, which was filled with billows of crinolines and satin and lace. You started sorting through the gowns with an expression of martyrdom.

"Angela," I said, "I can tell you right now that you won't like any of those dresses. In fact, you'll despise them."

You dropped your arms in defeat. "Is that right?"

"Look, I don't have anything here right now that would suit you. I wouldn't even *let* you wear one of these gowns—not you, the girl who was fixing her own bicycle by the time she was ten. I'm an old-fashioned seamstress in one regard only, my dear: I believe a dress should flatter not only a woman's figure, but also her intelligence. Nothing in the showroom is intelligent enough for you. But I have an idea. Come sit down with me in my workroom. Let's have a cup of tea, if you've got a moment?"

had never before taken a bride into my workroom, which was at the back of the shop, and full of mess and chaos. I preferred to keep my customers in the pretty, magical space that Marjorie and I had created at the front of the building—with the cream-colored walls and the dainty French furniture, and the dappled sunlight streaming in from the street windows. I liked to keep my brides in the illusion of femininity, you see—which is where most brides like to abide. But I could see that you were not somebody who wanted to abide in illusion. I thought you might be more comfortable where the actual work was done. And there was a book I wanted to show you, which I knew was back there.

So we went back into my workshop, and I fixed us each a cup of tea. Then I brought you the book—a collection of antique wedding photos that Marjorie had given me for Christmas. I opened to a picture of a

French bride from 1916. She was wearing a simple cylindrical gown that came to just above her ankles, and was completely unornamented.

"I'm thinking of something like this for you. Nothing like a traditional Western wedding gown. No flounce, no whim-whams. You could be comfortable in this, and move about with ease. The top of the dress almost looks like a kimono—the way the bodice is just two simple pieces of fabric that cross over the bust? It was the style in the teens for a while, especially in France, to imitate Japanese clothing in wedding design. I've always thought this shape was beautiful—not much more complicated than a bathrobe, really. So elegant. It's too simple for most people, but I admire it. I think it would suit you. Do you see how the waist is high, and then there's that wide satin band with the bow on the side? Something like an obi?"

"An obi?" You were legitimately interested now.

"A Japanese ceremonial sash. In fact, what I would do is make you a version of this dress in a creamy white—to satisfy the traditionalists in the room—but then, on your waist, I'd give you an actual Japanese obi. I would suggest a sash of red and gold—something bold and vivid, to signal the unconventional path that your life has taken. Let's stay as far away from the 'something borrowed, something blue' cliché, shall we? I could show you how to tie the obi in two different ways. Traditionally, Japanese women use different knots, whether they are married or unmarried. We could start you off with the unmarried knot. Then perhaps Winston could untie the sash during the ceremony, and then you could retie it, with the knot of a married woman. Maybe that could *constitute* the entire ceremony, in fact. Up to you, of course."

"That's *very* interesting," you said. "I like this idea. I like it a lot. Thank you, Vivian."

"My only hesitation is that it may be upsetting for your father, to see the Japanese elements in the design. Given his history in the war, and all that. But I'm not sure. What do you think?"

"No, I don't think it would bother him. If anything, he might appreciate the reference. Almost as if I am wearing something that represents a bit of his history."

"I could see him thinking that," I said. "One way or another, I'll talk to him about it so it doesn't catch him by surprise."

But now you seemed distracted, and your face became sharp and tight. "Vivian, may I ask you something?" you said.

"Of course."

"How is it that you know my father, anyway?"

God help me, Angela, I do not know what my face revealed in that moment. If I were to guess, though, I would imagine that I looked some combination of guilty, afraid, sad, and panicked.

"You can understand my confusion," you went on, seeing my discomfort, "given that my father doesn't know *anybody*. He doesn't talk to a soul. He says that you're his dear friend, but that doesn't make any sense. He doesn't have any friends. Even his old friends from the neighborhood don't socialize with him. And you're not even from the neighborhood. But you know so much about me. You know that I was fixing bicycles when I was ten. Why would you know that?"

You sat there, waiting for me to answer. I felt completely outgunned. You were a trained psychologist, Angela. You were a professional dissembler. You'd been around all sorts of madness and lies in your work. The feeling I got was that you had all the time in the world to wait me out—and that you would instantly know if I was deceiving you.

"You can tell me the truth, Vivian," you said.

The look on your face was not hostile, but your focus was fearsome.

But how could I tell you the truth? It wasn't my place to tell you anything, or to violate your father's privacy, or to possibly upset you right before your wedding. And how could I possibly explain Frank and me? Would you have believed me, anyway, if I'd told you the truth—namely, that I had spent several nights a week with your father for the past six years, and that all we did was walk and talk?

"He was a friend of my brother's," I finally said. "Frank and Walter served together during the war. They went to Officer Candidate School together. They both ended up on the USS *Franklin*. My brother was killed in the same attack that injured your father."

Everything that I said was true, Angela—except for the part about your father and my brother being friends. (They had known each other, yes. But they were not friends.) As I spoke, I could feel tears standing in my eyes. Not tears about Walter. Not even tears about Frank. Just tears about *this situation*—about sitting alone with the daughter of the man I loved, and liking her so much, and not being able to explain anything. Tears—as with so many other times in my life—about the intractable dilemmas in which we can find ourselves.

Your face softened. "Oh, Vivian, I'm sorry."

There were so many more questions you could have asked at that point, but you didn't. You could see that the subject of my brother had upset me. I believe you were too compassionate to keep me cornered. Anyway, you'd been given an answer, and it was plausible *enough*. I could see that you suspected there was more to the story, but in your kindness, you chose to believe what I had told you—or at least not to chase any further information.

Mercifully, you dropped the subject, and we went back to planning your wedding dress.

What a beautiful dress it was, too.

I would spend the next two weeks working on it. I searched the city myself for the most stunning antique obi I could find (wide, red, long, and embroidered with golden phoenixes). It was criminally expensive, but there was nothing else in New York like it. (I didn't charge your father for it—don't worry!)

I made the gown itself out of a creamy, clingy, charmeuse satin. I fashioned a fitted slip beneath it with a built-in brassiere that would subtly make you feel more held together. I wouldn't let my assistants, or even Marjorie, so much as lay a finger on that gown. I sewed every stitch and seam on my own, bent over my work in something like prayerful silence.

And as much as I know that you hated ornamentation, I could not help myself. At the spot where the two bands of fabric crossed your heart, I sewed one little pearl, taken from a necklace that had once belonged to my grandmother.

A small gift, Angela—from my family to yours.

THIRTY-THREE

t was December of 1977 when I got your letter saying that your father had died.

I'd sensed already that something was terribly wrong. I hadn't heard from Frank in almost two weeks, which was highly unusual. In fact, in the twelve years of our relationship, it had never happened before. I was growing concerned—*very* concerned—but didn't know what to do about it. I had never called Frank at home, and since he had retired from the police force, I couldn't phone him at the precinct. He didn't have any friends that I knew of, so there was nobody I could contact, to ask if he was all right. I couldn't exactly go knocking on his door in Brooklyn.

And then came your note, addressed to me, care of L'Atelier.

I've saved it, all these years.

Dear Vivian:

It is with a heavy heart that I write to tell you that my father passed away ten days ago. It was a sudden death. He was out

460

walking one night around our neighborhood, as he was wont to do, and he collapsed on the sidewalk. It would appear that he had a heart attack, although we did not ask for an autopsy. This has been a great shock to me and to my mother, as I'm sure you can imagine. My father had his frailties, to be sure, but they were never of a physical nature. He had such stamina! I thought he would live forever. We held a small service for him at the same church where he was christened, and he has been buried in Green-Wood Cemetery, next to his parents. Vivian, I apologize. It was only after the funeral that I realized I should have contacted you immediately. I know that you and my father were dear friends. Surely, he would have wanted you to be alerted. Please forgive this tardy note. I'm sorry to be the bearer of such bad news and I'm sorry that I didn't get word to you sooner. If there is anything that I, or my family, can ever do for you, please let me know.

Sincerely, Angela Grecco

You had kept your maiden name.

Don't ask me why, but I noticed that right away—before I had even fully registered that he was gone.

Good for you, Angela, I thought. *Always keep your own name!*

Then the news hit me that Frank was gone, and I did just what you might imagine I would do: I dropped to the floor and I wept.

Nobody wants to hear about anybody else's grief (there's a level at which everyone's grief is exactly the same, anyhow), so I won't go into details about my sadness. I will say only that the following few years were a very hard time for me—the hardest and loneliest I ever experienced.

Your father had been a peculiar man in life, Angela, and he was peculiar in death, too. He remained so vivid. He came to me in dreams, and he came to me in smells and sounds and sensations of New York itself. He came to me in the scent of summer rain on hot macadam, or in the sweet perfume of wintertime sugared nuts sold by street vendors. He came to me in the sour, milky odor of Manhattan's ginkgo trees in springtime bloom. He came to me in the bubbling coo of nesting pigeons, and in the screaming of police sirens. He was everywhere to be found across the city. Yet his absence weighted my heart with deep silence.

I went on about my life.

So much of my day-to-day routine looked exactly the same, even after he had gone. I lived in the same place, I did the same job. I spent time with the same friends and family. Frank had never been part of my daily routine, so why would anything change? My friends knew that I had lost someone important to me—but they hadn't known him. Nobody knew how much I had loved him (how would I have explained him?), so I wasn't warranted the public grieving rights of a widow. I didn't see myself as a widow, in any case. That was your mother's position, not mine. How could I be a widow when I had never been a wife? There had never been a correct word for what Frank and I were to each other, so the absence I felt after his death was both private and unnamed.

Mostly, it was this: I would wake up late at night, and lie in my bed, waiting for the phone to ring so that I could hear him say, "Are you awake? Do you want to go for a walk?"

New York City itself seemed smaller, after Frank died. All those distant neighborhoods that we had explored together on foot were no longer open to me. They weren't places a woman could go alone—not even a woman as independent as myself. And in the geography of my imagination, a great many "neighborhoods" of intimacy were now also shuttered. There were certain subjects that I had only ever been able to talk about with Frank. There were places within me that he alone could reach with his listening—and I would never be able to reach those places on my own.

Even so, I want you to know that I've done just fine in my life without Frank. I grew out of my sorrow—the way people usually do, eventually. I found my way back to joyful things again. I've always been a lucky person, Angela—not least of all because my natural temperament is not one of gloom and despair. In that regard, I have always been a bit like my Aunt Peg—not prone to depression, thank God. And I've had wonderful people in my life in the decades after Frank died. Exciting lovers, new friends, my chosen family. I've never wanted for company. But I have also never stopped missing your father.

Other people have always been perfectly nice and kind, don't get me wrong, but nobody was *him*. Nobody could ever be like that bottomless well of a man—that walking confessional booth who could absorb whatever you told him without judgment or alarm.

Nobody else could be that beautiful dark soul, who always seemed to straddle the worlds of life and death.

Nobody but Frank was Frank.

So you have waited a long time for your answer, Angela, about what I was to your father—or what he was to me.

I've tried to answer your question as honestly and thoroughly as I could. I was about to apologize for going on so long. But if you are truly your father's daughter (and I believe that you are), then I know that you're a good listener. You're the sort of person who would want the whole story. Also, it is important for me that you know everything about me—the good and the bad, the loyal and the perverse—so that you can decide for yourself what to think of me.

But I need to make it clear once again, Angela: your father and I never embraced, we never kissed, we never had sex. He was the only man I ever really loved, though, with all my heart. And he loved me, too. We didn't speak of it, because we didn't need to speak of it. We both knew it.

That said, I do want to tell you that over the years, your father finally reached a point of ease with me where he could rest the back of his hand on my palm without flinching in pain. We could sit together in his car, in the quiet comfort of that touch, for many minutes at a time.

I never saw more sunrises in my life than I did with him.

If by doing that—by holding his hand all those times, as the sun came up—I took something away from your mother, or from you, I beg your forgiveness.

But I don't think I did.

So here we are, Angela.

I am sorry to hear about your mother's death. You have my condolences. I am glad to hear that she lived a long life. I hope she had a good life, and a peaceful death. I hope that your heart is strong within your grieving.

I also want to say that I'm so glad you were able to track me down. Thank God I'm still living at the L'Atelier building! That's the good thing about never changing your name or your address, I suppose. People always know where to find you.

Although I should tell you that L'Atelier is not a bridal boutique anymore, but a coffee and juice shop that Nathan Lowtsky runs. The building itself belongs to me, though. Marjorie left it to me after her death thirteen years ago, knowing that I would do a better job than Nathan at managing the property. So she put things entirely in my hands and I've taken good care of the place. I was the one who helped

Nathan to get his little business up and running, too. He needed all the help he could get, believe me. Nathan, dear as he is, will never set the world on fire. But I do love him. He has always called me his "other mother." I'm happy to have his affection and care. In fact, I am probably as embarrassingly healthy as I am for my ripe old age because he tends to me. And I tend to him, as well. We are good to each other.

So this is why I am still here—still in the same place I've lived since 1950.

Thank you for coming to look for me, Angela.

Thank you for asking me for the truth.

I have told you all of it.

will sign off now, but there's one more thing I want to say.

Long ago, Edna Parker Watson told me that I would never be an interesting person. She may have been right about that. That's not mine to judge, or to know. But she also said that I was the worst sort of female—namely, the type of woman who cannot be a friend to another woman, because she will always be "playing with toys that are not her own." In this regard, Edna was wrong. Over the years, I've been a good friend to a great many women.

I used to say that there were only two things I was ever good at: sewing and sex. But I have been selling myself short all this while, because the fact is that I am also very good at being a friend.

I'm telling you all this, Angela, because I am offering my friendship to you, if you would ever care to have it.

I don't know whether my friendship would interest you. You may never want to have anything to do with me, after reading all this. You may find me a despicable woman. That would be understandable. I don't happen to think I'm despicable (I don't think anyone is, anymore), but I will leave it to you to decide for yourself.

But do give my offer some thought, is my respectful suggestion.

You see, all the while that I've been writing these pages to you, I have been imagining you in my mind as a young woman. To me, you will always be that flinty, smart, no-nonsense, twenty-nine-year-old feminist who walked into my bridal shop in 1971. But I'm grasping only now that you're not a young woman anymore. By my calculations, you are almost seventy. And I'm not young either, obviously.

This is what I've found about life, as I've gotten older: you start to lose people, Angela. It's not that there is ever a shortage of people—oh, heavens no. It is merely that—as the years pass—there comes to be a terrible shortage of *your* people. The ones *you* loved. The ones who knew the people that you *both* loved. The ones who know your whole history.

Those people start to be plucked away by death, and they are awfully hard to replace after they go. After a certain age, it can become difficult to make new friends. The world can begin to feel lonely and sparse, teeming though it may be with freshly minted young souls.

I'm not sure whether you've had that feeling yet. But I've had it. And you may have that feeling someday.

All this is why I want to end by saying that—although you owe me nothing, and I expect nothing from you—you are precious to my heart nonetheless. And should you ever find that your world feels lonely and sparse, and that you need a new friend, please remember that I am here.

I don't know how much longer I will be here, of course—but as long as I remain on this earth, my dear Angela, I am yours.

Thank you for listening,
Vivian Morris

ACKNOWLEDGMENTS

So many generous New Yorkers (past and present) shared of them-selves in order to help me create this book.

Brooklyn native Margaret Cordi—who has been my brilliant and beloved friend for thirty years—guided me through my research, ac-companied me on all my field trips, tracked down my sources, and proofread the hell out of these pages in an insanely short amount of time. But she also stirred up my joy and excitement about this project when I was under deadline and under stress. Margaret: There is simply no way I could have written this story without you. Let's always be working on a novel together, okay?

I will be forever grateful to Norma Amigo—the most gorgeous and charismatic nonagenarian I ever met—for telling me all about her days and nights as a Manhattan showgirl. It was Norma's unabashed sensu-ality and independence (as well as her unprintable answer to my ques-tion "Why did you never want to get married?") that allowed Vivian to come into full and free existence.

For more background on the New York City entertainment world of the 1940s and 1950s, I am also grateful to Peggy Winslow Baum (actress), the late Phyllis Westermann (songwriter and producer), Paulette Harwood (dancer), and the lovely Laurie Sanderson (keeper of the Ziegfeld flame).

For help in understanding and unearthing a Times Square that will never again exist, David Freeland was an essential and fascinating guide.

Shareen Mitchell's insights and sensitivity about wedding gowns, fashion, and how to humble yourself in service to nervous brides completely shaped this aspect of Vivian's story. Thank you also to Leah Cahill, for her lessons in sewing and tailoring. Jesse Thorn served as an invaluable emergency contact for my questions about men's style.

Andrew Gustafson opened up the wonders of the Brooklyn Navy Yard for me. Bernard Whalen, Ricky Conte, and Joe and Lucy De Carlo helped me to understand the life of a Brooklyn patrolman. The regulars at D'Amico Coffee in Carroll Gardens took me on the most colorful trip through time you could ever imagine. So thank you to Joanie D'Amico, Rose Cusumano, Danny Calcaterra, and Paul and Nancy Gentile for sharing your stories. You guys really made me wish I had grown up in South Brooklyn back in the day.

Thank you to my father, John Gilbert (LTJG, ret., USS *Johnston*), for helping me to get the Navy details right. I am grateful to my mother, Carole Gilbert, for teaching me how to work my ass off and how to be resilient in the face of life's difficulties. (I never needed it more than this year, Mom.) I am grateful to Catherine and James Murdock for their keen copyediting skills. Because of you this book has five thousand fewer commas than it needed.

Without the Billy Rose Theatre Division of the New York Public Library, I would not have been able to read the papers of Katharine

Cornell, and without Katharine Cornell, there would be no Edna Parker Watson.

I am grateful to my great-aunt Lolly, for giving me those old Alexander Woollcott books, which set me down the path of this story. But most of all, Lolly, thank you for modeling the extraordinary optimism, cheer, and strength that make me want to be a better and braver woman.

I am grateful to my extraordinary team at Riverhead—Geoff Kloske, Sarah McGrath, Jynne Martin, Helen Yentus, Kate Stark, Lydia Hirt, Shailyn Tavella, Alison Fairbrother, and the late and beloved Liz Hohenadel—for publishing my books so brilliantly and boldly. Thank you to Markus Dohle and Madeline McIntosh for investing in me and believing in me. Thank you, also, to my friends and colleagues at Bloomsbury—Alexandra Pringle, Tram-Anh Doan, Kathleen Farrar, and Ros Ellis—for keeping things so bright and cool on the other side of the Atlantic.

Dave Cahill and Anthony Kwasi Adjei: I cannot run my world without you. I hope I never have to!

Thank you to Martha Beck, Karen Gerdes, and Rowan Mangan, for reading thousands of pages of my writing over the past few years, and for wrapping me up in the great big wingspan of your collective love. Thank you to Glennon Doyle, for sitting by my door all those nights. I needed it, and I am grateful.

Thank you to my sister-wives, Gigi Madl and Stacey Weinberg, for their love and sacrifice during such a hard season of pain and loss. I could not have survived 2017 without you.

Thank you to Sheryl Moller, Jennie Willink, Jonny Miles, and Anita Schwartz, for being enthusiastic early readers of these pages. Thank you to Billy Buell, for lending me the use of his fabulous name.

Sarah Chalfant: As ever, you are the wind beneath my wings.

Miriam Feuerle: As ever, I love rolling with you.

Lastly, a message to Rayya Elias: I know how badly you wanted to be here at my side while I wrote this novel. All I can tell you, baby, is that you *were*. You are never not at my side. You are my heart. I will always love you.